*L*IKE *S*APPHIRE *B*LUE

To Ann
Enjoy your read!
xo
Marisa Bellins

Mirador Publishing
10 Greenbrook Terrace
Taunton
Somerset
UK
TA1 1UT

LIKE SAPPHIRE BLUE

MARISA BILLIONS

Dedication

For my wife, Stephanie. Thank you for your constant love and support. Though this story is so wholly unrelated to us, I couldn't do it without you. This is a great love story in its own right, though ours is still the best.
– I love you – MOST

Also, for Maria "Bougainvillea" and Michele Dragon – My Pineapple Express. Thank you for encouraging me to keep writing.

Part I

Dinner for Two

~ *1* ~

Humble Beginnings

The Present...

DISCORD, MEANING A LACK OF harmony or unity by the definition. In a relationship it is that moment when the realization hits that there is no turning back and the damage is done. It's irreparable.

Why won't she look at me? Emma looked about the room. The table was set with the good china. Their favorite bottle of wine sat corked in the center, and across from her, was her beautiful wife. This was the woman that she spent the last two decades of her life with, and she won't even look up? *There was no way I was ever going to really fall in love with anyone else, you made sure of that. Whenever I thought you were out of my life, you miraculously reappeared every time.* With narrowed eyes, gripping the ends of the table she looked around in the dimly lit room.

The dining room was immaculate, crown molding lines the ceiling, and a tapestry of a French courtyard hangs on the back wall. A china cabinet delicately displaying the unused settings on the opposite wall. The dimmer switch was set to low and candles flicker in silver holders (inherited from her wife's grandmother, who inherited them from her grandmother and so forth and so on). Her wife was sitting, with her thick strawberry blonde hair in delicate waves down her back. Her favorite dress clung to her curves. She has a beautiful body, and not a lot of things look bad on her. Her chin was down, and her beautiful blue eyes are downcast, refusing to look at Emma. She is leaning back against the chair with her head down. She's there, but she's not.

Emma sat back, still staring across the table at her wife. One hand rested on the table, the other on the back of her chair. She worked so hard on this dinner. She made their favorite meal – eggplant parmigiana, pasta, home-made garlic bread. *Not even an acknowledgement of the fact that the bottle of wine costs what Bear used to make in two weeks working at Jessie's shop.*

Her wife just sat there unmoved. Unimpressed. Not looking. Not speaking. This was her schtick though. The cold shoulder. The silent treatment. It wasn't the first time she did this to Emma. But still, it was frustrating to her. *And to think, this woman has a PhD. You would think she has better coping mechanisms than the silent treatment.*

The dinner itself and the beautiful and impressive dining room it was served in, could not be a further cry from Emma's meager beginnings. To keep from looking at her silent wife, Emma looked around at the room.

"You had everything growing up. This dinner, and what I did to prepare it, probably don't mean much to you. But to make this, to have this, this is the world to me. What we built together, has meant the world to me." Emma's voice was quiet. Tears had welled up in her eyes.

The Past (1976-1991)

EMMA LANDRY NEVER KNEW HER mother. She didn't even know she had one until she was in kindergarten. She thought she only came to be because of one parent, her dad Frank, who she called Bear, short for Papa Bear.

She lived with her dad in a small trailer near the town. It was behind the auto shop that her dad worked at, which was owned by his brother, her uncle Jessie. The trailer was rundown, and there was a hole in the corner of the floor in the living room where she could see the ground beneath. In the winter time, she would stick a towel in the hole to keep the cold out, but sometimes the mice beneath the trailer would take it. Bear's room was located at one end of the narrow trailer, and hers was at the other. There was a small living room with a tv that had bootlegged cable running to it. The walls were lined with a dark, faux wood paneling. An old card table with folding chairs was where they ate from dull plastic plates with mismatched silverware and chipped ceramic mugs. The couch was old, cream colored with brown and orange flower print, sagged in the middle and smelled faintly of mildew.

Their trailer and the shop were located on a small, wooded plot of land. They didn't have neighbors, and she didn't have friends. Her friends were two plush animals, Teddy (a floppy eared dog) and Brownie (a threadbare cotton tailed bunny).

Bear worked for her uncle Jessie at the small garage providing oil changes, tire rotation and simple mechanical services for the locals who couldn't get in to have their services done at the dealerships. Before she was able to go to school, he would bring her with him to work. Sometimes she stayed with Jessie when Bear wanted to go out after work. Jessie would take her back to the trailer and make her macaroni and cheese from a box and tuck her into her small bed and tell her fantastic stories that he made up. He gave her books sometimes, too. She loved the stories, and she loved the books. Getting lost in stories that fueled her vivid imagination was her favorite thing. She could read before she started kindergarten.

Emma's life was simple with Bear. She grew up exploring in the woods, bringing Teddy or Brownie with her to keep her safe. They would watch sports together on the small television in the living room and sometimes sitcoms, too. Holidays were small and basic. They would go to Jessie's house and eat a dinner usually prepared by one of his girlfriends and she would get a small toy or a book or a new outfit to wear.

Bear was an awkward father. He never knew what to say to Emma or how to interact with her, exactly, however she never questioned his devotion to her, and knew he loved her and would do anything for her, and she always felt safe with him. He would always tell her that she was his princess, and she was Daddy's little girl. She loved sitting on the saggy couch and watching football with him. He taught her all of the calls and she rooted for his favorite team with a fervor that matched his.

He always bought her cute clothes from the Salvation Army. Pink tops and jeans with sparkly stuff on them. Shoes with pink and sparkly stuff to match. They were used, and out of date compared to that of the other girls in town, but that was no mind. He did his best.

Bear even learned how to put her hair in pigtails and braids, taught by one of Jessie's many girlfriends. "Just because we ain't got money, doesn't mean my little girl has to look bad," he would say as he brushed her thick dark hair gently.

When she was five, Bear taught her how to trap rabbits for dinner. She caught four that year. Bear cut one of the feet off and mounted it for her as a lucky rabbit's foot on her backpack.

When she got to school, she showed that foot to her classmates for show and tell. The teacher did little to hide her disgust, and the girls thought it was gross. She never talked about it again. Emma didn't understand why everyone thought it was weird or gross. She asked them how else they got food. "At the store!" they all laughed as they answered.

She would see the other little girls get walked in by pretty mommies and that was when she asked Bear for the first time about her own mother.

"Bear, some kids have mommies. I don't. Why?"

"Your ma couldn't stick around. She had some issues," was his reply. Simple and to the point was just the kinda guy Bear was.

"What do you mean? What kind of issues?" Emma pressed on.

"Issues that made her not want to be a mama or a wife."

"Was I not a good baby?"

"No, you was a great baby. Your ma just couldn't be a ma."

"But why?"

"Emma, baby girl… That's just not something a little kid needs to talk about or know about. You got me, and that needs to be enough." He sounded wounded in the last sentence.

That shut her up, but she never stopped wondering. She did learn that kids look like their mommies and their daddies. Bear was really tall, and really big, he was blond with coarse straight hair and deep, dark, blue eyes. She had dark hair that was silky and wavy, and her eyes were a very dark blue. Her skin

~ 4 ~

was darker than Bear and her features were not as big. She was taller than most other kids her age, like Bear, but she was slender and reed thin, not like Bear. She gathered her dark hair and complexion came from her mom, and also that she was so skinny, and her height and blue eyes were from Bear.

Bear didn't have family other than Jessie. Emma didn't have grandparents that could spoil her rotten. There were no aunties and cousins to play with. It was just her, Bear, Jessie, Teddy and Brownie. While she was young, she didn't mind as much. It was something that would bother her as she grew though.

Starting from the rabbit's foot episode, she didn't have friends either. The girls were afraid of her, and the boys didn't know what to do with her either. It didn't really bother her, because overall, she was a happy kid. With a vivid imagination fueled by books picked up at library sales or from Jessie, and the endless woods behind the trailer to explore she didn't need anything more.

WHEN SHE WAS SEVEN, BEAR bought Emma her first rifle. While her classmates were going to ballet lessons and playing sports, she was learning her way around the rifle. Cleaning it, loading it, and being safe with it. "Don't point that thing at me!" Bear would yell.

"It's not loaded, Bear!" she would say, pouting at Bear's displeasure with her.

"Never assume that!" he corrected her. "As far as you know, there is always something in there!"

Bear spent a year teaching her to shoot. He set up targets of soda bottles behind the trailer. He showed her how to hold the rifle and how to stand and brace for the kick.

Emma was far from being a natural with the rifle. She struggled for months, but Bear was a patient teacher. He took his time and helped her and cheered her on and praised her when she did things right.

When she was eight, he took her to hunt deer for the first time. He waited until she was able to hit every target he set up for her behind the trailer; one right after the other in rapid succession. She still was not a master, but she had definitely become skilled in her ability to use the rifle and hit the targets as they were lined up.

Up in the deer stand, in the early morning, she sat with Bear in silence waiting for a deer.

Anxious, with her heart thrumming loud in her chest she sat quiet in the stand. *Calm down, the deer can hear your heart beating! There's no way they can't hear it! They are not going to come, and Bear will be sad!* They were perched up in a home-made deer stand built into a large tree overlooking a small clearing. The early morning was misty, and frost clung to the surfaces of the deer stand and on the grass below them.

Steam came from her every exhale, and her ears were so cold she thought they might fall off her head. She sat quietly next to Bear, watching the puffy clouds of their breath, and trying to not complain. *I really have to pee. There's nowhere to go though.* Trying to not fidget with her discomfort because she didn't want to disappoint Bear, she distracted herself by trying to count the remaining leaves that hung from the tree the deer stand was propped in.

Finally, after what seemed like an eternity, Bear nudged her and nodded his head out to where she could see a large doe and her fawn grazing. She froze looking at the majestic animal. It was so big and so gentle with her large black eyes. Its ears flicked, and the fawn looked around before going back to its gentle grazing. *She's so beautiful! Look at that baby with her! I can't kill it. I can't. I don't want to.*

Bear nodded to her again, nudging her to do it. His gesture said, 'Go ahead, now!'

Don't make Bear mad. You have to. Just do it. Do it now. She looked through the scope and honed in right where Bear told her to. Her finger wrapped around the trigger, and her body braced for the kick. She took a deep breath in and going against all she was taught – she closed her eyes. On the exhale, doing as she was taught – she squeezed the trigger.

Her eyes opened as the loud bang echoed off of the trees in the clearing and she watched, almost in slow motion as the doe dropped and the tiny buck fawn ran off into the woods.

"Alright! Princess! Way to go!" Bear was on his feet slapping her back and cheerful.

She stood there frozen.

Bear was making his way down and out of the deer stand.

She couldn't move. She kept seeing the doe fall again and again in her mind's eye every time she blinked and her eyes closed. *What did you just do? Why did you do that? Oh, I need to pee so bad. That poor beautiful animal! Where is the baby? Where did he go? Oh, you killed her. You killed her in front of her baby!*

Tears were welling up in her eyes.

"Come on, Princess!" Bear called.

Her lip was trembling. Every time she closed her eyes to blink, she saw the doe fall and the fawn sprint off. She couldn't not see it. It was ingrained in her brain.

Where are you, little fawn? Are you scared? Are you looking for your mom? I know you have to be sad because I'm sad. I wonder where my mom is too. I'm so sorry, little fawn. You were just there with her and now she's gone. You are alone now. It's my fault. I'm so sorry, little fawn. Are you out there looking for her? I really need to pee. Why did I do that? How could I do that to that baby and that mama?

The tears were overflowing now. With shaking hands, she put her rifle down and crumbled to her knees sobbing.

Bear stood with his upper body still in the stand, "Emma, honey, why are you crying?" His voice was exasperated.

"I killed her, and she was a mama."

"That mama is going to feed us for all of the winter, Princess. That mama would probably starve during the winter anyway."

"That baby deer doesn't have a mama no more. I killed his mama." She was inconsolable, trembling with sorrow and cold. "I don't have a mama, and the baby deer doesn't now either, because of me." It was only the second time in her life she had brought up not having a mother and the first time she realized she was upset about it. She had peed her pants in her meltdown and only just now noticed it as the wind blew and she felt cold and wet.

"Listen," Bear was firm. "That mama deer was most likely going to die in the winter. She was gonna get killed by a car or starvation or another hunter. We need to eat. She is going to feed us for a long time. What you did was good. You need to stop crying and get over it. *Now*. I'm *not* going to listen to that sniveling all day. Get your ass out of this stand and help me load this deer into the truck."

Emma stopped the sound of her crying but could not stop the tears from flowing freely.

The snot poured out of her nose like a faucet and dried to her upper lip in the cold as she made her way across the ground to her first kill. Her legs and her bottom were cold from where she peed, and her wet cheeks felt cold every time the wind blew.

She felt every bit as lost and alone as that baby buck must be feeling now. *Where did you go, little fawn? Are you watching us? Do you know what I did to your mama? Are you scared?*

Bear field dressed the deer right on the spot. Slicing open her belly and pulling out the intestines and other now useless organs.

Steam rose from the organs as he pulled them out of the large gaping gash in her belly. Emma's head was swimming and she felt sick.

Eyes clouded with tears, she watched as his hands went in and heard the noise reminiscent of footsteps in sludge as he kept pulling them out. The acrid metallic smell filled the air around her. The world began to swim in her eyes and the ground was unsteady under feet. She fell to her knees and threw up. *I wish my mom were here. I've never met her, but I want someone to hold me right now. Tell me it's okay. It's not okay. Nothing is okay.* Bear ignored her as she continued to sob and kept on with his grisly task.

Don't look back. Don't look back. Eyes forward. Look ahead. Don't look back. She helped her father carry the doe to the truck, her small hands wrapped around the rope that attached to a sled that carried the deer, arms behind her, stopping frequently to rest. Bear heaved it up into the bed of his beat-up pick-up truck. Its tongue was sticking out, and its eyes were vacant and dull.

Bear got into the driver's seat, and she stayed behind looking at its face. She laid her hand on its neck and whispered, "I'm sorry. I hope your baby is okay."

"Emma! Get in this truck! *Now!*" Bear yelled.

How is he able to do this and not care? Why doesn't care about the fawn? Or me? With a heaving sigh she ran up and got into the truck next to Bear. She wiped the last of her tears and snot with her sleeve. *Don't look in the mirror. Don't look at Bear. If you look in the mirror, you will see the poor mama deer bouncing around back there with her tongue out. Don't look at Bear because you don't want to cry anymore. I can tell he's mad at me. So mad at me. I've never made him this mad before.* Bear stared straight ahead at the road, white knuckles gripping the steering wheel. She wasn't looking at him and he wasn't looking at her either.

The remainder of the winter, she refused to eat the meat that came from the doe. She made herself peanut butter and jelly sandwiches instead.

"Suit yourself," Bear would say. "More for me," he would say as he heaped venison stew from the large pot on the stove into his bowl.

The thought of eating that baby buck's mom made her ill, though she never said a word about it. The gamey smell of the meat cooking nauseated her, and the thought of the texture of the meat on her tongue made her head swim all over again as it did in the woods, and a clammy sweat break out on her forehead bringing her right back to the moment she watched her father field dress the doe. It was a visceral reaction she couldn't control, so she flat out refused.

Bear was angry at her insistence on wasting perfectly good meat and a meal he worked hard to provide. But he didn't know how to navigate the situation, so his compromise was that she had to provide for herself and prepare something else.

She outsmarted him by choosing to make peanut butter and jelly sandwiches for dinner. She didn't care that she had eaten it for lunch as well. It was better than the alternative.

AS SHE BECAME MORE SELF-sufficient, Bear would go out after work and stay out late into the early morning or sometimes all night long. Smelling like alcohol and cheap perfume with a dusting of glitter (most notably over the lap of his pants), he would come rolling in just in time for Emma to get ready for school. Emma didn't think twice about it. She liked being alone. She loved Bear, without a doubt, but it was just nicer when she was alone. She would watch television, eat her dinner and then brush her teeth and tuck herself in. She would read her books and she would talk to Teddy and Brownie about her day.

Although she was a good student Emma began to resent certain assignments in class that had to deal with family trees or talk about families. She didn't know if she had grandparents or family from her mom's side. Bear would refuse to talk about it. He said he would handle it with the teachers so she didn't get a bad grade for not participating. He would meet with the teachers or call them and sweet talk them about how it's a touchy subject and to please not require these things from Emma. Emma would be given alternative assignments instead, which was embarrassing to her, as she would be pulled aside by the teacher as they explained some meaningless task to keep her busy while her classmates looked at her and whispered while they worked on their family tree.

She would see the elaborate and pretty trees her classmates would make with pictures of extended family-grandmothers and grandfathers and great grandparents and so on. Jessie didn't have a wife or any kids. Sometimes he would have girlfriends. Pretty girls from the town, who would talk sweetly to Emma and play with her hair. But they never stuck around long, and Bear never had girlfriends, or at least none he would bring home to meet Emma. She wondered what it was like to have cousins and siblings. She wondered what it was like to be tucked in by a mom, or soothed and comforted when she was sick.

She resented that Bear wouldn't tell her where her mom was or why her mom left. She resented that he never talked about his own parents or where they were. Jessie never talked about it either.

She went from being a happy kid, to a quiet kid.

As she grew, the other kids noticed that Emma wore clothes that were faded and shabby. She didn't have the shiny and new toys or a bike, or new stylish clothes. Many of them remembered the rabbit's foot she had brought during kindergarten. She continued to have no friends to play with. They would pick on her for her clothes or the rabbit foot, and her lack of a mother. Unable to relate to the other kids as they talked about vacations and new stuff she kept to herself. They didn't try to befriend or relate to her either.

After school she would come home and draw pictures, read books, or wander the woods that were slowly losing their magic as she grew older and she had memorized each tree and stump and path around, or she would walk to her uncle's shop and hang out with Bear and Jessie and watch them as they worked on the cars. She began to learn the customers and would help out with the front desk and the register and books, or sweep up around the front. Jessie would toss her a few bucks here and there for helping.

Emma would use the meager earnings from helping out at the shop to buy herself a used bike from the thrift shop, and the food she liked so she wouldn't have to eat the rabbits and the deer that her father killed. She refused to kill another animal after her incident with the doe. Her heart couldn't take it. She wouldn't eat meat even if it was store bought, and especially if Bear killed it, she wasn't eating it. She refused to trap rabbits or join Bear in his hunting excursions.

"You know all food comes from something that died?" Bear asked her one night as she microwaved a frozen French bread cheese pizza. "Wheat plants and tomatoes died for that pizza you are going to eat."

Emma shrugged. "But I didn't see it be killed. I didn't see it dead in the back of your truck. I didn't kill it. I didn't make eye contact with it."

Bear didn't bother to argue with her.

AS MIDDLE SCHOOL BEGAN, BEAR was pushing her to do things that didn't require her staying around the trailer all day or the shop. He encouraged her to try out for various extracurricular activities and sports.

Emma started playing softball and basketball with the girls' teams. She wished she could try out for football since she and Bear loved to watch it together, but they refused to let a girl try out, even if it was just flag football.

It didn't stop her from attempting to try out. When she showed up for the football tryouts on the field, and the coach looked at her, "Cheerleading tryouts are in the gym."

"I'm not here for cheerleading. I'm here to play football." Emma was certain and confident.

The coach laughed and the boys waiting to try out joined him. Emma stayed stoic and narrowed her eyes at him so he could see she was serious.

The coach stopped laughing and so did the boys. "Girls don't play football." The coach was befuddled.

"Why not?"

"They don't. We can't have girls on the team. It's not ... It's not a thing." Now he was annoyed.

"I think there are laws against that."

"It doesn't apply to football."

The boys assembled for tryouts began to laugh again.

Head down, Emma sauntered off the field and walked to the shop. She sat in the office chair and spun around lazily.

"What's wrong, Princess?" Bear called in from under a customer's luxury sedan from the bay.

"I tried to try out for football, and I was told I can't because I'm a girl." She was pouting.

"Girls don't play football."

She crossed her arms over her chest and leaned back in the chair. "That's stupid."

Bear shrugged. "It is what it is. At least you tried."

Though she was on both the basketball and softball teams, she maintained her status as a lone wolf. She had managed the art of disappearing in a room full of her peers. She only spoke in class when called upon, and though she was a talented athlete and performed well on her teams, she didn't socialize with her teammates, as she had nothing in common with those girls. They would talk about their vacations with their families, boys, makeup, or the newest clothing trends. She couldn't relate, so she stayed quiet. The girls didn't try to include her, and she didn't try to be included.

For being a pretty girl who obtained great grades and was a talented athlete, she was invisible. Teachers never even acknowledged her unless they called upon her to answer questions. She had grown accustomed to flying under the radar. She sat alone in the hallway at lunch and aside from small talk in the locker room or mandatory group work in classes, she didn't speak.

After school and after practice, she would make her way home and stop by the shop to help out if anything needed to be done, and then home to the trailer. She would lay across her bed with a beat-up book she bought second-hand from the library sales or the thrift shop. She lost herself in the stories of lives she would never otherwise imagine and in worlds that had to be better than what she lived every day.

MIDWAY THROUGH HER FIRST SEMESTER of seventh grade, Emma was moodier than normal. Everything Bear did or said made her want to cry.

She could feel stabbing little pains in her lower abdomen and her pretty complexion was sporadically dotted with small pimples.

She avoided going to the shop after school lest she explode and yell at Bear or Jessie. They annoyed her constantly. Everything was annoying to her.

She couldn't stand her characters in the books she was reading. They were so predictable, and their worlds were bullshit. She would write in a notebook she used as a journal or lay across her bed and listen to the radio fantasizing about a different life.

It was a dreary mid-November day. The weather matched Emma's persistent mood lately. It was overcast, and damp outside. Emma was sitting in her science class at a black Formica table with a sink and Bunsen burners. Ms. Vasquez had been droning on about the biology of plant cells and Emma struggled to pay attention. She didn't feel well, and she could hear the boys at the table behind her whispering and laughing together. She was annoyed and just wanted to get done with the day so she could go home. The buzzing of the fluorescent lights was causing her head to ache and that annoying stabbing pain in her lower abdomen made her feel like she wanted to throw up. The cool black surface of the lab table felt strangely reassuring as she placed her palms flat and tried to breathe through the pains in her belly and stay focused on her teacher. *Just breathe. Inhale. Exhale. I wish Ms. Vasquez would stop talking. Why won't Rhys and his friends shut up? I wish she would do something about them or move me further away.*

Finally, the bell rang while Ms. Vasquez was mid-sentence, and Emma stood up to go.

The table behind her of three boys was snickering and leering at her.

She was not used to this attention, and she turned red with frustration. *What are they laughing at? They are so stupid. I'm definitely going to have to ask Ms. Vasquez to move me.*

As she was walking to the door, Ms. Vasquez's large chocolate brown eyes got big and her thick black eyebrows raised up, and she pulled Emma aside by grabbing her arm abruptly. "Emma, sweetie, you might need to go home and change." Her voice was discreet.

Emma looked at Ms. Vasquez confused.

"You started your cycle," she prompted, cocking her head to the side.

Emma still looked confused. *What is she talking about cycle? The wash?*

"You took sex ed fifth and sixth grade, didn't you?" Ms. Vasquez tucked a lock of her short dark bob behind her ear.

"Bear – my dad – didn't sign the forms so I had to go to the library."

"Did your dad or mom tell you about your period?" Ms. Vasquez asked.

Emma looked at her confused. "I don't have a mom. I mean, I guess, biologically I do, but I've never met her."

Ms. Vasquez took a deep breath and exhaled. Peeling off her brightly colored cardigan, she handed it to Emma. "Wrap this around your waist. You and I are going to go to the office and talk to the nurse."

Am I in trouble? Ms. Vasquez ushered her at breakneck speed taking long and fast strides weaving around the masses of students, down the hallway and to the office and into the nurse's office. "Ms. Wilson, this is Emma. Emma just got her cycle and doesn't know anything about it. She wasn't able to participate in Sex Ed and doesn't have a mom. I would stay and help her, but I have a class in one minute that I need to rush back to."

Emma looked at Ms. Wilson, the school nurse. *If I ever had a grandmother, I would want this woman to be her. She looks like she bakes cookies and gives good hugs.* She was stout, blonde, and had the sweetest round face with soft blue eyes that Emma could swear sparkled when she laughed. Ms. Wilson raised her eyebrows at Emma with concern.

Why am I even here? Did I do something wrong? This is so embarrassing. I wish everyone would stop looking at me like my dog just died. This is annoying. Just don't cry.

"Sit down, Emma," Ms. Wilson prompted. She proceeded to explain to Emma about becoming a woman and starting her cycle. She gave Emma a bag full of tampons and maxi pads and explained to her how to use them.

Emma sat and listened to Ms. Wilson as she spent the better part of the hour explaining menses, and she was mortified as she looked at the bag full of sanitary supplies.

"Can I go home and change my clothes?" Emma asked quietly.

"We have to call your parent and they need to pick you up. You can't just leave," Ms. Wilson informed her.

Stop looking at me like that. I don't want your goddamned pity. Emma started to cry despite herself. "I don't want to talk to Bear about this, and I don't want to stay here in messed up clothes."

"I am so sorry, Emma. I have to follow the rules, I can't just let you leave. There are laws and stuff, sweetie. Why don't you go clean up in the bathroom and you can stay in here until the final bell? I will call your teachers."

Emma composed herself and took a deep breath in. She nodded at Ms. Wilson. That was a far better plan than having to talk to Bear about her being a woman now.

She was self-conscious as it was about dealing with the fact she had boobs and was almost as tall as some of her teachers if not taller than a few.

After re-reading the instruction on the maxi pads (after looking at the instructions of the tampons she figured that was something she had no desire to try), and cleaning herself up, she went back into the exam room Ms. Wilson used, and grabbed the book she had been reading out of her backpack. She made herself comfortable on the exam table and read until the final bell rang.

Ms. Vasquez's brightly colored sweater stayed tied around her waist as she walked home. After having the rest of the afternoon to process what had happened in Ms. Wilson's exam room, she at least now understood why she had been feeling the way she had emotionally and that gave her some comfort. Her sadness and confusion had given way to anger and bitterness that ran deep. She was angry and bitter at not having a mom to explain to her these things, or that Bear was so ... Bear, and he couldn't be bothered to, or maybe he was too embarrassed to explain it to her. She felt as if she had been left to deal with this huge change on her own, and that just was not fair.

She tossed Ms. Vasquez's sweater in the wash with her clothes when she got home and stored the products she had been given by Ms. Wilson under the sink in the bathroom. She contemplated telling Bear about what happened but decided it would just be weird so she decided it would just not be discussed. It was just as well, as Bear never came home that night.

The next day, when Emma arrived in her science class, as she walked in, the table of boys that sat behind her started chanting in unison, "Bloody Mary! Bloody Mary! Bloody Mary!" as Emma took her seat.

"Absolutely *NOT*!" Ms. Vasquez shouted and slammed her hands down on her desk so hard it shook.

Rhys, the ringleader of the boys at the table, was laughing. "Have a sense of humor!" he said snidely.

Emma put her backpack down, walked around his table so she was standing in front of him and looked Rhys in the eye and said, "How's this for a sense of humor?" as she belted him with a right hook.

Rhys, not expecting it, went back and landed on his backside on the floor.

No one had expected it. Emma herself had not expected or planned her reaction.

She pulled Ms. Vasquez's sweater out of her backpack and brought it to the front of the class and set it on her desk. "I will take myself to the office."

Ms. Wilson brought her a bag of ice for her right knuckles as she explained to the vice principal, Ms. Jones, a young very pale blonde administrator who was new to the school, what she had done. Emma was unwavering as she looked at Ms. Jones in her pale watery blue eyes, who seemed so kind and quiet. "I started my period yesterday in class. These boys noticed it. I didn't even know what a period was... I just learned from Ms. Wilson because I don't have a mom or anyone to explain these things to me." Emma felt a twinge of emotion in the last line but swallowed it. *Just keep it together. Don't cry. Don't let them see how much it hurts.*

She was given two days of in-school suspension for striking Rhys.

After school, she made her way to the shop. She was sitting in the office chair swiveling back and forth, using her toes as a pivot.

"Wanna tell me what happened?" Bear asked.

Most definitely, I do not. Emma shook her head 'no' as she twisted back and forth in the office chair behind the desk.

"Did he deserve it?" Bear asked.

If you only knew, Bear. Emma nodded.

"Did he touch you?"

Gross. No. Emma shook her head 'no' again.

"Did he say something nasty about you?"

He most certainly did. Emma nodded her head.

"You ain't gonna tell me what he said?"

Nope. Nope. Absolutely not. No, sir. She shook her head 'no' again.

"Did you get him good?"

She grinned and nodded. *You taught me well, Bear.*

"Good girl." He ruffled her hair and went back to the bay.

Emma liked the in-school suspension days. The room was quiet, and it was just her and one other student who had been caught smoking in the girls' bathroom. The teacher seemed not to care too much and just doled out the work that was given to her from her teachers. The room had one small window that looked at the street and the houses across from the school. There were only about 10 desks lined up inside. Emma sat at one of the desks in the back of one corner, the other girl, a grade ahead of Emma, sat in the opposite corner. They looked at each other, nodded a greeting and had no further interactions. *Would it be too much to ask if I could just stay here the rest of this year and next? I like this room.*

The remainder of her middle school time no one bothered to mess with her. They would murmur about her, she would hear them, but they didn't dare cross her for fear she would lay them out like she did Rhys.

Middle school also saw the dawning of new love for most students. Emma would watch as they began to pair off in couples. She thought she should be envious of them, but she wasn't. There wasn't a single person who caught her attention that she would want to pair off with.

Dances were announced. Notes were passed asking classmates to go to the dances or to go steady.

Emma watched the goings on, curious, but distant, still invisible. She didn't want to be asked, and she didn't want to ask anyone. She could see couples in the hallways holding hands, and behind the school up against the walls making out. It made her slightly nauseous. Even that turd Rhys had a girlfriend that would hold his hand and kiss his slimy lips. Emma knew his lips were slimy, because she could remember the feel of them against her knuckles when she hit him.

Emma threw herself into her sports and her studies. She didn't have time for socializing, no one was worth detracting her from her goals. Jessie had told her that some students who were really smart and athletic could get scholarships to colleges and universities. That was what she wanted. She decided she wanted out and she wanted a new life. Her superpower was that despite all of her accomplishments, she maintained a level of invisibility. Even her teachers couldn't remember her name, even though she often had the highest scores in the class.

~ *2* ~

S o m e t h i n g   t o   B e l i e v e   I n

The Present...

THE LOW LIGHTING AND FLICKERING candles danced off of the crystal glasses. Through the sound system, Ellis Marsalis is playing in the background. Emma's wife loved Ellis Marsalis. They had seen him live in New Orleans a few years ago. She was now, seemingly unmoved by hearing him over the speakers. She was equally unmoved by the romantic ambiance that Emma worked so hard to create for this dinner.

Emma had pulled out the cloth napkins and polished the silverware. She had worked so hard. Why didn't her wife, normally a sucker for romance, care? *I didn't think my heart could hurt this much. I honestly thought it was so hyperbolic to say heartache. But it's real. I don't even know how you could do this to me.*

Emma stood up and grabbed her wife's plate and went into the kitchen. She stood silent and still for a moment before she scooped the eggplant parmesan on one side, and the pasta next to it. She poured the home-made red arrabbiata sauce over both and popped a piece of fresh hot garlic bread on the edge of the plate before heading back to the dining room and setting it down in front of her. She had spent the better part of the day preparing this food. Cleaning. Polishing. Cooking. Ignoring the calls that came in for her business to make this night special. The least her wife could do is acknowledge it. *Are you this over me that you can't even say one word to acknowledge what I put in for this night? Fuck. Not just this night. This life. How ungrateful.*

She went back to the kitchen and served her plate as well and sighed heavily as she went back into the dining room to set her plate down and uncorked the wine. Now neither of them were speaking. Emma was struggling to not cry. She poured two glasses and set one in front of the woman she loved for so long, and one in front of her own plate.

Emma sat back down and put her napkin in her lap and picked up her fork. She held back her tears and put the polished utensil back down.

"I get it. You don't want to talk to me right now. You don't want to discuss it. So, I will talk," Emma began. "I've spent the better part of my life invisible. Invisible by choice. Unimportant. No one ever *really* noticed me until you…" Emotion was gripping her voice and it shook as she spoke. "I became who I am, and did everything, in part, to provide this life for you."

The Past (1991-1992)

EMMA STARTED HIGH SCHOOL AND was selected to play varsity for the girls' basketball team her freshman year, which as a freshman was completely unheard of. Coach Adame had actually watched Emma play during her eighth-grade year, when her middle school played his daughter's school.

Bear was gone more than he was home anymore. At least three or four nights a week he didn't come home until early in the morning. Faint glitter dusted his pants and he smelled like cheap coconut oil and beer when he came wandering in. His eyes would be bloodshot, and he would grumble to Emma as she made her breakfast before school.

"Sorry, Princess."

She would shrug, "Good morning, Bear."

He would stumble over to the coffee maker where Emma had made a pot for them both to share and pour himself a mug.

He would plop into the chair across from Emma while she scarfed down toast and jam and drank her coffee.

"How's school, Princess?" he would ask.

"Good. I have all A's."

"That's my Princess!"

"I made varsity, Bear."

"You're a freshman! That's good."

Emma was now almost 5'10". She kept her hair long, but it stayed in a tight ponytail at all times. Her olive complexion was flawless, and her thin figure was envied by the other girls in the locker room. She was toned and taut from eating a predominantly vegetarian diet (she never recovered from the doe), and her extra time working out and practicing for basketball and softball. She was agile and aerodynamic on the basketball court and her fastball on the pitching mound threw more than one batter off regularly. She was naturally beautiful in her features. High cheekbones, and her piercing dark blue eyes were framed with dark lashes. She was aware of the other girls around her and she knew she was pretty and exotic looking compared to the others. She was confident in her appearance, abilities, and intelligence.

Beautiful. Talented. Smart. Still invisible. She didn't mind the invisibility, though.

"I have a game tonight, Bear, maybe you and Jessie can come?" she asked, hopeful.

"Maybe."

Emma sighed heavily. She loved being invisible amongst her classmates and teachers, but she wished Bear or Jessie would spend more time paying attention to her. She would like to have someone there for her in the stands when she played, cheering for her.

The girls in the locker room left her alone because they were all upperclassmen, and she was a freshman.

They would congratulate her on her big plays and her ability. They would clap her on the back, but that was the extent of the interactions.

She would listen to them talk in the locker room.

"Are you going to the party at Jilly-Bean's house this weekend?"

Who the hell willingly goes by Jilly-Bean?

"Yeah. Of course."

Because when in Rome, riiiggghhhtt?

"Do you think Brad will be there?"

Ohhhh... Brad!

"I hope so! Oh, my gawd... Did I tell you he asked me to hang out and help him 'study' tomorrow!"

Gag.

A gaggle of giggling and snorting and obscene gestures would follow, causing Emma to blush and feel awkward. *This is the type of stuff I expect in the boys' locker room, not the girls'. God, this is disgusting.*

Emma faded into the background as she changed her clothes and made her way to class.

She made her way amongst the halls, quiet and unnoticed, observing her peers detached. It was December of her freshman year and she had spent the better part of her first semester in high school flying under the radar.

As she made her way past a group of boys on her way to second period, "Hey! I remember you!" a boy in the center of the group called out.

There were about ten boys clustered around. She looked, unnerved that her cloak of invisibility was not working.

"I know you! Bloody Mary!" he sang out. *That stupid prick, Rhys.*

"Bloody Mary?" a boy in the group asked leering back, knowing Rhys must have a good story.

Rhys, let it drop. It's not even that funny and it's old.

"She started her rag right in class. Blood. Every. Where. Like that scene from *The Shining* where it's pouring out everywhere," Rhys exaggerated, laughing. His group laughed with him.

Oh. We are going there, are we?

She stopped and faced him, smirking. "Tell the rest of the story, Pussy Boy."

All the boys stopped laughing and looked at her.

"What's the rest of the story?" Rhys challenged.

"I clocked you. I hit you so hard, you fell down and hit your head. I almost knocked you out. I can do it again and show your friends how you got your ass handed to you by a girl, Pussy Boy."

"Oooooooohhhhhh…" his friends taunted.

"Is that true?" another one asked Rhys, hitting his shoulder. "You got laid out by a girl?"

"Whatever," was Rhys's only reply. "Keep moving, Bloody Mary. None of us want to talk to your weird ass anyway."

Emma flipped him off. "Whatever, keep it up. I will show you and your friends all over again."

She spun on her heel, pulled her hood on her sweatshirt up over her head and marched off to her class.

She was shaking and angry. She was trying to not let her anger show as she slumped into her desk in class. *Straight A's. Best female athlete in the history of the school. And this is what I have to deal with? All because Bear is too negligent to raise a girl. All because he couldn't be a good husband and keep my mom around. This is unfair.*

Emma sank deep into a brooding mood for days after this. Rhys and his cronies would taunt her as she walked by. "Bloody Mary." She would hear it hissed at her as she walked by.

Her heat and anger would burn as she walked by with her middle finger in salute as she passed.

As she was passing them one day, a hand reached out and grabbed her unexpectedly. *What is going on?* Before she could say anything or pull away, hands covered her mouth and other hands were holding her arms, bodies were barricading her in every direction, and she could feel hot eager hands groping her between her legs. *Stop. Just stop. Someone make it stop.* "Nope, she's not bloody!" They were laughing as they all let go and pushed her away down the hall and sauntered off laughing in the other direction.

Her eyes brimmed with tears and her body buzzed with hate. Even though they had let go of her, she could still feel their hands all over her, restraining her and groping her. *Of all the things I will be remembered for. Who the hell gave them the right to touch me like that?*

Her anger hummed through her the rest of the day. After the final bell rang she marched to the shop where Jessie and Bear were busy doing a brake job.

"Princess, what's up?" Bear sang out to her from the bay where he was working underneath a luxury car of some sort.

Just let it out. He needs to know. "You want to know what's up?" she shouted. "What's up is you never bothered to explain to me when I was younger that I was going to start my period. Or what it was. I got my period in school two years ago, and guess what? That's all I'm known for now. I'm called Bloody Mary. That's what they call me. You couldn't be there for me. You couldn't prepare me. I'm not known for any of my accomplishments. I'm known for starting my period in 7th grade. I have a mom somewhere out there. You won't tell me her name. You won't tell me who she is. I don't even know her god damned name, Bear! Tell me … Who is she? Who *is* she? *Where* is she?" Emma was crying, her face was red.

Jessie put down his tools. "Emma, sweetie… now is not the time for all of this. We have to get this car done. Why don't you go on home, and Bear will be there——"

"No. No! I'm not going! I'm not leaving! I'm so sick of you both! Neither of you have done anything for me! Who is my mom? Where is she?" Emma was shouting inside the shop. Her voice shrill and echoing off of the cement of the mechanic's bay.

"Princess, I'm going to tell you this one last time," Bear's voice was low and measured. "Your ma left. She gave birth to you, and she left. That's it. It doesn't matter who she is. It doesn't matter what her name was. She is the one you need to be mad at. Not me. I'm doing the best I can by you. You can show me a little bit of gratitude."

Of course. It's all about you. Emma narrowed her eyes, and lowered her voice to match Bear, "Tell. Me. Her. Name."

"Go. Home."

Jessie approached Emma and put his hands on her shoulders and tried to steer her back, "Emma, hon, I think you need to head home and calm down."

The last thing I need right now is someone else touching me. She spun from under his touch and focused her gaze and her anger on Jessie, "I'm not leaving until one of you tells me the name of my mother. You, Jessie, are just

~ 24 ~

as much to blame for all of this as he is. Neither of you can tell me... And why?"

"Emma, you are being very ungrateful," Jessie said quietly. "We've done everything we can for you. We don't know much about kids or babies or raising young ladies. But look at you. So what, your Bear didn't think to tell you about your period. Look at everything else. You have a roof over your head. You have meals that you don't even eat. You have clothes. So what, your ma left you? Why do you blame us for that? You don't thank us for what we did do for you, but you blame us for something we had no say in or control over?"

"Tell. Me. Her. Name." *It's really not that hard. You should remember her name in the very least.*

"Jayne Mansour," Bear said quietly. "Her parents were immigrants from somewhere."

Emma's eyes began to mist over, and her throat tightened. In her fourteen years, this was the first time she heard her mother's name. "Jayne Mansour," she repeated. "Was that so hard for you to tell me?"

"When she left us, Princess, it hurt me bad. I don't like to even say her name."

"Don't call me Princess anymore," Emma whispered.

Bear and Jessie were quiet.

Emma turned on her heel and walked out defiant, doing everything she could to hold back the floodgate of emotions that was threatening to burst. *I know her name. She had a name. Jayne. Jayne Mansour.*

She let herself back into the trailer and to her small room. She threw down her bag and laid across her bed grabbing Brownie and holding him tight to her chest. "Jayne Mansour," she repeated. "My mom has a name. It's Jayne Mansour." She was talking to Brownie, whispering in his ear. "I finally know who she is."

She sat up and grabbed a notebook out of her bag and wrote the name down, "Jane Mansore," the way it sounded with Bear's pronunciation.

Bear didn't come home that night.

~ 25 ~

In the morning, he came stumbling in again. Again, smelling of beer and cheap perfume. He poured coffee and sat at the table.

Emma sat across from him. *He's kind of gross. I mean, I can see why my mom left if this is what he's always been like.*

"Tell me about her."

"Nothing to say. She's gone."

Liar. Gross and a liar. "What was she like before she left?"

He shrugged. "I don't remember."

"Bullshit."

"Watch your mouth."

"No. I know you remember things about her."

"We are not doing this." Bear stood and took his coffee to his room and slammed the door.

Gross. Liar, and a chicken shit. Yep. That's exactly why she left. No one can blame her for that.

Emma took herself to school early and went into the library. She walked over to the librarian and asked, "If I wanted to find information about a person, how would I do that?"

"Do you have their name?"

"Yes."

"Follow me." The librarian took her to the back of the library where the stacks of journals, phone books, records, and microfiche were found.

The librarian sat her down and showed her how to search through the indexes.

She sat for over an hour, making herself invisible and disappearing into her search. The librarian forgot she was there, and she missed the entirety of her first period class searching for anyone by the name Mansour or any of its variations. She found nothing. No one by that last name, and no one that could possibly be linked to that name.

She researched the surname and learned that she had not spelled it correctly, and it was most likely some sort of Middle Eastern, Arabic or Egyptian name. She was excited by this information, as her olive complexion and dark hair now made sense to her. She felt a sudden connection to a past she was beginning to realize. She checked out books on the Middle East, Mediterranean, and Egypt so she could learn about their cultures.

After school she went to the city registrar's office and asked for a copy of her birth certificate.

She was dismayed that they didn't have it on file.

She walked down to the shop and confronted Bear again. "Where's my birth certificate?" she asked.

"Girl, I don't know what's gotten into you."

"I deserve to know who I am and where I come from. That includes my people."

"I don't know where it is. Jessie and I are your people."

"How do you not know where it is?" she asked exasperated.

"It's somewhere in the trailer in my paperwork." He shrugged. "You can go look for it."

He's hiding something. He has to be. There's no other reason he won't tell me anything. That's fine. I will get the information on my own. Emma took herself back to the trailer and went to Bear's room and opened his closet. Piles of dirty clothes lined the floor and the room smelled musty like beer and cigarette smoke. *It really stinks in here.* She saw piles of old paperwork stacked on the top shelf. *No wonder he doesn't know where anything is.*

She pulled the first stack down and took it back to her room. She couldn't stand the smell in Bear's room.

She sat on the floor and sat Brownie and Teddy next to her, out of habit from her childhood.

She sorted through the stack. Old bills. *Useless.* Letters from when Jessie was in the army. *Jessie was in the army? Why did I never know that? What else has he not told me?* More bills. Bank ledgers. *I knew we were poor, but damn.* Seeing the bank ledgers, sometimes with negative balances really showed Emma how poor. Drawings she had made Bear growing up. *That's actually kind of sweet.* School photos and other snapshots. *Who the hell are these people? None of these make any sense or have any context. Bear has had this whole life I know nothing about.* A few of Bear with some dead animals he killed. Some people she didn't recognize with no captions. She organized the stack and put it back.

She came back to her room and took notes on what she found out. She had kept some of the photos out so she could ask Bear about the people in the photos. None of them looked Middle Eastern to her, so none of those were her mom. But there were a few that looked like Bear and Jessie, so she assumed they were family she never met or heard of.

She laid back on her bed too tired emotionally to grab another stack and walk away with more questions. She would save that for tomorrow.

She heard Bear come in and go to the fridge and the pop and hiss of a can of beer being opened.

The trailer rocked with his heavy footfalls and with him collapsing on the sofa. *Look who decided to come home.*

She grabbed her notebook and heaved herself off of her bed and to the couch next to Bear.

"You have some 'splaining to do," she said imitating a character from a show they used to watch together as she sat next to him on the couch.

He sighed in defeat.

"Jessie was in the army?"

"Yes. He was in Vietnam." There was an undertone of pride in his voice.

"For how long?"

"He served two tours. He got a Purple Heart for getting hurt while he was saving one of his platoon members."

"Did you serve?"

"No. I hurt my knee playin' football. They wouldn't take me. I tried to go though."

"Why didn't you ever tell me about any of this? Or Jessie?"

"It never came up. I'm tellin' you now."

She sighed.

"Emma, what do you want from me?" He was frustrated.

"I just want to know. I want to understand." She looked back at her notebook. "So, you were injured and didn't serve. Jessie served. Who is this?" She held up a picture of a pretty blonde woman with a bouffant hairdo and a cigarette.

"That was my ma." He took the picture from her and looked at, his expression softening.

"My grandmother." Emma's voice was soft as she leaned over so she could further study the picture with Bear. "Tell me about her." Her tone went from soft to pleading.

"Not much to tell... She had Jessie when she was young. Very young. She was maybe fifteen or sixteen. She drank a lot. And smoked a lot. But she was a lot of fun. She made me laugh a lot. She got the cancer in her lungs and her breast, and she died right after I graduated high school. Jessie was still in the war." His voice was quiet and hoarse. Emma could sense the pain in him as he spoke. "She would have liked you a lot. She would have been proud of you."

Emma held her breath. *Keep talking there has to be more! I want to know it all!* But instead, he just heaved a deep breath and took a swig of his beer and stopped.

"What was her name?"

"Emily. I named you Emma in honor of her. Your eyes remind me of hers. They were like a dark blue, like yours sometimes look. Yours are darker blue, I think. But it's been so long. Maybe they were the same."

Emma felt grounded for the first time in so many years. She had a whole family with a back story, and she was learning it.

"Why haven't you ever told me about her? Told me stories about her?" Emma was not confrontational, but quiet.

"It hurts to talk about her. I miss her a lot. Princess, I never thought that you would need this information. I thought Jessie and I could be enough for you."

She looked away from the picture and away from Bear. She looked down at her notebook and the other pictures she had pulled from the stack.

She pulled a picture of Bear with a man that looked just like him, but older, standing with a large dead buck. She held it up for Bear to see.

Bear took it with shaking fingers. "That's my pa and me."

"Where is he?"

"Dead, too. Not long after my ma. He drank a lot. Gambled a lot. When Ma died, he drank more. He was driving home from the bar after drinking too much. He ran a red light, they say. He died. Neck snapped. But you didn't miss much. He was a mean man. A mean drunk. Used to beat my ma and us when he drank too much and lost money when he gambled."

She had never seen Bear so quiet and so emotional. Hearing all of this new information, gave her a whole new sense of who Bear actually was. So much about him made sense to her now.

"What was his name?"

"Asshole. That's what I called him. But his name was Thomas." His voice was still low, and his hand was still trembling as he held the picture. His eyes were far off.

Emma threw herself into his arms and hugged him tight. "Thank you, Bear. Thank you for telling me about them." Her eyes were damp with tears. *You make sense to me now. At least more than you did. I can't be mad at you. You've been hurt for so long. Everyone you loved is dead or left you.*

She put the research on her mother on hold, having a new sense of connection to her family through Bear.

Every year they had Christmas at Jessie's small house down the road from the shop. He had a small tree with a few chipped bulbs and flashing colored lights. His house reflected that he was a lifelong bachelor. An army flag hung over the tattered couch. Posters of women in bikinis with fake boobs and beers hung on the walls.

After Christmas dinner, she cornered Jessie to ask him about his time in the army.

"Emma, I don't like to think about it. That's why I don't talk about it. I get nightmares. I wake up in the middle of the night thinking I'm back there. I hear fireworks and I feel like I'm back in the jungle. I wake up screaming sometimes. Seeing blood. Seeing my friends blown to bits. Seeing kids with bombs strapped to them…"

"Why haven't you ever gotten married or had kids?"

Jessie sat back on the couch. He pondered the question for a moment in silence, took a sip from his long neck beer bottle and looked at her. "I haven't found a woman who can deal with me. I told you I have those nightmares. It's hard for most women to put up with that. They don't like that I don't have much money. They don't like that I've been a bachelor so long I don't want to change my ways."

Emma looked around at his house for the first time from the perspective of a young woman and not as a place she had always spent a lot of time. *He's not lying. This place screams 'single for life'.*

"Do you want a wife and kids?"

"Your Papa Bear and I didn't have the best example growing up of how a husband and dad should be. I don't know that I even really want all of that anyway. I guess it would be nice to have a wife, but I don't need no kids. I have you." He smiled and ruffled her hair.

"Stop!" She pulled away giggling and smoothing her hair back out. "I'm serious though."

"So am I. If one comes around and sticks around, yeah, that would be great. But I'm too old for any kids or stuff."

Emma felt content in her new knowledge of her family, and she felt like life made sense again.

When school came back from the holiday break, she moved back into the tranquil flow of her invisibility. She did her homework, and she went to her classes, and she went to practice and her games.

By March, her basketball team had made the state championship finals. She was agile, graceful and aggressive on the court. She convinced Bear and Jessie to come and cheer her on. It was a big deal for their school to make it as this was the first time, and she was the first freshman to ever make varsity and it was because of her that they even made it this far. It was nice to know that she would have people in the stands cheering just for her for once.

During the game, she was given a chance for three penalty shots.

She stood at the line, and she looked at the basket. The crowd in the stands had faded from her vision, and she could no longer hear them either. The only sound she could hear was her heartbeat in her ears. She felt as she did the moment she zeroed in on the doe in the deer stand. Her breath was caught up in her chest and she felt the rubber of the ball against her fingertips. *Breathe. You need to breathe.* She dribbled the ball in sync with the beat of her heart.

She exhaled and shot the first one. She made it. She grinned with self-satisfaction.

She made the other two, looking smooth and confident as she did, which gave her team the margin to win.

After the game, as she was meeting up with Bear and Jessie in the parking lot, her coach, Mr. Adame, approached them. He was a former college athlete who missed going professional due to a knee injury. Tall, and self-assured he was a favorite teacher of most of the female student body. Most girls did all they could to get into his Algebra class and attend his after-school tutoring as well. Emma never paid him much attention, as she still had no interest in anyone. When her classmates would whisper and giggle and make borderline inappropriate comments about him, she would blush and do her best to shut them out.

"Landry!" he called out trotting up to her and Bear and Jessie.

She stopped and turned to face him. "Mr. Adame, this is my dad and my uncle Jessie."

He shook their hands in the order she had introduced him. "Joseph Adame. Nice to meet you both."

"How 'bout my Princess!" Bear called out slapping Emma on the back.

"That's what I want to talk to you about. Emma is quite the athlete. She's a natural. I've never seen another girl on my team move like she does. I've never recruited a freshman for varsity before. Look, college coaches are not allowed to recruit kids until their junior year – but—"

"Hey, Coach. Not to cut you off, but I wanted to take Emma for some ice cream to celebrate. Why don't you join us and tell us what it is you want to tell us over dessert?" Bear interjected.

Mr. Adame nodded, "Yeah. Okay. I will follow you."

Emma was excited. Bear only ever took her for ice cream for her birthday.

Sitting across from Bear and Jessie with Mr. Adame in the booth with them, Emma felt very self-conscious all of a sudden.

She looked down at her chocolate malt as Mr. Adame and Bear talked small talk for a moment. "Look, I don't know how much you or Emma know about me personally…" Mr. Adame began.

Emma shrugged.

"I don't know shit about you, man. You are Emma's coach. You teach at the school," Bear said.

Oh my god. Shut up, Bear. Don't embarrass me.

Jessie had gotten up and excused himself to go and flirt with the waitress working the counter. *I wish I could just get up and go to the counter, too.*

Mr. Adame half smiled at Bear's curtness and continued, "I came from nothing. My mom was a single mom. We lived off the system—"

"I don't take no handouts," Bear cut him off. "We may not have a lot of money, but I refuse to take a dime from the government."

Just listen and stop embarrassing me.

"No, that's not where I'm going. I'm telling you, we didn't have a lot. And I had two younger sisters, also. So, my mom, she worked two jobs and had government assistance. College was not in the picture for me. But I was a natural athlete like Emma. I started playing sports. I had to. It was that or start running with the rough kids. Selling dope and whatnot. I was recruited for the university, and it changed my life. The recruiters can't reach out to Emma until she's a junior, but she can still secure herself a scholarship and a future. One of my friends is the women's coach at State. If Emma is interested in going there, she can reach out to him, and they can set up some meetings, put herself on the radar with him. She can get the ball rolling and secure herself a spot and a future. It can change her life."

Emma looked at Mr. Adame for the first time since they sat down. *I can get away from this life. I can be something more than where I come from. I want to go to college. I want a better life. I don't think it will ever happen though. Those kinds of goals, those things don't happen for people like us.*

Bear was quiet.

"Think about it, Mr. Landry. This could be the opportunity of a lifetime for Emma."

Emma shifted her gaze to Jessie and the waitress at the counter. She was leaning over the counter seductively as they talked, and Jessie was grinning at her. The waitress was playing with Jessie's ponytail. *Gross. I don't understand what women see in him.*

The speakers were playing pop hits from the 1950's, and there was a soft murmur from the surrounding tables.

He's only talking to Bear to be polite. This is directed at me. Honestly, it doesn't matter what Bear thinks or what he wants. I'm going to do it. I'm getting out of here. I want to go to college. I want a career. I want a life where I don't deal with this hillbilly bullshit or my fucked-up history, or this town where I'm looked at like I'm nothing. I can see it. If I do what I need to do, and play it all right, I can see the light at the end of the tunnel. I know what my potential is. I know I'm more than what they see me as.

"Thank you for the information, Mr. Adame. Emma and I will talk about it."

That's a lie, Bear. You will never bring this up with me. Not ever. This is my decision anyways. Not yours.

Going back to school after the state championship game, Emma found a new notoriety. Several of the students congratulated her and high-fived her. She was humble and shy in this praise.

As she walked into the lunch room to get her free lunch, she heard, "All Hail! Bloody Mary! The Hero of the Girls' Varsity Basketball Team!" Rhys was standing on a table, calling out with hands to his mouth to amplify his already loud voice. His table of minions began chanting "Bloody Mary! Bloody Mary!" and it began to pick up and carry throughout the cafeteria.

The cafeteria was lined with long tables that could accommodate roughly ten kids per side on each table on long bench seats. There were approximately ten tables, packed in the cafeteria, each full with students eating their lunches. Emma assessed where she was standing by the entrance, and where Rhys was perched on top of his table with his minions chanting and pounding the table below him. There was a table between where Emma was standing near the entrance and the table Rhys stood upon.

Emma looked down and bit her lip as she shook her head; *Oh hell no. Not this shit again.* She sat her bag down by her feet and evaluated the clearance between herself and him and how best she could get to him. Before she could think twice, she sprang from the floor to the bench seat, nearly pushing a boy to the floor, to the table top closest to her and then leapt across the space like a panther, tackling Rhys. The both of them went sailing downward tumbling to the floor – Rhys taking the brunt of the fall below Emma on his back.

The wind was knocked out of him from the force of her weight landing on top of him. It was apparent he was stunned by the swiftness and severity of her attack. He stared up at her with large eyes, telling her that he knew she bested him yet again. Sensing his fear, she sat up with her knees straddling his chest, pinning him to the floor. He was gasping for air under her weight and from the strain of the hit.

The crowd in the lunch room was shouting and cheering as they formed a circle around her and Rhys to watch. They were shouting for Rhys to get up and fight back, some were just chanting "Fight! Fight! Fight!" Emma heard none of it. She only could hear the loud humming in her head.

She cocked her fist back and nailed him once good and hard. She felt his teeth against her knuckles and heard a snap. Before she could pull back and hit him a second time, she was being forcibly pulled off of him and to her feet by the principal, Mr. Barrett. She could smell his strong cologne spicy and musky as he dragged her back. His bright bald head was reflecting the light into her eyes.

The school security guard was helping Rhys to his feet. He was muttering, "Crazy bitch! That crazy bitch hit me," Rhys spit as blood was pouring from his lips. The broken fragments of his teeth were on the floor by his feet.

"Who's bleeding now? Call me Bloody Mary again!" she shouted at him. "I kicked your ass in seventh grade, and I kicked your ass just now. I will kick it again. I dare you!"

Mr. Barrett and now his vice principal Mr. Stone were both pulling her back. "Hush!" Mr. Stone coaxed. "Girl, do you want to throw away your whole future on some worthless little shrimp?" He was trying to de-escalate her. Both Barrett and Stone were huge, bald men. She was being dragged away between two pool balls she imagined. "You have a brilliant future. That boy only has his daddy's money. He ain't gonna amount to much aside from that. He is not worth it." He was whispering in a steady stream as her feet began to finally move under her instead of being dragged.

She righted herself and pulled out from the grasp of the two older men and walked upright and proud between them instead. Her breath was still shallow, and her adrenaline was coursing through her. She had zero cognition of her knuckles bleeding and open from their direct contact with Rhys's teeth.

She sat in the principal's office while they called Bear. Her arms folded across her chest, she was only just now becoming aware of her knuckles bleeding from where they had met Rhys's perfect pearly whites. She had refused the ice pack they offered her as she was escorted into the office. Her right leg vibrated with anger and anxiety.

Mr. Stone and Mr. Barrett sat across from her. Neither of them said a word to her. Mr. Stone looked concerned, and Mr. Barrett looked annoyed.

When Bear arrived, an older secretary led him in, and he took his seat next to Emma.

She looked at Bear defiantly and he looked back at her with a mixture of concern and confusion.

"Mr. Landry, we called you here today because we need to suspend Emma."

"Suspend Emma? Why?" Bear asked, taking a seat next to Emma.

"She attacked another student. She tackled him and beat him to a pulp," Mr. Barrett informed him.

"You are leaving out that he is calling me Bloody Mary for starting my period in seventh grade. Humiliating me in front of the entire school. He needs to learn when to let it go and to shut up." Emma was seething at a low boil, her knuckles were beginning to swell and really hurt, causing her to regret declining the ice pack.

"Is the boy going to get any punishment for humiliating my daughter?" Bear asked.

"He's going to need to see a dentist, and a doctor for his injuries. Don't you think that's punishment enough? He got beat up by a girl," Mr. Barrett said deadpan.

"How long is Emma suspended for?"

"Three days. If she does this again, we will have to consider expulsion."

Bear turned in his chair and faced Emma. "Girl, I don't blame you for what you did. But I'm not happy with this. Not one bit. You have a chance in life to be better than anyone else in our family. You heard what that coach said last night. You want to piss all that away?"

Emma's eyes brimmed with tears. She looked down and away, staring at the floor. *This is why when I think about what life could be for me, I know it is just a wish. I will never escape this. I can't escape it. Don't pretend like you think I will actually make it out of this.*

"What about her homework?" Bear asked.

"I sent an office aid to collect it for her."

Emma turned in her seat and saw Rhys bloody, with what she presumed was his mother comforting him. She made eye contact with the tall, elegant woman in high heels and a fine skirt. Her blonde hair was swept up in a French twist, and her diamond earrings dazzled in the fluorescent lights. Rhys's mom refused to break away from her gaze and marched into the principal's office without knocking.

"This is the little monster that beat up my son?" She was pointing her red lacquered nail at Emma.

"Your son is a little bitch," Emma snarled, staring Mrs. Mills directly in the eye, fearless.

Bear spun around and looked at Emma. "That's enough," he warned under his breath. Emma had never seen him kowtow to anyone before.

So, it's like that, Bear? You will bow down to this pretentious bitch and her kid? I am not ever going to bow down to these people. I refuse. I will not be like you. "No. It's not." Emma stood defiant and narrowed the gap between herself and Rhys's mother. *This bitch and her pathetic spawn will not get away with treating me like I'm anything other than worthy of the same respect they demand.* "Your son is a little pig. You know what he did to instigate this? He called me Bloody Mary. He called me Bloody Mary because when I was in seventh grade I got my period in front of the whole class. He thinks that it's funny. He's a pig. A classless pig. You need to do better." Emma pointed her finger back at Mrs. Mills. They were standing nearly toe to toe. Emma could smell her expensive perfume.

She narrowed her eyes on Emma. "Lay another hand on my son, and I will make sure the only school you attend is in the state pen. You need to learn to act like a lady. Get some class, you poor white trash loser." She looked at Bear and pointed to him, "I will send you the bill for Rhys's teeth."

Bear wiped his mouth with his hand and closed his eyes with an exhale. "You can't get blood from a turnip, lady, but you sure can go ahead and try."

Principal Barrett just remained silent at his desk. Incredulous, Emma looked over at him. *Why wouldn't he say anything to this woman?*

Rhys's mom turned on her expensive high heeled shoes and spun out of the office. "So, she's allowed to march in here and talk to us like that? Her son is allowed to say whatever?" Emma was frustrated and didn't understand.

"Emma, you can't let what others think of you get under your skin like that," Principal Barrett was quiet. "You can't react every time someone makes you mad. You will set yourself up to fail. People will instigate you, just to see you fail. Rhys is one of them."

"I'm not going to let people treat me like I am less than they are. Just because my dad doesn't have a lot of money. I'm not less of a person. I may not have a mom to teach me to be a fancy lady... But I'm still a person. I still matter."

"No one is saying you don't matter, Emma. But you can't go beating up everyone who makes comments you don't like," Principal Barrett said to her.

Bear stood up, "How long before this aid gets back with her homework? I think I need to get her home and calm her down."

A girl Emma recognized from her team came in laden down with books and papers. She set them down on Principal Barrett's desk and quietly excused herself.

Bear grabbed the stack off of the desk. "Let's go," he said quietly.

Emma walked two steps behind Bear to the truck and got in. Bear set the books on her lap and let himself into the driver's side. He didn't say a word to her on the way home.

She didn't look at him. When they pulled up in front of the old run-down trailer, she got out with her books and went to her room and slammed the door.

She turned on her radio and Nirvana was crackling through the static of the speaker. She laid across her bed and stared at the ceiling.

This isn't Bear's fault. Maybe it is. He should have stood up to that bitch Mrs. Mills. He's so spineless around the rich people. He just bends over and takes it from them. What a weak suck. That's probably why my mom left him. Maybe my mom left him because he is poor and didn't do anything with himself. Maybe if he had done something more than just go work on cars for Jessie we wouldn't be so poor. If we were not so poor maybe my mom would have stayed. Maybe if she had a husband she could have been proud of, that could stand up for who he was and who we are, she would still be here. This all comes back on Bear. This is all his fault. Whatever.

She didn't move. Songs changed on the radio. The DJ left and another one came on. The sun moved across the sky and her room grew dark. *That's fine. The dark works. It matches my mood.*

It's time I start looking for my mom and her family. Maybe they will take me in. Maybe they will love me and maybe she's there with them, or they at least know where she is. Maybe my mom is wondering where I am, too.

After Bear left for work the following morning, Emma came out of her room and began going through the stacks in his closet again.

In the middle of a stack full of outdated bills, shut off and collection notices, she found a newspaper, yellowed with age and a blurry, inky picture of a pretty woman. 'Local Woman Missing', read the headline.

'Jayne Landry (née Mansour), 22, mother of an infant girl who is only three months old is missing. Police have questioned her husband and father of her infant daughter, Frank Landry, 26. Landry's alibi was solid, and they are no longer considering him a person of interest.

Landry was out hunting with his brother, Jessie, 32 when his wife went missing. "I came home, and the baby was crying in her crib, and Jayne, my wife, was nowhere to be found. It's not like her to leave the baby."

There were no signs of a struggle, and Mrs. Landry's car was gone as was her purse, jewelry, and other items of importance to her.

Her parents, Leyla and Amir Mansour declined to comment at this time'.

Emma looked at the picture again. Studying it close. The woman had her delicate bone structure and full mouth. She had long wavy black hair and her large eyes looked light in color in the black and white photograph. *I look like her. But where is she? Where could she have gone? Did she just up and leave?*

She read the names Leyla and Amir Mansour.

She kept the newspaper, setting it aside, and continued searching the closet. At the very back was a stack of pictures. Bear in a powder blue tux with a ruffled shirt front, and there she was in faded color, her mother in a beautiful white dress. Her vivid golden eyes and olive skin resplendent as she looked at Bear as they cut the cake. She was beautiful and looked so happy as she beamed up at Bear. Bear had never looked happier. *Bear really loved her. I've never seen him that happy. She looks happy, too. And yet she's gone, and no one knows what happened to her.* His features were soft with youthful love and promise as he gazed down at her mother.

Emma swallowed the lump in her throat as she looked at her mom in full color. *I have grandparents with a name I have never met and a mom that was gone somewhere in the wind. I have so many questions and no answers. No one has the answers. Where are Leyla and Amir Mansour? Why didn't they ever come to see me? What happened to Jayne, my mother?*

Behind the picture of Bear and Jayne, there was a picture of Jayne holding her, newborn, in the hospital.

The tears escaped Emma as she sat back against the wall in Bear's room looking at a happy and proud Jayne staring down at a tiny, bundled Emma. Her hair was in a ponytail on top of her head, and her face was clean of makeup, but still beautiful. Emma held the picture to her heart and cried. *You look like you loved me. You were happy to hold me. It shows. I want to know you. I want to ask you questions.*

No one can ever understand how alone I am right now. What would possess this mom who looks so happy and in love with her baby to leave? What kind of mom does that? Why haven't these grandparents ever tried to meet me or know me?

Emma gathered herself together and took the two photographs and stashed them safe in her room. Those were hers now. She would not let them be buried in Bear's closet any longer.

She dug the white pages out of the drawer in the kitchen and looked up Mansour. There was no one by that name locally.

I wish this rain would let up. Emma looked out at the weather. *I've ridden my bike in worse. I could go to the library still, but I really just don't want to, it's three miles in a torrential downpour. I will just sit and wait for Bear.*

She went back to her room and set the pictures where she could see them next to the speakers of her radio.

She turned on the radio and laid back on her bed, looking at the propped-up pictures. *I should do my homework, but I can't focus on that right now. I need answers about my family.* She watched the rain pour down outside her window and hugged her bears to her chest. *I am going to find Leyla and Amir. They will give me answers. They have to know something.*

She heard Bear come home and went out with the newspaper in hand. He stood still, frozen and looked at her with eyes large. *He looks like he just got caught in the cookie jar. That tells me he knows something. He knows more than he lets on.*

"You don't know where she is?"

He shook his head slowly, eyes downcast.

"What about Leyla and Amir?"

"I know where they were 15 years ago. I don't know if they are still there."

"Will you tell me?"

"Look, Princess. You need to know some things. I was hoping I would not have to tell you... I hoped this conversation never would come to be."

"Tell me all of it. I deserve to know. This is my story, too."

"Your ma's folks, they didn't like me. Not one bit. They didn't approve of her and me. So they wanted no part of it once she married me. They tried to stop us from being together. They told her, if she married me, they would disown her. They had some money. Amir owned a jewelry store or something. They wanted to see that she married people more like them. From the same place. They don't even know you exist."

"If they read the papers, they know I exist," she countered.

"I will give you the information I have, Princess. But if they don't want nothin' to do with ya, I don't wanna hear a word about it. They ain't what you think. I can promise you, Leyla ain't gonna be baking you no cookies an' shit."

"Maybe. Maybe they know what happened to my mom. Maybe, they will look at me and see her, and want to know me, especially if she hasn't been found."

He sighed heavily. "I want that for you, Princess. I do. I can see that I've let you down. But I know them. They ain't nice folk."

"Maybe they've changed. I need to see for myself."

He left the room and she sat at the table looking at the picture of her mother in the newspaper. She had memorized the picture at this point. If she closed her eyes, she could recall her face. So much like her own. *What did your voice sound like? Did you sing to me? If I saw you now, would I recognize you or your voice?*

Bear came out of the room with a frayed piece of paper. He had scribbled Leyla and Amir's name and address on it. "I won't take you there. But I will give you bus fare."

Emma took the paper and nodded. "I need time to figure this out. I need to know what I will say and how I want to do this."

~ *3* ~

Rising Star

The Present...

EMMA SAT BACK IN HER high back cream colored fabric chair, picking up her fork, and pushed the food around on her plate. "I had to deal with navigating the feeling of not being wanted growing up. I guess this is nothing new for me. I just wish I knew what it was that I did to make you feel the way you do. That makes me ultimately unwanted. Undesirable." She put her fork back down. "I never thought, though, that you would ever not want me."

A fly landed in the middle of the table, and she shooed it off with her cloth napkin, nearly spilling her wine. She quietly chuckled and looked at her wife before stopping, growing solemn again. "Normally, when I would do something like that, you would laugh at me. You would smile and tease me for being ungraceful, blame it on my past..." Her voice was mournful and cracked with emotion. She sighed and regained her composure.

"I'm so tired of fighting. I'm so tired of trying and being the only one who tries anymore... You are lucky. You were always wanted by everyone. I had to fight so hard to even figure out who my family was..."

The Past (1992-1993)

SUMMER VACATION CAME AND WENT, and Emma still had not pulled the trigger on meeting Leyla and Amir. She looked at the paper every day and looked at the pictures of her mom. She felt an odd sense of comfort in just knowing that she knew where her grandparents were and seeing her mom's face.

After meeting up with Mr. Adame at the beginning of the year, she reached out to his friend who coached at State.

She sat in Mr. Adame's classroom after hours and used his phone. Coach Donnelson's gruff voice on the other end made her nervous. She stammered into the phone, "Hi, Mr. Coach Donnelson… I'm Emma Landry. Mr. Adame is my basketball coach, and he told me I should reach out to you and talk to you about maybe playing up at State when I graduate in two more years…" Her voice was weak and trailed off.

"Hey, Emma Landry. Mr. Adame told me you would be calling. He also told me that you are one of the most talented players he's ever had. How would you like to come up to see the campus, watch my girls play and maybe talk?"

Emma's heart began to race. "I can… I can talk to my dad about that."

"You do that. Get some questions together for me and get back to me."

"Okay, sir. I will do that." She handed the phone back to Mr. Adame who placed it back on its cradle. He spun in the chair and looked up at her.

"Emma let's be frank. Last year was rough for you. I get it. Your grades were good, and your athletic skills were on point… But that stunt with Rhys in the cafeteria… We can't go forward this year or any other year with those kinds of antics. We need to keep your record clean. We need to make sure you get to take advantage of all that you are capable of. Do you understand?"

Emma looked at him wide-eyed. "Yes, sir. I understand. But what am I supposed to do? Just let Rhys and his cronies do and say what they want?"

"No, Emma. I'm not saying that. But instead of reacting, just come talk to me, or someone. I know you think we don't care. But we do."

Emma took a deep breath. "I got it, Coach. I will do what I can."

She ran to the shop after school and excitedly told Jessie and Bear about the trip. Bear agreed to give her bus fare to go.

Looking at the map, Leyla and Amir were on the route between home and

State. She decided she would stop and see them on the way to State. It was time. She was ready.

Emma got to school early the next day and rushed to Mr. Adame's room. "I'm going to go. My dad said I could go! Can you call Coach Donnelson for me?" She was gushing.

Mr. Adame came around the front of his desk and high-fived Emma. "You are going to do big things, Emma. I know you are." He was looking at her with admiration. Emma blushed. She wasn't used to people looking at her like that, or even being seen for that matter.

Emma and Coach Donnelson set up her trip for the first week of November.

In that time, she worked hard to ignore Rhys and his friends. They would taunt her as she walked by, but she didn't even so much as look at them. Inside, she would boil, but it wasn't worth it.

She was starting to get that sinking lonely feeling though. She could see that all of her peers were pairing up.

Dances were being scheduled and notes were being passed and hands were held in hallways.

Emma looked around at the boys in her classes. None of them gave her that spark of desire she read about in books.

She had caught a few of the boys checking her out. But she didn't feel the same.

She kept her nose to the grind and stayed focused on herself.

Days before the homecoming dance, in her World History class, one of the boys who sat near her looked at her nervously before the bell rang. He was looking at her intently, hoping she would say something to him. She pretended to ignore him by busying herself with her notebook and pen. *Get the hint. Not interested in anything you have to say.*

"Emma?" he asked fidgeting in his seat, tapping her shoulder, and looking at her expectantly. She knew his name was Brandon Fitzgerald, and they had been assigned to work in the same group for a few assignments. She had caught him staring at her more than once as they worked together. She had not paid him any attention in return though. However, the girls in the halls talked about him a lot though. Many of her teammates had mentioned him as boyfriend material. He wasn't an athlete, but he competed on the debate team.

She turned, showing obvious disinterest, waiting for the teasing or slurs to begin, though he had never been historically a part of Rhys's group of assholes. *Keep your calm, Emma. No matter what, stay calm. Don't fall for the bait.*

"Um… Are you busy this weekend?" he asked.

Reflecting on what she had overheard a lot of the girls in the school talk about how they thought Brandon was cute, she scrutinized his face and his features and tried to see the attraction. He wasn't bad looking, but he was not really appealing to her. He was tall like she was and had thick brown hair and dark brown eyes, and dimples when he smiled. Even some of the girls on her team, even though they were upper classmen talked about him being good boyfriend potential because he was cute, sensitive, smart and from a wealthy family. *I have no idea why this so-called boyfriend material is talking to me about weekend plans. This has to be a set-up from Rhys and his friends.*

"Why?" she asked with a tone of suspicion in her voice.

"It's homecoming. I don't have a date. And I think… I think you are … You know. You are pretty. Would you go with me?" His voice cracked as he asked. He was obviously very nervous.

"Are you serious?" she asked raising a skeptical eyebrow at him. *I'm positive this is a set-up.*

"Um. Yeah. Yes. Why?" He was so nervous. She was charmed by his obvious anxiety.

Maybe not. He seems sincere. He's like really nervous. That's not an act. She smiled at him. "Because… I don't usually get asked."

"Okay. So will you?" He was turning shades of crimson.

She nodded, "Yeah. I'll go." *Ugh. You just said yes. I can't believe that answer came out of my mouth. I'm going to a dance with a boy.* She forced an awkward smile at him.

"Can I have your number so we can make plans?"

She scribbled her number on a piece of paper and tore it out of her notebook to give him. He folded it and put it in his pocket hastily.

As she was finishing washing dishes after dinner, the phone rang. Emma paused before answering, "Hello?"

"Hi, is this Emma?"

"Brandon?" She grabbed the cordless phone and took it in her small room.

"Why did you think I'm not serious?" he asked her again.

"Because. I don't have friends, Rhys and his group—"

"Are assholes." He cut her off. "For what it's worth, I was cheering you on when you kicked his ass last year."

She laughed nervously. "Your words not mine." *Okay. You really aren't so bad. Extra points for that answer.*

"So, what time should I pick you up for the dance?" he asked nervously.

"Can we just meet there?" Emma asked. *Please just go with it. I don't want you to see this trailer. You will change your mind. You will see what everyone says, and you will not want to go.*

"Um… yeah… I guess so. I mean, won't your parents want to take pictures or meet me or anything?" he asked.

"No… My dad ain't like that."

"Okay… Well, meet me at the flagpole then? In front of the school at seven?"

"Yeah. Okay, that works." *Thank you for not pushing the issue.*

"Oh – and what color are you going to wear? I need to get you a flower thing."

Color? I need a dress now, don't I? Shit. "I don't know. I don't have a dress. I have to go buy one tomorrow." She was suddenly nervous. She mostly wore clothes from the thrift store that she bought with her earnings from helping Jessie and Bear in the shop. *Oh shit. I only have $300 saved. I was hoping to bring that to State. I hope I can find a dress for less than that. I don't want to blow all of it on a stupid dress.*

"Okay, well, cool. Maybe call me when you buy it and tell me?"

AFTER SCHOOL, EMMA TOOK THE bus to the mall and wandered around the shops trying to figure out where to even begin. She saw gaggles of the girls she went to school with hanging out and gossiping and shopping. *And this is a sudden reminder of why I never come to the mall. I need to get in and get out as fast as I can.* A few of them took notice of her curiously and she could see them side eyeing her and making comments. *I just pray that no one tries anything. I'm here alone.*

She ducked into a shop with bright lights and loud music and vibrant colors to avoid an approaching group heading her way. A sales girl approached her eagerly. She had an edgy haircut with vibrant bright blues and pinks streaked through it and a nose ring. Emma had seen girls dressed like that in punk rock videos on MTV. She found it hard to not stare at the girl in awe. *She's like some sort of pretty exotic bird! Stop staring! She's going to think you are weird!*

"Can I help you find something?" She was smiling eagerly.

Emma looked nervously around. "I need a dress for homecoming."

"You are stunning!" the girl announced looking Emma up and down. "You are going to look great in anything you choose."

"That's the problem. I don't know what to choose."

"Here! I've got some ideas!" The girl dragged Emma from rack to rack and pulling options for her. *This is too much. I can't deal with this right now.* She was pulling dresses on hangers from about the store and shoving them into Emma's arms while Emma followed her around the store clueless and overwhelmed. "Try these on!"

I should have never agreed to go to the homecoming. I just want to go to the shop or the trailer. I don't like being here. I don't like all of this going on around me. I want my peace and quiet. This is so stupid. I was stupid to agree to go. It's too loud in here. There are too many people around.

She ducked into the dressing room the sales girl opened for her with six different dresses.

She undressed and selected the first one off the hanger. It was black, long, and had long sleeves and a low back. Bear bought her dresses when she was little, but she hadn't worn any since before middle school. She liked jeans and t-shirts mostly, and the combat boots she picked up at the Army Navy Supply store just outside of town when she went with Jessie.

The dress hugged her figure, and she felt self-conscious. *I might as well be naked. There are five more dresses here. I don't really want to try those on either. If I try them all on, I have to stay here longer. I can buy this dress and be done with the whole ordeal.*

"What do you think?" the sales girl called out.

"Um, I like this one. I think I'm going to take it," Emma called out looking at the sales tag. It was on sale and just over $100. *I don't think I have ever spent this much money on one item of clothing. But I really want to go home. I can stay and look for other options or bite this bullet. I'm just going to do it. This is money I could have spent up at State though.* "Do you have shoes here?"

"Let me see which one!" The sales girl was over eager. "We have shoes!"

Emma opened the door self-consciously.

The girl took in a sharp breath. "My girlfriend said I should buy the same dress for a wedding we were going to attend. I didn't look half as good in it as you do, though!"

"I'm sorry?" Emma asked, confused. *I think she just said her girlfriend. She has a girlfriend not a boyfriend. That's interesting.*

The girl blushed and grinned. "I have the same dress. My girlfriend encouraged me to get it. But seriously, I don't have the figure for it like you do. It's made for tall, skinny girls like you. Not short girls, like me."

She was talking fast, and Emma was still confused. *I didn't even ever think that was an option.*

"It's all good. Don't worry about it." She waved her hand in front of her face, flustered. "Shoes... Heels? You are already tall, and they won't be comfortable... What size shoe are you?"

"Eight and a half."

"Be right back." The girl disappeared quickly, and Emma went back into her dressing room and peeled the tight figure-hugging black dress off.

As Emma came out of the dressing room with the black dress in her hand, the sales girl came back with a box containing black satin shoes with a low heel. "These are called a kitten heel. They will work with that dress because of how tall you already are." Emma grabbed the box gingerly and followed the girl to the register. "Do you need accessories?"

"Please, no. I just want to pay and get home."

"Is it because of what I said?" the girl asked suddenly. "About having a—"

"No. I just don't like this place. I don't like shopping. I just... I shouldn't have agreed to go to this dance. I don't even like the guy. I mean, he's nice. But he's not my boyfriend. I don't like him like that." Emma felt the need to share all of this all of a sudden.

The girl cocked her head to the side. "I get it. I just hoped I didn't offend you."

"You didn't." *Why would that have been offensive?*

The girl started to ring up the dress and shoes. "If it's any consolation, I went to more than one homecoming with boys. I didn't like them. I went to college and discovered I like to date girls better."

Emma blushed. "I don't think I like anyone, honestly." *I must be some sort of a freak.*

"You will. One day." The girl smiled.

She is so nice. Like genuinely nice. Emma smiled back at her. "Where do you go to college?"

"I used to go to State, but I was too obsessed with dating girls and not doing my school work. I got dropped for bad grades. I go to the community college now, and I'm the assistant manager here. My girlfriend still goes to State though. I go there on the weekends and hang out with her and all of my old friends when I don't have to work weekends."

"I'm going there in a few weeks to meet the basketball coach and tour the campus."

"Really? That's awesome! I'm Simone, by the way."

"Emma."

"Maybe we can meet up while you are up there."

"The coach got it arranged for me to stay in one of the dorms and stuff."

"Abby, my girlfriend, has an apartment near campus. Let me give you her number. Call us when you get up there." She pulled tape from the register and scrawled out 'Simone and Abby-' and the number.

Emma smiled. "Thank you so much." She put the number in her pocket and paid for her purchases and left. *I think I just made a friend.*

She got home and called Brandon. "It's black," she said when he answered the phone.

"Your dress?"

She laughed. She was in such a good mood after meeting Simone. "Yes, my dress."

"I like your laugh."

I wish you wouldn't say this kind of stuff. It's weird. She felt suddenly self-conscious again. "Thank you?"

"See you tomorrow at seven?"

"At the flagpole."

GETTING READY FOR THE DANCE made Emma feel insecure all over again. It would have been better if she did not have to wear the dress. She was confident in herself when she was comfortable, but she was beyond uncomfortable. *If I ever wished my mom were here it would be now. I don't know what to do with all this hair. I guess instead of my ponytail I can leave it down. This dress is strangling me. It's so tight. I don't understand how girls dress like this every day. I can't even hardly balance in these stupid shoes. God, I hope this night goes fast.*

Jessie dropped her off in front of the school at ten to seven. She sat on a bench near the flagpole waiting for Brandon. She and Bear had watched the movie *Carrie* together once. She was hoping that she wasn't being set up for something like that by Rhys and his minions.

Out of the corner of her eye, she saw Brandon come up carrying a box with a large white flower. He let out a low whistle as she stood up and tottered toward him with those unbearable shoes.

She smiled shyly and looked down. He opened the box with the corsage, "Let me have your wrist." His voice was soft, and he looked at her with soft, dreamy eyes.

Please stop looking at me like that. This is really uncomfortable. She held out her wrist and he slid the flower on her and offered his arm so she could take it as he escorted her into the gym.

Please don't let me fall. The DJ had loud dance music playing and the space was crowded with kids. *I've never wanted to go home more in my life.*

Some of the girls from her team saw her and approached. *Don't humiliate me in front of Brandon. Don't throw pigs' blood on me. Why are you approaching me now? You never even speak to me unless we are in group projects together.*

"Emma! We almost didn't recognize you. You look beautiful!" Tamara, the varsity captain exclaimed.

Emma blushed. *Say something! Make conversation!* "Thank you. You look amazing!"

"Have fun!" Tamara exclaimed as she kept moving.

Brandon beamed at her. "I do have the prettiest girl in the room on my arm!"

Seriously. Stop that. I don't even know how to respond to that. I could say you look nice, too. But that would sound patronizing. She just forced a smile in his direction. "Thanks…"

Eventually, she ended up relaxing and having a decent time dancing with Brandon and laughing with the girls from her team. Emma felt for the first time, a sense of belonging amongst her peers.

After the evening wound down, she and Brandon walked back outside. "I can give you a ride home," he suggested, hopeful with his voice trailing off.

She shook her head and stopped to take her shoes off. "My dad is going to pick me up in a few minutes."

Brandon grabbed her arm and pulled her into him. "Emma, you are so beautiful." His voice was soft as he leaned in and kissed her.

Emma froze and stiffened in shock as his lips met hers. *Oh no. Nope. Nothing about this moment is right.* When she regained her senses, she pulled back and away from him. "Brandon, you are so nice to have asked me. And I really had fun, but it's not like that for me."

He was turning various shades of red under the floodlights in front of the flagpole. "Emma, I thought—"

Good going, Emma. You hurt his feelings. She shook her head. "I swear, it's not you. Maybe everyone is right and there is something wrong with me. Maybe I am weird or a freak. I hear all of the girls talking about you in the halls and in the locker room. A lot of girls are really into you. But I'm not one of them. Please, don't be mad at me. Don't hate me." Her voice caught in her throat at the end.

Brandon took her hand and looked into her eyes. "Emma, I don't hate you. I can't hate you. I'm disappointed. Who wouldn't be? I put myself out there and you shot me down. Do you think you could try? Give me a chance?"

"I don't think that would be fair to either one of us."

He looked down away from her, still holding on to her.

"Brandon, please…" Her eyes were misting with tears.

He nodded at her. "I won't hate you. I will be your friend. But it will be hard. You are so amazing, and you don't even see it."

She pulled him in and hugged him. "Thank you," she whispered.

Being the gentleman he was raised to be, he sat on the bench and waited for Bear with Emma. She appreciated his effort to get past the awkward kiss and talk about their history class and some of their peers.

THE FIRST WEEK OF NOVEMBER on a Friday, she ran home from school, grabbed her duffel bag packed with a few days' worth of clothes and toiletries and Jessie dropped her off at the bus stop.

"Emma, girl, you know we are real proud of you," Jessie said as she sat in the truck next to him.

Wow. He's never really told me that before. She smiled at him. "I hope so. I try, you know."

He reached into his back pocket and pulled out an envelope and handed it to her. "It's not much, but it can help you, hopefully."

She looked in the envelope, and inside were two one-hundred-dollar bills. She reached over and hugged Jessie hard. "Thank you!" That money would help her pay for food while she was away on this trip.

Her first stop was to meet Leyla and Amir. She had considered calling them first but had chickened out each time she picked up the phone. *If I'm going to do this, I need to just do it. It will be harder for them to reject me if I'm standing right in front of them at their door.*

She got on the bus, sat near the window and watched the town fade into the distance and a different town creep into view ahead and fade out again. An hour and a half later, the bus rolled into another town. This one was more worn, and older, but nicer than her town in a more traditional and established way.

The houses were all brick bungalow style homes. Sturdy and solid. Strip malls and restaurants lined the main street, large trees shaded the walk ways of the streets, brilliantly plumed with fall colors. Emma had studied the map of the town before coming and knew the walk from the bus stop would be just under a mile. *This town is nice. I like it better than home. If all goes as planned, I should be at their house in 20 minutes and I can spend two hours with them before walking back to the bus stop to head to State. Ha. Two hours though. They might want nothing to do with me. If not, I will just come back up here and eat at one of the restaurants and whatever.*

She got off the bus and looked around. Plenty of the signs were in Arabic writing and there were three competing Middle Eastern restaurants. *What is that smell? Is that from the restaurants? It smells so good. If they turn me away, I will just come over here and eat. It has to be good if it smells like this.* She had never even known her heritage, much less tried the food. The exotic smell of the spices emanating from the restaurants was intoxicating and exciting to her.

Emma walked down the street away from the restaurants and strip malls and into a residential neighborhood.

The brick bungalow homes got larger and more ornate the further she went into the neighborhood.

The closer she got to Leyla and Amir's address, the more her anxiety ramped up. *Oh my god. I'm doing this. What am I going to say to these people? What if they don't want the intrusion? What if they are like what Bear said they are? What if my mom is there? Will she want me? I should just turn around and go back. This is stupid. I don't know what to do if they don't want me. I need to do this though. If I don't do this I will never know. I need to do this. Keep walking. Keep going forward. Bear has lied and been wrong about so much. I've seen that much.* She found their home. A large brick bungalow with gleaming windows and a large black Buick parked in the driveway. The door had a cobblestone A-frame around it, giving it a cottage style appearance, and the door itself was rounded and newly painted. A manicured garden and trimmed bushes lined the front of the house, and the lawn was perfectly well-kept. *Move. One foot in front of the other. You look like a stalker just standing here. Come on. Move, girl.*

With leaden legs, she finally took one slow, heavy step after the other up the walk, not sure she was even breathing.

Before she knew it she was at the door. She had to knock or turn and run away back to the bus stop.

Her fist rapped against the door on autopilot. She waited with her heart thumping hard in her chest, when an older woman with skin the same color as hers, and short salt and pepper hair answered the door. She was looking into eyes shaped exactly like hers, large, round, and framed with thick dark eyelashes. "Can I help you?" the woman asked with a heavy accent. The woman was staring at Emma as if she was not trusting what she was seeing.

"Are you... Hi, ma'am... Are you Leyla Mansour?" Emma's voice was tremulous.

"Yes. Can I help you?" She repeated her question, still staring.

"I'm ... I'm ..." Emma was shaking. *Damn it. Just spit it out.* She cleared her throat and closed her eyes. "I'm Emma Landry. I'm Jayne Mansour's daughter. I'm your granddaughter."

Leyla's hand flew up to her mouth. "I couldn't believe it, what I was seeing looking at you. I thought maybe... Do you know where Jayne, your mother is?" she whispered.

Emma shook her head. "I was hoping you knew."

Leyla stepped aside, "Come in."

Emma stepped inside tentatively. She looked around and saw photos scattered about on tables and walls. A nicely decorated living room and plush couch. Beautiful hardwood floors stretched the length of the room and into the hallway. They were polished and the home smelled of lemon and spices. *She is not like what Bear said. I've missed out on a lifetime of this woman.*

"Sit. Sit." She ushered Emma to the cozy microfiber couch.

Emma sat on the edge of the seat. She was still unsure if she had taken a breath yet.

"You look like my daughter, Jayne," Leyla said with her tremulous voice. "We've been looking for ... Well... I've been looking for her. My husband, her father, your grandfather... He passed away five years ago. A heart attack. So sudden while he was at work. Now, I'm alone."

She was seated next to Emma on the couch. She reached out and grabbed Emma's hands. Emma's eyes spilled over at feeling Leyla's hands in hers. *I want to memorize these hands.* Her skin was soft, and her hands were slight and bony and cold. Her knuckles were large with arthritis and the gold rings she wore slid around at the base of her fingers. Her nails were painted red. *The tenderness in her hands. The veins on the top of her hands. Look at how she is looking at me! She loves me.*

"But you don't know where my mom is either?" Emma asked.

Leyla closed her eyes and a tear slid out. "I made a big mistake with your mom. When she met your father, I was mad. I didn't like him. He was a no class, no education man. I thought my daughter could do better. I told her so. She was smart. She could have gone to college. She could have found a man with education and class. I told her, him or us. We had a nice husband picked out for her. A medical student from our country. Lebanon. Did you know that is where we are from? Lebanon, your blood is from. She chose him. But then, she had you. We didn't even know she was pregnant. She said she was coming back to us with you. She never came. You never came. A reporter called and said have we seen or heard from her. The police, they come, and they ask. But she never come. You never come. Not until today. We tried to call. Tried to see you. Sometimes no phone. Sometimes no answer. Sometimes, he just say no."

"You tried to see me?" Emma asked. *Keep your calm. Breathe.*

"We tried. When Jayne went missing. We knew you would need us."

Emma's tears began to flow. *You have no idea how much I've needed you.*

"You, you are here with me now. Allah blessed me with you now." Leyla smiled and pulled Emma to her. "I can't believe you are sitting here with me now. You will see more now, yes? You will come spend time with me? You will know me? I will know you?"

Emma nodded her head against Leyla's shoulder. *I need this. I need her.*

"You are so beautiful. Like your mother, my daughter, my Jayne. Such shame you never know her."

Emma pulled back and sat up and looked at Leyla. Leyla's hands went to Emma's face. "You have his eye color, but you look like my Jayne. I wish I know where she is."

"I wish I knew, as well. What do I call you?"

"Teta, is a way to say grandmother in Arabic."

"Teta…" Emma repeated.

"How much time do I have you?" Teta asked.

Emma looked at the clock on the wall. *Forever if I have my way. I want to stay here forever. I've missed so much already.* "I have about an hour and a half before I have to catch the bus. I am going to State for the weekend. I might go to college there and play basketball. I think they want to offer me a scholarship."

"So, you are an athlete? You play sports? How are your grades?"

Emma filled her in on her grades, classes and sports, while Leyla dragged her to a small dining room and sat her down. "You have dinner with me, and then I make sure you get to the bus station."

Teta put a plate of rice and rolled green things with a white sauce and a small bowl with a brown paste and strange bread in front of Emma. Emma looked at it puzzled. *Smells good, but what is it? This is what those restaurants must have been serving. It smells similar.*

"You never eat the food of your people before?" Teta asked.

Emma smiled shyly. *I've never even met "our people" much less ate the food.*

"That is rolled grape leaf, rice, leban, hummus, pita bread." Teta pointed to each item on the plate. "Healthiest diet in the world, Mediterranean. If my husband ate more of it instead of the fast-food American foods he would sneak all of the time, he would not have heart attack and die. He could have met you." She smiled brightly. "Eat. You need good food before you go on your big college weekend."

Emma ate the food and enjoyed it immensely. She watched how Teta did it, picking up the bread and ripping it and using it to pick up the food and dip it.

"This is so delicious," Emma said as she polished off her plate. "Can I please help you do the dishes?"

"No, no. Don't be silly. This is such a treat for me. Let me get some dessert and coffee, then I take you to bus."

Emma watched Teta scoot into the kitchen and come back with two cups full of hot coffee and a plate with pastries. "This is baklava. I make it better than the stores and restaurants here."

When they had finished the dessert, she drove Emma to the bus stop. "Please, promise me you will come and visit again soon?"

"I promise, Teta. I will come see you soon. Maybe in a couple of weeks? I will come on a Saturday so I can spend all day. I want to know you. I want to know more about my family, my culture. Who I am." *She wants me to be in her life. She wants to be a part of my life.*

Teta hugged Emma hard. "I love you. You don't know me. But I know you in your soul and your heart and your blood. I love you."

I've needed this woman in my life. I've needed these hugs. This love and tenderness. "I feel like I do know you. And I know I love you, too." *I've missed out on so much my whole life. You will be a part of my life from here on out for sure. I promise this to both of us.*

Emma boarded the bus with a new feeling of belonging. These past few weeks had brought her so much peace and confidence. She had a new friend in Brandon, and now she had her Teta, and now she was off to explore the possibilities of her future.

But she also had questions. Why didn't Bear allow Teta to know her? Why hadn't he allowed them to reach her? She pushed those thoughts out of her mind so as not to weigh herself down this weekend. She wanted to just enjoy her new connections and her possibilities without the darkness.

IT WAS DARK WHEN THE bus arrived at State. It was late, the buildings loomed large and dark over and around her with golden light spilling sporadically out of windows as she walked slowly to the building she was assigned to stay in for the weekend, following the map Coach Adame had drawn for her.

She checked in at a desk where a young woman was sitting behind a computer. She had black hair, and a lot of eyeliner with a long sleeved Soundgarden shirt and ripped jeans, reading a large text book with a highlighter in her other hand.

"Hi, I'm Emma Landry. Coach Donnelson set me up here for the weekend."

The girl reached back and grabbed a key. "You are on the third floor. Room 312. It has its own bathroom. There's a phone, but only for local calls, stairs are that way." The girl pointed to her left, all of this was said and done without her looking up from her book.

"Thank you." Emma took the key and headed up the stairs. When she got up to the third floor, she could hear music coming from under the doors as she passed by, and girls talking and laughing. Two girls came out of one room dressed up for what Emma presumed would be the bar, laughing. One smiled politely at Emma as they passed her.

She found the room and used the large heavy key to open the door. It was a basic room with a desk, a chest of drawers, and a small twin bed like the one she had at home. It was made up with a white comforter and two thin pillows. There was a digital clock on the nightstand and a phone as the girl promised. The small bathroom off of the room had white tiles, and a small standing shower, toilet and sink. Her only frame of reference to this point was either the trailer or Jessie's house, so though this was no frills, she still considered it an upgrade. She dropped her duffel bag on the floor and laid on the bed. She could hear muffled music through the walls and voices talking and laughing. She felt a sense of calm wash over her.

I really should call Bear and let him know I'm here safe and sound. With a sigh she rolled over and called the operator and asked to make a collect call, giving the operator the number.

Bear accepted the charges when he answered. "Hey, Princess." He sounded tired.

"Hey, Bear. I'm here. I'm safe."

"Good thing." His voice was low and flat.

He's either really tired or sad. I've never heard him like this before. "Okay, I won't keep you since it's collect. I just wanted to let you know so you don't worry."

"Okay, Princess. Have fun."

Emma hung up and rolled onto her back and fell asleep dreaming about a future that seemed to be calling her away from her roots.

THE NEXT MORNING, SHE MET Coach Donnelson for breakfast at a diner just outside of the campus.

Emma was nervous and fidgeted endlessly. *I don't know what to talk about. I don't know why I'm here. I don't deserve to be here.*

"I hear you have quite the talent. Honestly, in the last ten years, Adame has never once reached out to tell me about a student, so you have to have something going for you." Coach Donnelson was tall, and broad shouldered, his hair was thinning on top, and his gruffness reminded Emma a lot of Bear. He took up his side of the booth all by himself, he was larger than life to Emma. His eyes were sharp and so were his mannerisms and his way of speaking. He was sizing her up with his narrow eyes.

Emma fiddled with her fork. *Speak girl. Speak. Look at the man.* "I mean, that's what they tell me. I don't know how to respond... I'm sorry."

"Emma, the first thing you need to work on is your confidence. In this meeting, you need to be wowing me. Telling me how you are the best. Sell yourself to me. Tell me why you deserve to be here."

Emma sat back in the booth and looked at him. *Breathe. Don't blow this. You need this.* "I don't follow. I want to understand. I want to do what it takes. I want you to want to come see me play and offer me the spot for when I graduate. But I don't know what to say, how to do this." She was being honest with him.

"Adame said you come from nothing much. Neither he nor I came from anything. I grew up in government housing. Single mom. Same as Adame. So, I am guessing you haven't had a lot of experience in a lot of things."

Emma looked at her plate of eggs she hadn't touched yet. *Everyone knows you are poor white trash.* "This is my first time leaving my town."

"Emma, why do you want to come play for me here at State? What do you know about State? My team?"

Emma shook her head. *You look like an idiot. You are an impostor.* "I don't know anything about your team or you or even this school. I never even thought about it as an option until Mr. Adame talked to me. Honestly, I only ever thought that going to college or getting scholarships is a dream."

"What do you want to do when you graduate?"

Emma looked at him blankly. *Anything but stay in the trailer and work for Jessie.* "I haven't thought about it. Honestly, I thought when I graduated high school I was going to end up working at my uncle's auto shop. Like I said, I didn't really think about it. I didn't really think I had options. I thought anything more was a pipe dream."

"If you could do anything, if the world was to open for you, what would you do?"

"I just got done reading this book by John Grisham, and it has a lawyer. She's like the type of person I would like to be. Maybe a lawyer."

Coach Donnelson dipped his toast in his egg yolk and took a bite. *He's probably trying to not laugh at you.*

Emma kept talking. "Sitting here now, I feel like if I do things right, it's not impossible for me. I feel like if I do everything right – if I impress you – if I get a scholarship, my world will be bigger than the shop. I can be a lawyer. I can get out of that town where I'm nothing and my family is nothing. I can be so much more. So, everything rides on you liking me. You being impressed with me on the court." She was laying it all bare for him now.

"From what I understand, I will not be the only one knocking on your door to play for me. Why would you choose my team if you have other offers?"

"You are Mr. Adame's friend. I trust Mr. Adame." It was that simple for Emma.

"I tell you what, Emma Landry, one of my girls is going to meet us here. She is going to show you around today." He pulled two tickets out of his satchel and put them on the table. "These are tickets for the game Sunday. Watch my girls play. Take notes. When you go back, I want you to look up more about my team. My record. This school. Programs of study. I'm going to come watch you play when you get closer to being eligible for offers. After I watch you play, we will revisit this conversation."

Emma smiled at him. "Sounds like a deal, sir."

He paid the bill for them and a tall, beautiful girl with long braids came into the diner and made her way to the table.

"This is my current star player, Ali Jones," Coach introduced.

Ali offered her hand and Emma shook it. "Ready to look around?"

Emma stood up. "Yes, I got here last night, and it was dark, so I didn't see much."

"Have a wonderful day, ladies. I will see you again, Landry. Jones, don't scare her off."

Ali laughed and put her arm around Coach's shoulder. "I will do my best."

Ali and Emma made their way out of the diner and across the street, back onto the campus. Large trees shedding their colorful fall leaves lined the walkways. Ali pointed out the various buildings named after past alumni and what classes happened where. She brought Emma to the large old library and then down to the gym where they practiced as a team. She went to a rack where balls were stored and dribbled one, tossing it to Emma. *Show her what you got.* Emma instinctively dribbled it back and dodged around Ali, tossing the ball effortlessly into the hoop. *Ha!*

"Nice!" Ali commented, taking the ball and putting it back on the rack and taking her down to the other end of campus where the events center was. "This is where our home games are. It's never as sold out as the men's games, but it's pretty exhilarating."

"What's it like? I mean playing for Coach Donnelson?" Emma asked as they walked back toward the student union and dorms.

"He's cool, but he can be a dick, straight up. But it's all in the nature of the game. We are a championship team for a reason. If you stay on his good side, he is awesome. But if you are lazy, or slack off... He ain't have none of that shit."

"He called you his star player, so that says something. What are you studying?"

"Political Science, English minor. I just took my LSAT. I'm hoping to get into law school and then a career in politics. That's how you make a real change in this country for the people."

"What would you change?" Emma asked as they wandered up to a coffee bar in the student union.

"Everything. This country is shit for women, for poor people, people of color. I want to work to even the playing field for everyone."

Emma quizzed Ali on what she would do and how she would make changes, and why she chose her major and Ali patiently answered all of Emma's questions until she had to leave to meet a study group.

Emma took herself back to the dorms and up to her room. She pulled the receipt with Simone and Abby's number on it and dialed the number.

"Hello?" a velvety voice answered.

"Hi... I am looking for Simone?" Emma answered feeling self-conscious.

She heard the phone pass hands, and a familiar voice on the other end. "Hello?"

"Simone? This is Emma... From the store. You helped me find a black dress for my homecoming."

"Oh hey! Are you here for the weekend?" She sounded warm and friendly.

"Yeah. I'm here." *Okay. You sound lame.*

"Cool. We are having some friends over. Just a bunch of girls. Nothing fancy or big. I can come pick you up."

"Awesome. Sounds fun." *Play it cool, girl. Play it cool.*

"I will pick you up in front of the dorms around seven. Will that work?"

"Yeah. Cool," Emma said.

She looked at the clock. It was five, and she was hungry, so she made her way back to the student union and found the Taco Bell. She ate her meal there in the union taking in the buzzing life around her. *Everyone here is so different and interesting. I want so bad to be a part of all of this.*

She wandered into the book store and found a long sleeve t-shirt with the school logo on it. It was on clearance, and she decided to buy it in hopes for her new future.

She made her way back to the dorm and put her hair up in a ponytail and changed her shirt to the new one she had just bought and took herself back downstairs to wait for Simone.

Simone pulled up in a beat-up old Ford sedan. Her hair had changed color since Emma had met her. It was all jet black and teased out. She wore a dog collar with studs around her neck and a black sweater with gaping holes showing her dayglow pink bra.

Emma smiled at Simone. *She is so confident and fearless. I wish I had that confidence.* "Wow, you look different," Emma said.

"Is that a compliment?" Simone smiled.

"Yes. I like it. You are definitely brave."

Simone shrugged and lit a cigarette, offering one to Emma. Emma declined.

Simone cracked the window and made her way down the street. "So how do you like it here?"

"I like it. I can see myself coming here."

"Just don't screw it up, like I did if you come here. They don't play with your grades."

It was a short drive to the apartment complex. Emma followed Simone up the three flights of stairs and into the box-like apartment. Mismatched furniture and brightly colored art on canvas adorned the walls. Emma looked at the first painting facing her. It was a naked woman with garish bright colors swirling around her vulnerable body. Emma cocked her head and studied it. *That's beautiful, and interesting.*

"You like?" A stocky woman with a short pixie haircut, dressed in a button-down and jeans asked. It was the woman with the velvety voice from the phone.

"It's interesting," Emma confessed. *Think of something more intelligent or thought provoking to say about it.*

"Simone painted it. It's supposed to be me. Before I cut my hair."

Emma looked at her and back at the painting. "I see it now," she said quietly. *So, I've just been staring at you naked. Awesome.* Emma's cheeks flushed.

"I'm Abby." The woman extended her hand.

Emma took it. "Emma," she said, suddenly shy.

"Relax. Do you want something to drink?" Abby asked.

"No, thank you," Emma said, looking around at the other paintings. They were all of naked women. None of the others looked like Abby. But Emma wasn't sure if she should be looking at them. "Simone, you are a talented painter."

"I try. Of course, my biggest collector is Abby!" Simone flopped onto the couch.

"It's a little awkward considering all those are Simone's exes in a sense." Abby laughed.

Simone rolled her eyes. "Not *all* of them. Art has been a good way to get many girls to take their clothes off for me though." She grinned devilishly.

She wasn't joking when she said she was girl crazy. No wonder she got kicked out of here!

Emma sat next to her, and Abby went to the refrigerator and grabbed two beers, one for Simone and one for herself. Before she could sit down there was a knock on the door. She handed a bottle to Simone and answered the door.

Three other women came in, clapping Abby on the back and hugging her. One other woman with a similar aesthetic to Abby, with close cut short hair, and loose jeans with a button-down shirt. Hers was flannel, and she sported shiny new Doc Martens. The other two girls were dressed similarly but with longer hair. One of the girls sat close to Emma and smiled at her with a side-eye glance. Emma felt butterflies in her stomach and blushed as she looked away trying to fix her gaze on something other than the girl sitting close to her.

They introduced themselves to Emma as they were seating themselves and getting comfortable. Simone got up and put on a Sarah McLachlan CD. The one with short hair and the flannel shirt said her name was Jackie, and the girl with long dark hair was her girlfriend, Heather. The third girl, the one sitting closest to Emma, was Heather's stepsister Zoe. Heather and Jackie were both attending their second year at State, and Zoe was a senior at a high school in a town that Emma had never heard of on the other side of the state. *Good luck keeping this all straight.*

"Babe, why are you putting that whiny shit on?" Abby asked. "No one wants to listen to that."

"It's chill. We are having a chill night, right?"

Abby came over and opened the CD player ejecting the disc and popping in Melissa Etheridge. "Let's be cliche." She grinned, kissing Simone on the forehead while Simone stuck her tongue out at Abby in response.

Abby sat on a big brown faux leather armchair and Simone curled up into her lap. *They are so cute together. I love how Simone looks at Abby.* Zoe kept glancing at Emma, with a look that Emma could not explain. It was somewhere mixed with curiosity and desire. *I would be lying if I said I didn't like the way Zoe keeps looking at me. Is this what I've been missing?*

"Is anyone else coming over?" Heather asked.

"No, this is it…" Simone said. "I'm going to order pizza." She dialed a number by memory into the cordless phone.

Jackie filled the silence by lamenting about her Sociology class and how she can't stand the discipline as a whole. "It's all about stereotyping and generalizing. It takes no account for outliers."

Emma sat and quietly watched and observed these women. *These women are all so confident and smart. Their conversation is even sophisticated. I totally don't belong here.*

I love Jackie and Abby's style though. I love the short hair. Sleek and almost masculine, but not. They are blending two ways of presenting themselves. I like it. I could do that. They look like the Calvin Klein commercials. I didn't think anyone did that in real life. And their girlfriends! They are so in love. I love how affectionate and sweet they are with each other.

"What's your story?" Zoe asked Emma, breaking her from her thoughts. Zoe's long hair was parted in the middle and dyed a reddish color with dark roots coming in. Her brown eyes were heavily done in eyeliner and dark shadow, making her skin look almost ghostly pale. Despite the paleness, Emma noted that she was pretty in an unsettling sort of way. She turned suddenly, sitting cross-legged facing Emma.

Feeling breathless under Zoe's scrutiny and intense attention, Emma tried to maintain a level of self-possession in her reply as she was studying Zoe's features. "I'm just here to preview the college. I might be coming here to play basketball on scholarship."

"How do you know Simone and Abby?" Zoe continued her interrogation.

"I met Simone a few weeks ago. She sold me a dress, and then invited me to hang out when I came up here."

"Are you a lesbian? Are you straight? What's your deal?"

Well, are you? Answer the girl. What are you? I don't even know. I know I like how you keep looking at me, though. The way you look at me kind of reminds me how Brandon looks at me. But I like it when you do it.

"Zoe! What the hell?" Heather reprimanded.

Think fast. Answer. "Are you studying to be a cop?" Emma asked, smiling, trying to find some humor to deflect the moment.

"No... I'm just trying to figure out how you fit into this gathering."

"Are *you* a lesbian?" Emma bunted the question back.

"I'm bisexual, as a matter of fact," Zoe informed her proudly.

Be honest. These women are smart. They can tell if you are lying. I'm safe here, I think. "Truth is, I don't know what I am. I mean, I'm not really attracted to anyone right now. I don't think I even thought about being gay or straight until Simone told me she had a girlfriend, truth be told."

"Well, you are really pretty. Like, have you had a boyfriend?" Heather asked sitting up on the edge of her seat and looking directly at Emma.

"I went to homecoming with this boy. All of my teammates think he's so hot. But it did nothing for me. He kissed me and it was just not... Well, it wasn't anything. I felt nothing. I've heard the girls in the locker room on my team talk... And I expected more." *You really put it all out there for these people. It felt good to say it though, and they seem to genuinely want to know.*

Out of nowhere, Zoe leaned in and kissed Emma slowly, her tongue teased against Emma's lips. A flame lit from the center of her being and warmed through her whole body. *Oh. This is it. This is what they talk about in the locker room. This is what I'm supposed to feel when I kiss someone.* As she finally felt it, her heart raced fast and hard and every nerve in her body had come awake at once. *This feels right.*

Zoe backed away grinning at Emma. The other girls were making cheering noises. "How was that?" she asked. "Did you feel something?"

Emma was blushing. She suddenly couldn't look at Zoe. *Are you serious? Did you not feel it? I want to feel that again. Now.*

"Well?" Jackie asked.

Emma laughed and leaned in and kissed Zoe compulsively.

Simone was laughing. "I think she's figured it out."

For the rest of the evening, Zoe and Emma followed each other around, out to the balcony, downstairs to walk around the complex and back upstairs.

"Do you come up here often?" Emma asked her as they strolled hand in hand around the complex for the second time. *That sounds so lame.*

"Not as much as I like. Heather doesn't always want her little stepsister

~ 68 ~

hanging around. But I try to tag along and come out here when I can. I like hanging out with Heather and the other girls. I learn a lot," Zoe said.

"So, like have you ever had other girlfriends?"

"No... I just know I like girls and boys the same. I see no difference. But to be completely fair, until I kissed you tonight, I had never honestly kissed a girl before, either."

"So, why did you kiss me then?"

"Because you are like, hot. I mean, you have to know you are. And I thought if I could help you figure it out, why not? Right?"

Grinning, Emma stopped in her tracks and pulled Zoe back to her. "I think I need more help figuring it out."

Emma and Zoe exchanged numbers at the end of the evening, though both of them realized the likelihood of seeing one another again was zero to nil. Zoe was going to attend college out of state next year and Emma still had another two years of high school to finish after this year.

Emma went back to her room later that night with a profound sense of self and determination. This was the weekend in which she learned and finally understood who she was and what she wanted. She was going to do everything in her power to rise above where she started in life and be more than anyone expected.

I need to keep this new friendship with Simone and Abby. I need women like them in my life. I want to be like them – confident and intelligent and thoughtful. I want to be able to have conversations like Jackie and Heather. All of these women know who they are and what they want. They all have futures. I want to have someone love and adore me like Simone and Heather adore their girlfriends. These women are my role models. I belong in this world that they are in. I fit somewhere finally.

Emma went to the basketball game on Sunday with Simone and was amazed at the fierceness of Coach Donnelson on the sidelines and how hard the girls played. She was committed to coming to State and being on his team from that moment. She enjoyed sitting in the stands with the small crowd but was jealous to not be in the game.

Simone refused to let Emma take the bus back and offered to drive her back to town. It was a much quicker drive without all of the stops of the bus. Simone introduced Emma to Siouxsie and the Banshees and The Smiths on the mixed tapes she had made in her car. They talked and laughed the whole drive home.

"I don't want to be a pest. But I want to hang out again," Emma said when Simone pulled up in front of the shop to drop Emma off.

"Nah. You aren't going to be a pest. You can be like my new kid sister. My pet project." Simone laughed. "You have my number. You can come up with me any time. You can crash on the couch or whatever. Abby won't mind, she loved you, too."

"I appreciate it. I hope this doesn't sound weird or crazy, but I never really had friends or anything. This weekend was really awesome, and I had so much fun."

"It's not weird. I had a good feeling about you when I met you. I felt like you needed a friend and that I could do that for you."

Emma leaned over and hugged Simone. "Thank you!"

"Call me, okay?" Simone called out as Emma hopped out of the car.

Emma nodded and walked away, past the shop and behind it to the trailer.

Emma looked at the trailer as she made her way across the gravel lot. *This is my beginning. My humble beginning, but not my end or my destiny. I have bigger things coming my way.*

~ 4 ~

The First

The Present...

EMMA SAT, LOST IN THE music. *I can't look at you. To look at you breaks my heart. You are so beautiful. We have so much history. How did you do this to us?*

The candle light illuminated her wife's pale skin, giving her an ethereal glow. Her strawberry blonde hair was falling in waves around her shoulders and her beautiful full cleavage straining above the top of her strapless dress. She looked stunning in the black strapless dress. Her favorite necklace hung delicately above her breasts. A diamond encrusted fleur de lis that Emma had bought for her at an antique shop in the French Quarter when they were there on vacation. It had cost a mint, but Emma hadn't cared. Anything for her beautiful and devoted wife.

The candle light was playing tricks off of the diamonds and Emma was entranced by them. It was hypnotic the way they glittered in the light. Her mind was numb, and her heart was aching in her chest.

The furnace kicked on with a hum and the breeze from the vents wreaked havoc on the flames of the candles.

Emma swirled the wine in her glass and sipped it. It was strong and full bodied. Her stomach was empty as she still hadn't touched much of her food.

"Do you remember the first time we met?" Emma tried to smile at her wife. "I think I knew. I kind of knew anyway… That first time we met that we would be together on some level. I maybe didn't know how, or when. But I knew. I felt it in the center of my being. And I think on some level, you knew, too. We were meant to be together."

The Past (1994-1996)

EMMA'S JUNIOR YEAR WAS SURREAL for her. She used her money that she had saved up to get her hair cut. She called Simone who went with her and helped her pick a style, explaining to the hairdresser the look that would suit Emma best. Her long, thick hair was shorn close underneath, and chin length on top. A look that was more popular with the boys who liked to skateboard, but it worked on Emma. Abby approved of Emma's new look. "You own it well, Baby Butch," Abby teased her.

She walked the halls with a new confidence. She knew who she was now. She no longer hid as the invisible girl. She spoke up in classes, and talked to her classmates in the halls and in the locker room after games.

Despite coming into her own and finding herself and becoming confident in herself, she kept her circle small. Brandon was her only real friend in her eyes at school. Since homecoming the last year, they had hung out regularly, usually at his house. Emma loved being in the large open kitchen and living room areas. His house was three times the size of Jessie's house and about twice the size of Teta's. Brandon's mom would come home from work and pop dinner in the oven and often invited Emma to stay and eat with them. She was not really sure what to make of her friendship with Brandon, but she was always warm to Emma. Emma and Brandon would hang out for hours after finishing their homework. They would sit in the plush living room and watch MTV or movies.

Emma confided in Brandon that she liked girls. He took it well, and he told her that the secret was safe with him. "I can actually handle that better than you think. It all makes sense now. It really isn't me; it really is you!" he teased her as they were hanging out in his kitchen after school working on their U. S. History project.

After understanding where Emma stood and the realization that he really did have zero chance with her, he would talk to her about the girls he liked, and they would plot out their future courses. Both of them were planning on becoming lawyers someday, Brandon choosing this course because both of his parents were attorneys.

"Fitzgerald and Landry. We will have our own firm someday," Brandon announced.

Emma shook on it. "We aren't going to do cheesy commercials though, are we?"

"I mean, if it works, why not?"

She continued to visit with her Teta once a month. Teta lived for the visits. She showed Emma all of the pictures of their family members and of Jayne. Teta explained that she named Jayne after the movie actress, Jayne Mansfield because it seemed very American, and when she and Amir first moved to the United States they saw a movie in the movie theater with her, and Amir thought she was beautiful. Teta did not like Emma's hair cut at all. "You look like a boy. You are a pretty girl. You grow your hair back out for your Teta."

Emma tried to not be a pest to Abby and Simone, going out to see them once every two months. She hadn't seen Zoe since they first met, but they talked on the phone sporadically. She was now out of state at her university.

Bear seemed more depressed than usual. He didn't come home as often, and Emma didn't mind. Since meeting with Teta, and the realization that she had missed out on 16 years of knowing her family, and being kept away, there was a slow erosion in her relationship with Bear. She loved him, but her respect for him or his opinions was diminishing seemingly daily.

Her room was now adorned with posters of Melissa Etheridge, and pictures of k. d. Lang in a barber's chair with Cindy Crawford draped across her.

She had researched the academic programs at State and talked to her counselor at the high school about what her chances of admissions and scholarships would be.

Coach Donnelson came out and saw her play finally early in the season.

After the game, Emma, Mr. Adame and Coach Donnelson went out to the local ice cream shop to talk.

"Landry, what are you looking to do after high school?" Coach Donnelson asked her again.

"I am looking to play for you, sir. I will study English and Political Science, like Ali did, in hopes of going to law school." She was confident and self-possessed in her answer and made direct eye contact with Coach Donnelson.

"Look at the difference a year makes," Donnelson laughed.

"Emma's really grown this last year."

"What are your grades like this year?" Donnelson asked.

"I'm on track to be the second in my class right now."

"I'm going to go back to State and put together the offer. I'm going to offer you a full ride to come play for me. Be ready, and you better not accept any offers from other schools!" He was laughing and the threat was not serious.

Emma laughed with him and shook his hand across the table.

It seemed all of the drama and darkness of her past, was just that. Her past. Though she still wasn't friends with the girls on her team or the girls at school in general, they regarded her differently. They didn't ignore her completely and she seemed to get along better.

Rhys had a new girlfriend, and his focus was no longer intent on tormenting Emma. Even his minions that would try to impress him by tormenting her had seemed to back off mostly. She couldn't understand why any girl would date Rhys though. Especially a girl as pretty as his girlfriend. She was new to the school this year, having transferred in from another town. *It has to be that she doesn't know what a troll he really is.*

Emma didn't have any classes with her, and didn't know her name, but would see her at a distance sucking face with Rhys in the hallway. Her thick strawberry blonde ponytail with Rhys's arm slung underneath it, her cute little nose smooshed against his.

Emma would cringe as she saw them together. *He is so over-chicked. Something has to be wrong with her. Whatever. As long as he is leaving me alone, I can focus on me and what I need to do. Soon this place and that douche bag will be a thing of my past. A memory. There is a definite light at the end of this tunnel.*

Second semester she had selected an Art class for her elective, and it was her first period of the day. As she walked in, the teacher was assigning students to sit at tables of four.

She found herself seated with Rhys's girlfriend. Emma sat and looked down at the table, refusing to make eye contact or conversation with the girl to her left. *Birds of a feather flock together. There's no way this girl could be worth conversation or time of day.*

Two other students were seated at the table that Emma didn't really know well, though they were excited to be seated together and held a steady conversation. Emma ignored them, too.

Rhys's girlfriend turned to her, "I'm Bailey Frankson."

Emma rolled her eyes. "Hi, Bailey Frankson." *Oh. You want to be friends.*

"What's your name?" Bailey asked.

"Ask your boyfriend. He has a nickname for me." *Ha. I'm sure you already know it.*

"What do you mean?"

"Nothing. No offense, but I have no desire to befriend someone with such bad taste in partners. You know… Birds of a feather. So, save the niceties. I don't have time."

"Wow… Okay."

Emma busied herself with reading her novel while she waited for the Art teacher to start talking.

"For the record, I think it's awfully rude of you to assume that whatever issues you have with Rhys, you should have with me," Bailey said.

Really? "Like I said, in my experience, birds of a feather. Assholes stick with assholes." Emma was trying to not be distracted by Bailey's polished appearance. *She is perfect. Flawless. How can a troll like Rhys land someone so stunning? She has to be stupid. Like brain dead stupid. That's the only logical explanation.*

~ 75 ~

The next week, after icing Bailey out each day, Emma took her seat at the table in the Art class, and Bailey sat down shortly after. "I asked Rhys what he called you. I think it's disgusting and rude," she said as she took her seat.

Emma's eyebrows shot up. *You really didn't know.*

"He also told me you attacked him."

Emma grinned. "I kicked his ass twice." *Knocked his goddamn teeth out. It was beautiful.*

Bailey smiled in response. "It sounds like he deserved it."

Okay. I wrote you off too quickly.

The bell rang and the teacher began, "Class, today we are going to begin work on chalk pastel portraits. Remember to use the techniques we had been discussing throughout the last week. You are going to pair up with a classmate at your table, you will first sketch them, and then you will work on filling the colors using the chalk pastels."

The two other students at the table (who Emma decided she couldn't stand because they reminded her of squawking hens with their incessant chatter) having an established friendship partnered immediately, leaving Emma and Bailey.

The teacher put the large papers and pencils on the table in front of Emma, who dispersed them around.

Bailey looked at Emma, "Please don't make me look like a monster because you hate Rhys." She was grinning.

As if anything could make you look like a monster. Emma smiled back at her. "I wouldn't sabotage my own grade just to piss you or him off."

Both girls went quiet as they began to sketch.

"Your eyes are amazing..." Bailey said looking up at Emma. "I've never seen a blue like that."

"Blue? Like what? They are just blue. Your eyes are the same color as mine." *Don't stare like an idiot, Emma. You don't want to look weird. Play it cool.*

"No... Yours are bluer, darker. What color would you say 'our' eyes are?"

Her voice is even beautiful. "I don't know. Like sapphire blue."

~ 76 ~

"I like that. Like sapphire blue…" Bailey's lips curled into a soft smile as her voice trailed off.

She has a pretty mouth. Emma blushed suddenly as she noticed Bailey was intently studying her. She took notice of Bailey's fine features, and how her strawberry blonde hair was swept up in a perfect ponytail. Her own bright blue eyes were rimmed with heavy black liner, and she had a dimple in her left cheek when she smiled. *Stop looking at her. She's going to think you are weird or creepy. I literally have no clue how Rhys got her.* Emma broke her gaze away so as not to come across as abnormal in staring too long.

"Why are you with Rhys?" Emma blurted out of nowhere, putting her pencil down.

"He's cute. He's funny. He's not that smart, but he's got a good future. Why not be with him – Aside from the fact you hate each other over something that happened in 7th grade."

"And ninth grade and tenth… He's such a douche and you seem like you are not a douche."

Bailey laughed and shrugged and kept sketching.

What would it be like to kiss you? God I hate Rhys even more now.

"What?" Bailey asked as she caught on to Emma's intent gaze.

"Nothing… I'm not a good artist, and you asked that I not make you look like a monster. I'm just trying to figure out how to draw you and do justice…" *Quit staring at her.*

Bailey leaned over and looked at Emma's paper. "Based on what I see, it doesn't look bad."

Emma shrugged and picked up her charcoal pencil and kept drawing.

Now that she had gotten to know Bailey, she noticed her everywhere. She had not even realized it, but due to the new semester and a schedule change, she was now in her American History class.

When Emma came in and sat down at her desk, Bailey rushed up and sat next to her. *Oh. She's in this class, too? Damn you, Brandon for switching out of this class and Bailey for the schedule change. And damn this teacher for wanting to be the "cool" teacher and not giving assigned seats. She smells good. What is that? Sweet strawberries? It makes sense with her hair. I really want to kiss her. I need to stop thinking about her. I need to leave it alone. I have to. But damn... now she's all I can think about. I'm losing my damn mind.*

At practice she was distracted thinking about Bailey. She missed shots that would come easy to her. She missed plays. She was all head in the clouds and not focused because of Bailey Frankson. Mr. Adame pulled her aside.

"Emma, what's going on? Donnelson will pull his offer if you keep playing like this!"

"I'm so sorry, Coach. I will get it together."

After practice, Brandon met her to give her a ride home and hang out. She had long gotten over her embarrassment of her trailer with him and since Bear was gone all of the time, it was ideal for them to sit and hang out and talk.

"I have a crush!" she informed him. "And I don't know how to handle it."

"Who?"

"Bailey Frankson."

"Rhys Mills's girl?"

"Mmmhhmmm."

"*The* Rhys Mills whose ass you kicked twice?"

"The very one."

Brandon gave a low whistle. "What are you going to do?"

"I don't know. I don't know if she even likes girls. I can only assume she doesn't since she's all about Rhys."

Brandon shrugged. "You never know until you try... Think about it. You could totally steal her away from Rhys. That would be even better than kicking his ass, stealing his girl."

Emma cocked her head to the side and then turned in her seat to look at him directly. "I like the way you think. Except I have no game. None. Nada. I wouldn't know the first thing to do or say."

"Just act natural. Act like she's that Zoe girl. You had plenty of game with her. Call your friends up at State and get some advice from them."

EMMA CONVINCED SIMONE TO BRING her up to State to stay with her and Abby that weekend. It was easy to convince Simone when she told her she needed advice about a girl.

While they were having breakfast Saturday morning Emma looked at Abby. "I have a crush and I don't know what to do."

"There's no knowing 'what to do'. Just be you. Who is she?"

Emma ran Abby through the whole story.

"So... yeah. Don't go there."

"Why?"

Simone poured herself a giant mug of coffee and added a ton of cream and sugar to it. "Don't go after straight girls. It's a recipe for disaster." It was hard for Emma to take her seriously with her coffee made like that.

"What if she's not straight?" Emma asked. "Zoe is not straight."

"Zoe is 'bisexual'," Simone said using air quotes. "She just doesn't want her mom and dad to think they failed by having two gay daughters, or that Heather was a 'bad influence'. But that girl is as gay as the rest of us. She hasn't even looked at a dude since she got to college, according to Heather."

"What if Bailey is bisexual or gay and just hasn't figured it out yet? I didn't fully know until I knew. It took Zoe kissing me to know."

"It's just that people get weird about that sometimes. You can get hurt. Not just emotionally, but physically. People will go after you and hurt you. Gay girls get raped, beat..." Her voice trailed as she sighed. Abby shook her head, "I've known people who have endured really bad things. Emma, don't."

Emma sat at the rickety table and sipped her coffee, pouting. *Not what I wanted to hear. Thanks for killing my hopes and dreams.*

"I know it's not what you want to hear. But you are like this wonderful baby sister that I always wanted but never had. I don't want to see you get hurt in any way," Abby continued, sitting down.

THE FOLLOWING WEEK, SHE WAS irritable and annoyed as she saw Bailey and Rhys making out in the hallway. *The fact that you willingly choose such a piece of shit should be enough for me to leave you alone. What does that say about you, ultimately? I don't need you in my life. I don't.* She was curt with Bailey in classes. In Art class, as they were adding color to their sketches, Bailey lamented, "There isn't a blue that's blue enough for your eye color. There's no, *like sapphire blue.*"

Emma tried to not read into that. *Um, excuse me. You are hanging on to something I said over a week ago. Like sapphire blue. Okay. That's something. It has to be.* Emma raised her eyebrow at Bailey. "Your eyes are the same color as mine," Emma reminded her with a tone of irritation.

Bailey met her gaze, locking in. "Not really, but okay." Bailey selected a black pastel and started filling in Emma's hair.

The way you just looked at me, it's like you really see me. You hear me. There is definitely something there. Maybe Abby and Simone are wrong.

The teacher came by and sang Bailey's praises.

Bailey continued to sit near Emma in American History. She would make comments under her breath that would make Emma giggle, wearing down Emma's guarded attitude, as the teacher droned on about the Roaring 20's.

Stop it. Ignore her. Stop trying to read into everything she says and does. Abby and Simone know these things. They've been there. They have friends that have been there. Leave it alone. Find someone else to obsess on. But damn. She's looking at me again. Why does she look at me like that? She looks at me like I look at her. I need to leave it alone.

The day after she sprung for her hair to be refreshed with her undercut freshly shaved, she had put her longer hair in a ponytail.

As she was sitting in History, Bailey reached over and rubbed the shorn underside under the ponytail. "I love your hair, it's so cool," she whispered.

Electricity ran through Emma's body, and she forgot to breathe. *I'm on fire. My whole body is on fire. I think my heart stopped.* "Thanks," she muttered, playing it cool somehow.

As she rode home with Brandon that afternoon, she made a resolution. "I'm going to go for it. I'm on a mission."

"A mission for what?"

"Bailey Frankson. She will be mine."

"How? Didn't your friends at State tell you to leave it be?"

"I think she likes me. Like, likes me likes me. So what they said is now moot."

"How do you know? What makes you think this?"

"She looks at me. Like all of the time. She is always finding excuses to touch me. She remembers everything I say. I just know. I have a feeling."

"How are you going to do this?"

"Valentine's Day is next week. I'm going to do something. I have a plan."

She had Brandon drive her to Jessie's shop. She popped into the shop with Jessie and Bear, Brandon in tow. "Jessie, can I get paid for the stuff I did last week? I need to buy some stuff."

"How many hours did you work last week?"

"Like 10 hours," Emma said.

"Here, here's fifty." He pulled a fifty-dollar bill from his wallet and handed it to Emma.

Emma grabbed Brandon by the arm and dragged him back to his car and directed him up to the main street area and into a florist shop.

"Do you guys do the dyed colored flowers?" she asked. "Like, can you make them dark blue... Like sapphire blue?"

THE MORNING OF VALENTINE'S DAY, she swung by the florist shop before school. She had managed to convince the florist to meet her there so she could pick up a single long stem rose dyed sapphire blue, with a blue satin ribbon tied around it, wrapped in blue and white tissue.

Emma paid the florist and all but ran to the school. She got into the classroom fifteen minutes early, and merely laid the flower wrapped in tissue across Bailey's section of the table, before exiting. *Don't ask me any questions, man. Just go with it.* Her Art teacher was looking at her puzzled, she just blushed as she walked back out.

When the bell rang she walked in slightly behind Bailey and they found their way to their table toward the back corner of the room nearest the window.

Bailey looked down at the flower wrapped in paper and picked it up. She peeled the paper back to reveal the dark blue rose bud and ribbon. She smiled and whispered, "Like sapphire blue." She looked at Emma with that subtle smile that made her heart flutter. "Is this from you?"

Emma gave a bashful smile and shrugged. *She likes it. She likes me. I can tell. I'm not imagining this.*

"Rhys didn't even tell me happy Valentine's Day. Thank you." Her voice trailed off.

I told you he's a douche. The way you are looking at me right now, I think I've got a shot. "You're welcome," Emma said with downcast eyes, continuing to smile.

Bailey carried the flower with her all day, keeping it close and protected. During their last period History class, Bailey smiled at Emma as she came in and took her seat. "I feel bad that I didn't get you anything though. I didn't think about getting anyone but Rhys anything."

Of course, you only thought of that dickwad. "I don't need anything," Emma said matter of fact.

"I know, but this was like, really thoughtful."

"You deserve to be thought of," Emma replied. *And that is the truth.* "Honestly, it's more of an apology for being such a bitch at the beginning of the semester."

THE NEXT MORNING AS SHE was walking into school, Rhys was waiting for her in front of her locker. "Why are you buying my girlfriend flowers?"

"The question is not why am I buying her flowers, the question is why are you not?" Emma deflected right back to him. "Excuse me, now, or I will kick your ass a third time. You don't deserve Bailey."

Rhys moved around and grabbed Emma by the shoulders and pushed her into the locker, nose to nose with her. "Stay the fuck away from my girlfriend, Bloody Mary."

Emma cocked her head to the side, "I can't help it if she won't stay away from me."

Rhys cocked his fist up, and Emma braced for the impact. *Hit me,*

~ 82 ~

motherfucker. I dare you. Give me an excuse to kick your ass again, this time, Bailey can watch. Her heart was pounding hard in her ears as she watched as his fist was coming toward her. Before impact was made, two school security officers jumped in and pulled Rhys back.

Emma just laughed as they pulled him away. *That was close. I almost lost it. I need to keep myself under control. I have too much to lose. I can't keep getting caught up in this bullshit. Coach already warned me. But damn. That short shit thinks he can take me. He doesn't quit.* She stowed her coat and grabbed what she needed for her Art class and made her way to find Bailey sitting looking downcast.

"Your boyfriend tried to punch me in the face," Emma said as she sat down next to Bailey.

Bailey shook her head with her eyes glassy with tears.

"Bailey, what's wrong?"

"When he asked me about the rose, I told him it was from you. He was so mad. He told me to throw it away. That it was weird you would buy me something. I told him no, because it was beautiful. And it was thoughtful. I told him that if he was so concerned, he should have thought of me on Valentine's Day... He told me not to talk to you anymore..." Now her tears were flowing.

Emma stood back up and grabbed Bailey by the arm. "Come on..." She looked at the teacher. "She's having a crisis. I'm taking her to calm down." She didn't wait for a response and just took Bailey out of the room and down the hall to the girls' bathroom.

Bailey just cried and Emma brought her in close. *Kiss her. You can make your move now. But don't. She's in crisis now. Just let her cry. She feels so warm and soft. She smells so damn good. I fucking hate Rhys. Just let her cry. She has to come to this on her own. Don't push it.*

"He took it and ripped it and threw it away," Bailey cried.

"It's okay... It really is," Emma soothed her. "I didn't mean to cause any problems between the two of you. I just wanted to do something special for you, since you have always been so nice, and I was such a bitch."

Bailey laughed, trying to compose herself. She wiped her eyes. "You really were kind of a bitch."

"You wore me down," Emma laughed with her.

Bailey moved away from Emma to one of the sinks and ran the cold water and threw it on her face.

You are even beautiful when you cry. Red and puffy eyes and all. "We should get back to class," Emma said, her voice quiet. *I hate that I am doing the right thing, when all I want to do is take you and run out of here.*

Bailey nodded and followed her back. No sooner had they both sat down than Mr. Stone, the assistant principal, had come in. "I need Emma Landry in the office," he announced to the teacher.

The class made an "oohhhh" noise to indicate the drama. Whispers began to fly around. A kid from the other side of the classroom threw out a, "You're in trouble!"

Emma made eye contact with him. She hadn't seen him since the day he pulled her off of Rhys. "Miss Landry... Come on..."

Emma got up and gathered her things and looked at Bailey. "Are you going to be okay?"

Bailey nodded, looking at Emma concerned.

She waited until she was in the hallway with Mr. Stone to ask, "What's up?"

He shook his large bald head. "What is the deal with you and the Mills kid? Why can't you leave each other alone?"

You have to be kidding right now. I should have kicked his ass anyway if I'm going to get in trouble for it regardless. "I didn't do anything, sir," Emma said taking two steps for his every one to keep up.

Emma followed him into the office where Rhys and his mother sat. *Of course. There's mommy dearest here to bail baby brat out. He's such a pussy.*

Before Emma had taken two steps into the office, Mrs. Mills sprang up. "This little piece of instigating white trash needs to be expelled. She constantly harasses my son and provokes him. She's attacked him twice already. Are you going to continue to let this stand?"

Rhys sat looking smug in his chair, refusing to look at Emma.

"Oh, of course, little bitch boy, can't handle himself so has to set his big bitch mommy on me to handle it." Emma just couldn't help herself.

Mr. Stone grabbed her arm and dragged her into the office and slammed the door. "Miss Landry!"

"Sir, he has gone after me. Ruthlessly. Since the seventh grade. He's harassed me. His friends have groped me. He has continuously humiliated me. I did kick his ass twice. But today, I didn't do anything. He's mad because I bought his girlfriend a flower on Valentine's Day, he didn't do anything for her. I showed him up. Again. He came to my locker. He tried to hit me."

Mr. Stone sat behind his desk calm and quiet. He sighed before saying, "It's your word against his. And we can't have his parents breathing down our necks for action. I'm going to have to do something."

"You can't expel me, Mr. Stone…" Emma was frantic.

"No… No… I'm not going to expel you. You are a star athlete and student. Your only issue is this Mills boy." He picked up the phone and dialed. "Mr. Landry, please. …. Yes. This is Mr. Stone, the assistant principal at Kennedy High. Yes, sir, Emma's school. I have Emma up here. Can you come in please and have a talk with us? Thank you, sir."

It seemed like forever before Bear arrived. Emma sat in Mr. Stone's office looking up at the picture of his Alma Mater over his head while she waited. *Keep your mouth shut. Don't say anymore. You are in control of how you react.* When Bear arrived, he received a verbal lashing from Mrs. Mills for never reimbursing her for Emma breaking Rhys's teeth, as he walked in and made his way to Mr. Stone's office. Bear simply ignored her as he walked past.

"Princess, what did you do now?" he demanded, furious as he entered Mr. Stone's office.

"Follow me, both of you." He led them into a conference room. The principal, Mr. Barrett came in, followed by Mrs. Mills and Rhys.

Everyone was seated and Mrs. Mills opened her mouth first. "If you do not expel that little piece of white trash from this school, I will pull all of my involvement with the boosters, and I will put Rhys in a private school."

This bitch needs to shut up. And please, put your piece of shit kid in a private school. Do us all a favor.

Mr. Barrett kept calm and ignored Mrs. Mills's demands. "Mrs. Mills, we've compiled a lot of witness statements. Not just from this incident, but also from previous incidents. We've reviewed the files. Your son has been the instigator in all of the situations. That does not excuse Miss Landry's reactions or how she has composed herself. For the rest of today and the next two days, both of them will be assigned to in-school suspension. But this is a warning. The two of them need to mutually agree that while they are on school property, or attending any school function, they will leave each other alone. If they can't leave each other alone, and more incidents arise, we will take more severe consequences for either of them. Up to and including suspension or expulsion."

"He was going to hit me. If school security didn't pull him off of me, Mr. Stone, he was going to attack me. Why am I getting punished for what he was going to do to me?"

"Emma, Princess... Shhhhh." Bear put his hand on her back. "We will talk about this at home."

Emma sat back in her chair. *This is ridiculous. I didn't do anything wrong.*

"That's fine, Mr. Barrett," Bear said. "I promise, no more issues with Emma."

Wait! Bear, stand up for me!

EMMA SPENT THE REST OF the day in the in-school suspension room. A bleak and dreary room with nothing on the walls. A window that looked over the staff parking lot, and a desk with a grumpy old teacher who never said much; her gray hair put into such a tight bun it looked like she had a botched face lift.

Emma took a desk near the door, and Rhys took a desk as far away from her as he could on the other side of the room. *That's right. Stay far away from me and don't even think to look at me. Weasel.*

After a long day of boredom, as she made her way to her locker to get her things, Bailey was standing there waiting for her. "I heard what happened. I'm sorry. This is all my fault."

Ha. Yeah, apologize for him. Really? "Don't blame yourself. It's Rhys not you. We have history. Just, for the next few days, I will be in lock down with him. After that, we have no choice but to leave each other alone or we are both suspended or worse. It will be fine. A little distance is good." *Maybe I need to leave you alone, too. Seriously. If you are going to apologize for him and take the fall for him, it's just as well.*

Emma left Bailey at that spot without another word and made her way to the shop where she sat behind the desk and filed invoices for Jessie.

Bear came in and wiped his hands on a towel. "Emma, you are getting punished because of nothing more than the fact that they have money and resources, and we don't. I'm sorry that I didn't do better by you."

He speaks. He has something insightful to say after all. "That's fine, Bear. Honestly, it just makes me committed to doing what it takes for myself. I will get out of here and I will do better on my own." *I'm going to make something of myself personally despite you and despite this shit show of an upbringing.* She was matter of fact in her response and just kept filing invoices.

AFTER A MONTH OF LAYING low, and winning the state championship, and doing her best to keep her feelings for Bailey at bay, Emma found herself partnered on a project with Bailey for History since she insisted on always sitting next to Emma. *Great. The last thing I need.*

"Can you come over after school and we can work on this?" Bailey asked.

"I guess so... Today?" Emma asked. *Yes. I can totally come over. I want to come over. I need to not want to come over, though.*

Bailey nodded.

"Your boyfriend is not going to be happy." *You had to go there. God, Emma. Leave it alone.*

Bailey rolled her eyes. "It's for school. Meet me at my car after school." *Of course. It's for school. It is. It's that simple.*

Emma complied and after dropping off the things she didn't need and grabbing the necessary supplies for her homework and the pending project at her locker, she met Bailey at her car. It was a new BMW Z3, shiny and sporty and expensive, in black.

Naturally, this is her car. I've never really thought about what kind of upbringing she had. She's rich. Like Rhys. That's why they are together. They make sense. They are expected to be together. Trust fund babies go with other trust fund babies. They are birds of a feather. Very expensive feathers.

Emma tried to not feel intimidated and self-conscious as she got into the passenger seat. The soft tan leather held her close as she put on her seatbelt.

Bailey zipped the little roadster out of the parking lot and down the street. "Oh my god. You are going to get us killed," Emma groaned holding on to the dash in front of her.

Bailey giggled. "I love this car. My dad got it for me for my birthday."

"Of course he did."

"What does that mean?"

"Nothing. I'm just a little jealous is all." *I barely got a bike as a kid, much less ever getting a car as a gift. I think the last bank statement I saw, Bear was overdraft.*

Bailey pulled into the long driveway of a large home with a grand portico and columns. Emma looked at the large trees with pink blossoms coming in. She had never been on this side of the town, or in a home like this. Even Brandon's house was not this nice.

"This is your house?" *It looks like The White House. Well, not exactly, but close. I can fit the trailer ten times over in this place.*

"Yeah. We just moved here."

"What does your dad do?"

"My dad is a real estate developer, and my mom is a neonatal specialist. They both work a lot."

Emma nodded her head and followed Bailey into the entry. She looked around at the shining and perfect surfaces. *This place is like a museum. Like the one we went to on that field trip freshman year. Don't touch anything,*

Emma. You can't afford to even breathe on any of this much less break it. "I feel like I'm in a museum. Like I can't touch anything."

Bailey shrugged. "It's just what I've grown up with. It's home. Let's go up to my room."

Bailey's bedroom was almost the size of her whole trailer, or at least it seemed that way. Her dresser was neatly organized with framed pictures of her with her friends lined up neatly on the top against one wall, and facing the window along another wall, a large desk with a computer on it and a vanity table with neatly organized lotions and cosmetics. Emma had only seen computers at the library and in the computer lab at school. She didn't realize people had them in their homes, too. Pink and cream, everything was in pink and cream. The wood was a silvery white, and soft pink curtains, the hardwood floors had fluffy pink area rugs that matched the curtains. Bailey's bed had an ornate headboard that matched the silvery white wood of the dresser, vanity table and desk. On top of the bed were tons of pillows in soft pink and white. Emma contrasted this with the dark paneling of her bedroom (and all of the rooms) of her trailer and hodgepodge mismatched wooden furniture. The cream and pink imagery surrounding her, combined with the sweet smell of strawberry that seemed to hover in this room and surround Bailey herself, intoxicated Emma.

"Do you actually use all of those pillows?" Emma asked.

Bailey giggled. "Sometimes... But mostly, no... I throw most of them on the floor. It just looks cozy." She flopped herself on the bed and sprawled across it.

Emma sat in the chair at the desk and put her feet up on the desk. "I like your room. It's very you."

"I'm breaking up with Rhys," Bailey said, sudden and out of nowhere.

"I think that's smart." Emma played it ice cold, though inside she was cheering with joy.

"Do you want to know why?"

"Sure."

"I like you. I like spending time with you. I can talk to you. You have

~ 89 ~

ambition. Rhys is mean. He's controlling. He lacks ambition because his parents give him everything. And his mom is a complete monster. I don't like that he hates you for no reason."

"I think that's all an accurate assessment." Emma was grinning.

"Prom is next month. Since I no longer have a date, a bunch of us were just going to go as a group of single girls. Do you want to come with us?"

Emma had only gone to the one homecoming. *If anyone else had asked me to go, I would say no. I have no desire to be part of that. But for you, Bailey Frankson... For you, anything.* She paused for a moment. "Yeah, but I don't want to wear a dress."

"Lots of women don't wear dresses. Wear a suit or a tux? Like Marlene Dietrich or that other actress who wore one on the red carpet. It would be cool! Edgy!"

"Do you already have your dress?"

"No, I'm going shopping this weekend."

"Can we invite Brandon? I know it's a girl's thing, but if he doesn't have a date, and if I don't, he might ask me to be his date again."

"Yeah... about that. He's cute. Why don't you go out with him?"

Emma froze. *Oh. Yeah, we've never discussed that. I'm not sure I want to talk about this. Not now. Not with you.* "I'm just not into him like that. We went to homecoming together last year, and we kissed. It was awkward. He's like a brother to me." She paused and got up and made her way to the window. "I'm into someone else."

"Who?"

Don't act like you don't know deep down. "I thought we were here to work on the project?"

"You aren't going to tell me who?" Bailey was up on her knees staring directly at Emma.

Emma shook her head and grinned. "Nope. I don't talk about that stuff. Brandon knows and that is it." *I think you do know. You suspect it anyway. On some level.*

"Yeah... I guess. Invite him then. But I will get you to tell me who it is you like. I'm good at that stuff. I am also good at putting the clues together."

Then you must know, Sherlock. "If you think you figure it out, let me know." Emma forced a smile.

AFTER CALLING ABBY, SHE BEGGED them to meet her for help. "Emma, we talked about this. This is going to blow up in your face," Abby warned after Emma brought her up to speed.

"Can you just help me figure out what to wear? I like your style. Help me!" Emma was almost whining.

"What's your budget? Are we going thrift or are you going classic tux and renting?"

"I don't know! That's why I'm here. I have like $200 saved."

Simone piped in, "Tuxedo. Rent the tux. It will be awesome. Get your hair cleaned up, slick it back in a ponytail. A little eyeliner on those eyes—"

Abby shot Simone a look and rolled her eyes. Simone shrugged and winked.

They strolled into a tuxedo rental shop after lunch. The salesman was confused when he saw the three young women walk in with no males present.

Emma walked up to him and announced, "I'm looking to rent a tux for my prom."

"How very Marlene Dietrich of you!" he proclaimed.

"That's what my friend said, who suggested it."

"Well, he or she has a good eye. You will look fabulous, come." He ushered Emma to a block and urged her up where he began measuring her.

"What color tie and vest?" he asked as he started pulling a jacket and pants off the rack.

"I don't know."

"What's your date wearing?"

"I don't have a date. I'm going with a group. Blue?"

He hung up a shirt, jacket and pants in a dressing room and grabbed samples with fabrics and colors and handed them to her. "Pick."

Simone and Abby sat over her shoulder and looked. "That one!" Simone picked out a deep blue. "Like your eyes."

Emma looked at the color labeled below. 'Sapphire Blue' it read. She grinned. "It's kismet. That one." She pointed to the sapphire blue sample.

"Shoes?" the salesman asked her.

Abby picked up a pair of spectator shoes, "These."

Emma nodded.

She was fitted and styled and had the date to come pick up her suit the day before prom.

She was elated.

That night after riding back up to State for the night with Abby and Simone, she called Bailey to tell her. "I'm going with your recommendation! I got a tuxedo 'like Marlene Dietrich'."

"I got my dress today! Oh, and we are renting a limo. But don't worry about paying. I already have it covered."

"You got your dress?"

"I did."

"What color?"

She laughed.

"What color?"

"Blue."

"What shade? There are a lot of blues." *I feel like I know this answer.*

She laughed, and Emma smiled. Simone and Abby were watching her on the phone shaking their heads. "I don't know... Like sapphire blue."

"For real?" Emma asked, putting her hand over her heart. *You do know. You know. And you feel the same way.*

"Yeah."

"We are going to match like twins. My vest and tie are the same color."

"That's so cool!"

Emma hung up shortly after and looked at Abby and Simone. "You guys, I can't help it. I think I might be in love. Like really truly. And I think she likes me. I don't know why."

Abby sat her down on the couch and grabbed her hands. "Emma, you have to understand. Girls like attention. It doesn't matter where it comes from. But once it goes past a certain point, they will get weird, and they will disappear or reject you or whatever. Be careful that you don't put too much into this."

Emma looked away from Abby. "I don't think Bailey is like that." *I feel this from the depths of my soul. She has real feelings for me. I'm not imagining this.*

"I hope you are right," Abby said. "But please, just be careful. I don't want to see you hurt."

Emma couldn't be mad at Abby for her warning. She appreciated having her in her life and her guidance.

BAILEY HAD ENCOURAGED EMMA TO come over for prom early, since the limo would be meeting them at her house before picking up her three other friends and Brandon for dinner. Acting on encouragement from Simone and Brandon, Emma had gone back to the same florist who created the blue rose for Bailey to have a corsage made for her.

The florist encouraged her to go with a white rose with blue tips and blue and white ribbons. It was gorgeous and Emma couldn't have been more thrilled with it.

Emma was suddenly nervous as she had Jessie drop her off at the end of the driveway of Bailey's house. "Damn, kiddo. Your friend is fancy."

"Yeah, wish me luck."

She got out of the truck and walked up the long driveway. She was sweating under the shirt and jacket, holding her breath as she knocked on the door.

She had slicked her hair back into a smooth ponytail like Simone had suggested and Simone had shown her how to put on eyeliner and mascara. When she had looked at herself in the mirror, she felt confident and proud. Bear was confused by her choice of attire for prom but didn't really push the issue. Emma was sure that Bear had a good idea that she was not straight, but they had never had a formal conversation.

The door opened, and a woman who looked almost exactly like what Emma figured Bailey would look like in 25 years opened the door. Her eyes were more green than blue, and she was shorter than Bailey, but her hair was the same distinctive strawberry blonde, and her complexion was milky just as Bailey's, and she had the same pouty full lips.

"Hi... Mrs. Frankson. I'm Emma... Bailey's friend. I'm supposed to be meeting her here for prom." Emma's voice was shaking.

"Dr. Frankson," she corrected with a polite smile. "You can call me Mary Anne. You must be Emma! Bailey has told us a lot about you. You are the girls' basketball star and second in your class, she says."

Emma blushed. "I... yeah."

"And you are humble, she said that about you as well. Your parents must be proud."

She was so nice, Emma wasn't sure how to handle it. "It's really nice to meet you. Your home is very beautiful." *Wow. Smooth, Emma. That's the best you could do.*

"Thank you! Do you remember your way up to Bailey's room? She should be almost done getting ready."

"Thank you very much, ma'am." Emma walked up the stairs and to Bailey's door and knocked. *Be cool. Be cool. Be cool. Breathe.*

Bailey opened the door, and the sweet scent of strawberries came wafting out. Emma took a deep breath and savored the scent.

Emma's breath caught in her chest as she looked at Bailey. Her chest was tight, and she just wanted to touch her to make sure she wasn't dreaming. She forced a smile.

"Oh, my gawwwdd!" Bailey exclaimed. "You look amazing!" She stood out of the way of the door and Emma came in past her.

She turned and faced Bailey, "You look... I mean... Wow!" Bailey's hair was piled in loose flowing ringlets on the top of her head, with loose curls framing her face. The sapphire blue dress brought out her eyes and complimented the creamy complexion of her skin. The dress was tight in the bodice and flowed loose to her knees. With the high heels she was busy slipping into, using the footboard for support, she would be almost as tall as Emma.

Speak. Breathe. Don't act like an idiot. Emma cleared her throat. "I… Uh… I felt bad that you didn't have a date because you were standing up for me. So… I uh… I brought you this." She handed the package with the corsage in it to Bailey. Her throat was dry, and her heart was beating so loud she thought Bailey could hear it.

"Oh my god. You are so sweet!" Bailey gushed. She rushed over to Emma and took the box. Her face full of surprised joy. "I think you are supposed to put it on me?"

Emma opened the box and pulled it out. "Hold out your wrist…" Bailey complied, and Emma was shaking slightly as she put the flower on Bailey's delicate wrist.

Bailey angled her hand around so she could admire it. "It's so pretty! And it matches!" She threw her arms around Emma.

Emma held her close and nuzzled slightly into her neck to soak in the sweet smell of Bailey. *You could totally make a move now. What are you so afraid of?*

"Girls?" Mary Anne called from the hallway. "I want to grab some pictures of you before the limo arrives."

Lingering in the embrace, Bailey looked up at Emma for a moment before backing away. "We're ready, Mom!" Bailey grabbed a silver sparkling purse and popped a lip gloss and her wallet inside. She turned to Emma, "I'm buying your dinner tonight because you have been so thoughtful to me! You really always make me feel so special."

Emma shook her head, "You don't have to."

Bailey shrugged. "It's nothing. Come on!" She grabbed Emma's arm and dragged her back out of the room and down the staircase.

Mary Anne had her camera ready as she directed the girls to stand at the bottom of the stairs. "Emma, I just love the bold choice to wear a tuxedo! It's really chic and edgy!" she gushed. "Here, you stand here, and Bailey, you stand on the other side. Each of you put one hand on the side banister!

Beautiful!" She clicked. She took several more pictures in the house and then outside under the flowering cherry blossom trees.

When she was done and the girls were in the back of the limousine, Emma looked at Bailey. She did what she could to soak in the moment and memorize each detail of her smiling face and the sound of her laughter.

"I've never taken so many pictures in my life!" Emma exclaimed.

"My mom is a bit over the top. I'm the only girl in the family, so she feels like she has to go overboard for every event in my life. There has to be like a million pictures of my first birthday, and me riding a bike." Bailey rolled her eyes.

"You have a brother, or brothers?"

"Just one. CJ. He's four years older than me. Charles Jr, actually. He's out east attending Daddy's alma mater." Bailey rolled her eyes and Emma could tell it was a contentious topic, so she let it go.

They picked up Bailey's three girlfriends – Sara, Ria, and Leanne before picking up Brandon and headed to an Italian restaurant.

The other girls were the type that Emma never enjoyed being around and for the most part, they ignored her, and she ignored them. She caught them side eyeing her and whispering amongst themselves, but she rose above it. It was not worth ruining the night for everyone.

Brandon was in heaven as Bailey's friends jockeyed for the seats closest to him at dinner. He whispered a sly "Thank you," to Emma as they walked to their table.

At the venue for the dance, as they walked in, Bailey took Emma's arm. Emma smiled coyly at her.

As the music reverberated through the banquet hall and the students socialized, Emma caught up with a few of her teammates and kept a steady eye on Brandon and Bailey – her two anchors in this situation.

She caught sight of Rhys and his date for the evening on the other side of the venue. He was eyeing her every move like a hawk. No matter where she went, she could see him watching her.

She pretended to not notice him as she found her way back to Bailey.

Without a word, Bailey grabbed Emma and dragged her on to the dance floor. Emma moved with Bailey to the beat of a poppy dance song.

Rhys had not stopped eagle eyeing her. She could feel his contempt from across the room.

After a few upbeat dance songs, the song switched to a ballad and Emma considered moving off of the floor, but acted on impulse and pulled Bailey close to slow dance.

Bailey snaked her arms up around Emma's neck, as Emma's arms wrapped around her waist. *This feels right.*

As they spun on the floor, Emma caught sight of Rhys with clenched fists on the table. *Poor little pathetic weasel. He's jealous.* He made direct eye contact with her. She smiled at him as she made eye contact. She knew she shouldn't have done it, but she couldn't help it.

She spun Bailey around and pulled her back in. As she was coming back into Emma's embrace, she was smiling at Emma in a way that Emma could not interpret other than one of love or interest.

"Let's go outside!" Bailey called over the music.

Emma nodded and Bailey grabbed her arm and dragged her off the dance floor.

Once outside, the coolness of the air felt refreshing from the heat of the crowd indoors. The night was clear, and the sky was brilliant with stars and a crescent moon.

Bailey continued to walk away from the venue and toward the limo. "Let's go sit in the car for a bit. I need a break from all of the people."

She wants us to be alone. I see where this is going.

The driver got out and opened the door for the two girls. Emma got in behind Bailey.

The moment Bailey sat inside, she kicked her high heels off and sighed.

Emma laughed, "I don't know how you've managed all night in those."

Bailey was sitting on the seat diagonal to Emma looking at her intently.

"Emma, I need to tell you something. Remember when I told you that I would get to the bottom of who it is you like? I've gotten to the bottom of it."

Moment of truth. She either is freaked out or she wants this, too. Emma held her breath and nodded at Bailey.

"It's me. And I feel like … I feel like … I like you. Like more than I should as a friend. I feel like I want to be with you. I know it's weird. At least I'm making it weird now. And I understand if you don't want to be my friend because I just made things all weird."

I knew it. Be honest and don't play games and leave her hanging. "It's not weird. I've felt that way about you since we first started hanging out."

"This is supposed to be wrong, though?"

"I don't think so."

"I was just raised to think that it is not normal. It isn't right. It's a sin and unnatural. But being with you. It feels like it's right."

Emma got up and moved over next to Bailey and took her hand. Her fingers laced through Bailey's, she felt the heat and electricity from their fingers through her chest. "If it feels right, it's right."

Bailey moved faster than Emma was prepared for and put her lips on Emma's.

Emma kissed her back, pulling her closer to her. She was drawing in that sweet strawberry fragrance and the warm, soft feeling of Bailey in her arms. *Nothing can be more right than this. This is all I can ever want or ask for.* Kissing Zoe was eye opening, and enjoyable for sure, but this was deeper. This kiss held promise and meaning that Emma – though she could not decipher, she could feel in every fiber of her being.

Bailey pulled back from Emma. "I… I mean… Wow," she whispered.

Emma looked at Bailey contemplating, trying to read her. "Are you weirded out now?"

"Have you ever kissed another girl before?"

"Just one. Last year. When I went up to State for the first time."

"Was it weird then?"

"No. It made a lot of sense to me about who I am, and who I am supposed to be. Was it weird just now for you?" *Please don't say that it was. I will die.*

"I've only ever kissed boys before. I never thought about girls before, at least not until you. It wasn't weird. It was different. Sweeter. More intense. More sexy. I want to kiss you again." Bailey leaned in and poured herself onto Emma.

Emma was overwhelmed by Bailey's intensity. Before she could think twice, she was on top of Emma, straddling her, with her dress riding up.

Emma took her hands to Bailey's waist and pulled her back slightly. "Bailey, I think the world of you, but I don't think this is the place—"

"Spend the night at my house tonight." Bailey was grinning with a devious look in her eyes. "When Rhys and I would, well you know, we had to be strategic around our parents' schedules. But my mom won't think twice about you sleeping over."

Emma laced her fingers through Bailey's and leaned back against the seat. "Maybe... I've never... and I don't know..." She was blushing and embarrassed.

"I want to know what it would be like to be with you," Bailey whispered as she kissed Emma again.

This went from zero to one hundred super-fast. Not at all like what I expected. I am not ready. "Let's go back in," Emma said breaking from the kiss. "And I will think about it. I don't want to rush something just because—"

"There is no 'just because'. It's prom night. We look amazing. We are having fun." Bailey was working every angle to persuade Emma.

She is not used to getting told no. It shows. "I'm not saying no. I'm saying let me think about it. I don't want to ruin our friendship over an impulse."

Bailey nodded and kissed Emma again.

Girl, just say yes and go. This is what you wanted. You want nothing more than for her to be yours. Why can't you just say yes? What's holding you back?

Bailey moved off of her lap and opened the door to the limo moving out gracefully.

Emma followed behind her and steadied her as she slipped her shoes back on.

In the coolness of the night, looking at Bailey under the spring moon, she pulled her back to her and spun her so that her back was against the car. *Nothing can be more perfect or right than this moment.* She kissed Bailey again, not even considering there could be others around.

"Yes, I will spend the night with you," she whispered into Bailey's ear.

"Fucking freak!" she heard a male voice from across the parking lot.

Bailey and Emma looked to see Rhys and his date standing a few spaces away. *Of course. That little shit ruins everything.*

"Fuck off, Rhys," Bailey yelled.

"You think you are going to replace me with a freak? You think your parents, or your brother are going to be okay with that?"

Emma straightened herself up, slid her jacket off and handed it to Bailey. *I'm not taking his shit tonight.*

"Are we doing this?" Emma asked.

"Doing what?" Rhys asked.

"Am I going to humiliate you in front of your date? It's no wonder Bailey wants me and not you. It's no wonder she dumped you and came running to me. I'm better at everything than you are."

"Emma... It's not worth it," Bailey called.

"Oh, but it is," Emma said walking in smooth strides to draw nearer to Rhys. "I've had enough of you. Of people like you. You think you can just have everything your way, all the time. And I'm here to tell you – You. Ain't. Shit." She stopped and looked at Rhys's date and made eye contact with her. She smiled sweetly at her and winked. Rhys's date blushed and looked away. *Give me a minute and I can probably have you, too.* Emma rolled up her sleeves.

Rhys moved his date behind him. *He's such a joke.*

"I feel sorry for her..." Emma said trailing off. "Here you are, on a wonderful night, and you are shitting all over it for her. Making her feel like an afterthought. That you are still hung up on your ex-girlfriend. Jealous because she's moved on. Upgraded."

"There's no way you could satisfy her. Not after me. Not after what I gave her. She will walk away from you begging to be back with me." Rhys grabbed his crotch.

He's really that delusional. He believes his own bullshit. "Not likely. If you were so satisfying, why is she here with me?"

"Emma, let's just go," Bailey begged.

More students had come out and were surrounding Rhys and Emma, watching.

"Freak. Dyke. You are pathetic. You will never be anything more than you are. A freak of nature," Rhys taunted.

That's the best you can do? You never answered the question.

One of the chaperones came out, a teacher Emma had never had. "Mills. Get. Over. Here," she demanded.

Still has to be saved by a grown-up. Such a pathetic child.

Mr. Stone came running out of the doors. "Emma!" he shouted; his tone carried a warning to her.

Emma looked up at him. She caught his gaze and was pulled away from her focus.

Rhys hawked a loogie and spat it on her. It landed slimy and hot on her cheek.

You asked for this.

"Mills!" Mr. Stone shouted as he entered the circle where they stood.

Emma's knee went reflexively into Rhy's crotch, sending him doubled over. As he was crouching in on himself, Emma elbowed him across the back and sent him to the ground.

"If I'm such a loser and such a freak, why are you so threatened by me?" Emma asked, looking down at Rhys's crumpled figure on the ground. "I would think if I'm so lowly, you wouldn't even be concerned with me, but here we are again." She wiped the spit from her cheek and rubbed it off on the side of her pants.

With that, she turned and walked back to Bailey who was shivering in her tux jacket. She finally felt herself breathing again. Her head was starting to clear. *I just want to go back to Bailey's house and be with her. Alone.*

The rest of their group was standing with her, Brandon behind her, clasping the hand of Ria (the prettiest of Bailey's friends, and least bitchy). *Good for you, Brandon.*

"Let's just go…" Brandon said quietly.

Emma nodded. "I'm ready to leave. So ready."

"I can't believe he is so obsessed with you," Leanne said. Emma wasn't sure if it was directed to Bailey or herself.

"He's such a creep!" Ria said, clinging to Brandon. "The best decision you ever made was to dump his ass."

"Not so fast, Landry. You are coming with me." Mr. Stone grabbed Emma's shoulder and steered her toward the building. *No. No. No. This is so unfair.*

Rhys was directed in the opposite direction by the principal. Emma looked at him over her shoulder. *I get it. I fucked up. But at what point do you people see that I have to stand up for myself? You people sure as shit never stand up for me. I'm going to lose everything now, because of that little entitled piece of shit.*

"Hold on. I need to let my friends know they can go without me." Emma turned around and looked at Bailey, who was wrapped securely in her tuxedo jacket.

Bailey looked back at her.

You are disappointed. I get it. I'm so sorry. I ruined this for you. "Just go without me," Emma called to her. "I will figure it out."

Ria was clinging to Brandon. "Are you sure? I can—" Brandon called out.

Emma shook her head. "Nah. I'm good. Just go." She turned around and followed Mr. Stone.

"You know what's going to have to happen." Mr. Stone's voice was ominous.

You need to try to talk this situation down. You can't leave it up to Bear. He won't do anything other than let these people steamroll you and keep you trapped in a cycle of poverty and misery. Emma followed him into a small office back inside the venue. "If my dad disenrolled me first thing Monday morning, can we avoid this being on my permanent record? Avoid it reflecting as an expulsion?" Emma pleaded. "I know what I did was wrong. I know I fucked up. I should have walked away. But when he spit on me, I just... I reacted before I could think. Mr. Stone, don't let him ruin my whole life."

"Emma, your inability to control your temper is what is going to ruin your whole life. But I will handle the paperwork on this. I will be discreet. If you can get your father in my office by the start of the day, Monday, I will make this happen for you. I will keep this off of your record."

She walked the five miles home in the dark alone from the venue. Mr. Stone did not let her leave until he knew Rhys was gone, and for that she was grateful. She plotted her course with each step she took home. Something had to give, and she had to make a change.

The trailer was empty as she let herself in. Bear was nowhere to be found. She grabbed the cordless phone and called Brandon to fill him in on her night and her plan. In response he gave her a play by play of making it to third base with Ria in a back bedroom of Rob's house at the after party.

After hanging up with Brandon, Emma laid awake in her bed in the dark and empty trailer. *My only option is to hope that I can live with Teta and go to school over there. Dear God, I don't ever ask for much. Please let this happen. If you make this happen, God, I swear I will never talk to Bailey Frankson or think about her again. I will stay out of trouble and just focus on living my life and achieving my goals. Please, God. I know I've never been to church or prayed before. But please. If you are there, if you exist. Help me get out of this.*

She called Teta first thing in the morning and ran to the bus stop without even having breakfast. Teta met her at the bus stop and drove them to a restaurant for breakfast.

"Teta, my school is not safe for me. There's this bully. He won't leave me alone. He's been tormenting me since seventh grade. Can I come live with you? Go to school with you? I promise you, I will be no trouble. None." *Please. Please. Please!*

"Have you talked about this with your father?" Teta asked, sipping her coffee.

Emma's hands wrapped around her coffee mug. "No. But I don't have any other choice. If I don't go willingly, they are going to expel me, and my future is over before I can even live it."

"I have no issue with you living with me. I would love it. I just don't know that your father will be okay with it."

"He has no choice unless he wants me to stay stuck and without an education."

They finished their breakfast and went back to Teta's home.

She dialed the shop and Jessie answered. "I need to talk to Bear."

She heard Jessie put the phone down and call Bear over.

"Bear, I'm at Teta's. I am moving here. I have to. I can't tell you everything. I don't want to tell you. You have to understand me. You have to do this for me. You have to let this happen."

"Princess—"

"Stop calling me Princess."

"Emma, this is what I've been fearing since you were born."

"Bear, please hear me. If you love me, let me go."

"Emma, let's talk about this."

"No. I can't discuss this any further. Just know, it's not safe for me at that school. It's not okay. Some really bad stuff has been happening. I just need to be away from it. I'm leaving next year for college anyway. You would be saying goodbye then. It's just a year early."

Silence on the other end.

Teta grabbed the phone. "I promise you, Frank. I will take good care of her. She will come to see you. She will be fine. My Jayne was taken from me. Let me have some time with my Emma."

Emma didn't hear Bear reply.

She walked from the room and out to the porch. She sat on the first step feeling the warm sun on her face. *If he says no, what can I do? Can I run away? File for emancipation so I can come here anyway? What are my choices?*

She waited for Teta to come back out and give her the verdict.

"Your father, he say yes. He say you stay here. He say come get your things and he will do paperwork tomorrow."

Emma let out a sigh.

She called Mr. Adame to let him know she wouldn't be playing next season for him and what school she was transferring to.

She called Simone and Abby and told them she would be up next weekend to let them know what happened.

Teta drove her in her large black Buick to the trailer. Emma threw all of her possessions into a few garbage bags and put them in the trunk of Teta's car. "This how you lived?" she asked puffing on a cigarette, wrinkling her nose in obvious disdain.

Emma looked around at the front of the trailer and the woods behind it, the shop on the other side. "My whole life. This is all I knew." Her throat was tight. It was bitter sweet to leave it all behind. *This is no longer home.*

MONDAY MORNING, BEAR MET HER and Teta at the school so she could be unenrolled. While Bear was filling out the paperwork, she went to her locker to grab her things. When she opened it, hundreds of tampons came flooding out around her feet. She didn't let it ruffle her. She didn't bother to pick them up, either, as she ignored the classmates giggling around her. She heard the familiar epithet "Bloody Mary" being whispered. It was still thirty minutes before school started. She took the books back to the library and dropped them off. *After today I will never hear that again. I will never have to see these people ever again. This chapter is closed.*

Emma still had time, so she decided to see if Bailey was in the Art room. *Bailey deserves to hear it from me that I will be gone.* As she made her way down the hall, she felt a hand go over her mouth and another over her eyes. The hands were large and dry – masculine. She was brought back to the moment her freshman year when Rhys's friends grabbed her and groped her. More hands held her arms and pulled no matter how hard she tried to fight. There were too many. She tried to fight her way out but was outnumbered.

She felt herself dragged backwards swiftly. When the hand over her eyes moved, she saw she was in the supply closet in the hallway near her locker. She was surrounded by Rhys and his minions. One was holding her arms tightly behind her, and another was keeping his hand firmly against her mouth. He was pressing so hard her lips were bleeding against her teeth.

"You think you are better than me, dyke?" he asked.

She just stared at him defiant. *I'm so over this. You don't even deserve a response.*

"You need to learn your place. You don't belong with Bailey. You don't belong here." Rhys continued, "You think Bailey actually loves you? She is just confused, and you are just an experiment for her. You are disgusting. And she will open her eyes and realize it. Now, just stay clear of her, or you will regret it. Understood, Bloody Mary?"

She moved her head managing to free herself from the hand over her mouth. "What are you going to do? Have your buddies gang up on me? Your mommy to come fight your battle for you again? What?" Emma asked.

Before Rhys could say anything, the janitor opened the closet door and saw them piled in.

"What are you up to in here?"

"Nothing, sir," Rhys's voice was sticky sweet and patronizing. "We were just concerned for our friend here and trying to help her understand some things better. Weren't we?"

Don't say a word. If this escalates, if you let on anything nefarious is going on, Mr. Stone could renege on your deal, and you will be expelled and that's it for your future. Just keep your mouth shut, girl.

She pushed past Rhys and his friends and past the janitor out the door and went to the Art room, where she hoped to see Bailey.

She sat at their table until the bell rang, and when Bailey never showed, she got up and walked out; the Art teacher called after her down the hall.

"It's okay, I'm not even a student here anymore," Emma said quietly as she walked off back to the office.

EMMA LOVED LIVING WITH TETA. She would come home from school and help Teta cook in the kitchen, listening to music from Teta's homeland in Lebanon on old vinyl records.

She relished the smells of the spices and rich flavors of the food. They would sit in the evenings and watch sitcoms on the television together. She loved Teta's hearty laugh. When Teta laughed, she laughed from the center of her soul. It didn't matter how Emma was feeling. When Teta laughed, she smiled at the very least, but usually would join her in laughter.

Her life was drama free, and she pushed hard to forget what she left behind. She pretended she had never known Bailey.

Brandon would come out to visit her occasionally and they would sit on the porch when the weather was nice or if it was rainy in the living room across from each other.

"Have you seen Bailey?" Emma asked one afternoon.

"I heard she's at a private school now. She disappeared all summer. Ria didn't even hear from her."

"Private school, huh?"

"Yeah. I did see her briefly a few weeks ago. Ria and I were at the mall. Bailey was there with some girls from her new school. She asked about you. I didn't tell her anything about you though. I just said I hadn't seen you. She knew I was lying though, because Ria told her I come see you all the time."

Emma didn't ask any further questions. In her mind, the sooner Bailey was a thing of the past, the better. Brandon left shortly after this topic fell.

"He a nice boy. You don't think so?" Teta asked after he left. She had high hopes every time Brandon came over that Emma would fall in love with him and be his girlfriend.

"Teta, it doesn't work like that," Emma would sigh.

"I try."

Brandon loved Teta and would bring her flowers occasionally when he came to visit. He would fill Emma in on the goings on at her old school. He was careful to never mention Bailey again.

She kept her promise going to visit Jessie and Bear at least once each month, borrowing, Teta's large black Buick. They would sit at the shop, or out back of the trailer or Jessie's house and barbecue.

Emma kept her head down and maintained her focus on her academics and her new basketball team. She felt slightly bad when her new team beat Mr. Adame's team in the regional playoffs. After the game, she hugged Mr. Adame and thanked him for all he had done for her.

Even though her grades were excellent and her skills on the basketball court were exemplary enough to take her new school to the state championships, she flew under everyone's radar.

Abby graduated from State and took a job out of state, moving her and Simone four hours away. Emma was heartbroken that her closest confidants would be gone when she arrived in the fall, but she had met enough of the other girls in their circle to know she would be okay.

She declined the honor of speaking as Salutatorian at the graduation commencements. Jessie and Bear came, but did not sit with Teta. They took her to dinner after the ceremony, where she tearfully thanked them for being there for her and raising her.

She moved into the dorms her freshman year and continued to excel in her classes and on the basketball court. She wasn't so invisible though and became the target of every single young lesbian (and a few 'straight' girls, too) on campus, not that it was a super large network, but it was big enough that Emma became the one everyone wanted.

She had cut her hair to a short pixie cut, close cropped. She came into her own with her fashion, opting for an androgynous look wearing mostly men's clothes which combined with her touch of eye liner and mascara (thank you, Simone!) gave most people pause to look twice at her. She was beautiful in a way that was unsettling to most people. It made men uncomfortable to leave their girlfriends alone around her, as they always found them flirting with Emma. She looked like she could have been recruited for Calvin Klein's One campaign.

It was not uncommon for Emma to not return to her dorm room each weekend as she found herself with a new girl each Friday night. She prided herself on being upfront with each of them. She had no interest in falling in love. She had goals and she had to stay focused. She had zero time for relationships.

Most of the girls were understanding, some not so much. She would find a few sitting in front of her dorm room door waiting for her, or outside of her classes.

She would call Abby and Simone and tell them about her crazy girls, and they would laugh. "Be careful! If you get too wrapped up, your grades will slip, and they will kick you out like they did me!" Simone warned, laughing.

She would visit Teta once a month and occasionally Bear and Jessie. She would coordinate with Brandon for weekends at home and they would hang out, as he was going to school out of state. Emma was too busy for love.

Second semester, she was home for the weekend and she and Brandon were having lunch at a small diner near the center of town when Bailey walked in. She was as beautiful as Emma remembered. It had been almost two years since prom. Emma slunk down in her booth. *Please don't look over here, Bailey. Don't see me.* "Bailey Frankson just walked in," she whispered to Brandon.

Brandon was extremely obvious as he spun and looked, making direct eye contact with Bailey.

Emma mortified, kicked him hard under the table. "Way to go. Fuck. She's coming this way." *What do I do now?*

Bailey came over, smiling brightly and sat herself down at the booth next to Emma. *God, she smells good.* "Hey!" she chirped. "I've been missing you." She was looking directly at Emma. "I love the shorter hair." She reached out and touched Emma's hair. *I just want you to touch me again. I wanted to forget about you. But damn. It's hard.*

"Hi. Um. Yeah. I tried to find you the day we came back after prom, but you didn't come to school."

"You had my phone number." *I forgot she's smart, too.*

"Yeah. I did." Emma sighed.

"You," she looked at Brandon. "Wouldn't tell me anything."

"Loyalties." Brandon smiled. He got up out of the booth. "Excuse me, ladies. I will be right back." *Don't go! Sit back down! You are supposed to be my best friend.*

Emma picked at her sandwich and did her best to not look at Bailey.

"Are you at State like you had always planned?" Bailey asked.

Emma nodded her head. *If you look at her, you are going to fall back in love. You don't need that.*

"I'm at the university. I love it." Bailey tried to make conversation.

"Good for you," Emma said quietly.

"Are you dating anyone?"

Emma smiled slyly. "Not really any *one*. A few girls. You?"

"Believe it or not, Rhys and I got back together right after senior year. But it's… Well, I mean he's out of state, East Coast where his dad went. It's … It is what it is." *By all means. Of course, you did. I should have guessed that.*

"You do you."

"What's that mean?" *Needless to say, she's offended. That was bitchy. But it's true.*

"You guys make sense together. I'm not a part of that world."

"I've missed you," Bailey said turning herself in the booth to look at Emma.

Emma continued to look at her plate.

"Look at me, Emma."

Emma looked at Bailey. "What do you want from me?" *I really want to kiss her again. Feel her lips on mine.*

"I held out hope that I would hear from you. That I would see you again. What I felt for you, what we talked about, it was real." Her hand gently rested on Emma's knee. Emma could feel a current of warmth from her touch straight to her chest.

Emma touched Bailey's hand and then pulled away as if she were burned. *Don't touch her. You are just going to be sucked back in.* "Well, you are with Rhys again and everything is right with the world again." Her tone held more acid than she intended.

"Seeing you, I know it's not. I want to give us a chance. There's a reason I came home this weekend. I wasn't going to, but I felt compelled. And here you are. That means something, right?"

Emma inhaled. *Brandon sure is taking his dear sweet time.*

"Have dinner with me tonight."

"Will Rhys be there, too?" Emma said with a bite. *Stop being such a bitch.*

"No. He's not home this weekend. Please, Emma. I feel like there is something we need to explore. You and me. We deserve that chance."

Emma exhaled and looked at Bailey's big blue eyes. *I never could say no to her. I'm not going to start now.* "Fine. Okay." As she said it, Brandon exited the bathroom and made his way back to the booth, grinning sheepishly. *Thanks for having my back. Some best friend.*

Bailey slid out of the booth after leaning in and planting a sweet, subtle kiss on Emma's cheek. "I will see you later."

"What time and where?"

"Seven, at the Italian place we ate at for prom."

Emma conceded and Bailey left.

"What the fuck, Brandon? Did you know she was going to be here?"

"No. Honestly. But I think it's good that you saw her. That you are going to see her."

"She's back with Rhys. She wants us to explore being together though."

"You never really had a chance. That might be good for you both."

Emma rushed home to Teta's and changed and freshened up for dinner. She went with a pair of jeans and a black button-down shirt and the new Doc Marten's Teta had gotten her for Christmas.

She kissed Teta goodbye and told her she would be back later that night and to not wait up.

Emma got to the restaurant and sat in her car for a good five minutes steeling her reserve to go inside. *There's no reason to be nervous or be afraid. She's just Bailey. You had a crush in high school. You nearly threw away your future over her. But you are older now. Wiser. Nothing to fear.*

When she walked in, she saw Bailey was already seated at a booth near the back. Her hair was in a high pony tail and her black turtleneck was tight, not leaving a lot to the imagination. Emma smiled at her and hung her head for a second before making her way over. *There's literally no resisting this girl.*

Bailey stood and Emma leaned in and discreetly kissed Bailey on the cheek, letting her lips linger near Bailey so she could drink in her essence. *You are a fucking fool where she is concerned.*

The talk was light, and they exchanged stories about their college life and goals. Emma regaled Bailey about the recent championship game and the close of the season.

The restaurant was located on the main drag of the town, and they left for a walk around the darkened streets. Even though it was cold outside, neither of them were ready to call it a night. Bailey led them to the park where she stopped and grabbed Emma's hands.

Emma bit her lip and held her breath before saying, "Bailey, I don't think this is a good idea."

"I called Rhys and broke up with him on his voicemail after I saw you. I don't know what it is, but we are supposed to be together. I know you know it. You can hardly look at me without your eyes giving it all away."

She's not wrong. Not at all. It's stupid to keep fighting this. She pulled Bailey in and kissed her. Bailey's body melted into her, warm and sweet.

Bailey broke away from Emma. "Stay the night with me," she whispered.

Emma nodded her head and followed Bailey back to the parking lot to their cars. *If you are smart you will take this car back to Teta's and not follow that girl back to her house.*

She parked in the large circular driveway and followed Bailey in through the darkened home. *It's still the same as I remember it.* "CJ is back East at grad school, and Mom and Dad are out on date night," Bailey explained as she led Emma up the familiar stairs and into her bedroom which still looked the same as it had two years ago.

EMMA SLEPT LIKE A BABY after she and Bailey spent the better part of the night exploring each other. It was every bit worth the wait of two years. Bailey was curled up next to her, and Emma was wrapped around her. Piles of pillows were around them and on the floor. She woke up smelling baked goods and bacon and coffee. Her stomach growled.

Bailey stirred in her arms and rolled onto her back. She smiled up at Emma. "That might have been the best night of my life." She kissed Emma softly as she moved out of the bed.

Emma blushed. *Most definitely mine as well. But I will never admit that to you. I still don't think I should even be here.*

"My mom is big on Sunday breakfast. Let's go down and eat." Bailey slid a t-shirt on and some sweatpants. She handed Emma a pair of pajama pants and a t-shirt to put on.

Emma looked around at the scattered clothes on the floor. "We should clean this up so it doesn't look like we …"

Bailey giggled. "They won't think anything." She moved the sheet and blanket away from Emma's naked body and caressed her. "God, you are beautiful…" she whispered.

Emma pulled her back in kissing her. Her belly grumbled again. "Okay. Breakfast," she said.

Emma sat at the table in the sunny breakfast nook. Mr. Frankson looked at her twice. "Aren't you the girl that used to work at Jessie's garage?"

"Yes, sir. Jessie is my uncle."

"Emma and I ran into each other last night. We had so much fun hanging out, she spent the night."

Mary Anne served plates heaped with eggs and home-made muffins and crisp bacon. Emma passed on the bacon. "We haven't seen you since Prom! You look great. Are you in college now?"

"I'm sorry. I don't eat meat. But yes, I am at State, on scholarship."

"Emma's been a vegetarian since she was eight years old," Bailey informed them.

She remembers!

It was a delightful breakfast with Mary Anne and Bailey. Emma couldn't read Mr. Frankson, he was gruff and not warm at all. She maintained referring to him as Mr. Frankson throughout the meal (never Charles).

As she drove back to Teta's she was buzzing inside, reliving every inch of Bailey's body in her mind. She was walking on air and her heart was singing. All of a sudden, the love songs on the radio made sense to her. *I swore that I was not going to get involved. I would not be detracted from my goals. I would not fall in love. And here, I am risking it all for Bailey again. I owe this to her and to myself to see where this goes though. There's a reason for all of this. A reason we keep coming together.*

For the next six weeks, much to the dismay of the girls at State, Emma was off the market. She was smitten. She would tie up the line in her dorm room talking to Bailey every night. Her roommate didn't mind as she was a recluse. She would pull the blanket over her head and roll onto her side while Emma would sit kicked back and talk late into the early morning with Bailey.

Weekends, Emma would either head to Bailey's apartment, which was near Teta's house, or stay with Bailey at her parents' house. Her parents were none the wiser of the true nature of their relationship. They just assumed Emma and Bailey had rekindled their high school best friendship.

Mary Anne loved Emma. She started making sure vegetarian meals and options were available when Emma was present and doted on Emma as if she were one of her own. Mr. Frankson (never Charles) was hardly ever around, and Emma was grateful for that. He made her uneasy. She didn't like his gruffness or the way he talked to her or Bailey, like they were an annoyance. When he was around, Emma was extra quiet and did her best to tiptoe around his presence.

Emma had grown accustomed to the grand house and its big spacious and bright spaces and light colors. She had grown accustomed to Mary Anne's baking on Sunday mornings and most of all, falling asleep with Bailey in her plush bed with too many pillows whether it be at the big house, or Bailey's tiny cozy apartment near the university.

One Friday afternoon, near the end of the semester, Emma met Bailey at the big house. Ria and Leanne and Brandon also were in town and meeting there before a night out at a local barbecue joint.

Ria quipped out of the blue, "Why don't you get back with Rhys? You know he loves you still. I mean, he was kind of a prick, but maybe he's learned his lesson."

Brandon side eyed Emma who bristled with the comment. *I'm not saying a word. I'm staying out of this.*

"He's a dick." Bailey was calm. She didn't look at Emma, she just looked at her fingernails.

"Yeah, but you guys were cute together. It's been a few weeks. Just forgive him," Leanne pressed.

She's left him twice for me. I don't think that she agrees with you. I better excuse myself before I say something I shouldn't.

Emma got up and went inside to the powder room off of the kitchen. She could still hear them through the open window.

"What's her deal with Rhys anyway?" Leanne asked. "What's your deal with her?"

"He tortured her relentlessly since the seventh grade. He nearly got her expelled, which would have ruined her whole future. He went out of his way to make her life miserable." Brandon was defensive.

And this is why you are my best friend.

"I mean, I know she's your friend and all, but I get it. She's kind of weird. Intense and brooding and stuff," Ria said.

Watch yourself, little princess. He doesn't take too kindly to people talking shit about me.

"Rhys told Phil that she's a dyke. Is it true?" Leanne asked.

And here we go.

"If it were, what difference does it make?" Brandon asked, his own irritation beginning to surface.

Bailey, are you going to step in any time here, or is Brandon the only one who really has my back?

"I mean, you spend a lot of time with her. Do you want people to think that about you, Bailey? And what if she hits on you?" Leanne asked.

For the record, she hit on me first. But you will never know that.

"Sounds like a Bailey problem and not a Leanne problem," Brandon was quick to the defense.

Again, thank you, Brandon. I think I need to just go home. These bitches are going to be the end of me tonight. I can study and not be part of this circle jerk. Emma left the bathroom and stood in the doorway, "I think I'm going to head home. I don't feel great. Plus, I have finals coming up."

Bailey leapt up. "I thought you were staying the night?" she asked, disappointment clear in her eyes.

No. You enjoy those friends of yours. Emma shook her head. "I'm going to head home."

An hour after she got back to Teta's, Bailey called her. "Hey. What happened?" she asked.

"I told you. I don't feel good. I wanted to go home." Emma was defensive. *You sat and let your friends talk shit about me. You didn't say one thing to shut them up.*

"No. Something happened."

Emma was quiet and Bailey didn't say anything either. *She's going to sit and wait me out endlessly. I need to tell her the truth.* With a sigh after a considerable silence, Emma finally spoke. "Fine. Rhys, first and foremost. The fact that your friends all think his attitude is okay and that you should get back together with him. He's a pig. He's an asshole. He's a really evil dark person. He has a shitty soul. I get that Leanne and Ria don't need to know how you and I are together, but it bothers me. Then... I could hear everything while I was in the bathroom. You didn't stand up for me. That hurt. A lot."

Bailey was quiet. Too quiet.

She's mad. "Are you still there?" Emma asked.

"Yeah." Her voice was soft.

No. She's hurt. "Bailey, this situation is too complicated. I don't know that we need to be doing this right now."

"No. Don't say that. Come back over and let's be together and talk about it."

"Because we won't talk. You will start getting all sexy and flirty and then

~ 116 ~

we won't talk about it, and it will just get buried." *Not that that would be the worst thing in the world.*

"Exactly."

"No, Bailey. I can't." *I really don't need this drama.*

She could hear Bailey sniffle on the other end.

Great. She's crying. "Are you crying?"

"I don't want to lose you. What do I have to do to not lose you?"

She is definitely crying. "Stand up for me when I'm not there. Fight for me like I have fought for you. I would fight the world for you. I nearly got expelled for you. That doesn't mean you have to tell them we are together. Just don't let people talk shit about me like that. It hurts that Brandon and not you stood up for me."

"I will. Just come be with me tonight. I need to know we are okay."

And I'm a total fool for you. Anything to make you smile.

Emma hung up and made her way out the door. "Teta, I'm going back to Bailey's."

"You are there more than you are home. I miss you being around," Teta grumbled. *There's no way to explain this to her. She's waited my whole life to have me and I'm blowing her off for Bailey.*

Emma shrugged. "I'm sorry! I promise we will do something Sunday!"

By Sunday morning, it was like Friday afternoon had never happened. Emma was seated at the family breakfast table eating a home-made vegetarian quiche that Mary Anne labored over all morning. Mr. Frankson (still not Charles) was sitting at the head of the table and Bailey across from Emma.

"Emma, we are getting ready to go on up to our cottage on the lake for a few weeks. I'm sure Bailey would love it if you joined us." Mary Anne was smiling. "We leave after Bailey finishes finals next week. We go every year. It's the only time we can really get Charles to leave work and relax. And our son CJ will be meeting us there."

Emma looked up at Bailey who was smiling brightly, nodding in encouragement for Emma to say yes. "Thank you so much for the invitation,

Mary Anne. I was going to enroll in summer session. I don't know. Let me think about it."

"You can take the train back in time for summer session!" Bailey exclaimed. "Come with us!" Bailey's foot climbed up Emma's calf under the table.

I need to learn the word no. This is bordering on ridiculous. Emma sighed as she smiled. "Okay. Yeah. I would love to join if I can still make it back for summer classes."

She left shortly after brunch and took Teta for a pedicure. While they were sitting in the chairs at the nail salon, Emma told Teta that she would not be home between spring and summer session because she was going to the lake with Bailey and her family.

"You spend a lot of time with this Bailey. What about Brandon? You two make such a beautiful couple," Teta said woefully.

She still has no idea. Or at least she pretends to have no idea. "It's not like that, Teta. I don't love Brandon. And Brandon does not love me like that. We are like brother and sister."

"I know. I know. You tell me all the time. It just strange, boy and girl friend and there no love feeling."

"I can't make you understand, Teta." *Don't make me say it.*

"I think I do. I still love you. I still happy you in my life." She smiled and patted Emma's arm.

How can I not love this woman? She's what I've needed my whole life.

AS SOON AS EMMA AND Bailey had finished with their finals, they met at Bailey's parents' house and were in the back of Mr. Frankson's highline SUV heading north to 'the cottage'.

Emma watched as the suburbs melted into tree lined open highway and farms. She caught Bailey watching her intently. *I can see the way you look at me. You love me. I wish I could take your hand right now.*

When hours later they pulled into the driveway of 'the cottage' (which was more of a somewhat smaller, country version of the large home they already lived in), a small red sports car was parked in the driveway. "Look! CJ is already here!" Mary Anne exclaimed.

"Great," Bailey sighed under her breath.

Emma looked at her. *I sense drama.*

"He's a dick. He loves Rhys. They are besties. *They* are birds of a feather," she whispered.

Emma rolled her eyes. *Great. It's to be expected with this crowd though.*

Mr. Frankson opened the back of the SUV so everyone could grab their bags.

Bailey led Emma up to her room, which was done in a teal and cream beach motif, and flopped on the bed while Emma opened the curtains to reveal a balcony overlooking the large expanse of water. "Wow... this is so beautiful." Emma opened the latch on the door and stood outside.

Bailey got off of the bed and came out and stood next to Emma.

"I forget you haven't been to a lot of places," Bailey said. "I take this place for granted. But seeing it with you and seeing how you must see it, I can appreciate it in a whole new way."

Emma could hear the shore lapping beneath them, and the glittering waves mesmerized her. "I don't ever want to leave," she whispered.

"It's really nice at night. I leave the door open and fall asleep to the sound of the water."

Emma pulled Bailey into her and nuzzled her hair. "One day, when we are done with school and everything, I'm going to build us a house like this. On the water."

"You think we will be together then?"

"Why wouldn't we be?"

"I was just surprised because I kind of think that we will be. I can't imagine my life without you in it. I didn't know you felt that way, too. You don't exactly tell me how you feel all the time, and I can't always read you. Can I just say it? I've wanted to say it, but I was scared. I'm going to say it. I love you, Emma Landry."

She doesn't understand how I came up in this world. It's hard. I don't talk about my feelings. I wasn't brought up that way. Emma dragged Bailey inside so she could kiss her. "Of course I love you too, and I do feel the same way." *I've always loved you. I don't ever see myself not loving you.*

At dinner that night, Emma met CJ and saw exactly what Bailey had meant. As he was passing her the bread bowl with biscuits in it he said, "So you are the grease monkey girl at the garage in town? I recognize you. You rang me up when I brought my car in for an oil change a few summers ago."

"It's my uncle's shop. I haven't worked there in over two years," Emma said, not letting him ruffle her. *You will not get me to react. I see what you are doing.*

"How are you two friends?" he asked Bailey, showing his obvious distaste with narrowed eyes.

"We were in a couple classes together in high school. We reconnected while we were home for a weekend. We just clicked. Emma's like my best friend."

"Where's Rhys?" CJ asked with obvious abruptness.

"They broke up," Mary Anne intervened. "Emma is delightful. She and Bailey have been inseparable."

"She's like Mary Anne's new project," Mr. Frankson gruffly added.

"Charles," Mary Anne nudged.

"She's not so bad. It's just like we adopted a whole new daughter. One was enough." Emma couldn't tell if he was joking or if he really thought she was a whole new incidental. "I'm surrounded by women all the time now."

Mary Anne made a face at him. "CJ, how about you? Any girls or love interests? Are you dating anyone?"

"I'm dating all of them," CJ leered.

In any other situation, we could bond over that.

"Gross," Bailey snorted.

"Good for you, son!" Mr. Frankson laughed. Emma had never heard him laugh once. She smiled at him. "See, even Emma thinks it's good for you."

CJ looked at her with his eyebrow raised. He was assessing her. "I'm sure she does."

Emma stopped smiling and narrowed her eyes at him. *Oh. You think you're clever.*

For the next few days, Emma and Bailey relaxed and unwound. They whiled away the days laying in the sun on the small shore of the lake, rode bikes around the small town and did just about everything to avoid time with CJ.

Emma did not like being around him or Mr. Frankson (still not Charles). CJ was pedantic, abrasive, and downright rude to Emma. He literally looked down his nose when he spoke to her or interacted with her. Bailey, being protective of Emma, did all she could to keep Emma away from him.

Almost a week into the trip, early in the morning, while Emma and Bailey were snuggled up in the bed still soundly sleeping, CJ came in without knocking. He snorted loudly causing them to wake up.

He closed the door behind him as Bailey and Emma sat up pulling the blankets around and up. "What the fuck, CJ?" Bailey asked.

"I talked to Rhys last night," CJ said straddling the chair at the vanity table and facing the two girls. "I wanted to know what happened that you two would break up. He said that there was some weird shit going on between you two in high school and that it probably started back up. You broke up with him right around the time you two reunited. I was already kind of guessing it, the way you two follow each other around, and the way you look at each other. It's weird. And Emma is kind of obviously a whatever. So, I figured I would see for myself. Oh. Dad is going to be *pisssssseeeddd.*" He drug the last word out.

Shit. Think fast, Emma. Say something.

"CJ," Bailey pleaded. "Don't. You don't understand. You don't."

"Bailey, there is something deeply wrong with you. This is unnatural. And I'm so telling Mom and Dad. Grease Monkey, pack your shit. And stay away from my sister." He got up and left the room.

Emma looked at Bailey. Her eyes were huge. She just shook her head. *So much for standing up.* "Bailey, what's going to happen?"

"I don't know. It's not going to be good." She was whispering and tears were falling from her eyes.

Emma could hear voices outside below. The living room patio was below Bailey's balcony. She threw on a sweatshirt and pants and opened the door quietly, sitting on the floor to listen. Bailey followed suit.

"You saw what, exactly?" Mr. Frankson asked.

"Dad, listen. Let me explain from the top. Rhys called me last night. He was returning my call, because I wanted to know what happened with him and Bailey. He was good for her. They were good together. I liked him. He told me some weird stuff was going on between Bailey and that Emma. He said he saw them *kissing* at prom their junior year. He said Emma and Bailey had reconnected and that same day that Bailey called him and broke it off with him. He said it was shady and they were probably up to something immoral. I needed verification. It didn't sound like my sister, you know. So, I walked into her room this morning and I saw the two of them. They were naked and in the bed together. That white trash grease monkey girl is *corrupting* my sister."

Mary Anne jumped in, "You had no business walking into your sister's bedroom like that."

Awe, Mary Anne! God bless you.

"Mary Anne, please," Mr. Frankson said. "He was worried about his sister. He did the right thing."

He can't be serious?

It was quiet after that. Bailey looked up at Emma and kept shaking her head. Before they could say or even think of anything else, there was a knock on Bailey's door. "Bailey Anne Frankson! You and your *friend* need to be downstairs in five minutes," he was ordering through the door.

Emma, you need to smooth this over.

Bailey leaned toward Emma on her hands and knees on the floor. "Just know that no matter what happens, I love you. I love you so much. I didn't think it was possible. But I do." She was crying as she kissed Emma.

Emma held her for a moment. "It can't be that bad. It can't. Your mom sounds like she's reasonable. And Bailey, it's not like we are kids anymore."

"She has literally no say in this household. It's all Dad. And CJ has Dad's ear. He listens to everything CJ says," Bailey said hopelessly as she stood. "We may not be kids anymore, but you don't get how this family operates. How my dad operates."

Emma followed suit getting to her feet. She followed Bailey down the stairs and to the living room and out to the patio where CJ, Mary Anne and Mr. Frankson (definitely not Charles now) were seated at the patio table. A carafe of coffee sat in the middle of the table.

"Sit down," Mr. Frankson ordered.

I feel like I'm back in the principal's office.

Emma and Bailey sat.

"What is the nature of this *friendship* exactly?" he asked. He was looking at Emma, not at Bailey.

Bailey opened her mouth to answer, and he held up his hand and cut her off. "Not you. I want Emma to tell me," he barked.

Emma knew better than to lie, or attempt to lie. Especially with CJ sitting there. "I love her, sir." Emma was not lying, she was looking at Bailey, not at Mr. Frankson (will never, ever be Charles).

His face went to a deep shade of crimson. "You've been coming to my home, staying in my home. Eating my food. All the while *corrupting* my daughter." It was not lost on Emma that he used CJ's words.

"I know it looks that way but—" Emma didn't know what to say, but Bailey cut her off.

"I 'corrupted' her. For the record, Daddy." Bailey was pissed.

You are standing up for me. For us. Against the person you fear most. You truly love me.

He slammed his hand on the table so hard his coffee cup jumped and rolled off the table to the floor shattering. "Enough. I will deal with you later." He looked at Bailey seething.

All the while Mary Anne sat, looking down at her lap. *How do you live like this? With this brute? You truly have no voice in this life. You are going to let him run over your daughter.*

"I want you to pack your things. I will take you to the train station. I will pay for your ticket. You will get on the next train back to State or your trailer or whatever. You will never, not ever, speak to my daughter or my family again. You will regret even thinking of her. Do you understand?"

Emma's jaw dropped. "Are you threatening me, sir?" *He can't tell me or his grown daughter who to see or spend time with or love.*

"I don't make threats. I make promises. My influence and my reach is far and deep. Trust me. You will be in a world of misery if I catch you near my daughter. Go. Now. Pack your shit. You are out of here and out of our lives."

He literally means business. He will ruin me over this.

Emma got up quietly, not knowing what else to do or say. Bailey moved to follow Emma. "No. You stay. You don't go within fifty feet of her," Mr. Frankson growled at Bailey. Bailey looked at Emma longingly as she sat back down.

Her legs felt heavy as did her heart as she dragged herself up the stairs. Emma slowly and quietly packed all of her things back into her bag. She saw a piece of paper and a pen sitting on the vanity table. *If I write a note, the likelihood it's confiscated or causes more problems is too great.* She went back into her bag and pulled out her favorite dark blue t-shirt and folded it up and left it on Bailey's bed. *Bailey will understand the significance.*

She didn't say one more word to Mr. Frankson or anyone else. The drive to the train station was silent while she looked out the window to avoid looking at him. *I thought I couldn't hate anyone as much as I hate Rhys. I was wrong. This man is a demon.* She boarded the train and stared out the window silent, unable to even think of anything, holding back tears, until she got off at the stop nearest to the campus, close to midnight, and walked back toward the dorms.

Clouds obscured the moon, and the stars were mostly obstructed. The streets were dark, and the street lights were scant. As she walked slowly with her heart in pieces, she heard footsteps behind her. She turned and looked behind her. *No way. Absolutely no way. Of all days.* She saw Rhys and his pack of minions behind her. His features had matured a little, but it was still definitely the same weasley, hateful asshole. "Hey, Bloody Mary," he leered.

They had gained ground when she stopped to turn around and see what or who was behind her. She thought to drop her bag and run, or throw it at them, but instead she opted to just walk away.

She turned to keep walking. *I can't handle this tonight. Not now. I don't want to deal with him. I just want to go back to my room, take a shower and sleep.* She tried to pick up her pace and keep walking. Before long, she felt hands all over her pulling her and dragging her as they did the day they dragged her into the supply closet. His minions held her tight. She couldn't move her arms and there was a hand over her mouth to keep her from yelling. Someone had yanked her bag away from her, she heard it hit the ground and skid feet away.

They pulled her into an alleyway behind a dumpster. The orange street light provided a flickering light and shadows enveloped them. Rhys was leering at her and his teeth gleamed in the flickering orange light. "CJ told me what train you would be on. He told me to send you a message that would keep you away from his sister." He undid his pants and exposed himself to her. "You think you can compete with this?" He was erect and it was pointing at her. He nodded to his other friend who undid her pants and pulled them down, ripping her underwear as he pulled them down. "They say that women are only carpet munchers because they haven't had the right dick yet. So I'm going to do you a favor..." He approached her as his friends held her, spinning her around, bending her over their backs.

She closed her eyes and held her breath; inside she wanted to cry and to vomit and to run. She held herself defiant and composed. She wouldn't let him see her react.

He brought himself up to her, body to body and she could feel him between her legs. She felt the hot tearing sensation as he entered her. She wanted to throw up as he pumped himself inside. His clammy hands gripped her hips, fingers pushing hard into her flesh. She looked up at the street lamp and focused on that. She was not going to let him see her react. Her mind was buzzing, and her body was on autopilot.

Shaking with a groan, he was over in a matter of a minute, and he laughed as he backed away. "That's a tight little pussy you have. Now maybe you will know how to use it and who to use it with. By the way, stay the *fuck* away from Bailey." He was zipping his pants back up. "Any of the rest of you guys want a turn on her? It's not bad," he offered.

They declined and the one holding her mouth shut backed away. Emma turned and spat on Rhys with blood-tinged spit. "Your pathetic little peen did nothing for me. Just like it did nothing for Bailey. You couldn't handle me on your own, so you had all of your little friends here to help you with your desperate display of masculinity. You are pathetic."

Rhys silently wiped the spit from his face and leered at her. "Come on, guys, let's go since none of the rest of you wanna go at her." They laughed and made comments as they wandered out of the alley, leaving Emma to gather herself and make her way back to the dorms, shaking, broken and alone.

~ 5 ~

Building a Life

The Present...

MUSIC POURED OUT OF THE speakers. Emma had lost herself in reverie and the sweet sound of Ellis Marsalis playing in the background.

"I was so broken-hearted leaving you that day. But I was afraid of what your dad might do. Or Rhys. I loved you so much, but I had to let you go."

Bailey was looking down at her plate. She was quiet, contemplative it seemed to Emma.

"Falling for you back then was a huge distraction. And Rhys... What he did to me... Well, it could have broken me for good. If I was a lesser woman, I think it would have. But it pushed me to do what I needed to do, which was to leave you alone. I was able to focus on finishing school, being the star athlete and scholar. Pass the LSAT and focusing on making something of myself." Emma laughed quietly.

She pushed the food around on her plate with a corner of her garlic bread. She took a bite, but the flavor held no joy for her.

She forced herself to chew it and to swallow. She followed it by a large drink of her wine. It all just sat like a heavy lump in her gut.

Closing her eyes, she put herself back in time. Back to when her life seemed to have so much promise. Not the steaming pile of shit it had turned into most recently.

The Past (1996-2000)

AFTER RHYS'S BRUTAL ATTACK ON her, she only told Abby and Brandon. She kept to herself on campus the rest of the summer, pouring herself into her studies and working out. Brandon and Abby had encouraged Emma to report Rhys's attack to the police, but Emma opted to not, knowing that nothing would happen, and he would just get away with it. She buried the trauma into a small compartment in the back of her brain and moved on.

She tried twice to call Bailey after she knew Bailey would be back from the lake. *We need some semblance of closure. To end this forever and know that we did our best and tried.* The first attempt there was no answer and the second attempt, her phone was disconnected.

She did not date the rest of the summer though she had plenty of opportunity. *The idea of being with anyone other than Bailey makes me ill. I just can't right now.*

At the beginning of sophomore year, Emma rented a house off campus with three of the other girls she knew from school. Two from her team, Jenna and Rebecca, and one from her network of fellow gay students, Meg.

She had set Brandon up with Rebecca after he and Ria broke up a few months ago, and he transferred from his school to State to be closer to her. He was there almost every night as well and it wasn't long before he was living in Rebecca's room, too.

Emma loved her life. She loved how busy she was. She loved her network of friends and her teammates and her classes. She loved her work study job and the second job she had picked up at the local bar waiting tables on occasional evenings. She slowly began to date again, picking up her old habit of refusing to tie herself down to just one girl. Soon, she was too busy to miss Bailey.

Emma felt the promise of her future in a whole new way. She felt like who she had started out in life as, had shed away like old skin.

Midway through her fall semester of sophomore year, she called Teta's house to check on her. With her new job waiting tables, she didn't get to make it back to Teta's every weekend. It had been six weeks since she had been with Teta, and well over a week since they had last talked. The answering machine picked up. It was an odd time for Teta to not be home. *Maybe she has gone out to dinner with one of her girlfriends.*

The next day, Emma tried again twice. Again, getting the answering machine and still no call back from Teta's rich voice. *Teta, where are you? You haven't called me. You aren't answering.*

The third day she expressed her concern to Brandon. "You want to drive down there and check it out?" Brandon offered.

Emma looked at her watch (a graduation present from Teta, and her only piece of expensive anything). "I have class in an hour."

"You can afford to miss a lecture. This is Teta. Let's go."

Rebecca grabbed her purse, "Come on, Emma... You won't be able to focus anyway."

Emma nodded her head and the three of them piled into Brandon's car. He put on a Dave Matthews CD and made his way south on the freeway.

Emma bit on her nails in the backseat trying to explain away the feeling of foreboding in her gut. *This is not right. Something has happened to her. I can feel it. She never goes this long without calling me back.*

They pulled up into Teta's driveway and Emma hopped out of the car and up the steps of the porch. She pulled her key out of her backpack. *I remember it like yesterday, how scared I was the first time I came here and knocked on this door. Coming here for that first time was the best move I ever made. Teta, you need to be okay. You were the first person to love and accept me wholly. The first and only truly functional relationship I've ever had.*

She took a deep breath and unlocked the door. "Teta! Teta!"

Silence.

Answer me! Come on!

As she crossed the threshold and walked in, the smell overcame her. It was a smell she knew well from encountering dead things in the woods behind the trailer growing up.

Pulling her sweater up over her nose to mitigate the powerful odor, she turned on the lamps in the living room and made her way to the small hallway and saw Teta's body collapsed and alone on the floor. *This can't be. I can't be seeing this. I can't.*

Brandon and Rebecca had let themselves in behind her.

She backed up into Brandon who caught her as her knees went weak underneath.

"Come on. We need to call the police and an ambulance," he said quietly, helping to steady her.

She nodded as the silent tears came from her eyes. *I missed out on having her for so long and now she's gone.*

"I'm so sorry, Emma..." Rebecca put her arms around Emma and guided her out to the porch.

Brandon went to the phone in the kitchen and dialed 911 to report the body of Teta in the hallway of the house.

The three of them closed the door gently and sat on the porch. The sun was setting, and the temperature was dropping. Brandon went back to his car and grabbed a flannel blanket from his trunk and wrapped it around Rebecca and Emma. Emma kept her head on Rebecca's shoulder. *Thank God for the two of them being here.*

The police and an ambulance came pulling up, their flashing lights glaring and gaudy against the darkening street. The temperature had dropped significantly but Emma didn't care, she was numb and couldn't put together a single thought. She just watched the flashing lights as they grew brighter and approached. Brandon escorted the police and the coroner and paramedics into the house and explained the situation to them.

Neighbors came out to their porches. One of them, an older Greek lady that used to occasionally play cards with Teta, but whose name Emma could never remember, came across, "Leyla?" she asked.

Emma shook her head.

"Oh, dolly, I am so sorry. She was so happy you were in her life. She looked for you for so long." The woman held her close in her boney embrace. "These last three years you were around she was so happy."

Emma choked back a sob. *I was so happy, too.*

"What happened, dolly?" she asked.

"I don't know yet," Emma managed.

She watched as the coroner came out followed by the paramedics with the body bag on a stretcher. "It doesn't look like foul play. We have to do an autopsy though."

Emma nodded at him and wiped her tears.

The police officers came out. "There was no sign of a struggle or broken doors or anything."

The officer and the coroner both gave her their cards.

"I don't even know what I'm supposed to do now," Emma said after they left.

"Do you know if she had a will or life insurance or funeral plans?" Brandon asked.

Emma shook her head. "We never talked about that."

"Does she have a desk or a filing cabinet?" he asked.

Emma nodded.

"Come on." Brandon led her back inside and Rebecca went through and opened windows and doors and turned the fans on to let the fresh air in.

Emma led Brandon to the small room Teta used as an office with an old pine desk and leather mat across it. At one point in time, this had been Jayne's bedroom.

Brandon opened the drawer in the bottom of the desk. Teta kept immaculately ordered files and there was one listed 'funeral, emergency, insurance'. Brandon pulled it out and handed it to Emma.

Teta had pre planned her funeral when Amir had passed. Her plot was paid for and so was her casket and stone. There was even a stone and plot for Jayne, should she ever be found. She had a small life insurance policy, which she had changed the beneficiary to Emma once they had reunited. Emma also got the house and all that was in it.

"This was very generous of her. But it's worthless without her," Emma cried.

"Are you going to keep this house?" Rebecca asked, looking at the plaster walls and hardwood floors. "It's in great condition. It's beautiful, actually."

Emma shrugged. "I don't know right now. I don't even know where I plan to live or where I'm going to get into law school."

"If you go to the university, it's down the road. You should keep the house. It's got to be paid for."

"I don't want to think about that right now," Emma said putting the papers back in the file and handing them to Brandon.

THE CORONER CAME BACK WITH the results of the autopsy a few days later. Teta had a massive brain aneurysm, and it ruptured so fast, she most likely had not felt a thing. He described it like a massive power outage in her brain and it just went dark. He said even if Emma were home, she couldn't have helped her. Though rare, these things happen, he said to her.

Teta's attorney reached out to her a day later while she was making funeral arrangements and contacting all of the people in Teta's phone book. He confirmed Emma was the sole beneficiary of all of Teta's assets.

Her professors were lenient with her given the circumstances and gave her a week of excused absences and work.

She laid Teta to rest, and after the funeral, finally went through the house room by room. Jayne's old room first.

Nothing in there of interest. Anything like journals or diaries had been searched for by the police when Jayne went missing. Teta had donated all of Jayne's old clothes, years ago when it was evident she was never coming back. It was mostly used as Teta's office space. It held her desk, Jayne's old bed and dresser and an empty closet.

The small room she had used when she moved in, nothing of interest.

Teta's room, a treasure trove of picture albums in the closet. Teta's jewelry. A box with an old, men's Rolex, engraved in Arabic, which Emma couldn't speak or read.

Emma put the watch in her backpack.

She pulled all of the old clothes out of the closets and dressers and put them in boxes. She had called the Salvation Army to come pick up the boxes from the porch.

She threw sheets over all of the furniture and grabbed the keys to the big black Buick.

Emma drove the Buick back to State and her heart felt heavy. She felt robbed of her time with Teta. She had envisioned Teta being there for her at graduation and years of learning how to cook in the small kitchen and evenings in the cozy living room watching sitcoms listening to Teta's throaty, soulful laugh. *This is on Bear. I had only a few short years with this amazing woman who loved and accepted me. A thoughtful and caring woman who took me in and taught me so much. The aneurysm is not his fault, but what I missed out on, what I was robbed of, that's all on him.*

No stranger to pain and disappointment, though, Emma pushed past it and translated it to fuel in the classroom and on the court.

She took the old Rolex to a jeweler who sized the band to fit her. She took it to the World Language department on campus to have the Arabic translated, it read, 'With Love, Leyla'. It became her signature piece.

TWO YEARS LATER, EMMA GRADUATED top in her class, and had taken the basketball team to nationals all four years, winning the last two consecutively. She passed the LSAT with flying colors and was accepted into the law program at the university. Emma used her busy schedule as a means of avoiding Bear and Jessie. She had less desire to spend time with them, holding Bear ever responsible for her lack of time with Teta.

After getting her acceptance to the university, she had tried to persuade Brandon to go to law school with her, but he opted to stay at State for his law program, so he and Rebecca could move in together in their own apartment.

She moved back into Teta's house, cleaning it out. Keeping most of the furniture and storing the possessions she didn't want to get rid of, but didn't suit her taste.

She made law review and balanced working at a busy gay bar on the weekends and keeping up with her studies, and of course the occasional tryst with a pretty girl here and there, when there was time.

It was her second year in law school, when she wandered into a coffee shop on her way to class that she was thrown off of her game. She was waiting for the barista to give her her order when she felt a tap on her shoulder and smelled the familiar scent of sweet strawberry. She closed her eyes and took in a deep breath, taking in the fragrance and all the memories that it brought. She knew without turning around who it was behind her. Every part of her being was fully aware before she turned around and met the gaze of Bailey Frankson.

"Emma Landry..." Bailey smiled warmly. "I thought that was you."

Emma's heart raced. Never in a million years did she ever plan to see Bailey again. "Hi..." She forced a smile. *I am supposed to stay away from you. I need to stay away from you. Your dad will ruin me.*

"It's me—"

"Yes, Bailey... I know who you are." She stopped smiling.

"I think I owe you an apology. A long talk. Something. Can we do dinner this week sometime? Are you local?"

We've already done this before. It has never ended well for us. "I live close by. I don't know. My schedule is tight." *I really don't want to open this wound again, or reopen those feelings. Bailey Frankson is nothing more than a distraction, and I don't need this right now.*

"Don't shut me out. You need to hear me out."

Ha. Just so your dad will find out and destroy what I've worked for. Emma took a deep breath. *I don't even know how this is possible. She's actually more beautiful than she's ever been.* Her long strawberry blonde hair was pulled back in a tight ponytail and her beautiful figure was wrapped nicely in low rise jeans and a tight t-shirt. Her deep blue eyes were set off by smokey coal liner. She smiled and the dimple in her left cheek was more pronounced.

If I could just kiss her one more time. Feel her. I wish I knew what it is about her that makes her so damn irresistible. It is not that she's just beautiful. I've actually had women who were at that same level. It's deeper than that. "Your dad made it clear I need to stay away from you."

"Brandon wouldn't even tell me where you were when I ran into him at home last weekend."

"Touché."

"Are you going to school here?"

"Yes. It's my second year of law school." Emma smiled proudly. "You?" The barista had called her name and she grabbed her coffee and moved to head to the door, Bailey doing her best to keep up with Emma.

"My first year of grad school. I'm getting my master's in Art History. Hopefully, my PhD after."

Bailey fell in step with Emma as she made her way up the street and toward campus.

"You know it's not my fault the way we ended. Everything I felt for you was genuine. I couldn't help what my father did."

"What happened? After he sent me away?"

"After you left with my dad to the train station, my mom cried and CJ booked it somewhere, the pussy that he is. But my dad came unglued when he came back from dropping you off. He sent me away to this program for like a month to 'make me straight.'"

"So... did it work?" Emma asked grinning at her. *I've spent enough nights with her to know there is no curing her and her insatiability.*

Bailey blushed. "I thought maybe, until I saw you standing in the cafe."

"What would your daddy do now?" There was a bitterness in Emma's voice.

"Funny. About that. Dad died a little over a year ago. He had a stroke."

"I'm sorry." *Okay, so that's a lie. I'm not sorry. Not in the slightest. Couldn't have happened to a nicer guy.*

"I'm not. Him sending me away like that ruined my relationship with him forever. I don't really talk to CJ either any longer."

"What about your mom?"

"She's good. She's going to sell the house and downsize. The big houses were never really her thing, that was all Dad. She's still practicing. She's busy."

"Would she be disappointed to see us talking right now?" *Mary Anne loved me. Who am I kidding?*

"No… I don't think she was mad. I think she was just going along with Dad. Seriously. Emma, what happened to you?"

Emma stopped in her tracks and took a deep inhale before answering. "I honestly was terrified of what your father promised to do. I did try to call you for closure, but you didn't answer and then your phone was disconnected. And then the whole issue of Rhys and his friends…" Her voice trailed off. *I am not going to tell you what he did to me. I don't want you to blame yourself for that.*

"Rhys and his friends what?"

"Nothing. It's nothing. Forget that part."

Bailey stopped in her tracks and grabbed Emma's arm. "Emma."

Here we go again. Emma looked at Bailey, conflicted. *I want nothing more than to run away with you. Pick up where we left off. But I swear it never ends well. It isn't meant to be. I pay the price every time.*

"Bailey, I'm going to be late. I have to go."

"We need to talk. Tell me. You were going to say something, and you just stopped. What? Rhys and his friends… What about them?"

Emma stood still in the bright sunshine, surrounded by the centuries old buildings of the university. Her eyes closed and she was instantly transported back to that moment outside of the train station in the alley. Rhys leering at her. She opened her eyes to rid the vision and looked at Bailey. "Rhys and his friends were waiting for me when I got off of the train. CJ called them."

Emma paused and Bailey's eyes were large. Emma moved them out of the walkway and into the shade of a large oak tree. "What happened? What did they do?" Bailey's hand was on Emma's arm.

"His friends held me down and Rhys raped me. He said it was a message to keep me away from you. He said he did me a favor. Bailey, I haven't thought of that since it happened. I don't want to think about it. It's done. We are done. It's all the past. It's not a part of me now or where I'm going. I don't want to talk about it. Think about it. I have to go. I have class. I can't be late."

Emma tried to move away, but Bailey held her arm. "Can I call you? You can't just drop bombs like that and leave."

Please don't. We've done this twice and it's ended badly for me both times. How do you not understand? "Yeah. I guess." Emma began to walk again.

"How? I don't have your number."

"Find it. It's not hard. You want it bad enough, show me." *I'm not listed. You won't find me.* Emma winked at Bailey and grinned deviously as she walked away. *I shouldn't have done that.*

TWO DAYS LATER, BAILEY WAS standing outside of Emma's class with a blue rose, with blue ribbons tied around it. She fell in step with Emma as she walked out of the building and across the bustling campus. She handed the flower to Emma. "Like sapphire blue," Bailey said, handing it to Emma.

She really remembers that. That was almost ten years ago. Emma smiled and shook her head. "You are too much," she said, taking the flower.

"You said it's easy to find your number. You are not listed."

That was the idea. Emma grinned. "Okay, you are persistent." She led Bailey over to a stone bench in the campus courtyard under a tree and sat down. Emma straddled it with her long legs, and Bailey sat cross-legged facing Emma as she dug in her bag for a paper. Emma scribbled her number down and handed it to Bailey. *This is a losing battle for me. Absolutely and wholly. I might as well give her the damn number. I don't typically answer the phone anyway.*

Bailey took the paper and folded it up, slipping it into her pocket. She reached over and grabbed Emma's hands.

I still remember how soft your hands are in mine. I'm going to play this cool though. "That's mighty presumptive of you, Miss Frankson."

"Do you have someone else?"

"Not any one in particular, no. But that's not to say I want a someone. I'm trying to get my foot in the door for my internship over the summer, and I have grades to maintain and work. I really don't have time. I mean that." Emma's eyebrow was raised. *I'm lying to you and to myself right now. I want nothing more than for you to be mine again. But you come with consequences that I always get stuck paying in the end.*

Bailey crossed her arms over her chest. "So, you are going to make it hard to just even be friends?" *Yes. Because I don't want the hurricane that comes with you being in my life.* She paused, and when Emma didn't answer, she continued, "Honestly, don't you think it means something that all these years later we never forgot each other and then here we are? Reunited by chance, by walking into a random coffee shop?"

I don't believe in that. Not when it comes to you. "I'm busy, Bailey. I'm working my ass off out here to maintain grades, scholarships, work. I don't have the luxury of having a social life and being friendly. I have to prove myself out here, and not just waltz in on a legacy. I can't be distracted by you." *That's the god's honest truth.*

"Dinner. No distraction."

That's rich. "You in and of yourself are a distraction to me."

"That's unfair."

So is every consequence I've paid for you being in my life. "That's life." Emma stood up. "I have to go. Thank you." She motioned to the flower. "It's sweet that you remembered that. I had forgotten." *Lie. I remember everything about us, no matter how hard I try to forget.*

EMMA WAS SLAMMED AT THE bar on Friday night. She had a line of women waiting for her to serve them. Most of them just wanted a chance to flirt with her, and she knew that. She collected phone numbers and heavy tips each night she worked, most of the phone numbers were tossed in the trash at the end of the night. Occasionally, if someone caught her interest, she would save the number and call from the bar phone after her shift (never from her home line in case they had caller ID, she didn't need anyone getting attached).

Emma's 'uniform' for tending bar per the club owner was jeans and a white tank top. She hated the job, and she hated the objectification, but the tips were helpful. She had burned through the small life insurance policy from Teta's estate on books and bills that were not covered by her scholarships, and taxes for the house.

As she was pouring drinks for a couple of older queens at the corner of the bar, she saw Bailey in the line. *For fuck's sake. This girl is obsessed. And we just made eye contact.*

Bailey pushed her way to the front of the bar once she realized Emma had seen her, pissing off all of the women she had cut in front of.

She's going to get her ass beat by these chicks. "You don't take no for an answer." Emma slid the drinks down to the gentlemen and slipped the tips into her pocket of her bar apron.

"When have I ever?" Bailey grinned. "I've tried calling you, and you don't answer the phone and you don't return calls."

You are not the first person to complain about that. I screen my calls because of crazy girls like you. Emma leaned over the bar to be closer to Bailey. "I'm starting to get concerned that you might be a dangerous stalker." *Stop flirting. Turn it off.*

Bailey leaned over the bar. Emma could see a gaggle of women checking Bailey out. They were nearly nose to nose, causing Emma to remember the nights where Bailey would be that close on the pillow. *Stop remembering these things. Turn it off.*

"Dinner. Sunday. I will even cook it for you. You don't even need to go anywhere. I will come over and make you dinner."

Say no. Just say no. Tell her to get lost. Leave you alone. "Fine. Fine. Will you get out of here now?" Emma said exasperated. *That's not what you were supposed to say.*

"Not even a kiss goodbye?" Bailey teased.

I want nothing more than that. "No. Get out. I'm working." *That's right. Stay strong.*

Bailey winked at Emma and straightened herself up and walked out.

SUNDAY AFTERNOON, EMMA PREPARED A fire in the fireplace to ease the autumn chill and settled herself in with her studies while she waited for Bailey. *I can't wait to see her again. I want to be able to have closure. I think that's what we need. To get involved with Bailey is certain disaster. It always is. No matter how good it is, she leads to trouble for me. But then again, it's been a few years. Her dad is dead. I hate that I have this weakness for her. I hate that I want her to be here, and I can't wait for her to be here. There is something seriously wrong with me.* Emma tried to soothe the butterflies in her stomach by opening a text book while she waited.

Bailey pulled up in the same little BMW roadster she had driven in high school. She balanced several bags of groceries and two bottles of wine. Emma opened the door and grabbed the groceries out of Bailey's arms.

"Thank you!" she giggled as she let herself in and looked around. "This is your house? Alone?"

"Yeah. It was Teta's. But I inherited it."

"That's awesome. Wait, inherited it? What happened to Teta?"

"Teta had a massive aneurysm and died in my second year of undergrad. I found her. It was actually awful."

"I'm so sorry. That's terrible. But it's a great house. A far cry from your dad's trailer."

Emma ignored that comment.

"Do you ever see your dad or uncle?"

"Not often. I'm busy. They understand."

Bailey nodded as she started pulling groceries out of the sack and organizing them on the counter. She pulled her jacket off and handed it to Emma. Emma went to the front closet to hang it up, and when she came back to the kitchen she noticed that Bailey was wearing the dark blue t-shirt that Emma had left on the bed of the cottage when she left. *That was my shirt. You loved that shirt on me. You still have it.*

Emma was quiet as she looked at Bailey in the shirt.

"I never could throw it away." Bailey understood that Emma saw it. "The few months we had together were everything. Even after the program Dad had

~ 140 ~

sent me to. I understood that no matter what, you loved me, and I loved you. Whenever I was sad, or feeling not so great, I would wear it. I would think of you, and remember what it was like to be in your arms, and feel better."

Don't go there. Please don't open that floodgate. "What are you making me?" Emma asked, changing the subject, trying to assess the ingredients as they were lined up. Two eggplants, salt, breadcrumbs, eggs, pasta, mozzarella, bread. She watched Bailey methodically unpack the load and line it up as she spoke. *I can't handle even thinking about that right now. I don't want to unpack those feelings. I stored them and put them away in a nice little box in my brain that will stay forever shut. Tonight is supposed to be about closure.*

"I remember you saying you didn't care for meat ever since you had to kill a deer when you were a kid. I'm making eggplant parmesan."

"I can't believe you remember that." *Yes I can. You always hung on every word I said. And you have an incredible memory.*

"I told you how I felt. I wasn't making that up."

"What did you do after I left?" Emma sat on a stool next to the counter to watch Bailey.

Bailey handed her a bottle of wine. "Open this, and I will tell you."

Emma got up and pulled out the corkscrew and two glasses. *Stop this, Emma. Don't get too cozy with her being here in the kitchen. The two of you together, acting like it's nothing. It's not nothing.*

"Rehab did a number on me. Dad sent me away for, of all things, sex addiction and perversion at some religious based program. It was frightening, to be honest. I was in there with these women who were much older, and much more depraved than I ever could be. I had this older male therapist who I swear was getting his rocks off after his sessions – he probably should have been a patient there himself. When I came back, I didn't want to date anyone. And I didn't for two years. Rhys tried to get back together, but I was not having it. I was so mad at what he did, going to CJ and getting him involved."

"How did you decide to date?"

"I minored in Psychology. I knew and understood after I really dug into my psych classes that I should have never gone to that program. I wasn't broken. I didn't have a problem. Loving you wasn't wrong and would never be wrong, it was my dad and CJ that had a problem. Not me. Once I came to that realization, I felt like I was ready to start dating and finding love again."

"But with guys?" Emma asked.

Bailey shrugged. "I don't think it has to do with male or female so much as the person. But to answer your question, yes, with men. You are still the only girl."

Emma rolled her eyes as she poured the wine into glasses. *I've been down this road before. Not only with you, but a lot of girls.* "So, was I an experiment for you? Am I still?"

"No... You weren't and are not. What I felt then and feel now is real. I mean, I let it go. I gave up hope of ever seeing you again and Brandon was so tight lipped about you every time I saw him."

Emma smiled and slid a glass to Bailey. "He's my boy." Emma lifted her glass in a toast.

"Seriously, though... I don't know how to express it to you. I loved you then. I did. And seeing you the other day... It ripped the band aid off of this wound I had worked so hard to forget about. We never got closure. I saw you and I ... I just wanted to be yours again." Her voice cracked with emotion.

"You were never mine." *Your dad made sure of that. Rhys made sure of that.*

"Don't say that. I was so completely yours. Just like you were mine."

Stop it. Just stop it. I don't want to feel that again. "We were kids."

"And now we are not. You can't tell me, Emma, that you have zero feelings for me."

"That's very true. I do feel something. Probably the unresolved puppy love crush. But I don't have time in my life. I told you that."

"What if I wasn't a distraction but someone who was there for you. To help you. You wanted a life with me once. What if we are being given a second chance at what was stolen from us? What if I'm not a distraction, but a partner in building a life together?" She was going through the kitchen drawers and pulling out supplies.

She still doesn't know the word no. And I won't be the one who gets her to understand it. "Who's in law school? You or me?" Emma laughed.

"I'm just saying, we never had a chance back then. We have a chance now."

"Maybe."

"Emma—" Bailey was slicing the eggplants on the cutting board.

"Bailey, I didn't say no. Honor me and my boundaries. I can't commit right now. If it's too much, you will need to understand." Emma sipped the wine. "Just like right now, I need to go back to my books while you cook. Remember, you are not supposed to be a distraction."

Emma left the kitchen and went back to the living room, threw another log on the fire and picked up her book and highlighter.

In the background of her studies, she could hear Bailey slaving away in the kitchen, and she smiled to herself. *This feels right. Just having her in the house with me. Her very presence near me is what I need. What I want. I can't keep fighting this. Bailey is right. She's absofuckinglutely right. We keep getting brought together because we are meant to be.*

She put her book down after annotating several passages and went to the doorway of the kitchen. She leaned in the doorframe and watched Bailey intently working over the slices of eggplant. *I'm not so sure she knows entirely what she's doing in there. Cooking was Mary Anne's thing, not really Bailey's.*

She's trying to look like she has it under control. She's so damn cute when she acts like that. She's an absolute mess. She could tell Bailey was flustered and pretending to not notice that Emma was there.

I'm so done fighting this. Emma made her way behind Bailey and slipped her arms around her. Bailey stopped what she was doing and just stood still in Emma's arms.

Emma drank in the smell of Bailey's strawberry fragrance. It was like coming home for her at that moment.

She spun Bailey around and kissed her softly.

Bailey looked up at Emma. "Thank you."

"For what?"

Bailey kissed Emma again. "For that."

Emma smiled. "I'm hungry. How much longer?"

Bailey shrugged. "I've never made this before, so I don't know."

"I'm going to let you concentrate then." Emma let go of Bailey and backed away.

THEY HAD FINISHED THE FIRST bottle of wine with dinner. Emma uncorked the second. She was buzzing from the wine and emotions. The conversation had flowed easily after she decided that to fight it was a fruitless battle, and Emma felt that the last several years of separation had never happened.

She cleared the plates from the dining room and stacked them in the kitchen and escorted Bailey into the living room. Emma's mind was surprisingly clear though she was slightly drunk from the wine and Bailey's presence.

Bailey set her glass down on a coaster and took Emma's and set it down.

She pulled Emma to her and began to unbutton Emma's shirt.

Emma's hand grabbed her wrists. She lowered her lips to Bailey's. *You don't get to be in charge anymore.* When they were younger, Bailey controlled everything. This was not going to be the case now. Emma lifted Bailey's shirt over her head. Her hands moved over Bailey's body gently. *There's never been anything more beautiful than her in this moment.* Emma felt the electricity from Bailey through her very being. Her skin, pale and glowing in the firelight, felt warm and velvety under her fingertips. She could feel Bailey's flesh respond to her touch with the small goosebumps that came up under her fingers, and Bailey's whole body trembled.

She unhooked Bailey's bra and let her lips tease over her nipples. This body was so familiar to her still, from the smell, to the taste, to her very responses. The feeling of her warmth emanating from her skin against Emma's lips and the familiarity of each curve and the sound of her breath as it caught in her throat released the avalanche of emotions that she had pent up so long ago.

Bailey took in a ragged inhale, her hands grabbed at Emma. Emma pulled her hands down again, and shook her head no, and Bailey acquiesced. *She does understand no, at least for this.*

Emma sat on the couch and pulled Bailey closer. She undid Bailey's jeans and pulled them down, her hands caressing Bailey's smooth firm legs, finding their way up to the warmth between. Her fingers found a rhythm over the fabric of her black cotton panties, rubbing gently as Bailey's breath quickened. Emma was teasing her, she knew right where to take her before stopping and slipping the skimpy black fabric away and letting her fingers slide up inside of her.

Bailey slid down on top of Emma straddling her as she moved and ground against Emma's hand. Her lips sought Emma's hungrily.

Emma moved gracefully around Bailey and pinned her beneath, burying herself between Bailey's milky thighs. Bailey cried out and arched against Emma, clutching at her. Emma felt lost in the heat and the familiarity yet newness of all of this. She had turned off her emotions all those years ago, and the rush of excitement as Bailey was moving beneath her, responding to her every touch was almost too much.

Bailey succeeded in grasping the collar of Emma's shirt and pulled her up. She deftly undid the buttons of Emma's shirt and with trembling hands, explored Emma's body.

Her eyes were glassy with tears as she looked at Emma, studying her every curve letting her fingers touch and explore.

Emma stopped her. "What's wrong?"

"I've just been wanting this. Missing you. Not even knowing—"

Emma kissed her deeply. "I missed you, too." For the first time in as many years, Emma let herself be lost in the moment and allowed for the release of all of her emotions to come to the surface as she lingered in each moment of Bailey's touch.

IT WASN'T UNTIL THE FIRE in the fireplace went cold and the hours of the early evening succumbed to early morning that they moved to the bedroom to sleep.

Emma was half asleep, groggy and giddy in class the next morning; an appearance no one had ever experienced on her before. She absolutely didn't care. Bailey Frankson was hers again.

Within a few months, just after the holidays and at the beginning of the new semester, Bailey had moved in. It was an adjustment for Emma who had grown to like her space and was particular about the way the house was kept. Bailey wasn't a slob, but she was not as neat as Emma. Emma found herself picking up piles of Bailey's clothes or wiping up the sink after Bailey put on her makeup, or doing the dishes behind Bailey who would leave her coffee cups in the sink when the dishwasher was only a foot away.

Emma took it in stride though. The petty annoyances were worth the feeling of having Bailey by her side in the night, or making the pot of coffee in the morning, or waiting for her to come home, happy to see her.

Bailey was always optimistic, and Emma's biggest cheerleader. When Emma was stressed or panicking about her interviews for her internships, Bailey was building her up. When Emma found out she had gotten into her first-choice firm for her summer internship, Bailey was waiting for her at home, with a "See, I told you! They would have been foolish to turn you down!"

Bailey had a tendency to make things around her beautiful and bright. She began to take on small projects in the house to make it more their own space. She repainted walls with brighter colors, she used money from her inheritance to update the furniture. While Emma was working dawn to dusk at her internship, Bailey had completely redone the upstairs bungalow space as an office for Emma. She installed shelves and had Brandon and his friends come move the desk from Teta's old space to the upstairs. She redid the lighting and potted plants around the window.

She made their house a home and it was one that Emma had dreamed of her entire life. One that was a place she craved to be and filled with the love of a person who made her the center of their life.

~ 6 ~

The Truth

The Present...

"IT'S FUNNY," EMMA SAID QUIETLY taking a bite of eggplant parmesan that was now cold, "this has always been kind of our meal. That dinner that brought us together. The dinner we make whenever we celebrate something special..." She chewed her food and swallowed it. It formed a cold lump in her gut. She took another swig of her wine. "When did this fall apart? When did *we* fall apart?"

Bailey was not making eye contact. She was stone silent and cold across the table. Her arms were resting in her lap and her head down. *The silent treatment. You are the master of that game. You've never been good about talking to me when you are upset. You know it hurts me more than any words that could fall from your lips.*

"I wish you could just look at me. Look me in the eye. Talk to me. Tell me what I did that led us here." Large tears were falling from Emma's eyes. "We had it all. Two decades of us against the world. If I knew this is how it was going to end, I would have never gotten involved in the first place. This is not what I wanted for us. Baby... I wish you would just look at me. I wish I could see your eyes..." *Look at me. Just look at me so I know we are okay. So I know we will be okay. I just need you to look.*

The Past (2002-2007)

EMMA GRADUATED LAW SCHOOL. SHE was in the top five of her class and was quickly hired by the firm she had interned for her second year specializing in corporate litigation. She was fully aware that she was a diversity hire. To absolutely no one's surprise, she passed the Bar easily on her first attempt.

Bailey still had one more year of grad school and had already been accepted to a PhD program. They had a tight network of friends that they would socialize with, but what they relished more than anything was that time together alone.

Being the most junior associate on the legal team, Emma had to work twice as hard and twice as long. She was the only female litigator and was in a position to prove herself. The only other females at the firm were paralegals and secretaries. But for Emma, that first paycheck made it worth her while. Aside from the life insurance check she received when Teta passed away, she had never seen a check that large. But she was not foolish with her paychecks. She listened to her older coworkers talk about investing and would make mental notes about how much and where and how.

She would come home from her long days and collapse into Bailey's lap. Bailey would caress Emma's head and run her fingers through her hair and honor the silence that Emma craved for a good ten minutes. Being with Bailey was a safe space where Emma could just be. She could be in the moment and not thinking about what next or strategy. It was her happy place.

As Bailey began her PhD program even those moments were limited. Emma would come home and retreat directly upstairs to her office space and Bailey would be spread out across the living room, with books and papers and her laptop.

They were busy building their careers and their lives together. They were there to support each other and lean on each other.

Bailey was initially reluctant to disclose her relationship with Emma to Mary Anne given the history. She had finally come clean with her mother about the nature of her relationship with Emma, and Mary Anne was not surprised and blessedly supportive. Bailey was all that she had since her husband had died and she was not close with CJ who had morphed into a full-blown junior version of his father, taking over the business and becoming twice the asshole his father had been, so she was not going to lose her daughter. She also could not deny how happy and satisfied Bailey was.

Five years into her career, and one year post PhD for Bailey, they had found a groove in their lives. Bailey had made excellent connections while she was interning and landed a coveted position working as a curator for the city's massive art museum downtown, and began teaching classes at the university part-time as well. Emma had won over the old guard men that she worked with and made a name for herself as a fierce litigator.

Emma's weakness had become having bespoke suits made to match her sleek and powerful style. Each quarter, as goals were met, a new suit was ordered as her treat to herself.

It was spring and the weather was unseasonably cool. Emma was in a meeting with clients, laying out their strategy when her secretary, Greta came in. "Ms. Landry, I'm sorry to bother you, but you have a phone call from a Jessie Landry. He says it's urgent and it can't wait."

I don't recall ever giving him my number here. Emma was annoyed. "It's going to have to wait. Please get his number and I will call him back."

Emma had been extremely lax about visiting and calling Jessie and Bear since Teta had passed. *I realize that I haven't been to visit in a long time. That's my fault, but I also still blame both of you for keeping me from Teta. She died before I got to spend a sufficient amount of time with her. Besides, the two of you really don't fit into my life any longer.* She had grown content with only seeing them once or twice a year for brief visits, or sending big checks in lieu of visits.

Greta, her secretary, an older woman with a soft demeanor who had been assigned to Emma on her first day in the firm, nodded her head and walked out. Two minutes later as, Emma was rolling back through her strategy, Greta was back inside the doorway. "Ms. Landry, he said it can't wait. He said," she looked down at her paper to make sure she was getting it right, "'Your father is in the hospital, in the ICU at St. John's. It doesn't look good. He needs to see you.'"

Her clients sat back and looked at her. *This couldn't be a worse time. Leave it to Jessie and Bear to throw a literal wrench in my life.*

She closed her eyes with her arms bracing her on the table and she took a deep breath. "Thank you, Greta." *She's just doing her job, bless her heart.*

Greta skitted out of the office. Emma was never harsh or mean to Greta, like some of the attorneys were with the secretaries. Greta was just subservient by nature.

Emma looked at her clients. *Please don't fire me. I promise you, I don't ever come with drama or put you on the back burner. I know where my bread is buttered.* "I'm so very sorry. I ... I think I need to deal with this." *The fact that Jessie doesn't have this number, I need to deal with this. This is urgent.*

"We understand. We all have families too." Her client was slightly monotone in his reply.

I know you are lying to me right now. You pay me to make you a number one priority. You pay me to put my life on hold for you. This can potentially cost me your business. You know it as well as I do.

Her clients got up and she said, "Please see Greta on your way out, and she will reschedule you for tomorrow morning before mediation. Just know I got this; you are handled."

They left the office and Emma picked up the extension, "Jessie..." she said, her voice trailing off, showing obvious annoyance.

"Emma, I understand you are a big shot now, and you are better than where you came from, but Bear – your dad – which you have only one... He loves you. He's dying and he needs to see you. He's asking for you." Jessie's voice sounded hoarse.

Was his voice always that hoarse? Is that age? Smoking? Or is that emotion? I can't remember what his voice is supposed to sound like. That's what I get for sending checks instead of visiting. She sat back against her chair and let out a sigh. *This better be a real emergency.*

"What's wrong with him?"

"He has cancer. It's in his chest. His esophagus they say. They didn't find it until it was too late. You know your dad is too stubborn to go to the doctor. Well, now it's not good. All he can say is he needs to see you. And it's high time you get yourself over here to see him before it's too late."

Emma's throat constricted. *I'm such an ass. I never thought about this happening. I never thought about Bear not being somewhere in the background of my life.* "I will be there in shortly. I need to handle a few things and I will be on my way." Her voice was barely a whisper.

She hung up with Jessie and called Bailey's office. *I need her. I can't do this on my own. I need her calm. I need her by my side.*

"I need you to come with me. I can't do this alone," she begged after filling Bailey in.

"I will meet you at home and we will go together."

Bailey was waiting near the door as Emma pulled up and she ran down the porch and into Emma's car.

"Are you okay?" she asked.

"I don't know how to feel right now. When I was little, it was just me and Bear against the world, until the world got bigger, and I understood. I've been so mad. So busy. So many things, and I haven't thought about this ever being a possibility. I took for granted that Bear would just always be there," Emma said as she navigated the car down the road and onto the freeway. She was operating on some form of autopilot.

Bailey reached for her hand and held it. Emma felt grounded and a greater sense of calm just having Bailey's hand in hers.

"Thank you for being there for me. I know you have a lot going on."

"Of course, baby… I understand what it's like to lose a dad. Even if you are not super close anymore, it's not easy." She squeezed Emma's hand firmly.

She was quiet for the remaining half hour until she exited the freeway and parked in the hospital parking lot. *I need to be prepared. This is serious. I need to forgive him for what he did in keeping me from Teta. He did what he thought was best for me. He didn't know the real her. He knew a different version of her. He loved me. He protected me.* She refused to let go of Bailey's hand as they made their way through the hallway and up the elevator to the ICU.

She was suddenly feeling very self-conscious as she made her way into the room where Bear was sleeping, and Jessie was reclined in a chair next to Bear's bedside. *When was the last time I made time for them? It was well over a year ago.*

Jessie sat up and looked at her with his eyebrows raised. His hair was all gray now, but still thick and long. His faded jeans and dirty work boots were the same as they had been when she was growing up.

She had walked in still in her bespoke suit for work. Fine black wool and high thread count button-down shirt with a fitted vest and jacket. Her hair was clean cut in a trendy faux hawk, and she still wore Amir's Rolex. "Look at you..." Jessie said. He didn't say it with contempt. He said it with pride and adoration.

They've never seen me in my work clothes. I can only imagine how portentous I look right now. He nodded at Bailey, who he had met only a handful of times before.

"Hey, Jessie..." Emma embraced him. *I should apologize for putting them on the backburner and not making time for them. It was so fucked-up of me.* She looked at Bear on the bed. He looked small and wasted. His hair was gone, and his body withered on the bed. He looked infantile and helpless. Not the big man with the booming voice of her youth. Larger than life and the center of her whole world for so long reduced to a shriveled being in a hospital bed.

"I'm going to let you be alone with him for a few," he said getting up. "I need a smoke and a soda."

Emma took over the chair Jessie had been sitting in.

"Frank... Hey... Wake up... Emma is here. Look at her. She looks beautiful." Jessie gently woke him.

Bear opened his eyes and he saw Emma. He sat up slowly and was straining.

"Bear, no…" Emma choked.

"I'm going to go with Jessie…" Bailey whispered in Emma's ear.

"Princess…." Bear whispered.

Emma forced a smile. "Bear, I'm so sorry. I'm so sorry." Tears were spilling from her big blue eyes. *I'm such a bitch. I can't take this back and make more time.*

"No, Princess. I need to talk to you. I need you to hear me. You are right to go away. I didn't deserve the time I had with you. I was selfish. I was stupid."

"No, Bear. Shhhhh…" *He thinks he deserves to suffer for the mistakes I made. That is selfless love. I am the worst daughter ever.*

"Princess, listen to me." His voice was weak. "I know where your ma is."

Emma stopped breathing, and she was sure her heart had also stopped. Leaning forward, her hands reached up and grabbed the metal rails of his hospital bed. *Wait. What?*

"I need you to listen to me though. I have prayed on this, and I prayed to God that you will forgive me all of it."

"I'm listening, Bear." Emma's heart was racing. *Skip the preamble and just tell me. I've been waiting my whole life for this.*

"When your ma and I got together, we was young. Real young." He was wheezing between words and his voice was weak and strained. "And I was crazy and stupid. I should have never messed with her to begin with. Her parents were not okay with us. They wanted her to marry a person like them, from their culture, not some low life hick like me. I should have left her alone. But I felt like I had to prove something. So, then we got married and I knocked her up. But she started to see I wasn't much. I wasn't ever going to be much. She knew it. She started talking about getting a divorce and going back to her parents. But you were born, and I didn't wanna lose you. You were precious and wonderful. And I wasn't going to not have you in my life. I would have lost you forever if she left. Especially back then. Courts didn't care about the dads getting rights to see their babies. Especially poor dads like me.

"So, I came home one night, I had gone out drinking and whatever. And

~ 153 ~

she was waiting up. You were just a tiny baby in your crib. And she was yellin' at me and sayin' how in the morning you and her was going to be at her folks' house and she was going to file for divorce. She was saying I wasn't never going to see you again. I lost it, Princess. I didn't know what else to do. I grabbed her by the throat…" He was struggling to breathe, and he clicked a button on the machine he was connected to. He was quiet for a second and his eyes closed as medicine was delivered into his bloodstream. "I killed her, Princess. I strangled the life right out of her."

Emma let go of the rails. *This is the drugs talking. This cannot be real.* "I can't breathe." She stood up and went to the doorway of the room. "You are joking, right? This isn't true. Maybe you wanted to kill her? But you didn't. It's just a morphine addled hallucination, right? Tell me it isn't true?"

He looked down, and tears were flowing from his eyes. "I couldn't lose you then. I knew I would lose you someday, and I did… And I understand why I did. I couldn't hold you back from what you could be, from what you became. Look at you. I'm so proud of you."

"Where is she?" Emma's voice was hard. "What did you do with her body?"

He was silent.

"Bear! What did you do with her body?"

"Do you remember where the deer stand is?" His voice was quiet.

"Yes…" Emma was crying, and she felt like the lost little girl in the stand the day she shot the doe.

"She's buried under the tree where the deer stand is. Jessie helped me bury her there."

"Fucking what?" Emma was still and her voice was like steel even though the tears were flowing free from her eyes.

He was sobbing. "Forgive me. I couldn't lose you. Forgive me." His whole body was shaking as he sobbed, and his monitors were going ballistic. *I can't deal with this right now. I need to get out of this room. These fucking monitors. His fucking crying. I can't breathe. This is too much.* "Princess, I'm dying. I can't die knowing you can't forgive me."

"You robbed me of my mother! You took me from her. From her whole family! You tell me this now... And I'm expected to just forgive you? Because you're dying?" Though she was never one to get shrill normally, she was bordering on it at the moment.

A nurse came bustling in. "I'm sorry. You can't be in here if you are going to argue and upset him."

"Fuck. Off," Emma told her.

"Excuse me?" she asked.

Bear grabbed the nurse's arm. "I upset myself. This isn't her fault. I told her some upsetting family things. Don't make her leave." He was crying, playing the victim.

You drop this bomb on me, and then play victim? I should choke the remaining life out of you like you did my mother. The fact he even has me thinking like this is fucked-up. The audacity of that man.

Emma spun on her heel and walked out of the room and to the nurses' station frantically searching her jacket pockets. *Where's my fucking phone?* "I need a phone. I need to borrow a phone." *I was in such a big hurry I left it in the car. Dammit.*

The clerk behind the desk looked flustered. "We are not supposed to let people use this line."

Emma was leaning over the counter looking down at her. *Don't play gatekeeper. Just give me your damn phone.* "This is urgent. I need this phone. Now. I need to call the police. I need to report a crime."

The clerk looked at a senior nurse who nodded approval. "Should I dial 911?"

Emma paused, "No... Just call the dispatcher or someone." She made her way around the desk.

She could hear Bear yelling for her in the other room "Princess! Princess! Forgive me!" he yelled between wailing sobs. *Someone needs to shut him up. God dammit.*

She looked at the nurse who was just in there with him. "Can't you sedate him? Knock him out? Call his doctor!" *Do your goddamn job,* she barked.

The clerk handed the receiver to her. She put her lawyer hat back on so she could compose herself as she told the dispatcher what her father had just confessed to her.

The clerk sat by listening intently. *I can't even imagine what you must be thinking.* Emma saw her pick up another phone discreetly and speak quietly into the receiver. *Great. She's calling security. We are making a spectacle of ourselves up in here.*

As she was hanging up with the dispatcher, she saw Jessie and Bailey making their way up the hallway from the elevator bank. *Jessie, you knew all this time. You knew. You protected him.*

Emma stood and made her way around the counter top and put herself in front of Jessie. She moved with the swiftness of a predator, and Jessie had no idea what Emma's motives were.

She shoved him back against the wall. Jessie was caught off guard as his back hit the wall with a thud. His eyes were large as his head went back and Emma was nose to nose with him. "You hid the body. He killed my mother and you helped him hide the body. You lied to me. You covered it up."

"Emma, babe? What is going on?" Bailey asked, concerned. She had not seen Emma this upset since prom night when she went toe to toe with Rhys in the parking lot. Emma was always cool, calm and collected; calculating in every movement, word and reaction.

Emma shook her head. Rage and pain were boiling off of her. Her mind was buzzing, and she felt as if she were not in her body.

"He's my brother, he's all I have left. What was I supposed to do, Emma?" Jessie asked as hospital security converged around them.

"What were you supposed to do? Really? What were you supposed to do? I don't know. Call the police. Not help bury a body. The body of my *mother.*" Her voice was loud, and back to bordering on shrill. A security guard came up and put his hand on Emma's arm and she shrugged him off.

Bailey was standing by with her jaw dropped.

"Come on, folks…" The security guard led them down the hallway. "We are going to take this episode of the Jerry Springer Show somewhere else."

The four security officers were herding Emma, Bailey and Jessie down the hallway and into a cluster of back offices. They put each of them in a separate office. "Just wait here while we sort this out. I understand the police are coming," the officer said as he sat her down at a desk and walked back out. Emma sat alone waiting for someone to come in and talk to her. She got up and began to pace the small office.

They have me in here like I'm a perpetrator. I mean, I did react inappropriately. But how is one supposed to act when they find out their father killed their mother and buried the body? Oh. And that their uncle helped. Where is Bailey? I need her here. I need to hear her voice. I need to feel her by my side. I need her to be my anchor right now. I need her calm.

As she paced, she kept visualizing Jayne, her mother, sitting in that dumpy little trailer alone, sad and angry and overwhelmed with a new baby. She pictured the whole scene of her father coming home drunk and rambunctious. She pictured them yelling at each other while she cried alone in her crib. She pictured her father's large, rough hands wrapping around Jayne's delicate throat. She pictured Jessie coming over and the two of them carrying her mother's body to the back of the truck, like the doe – vacant eyed and dead while her baby was lost and alone missing its mother, and driving to the clearing that led to the deer stand.

That's it. I've been cooped up in here alone for long enough. I'm going to find Bailey. She stormed over to the door and grabbed the handle to open the door when it opened, and a security guard and local detective were there.

She stepped aside to let them in. The detective moved and sat behind the desk. She was tall and stern, her hair slicked back in a short bob, and her shoulders stiff on her ramrod straight spine. Emma could tell she was no bullshit and, in most circumstances, would probably have liked the woman. But she was in no mood to be put on the spot right now.

"Hi, I'm Detective Kingman. I'm going to get to the bottom of this little kerfuffle y'all were having in the middle of the ICU. Do you want to tell me what is going on? You can start with your name," the detective got straight to business.

Emma sat down across from the detective, who pulled out her notepad and a pen. "My name is Emma Landry," she said resting her elbows on the arms of the chair and crossing her fingers in front of her body.

"Emma Landry... Okay, what is your relationship to the rest of these folks?"

"Frank Landry is my father. Jessie Landry is my uncle. Bailey Frankson is my girlfriend. Partner."

Officer Kingman looked up at Emma and nodded for her to continue.

"Frank is dying. We hadn't seen each other in a long time. You know, family stuff. And ... so, I came. And he told me that he killed my mother thirty years ago and hid her body under the deer stand in the woods behind his trailer. My mother has been missing since I was three months old. It's a cold case here, Jayne Mansour Landry. He killed her. He strangled her. Because she was going to leave him and take me away. And he killed her. He. Killed. Her." Emma was only now processing it. "Oh. My. God. He. Killed. Her." She was numb. She couldn't even feel the tears that were falling from her eyes.

"Do you know where this deer stand is?" Detective Kingman asked unfazed.

Emma nodded. Her hands went up over her mouth.

"And Jessie Landry? What does he have to do with all of this?"

Emma's voice came out in a thin whisper, "He covered it up. He helped bury the body."

"Imma be right back." Detective Kingman got up and stepped out leaving Emma alone with the hospital security guard.

Emma looked at him, "Can you please let Bailey in here? I really need her right now." Emma was doing all she could to keep it together, she was visibly shaking.

"I will see... Hold on." He got up and walked out too.

It seemed like an eternity before the door opened and Bailey was in the small room with Emma. "Baby, are you okay?" she asked as she sat down.

Emma shook her head 'no'. A flood of warmth spread through her just having Bailey near her. She didn't even realize she had felt cold. "My whole life is a lie. I grew up thinking my mother didn't want me. I grew up wondering why I wasn't good enough for her to stay around for. Bear killed my mother. He buried her. Remember I told you about him taking me hunting when I was little girl?"

"When you killed the doe?"

"Yes, when I killed the doe. Well, he buried my mother below that deer stand. I was standing above her corpse, crying for the mother of a fawn, while my own mother was rotting below my feet." Emma felt nauseous. Her head was spinning. She leaned over onto Bailey's shoulder.

Bailey wrapped her arms around Emma and kissed her forehead. "I'm so sorry, baby. I can't even believe this."

"Sadly, I can. This has been the life I have been working to get away from. Whenever I think it's behind me, this kind of hillbilly bullshit pulls me back in." There was a buzzing in her head and her thoughts were disjointed and scattered. Bailey just held on to her quietly as they listened to a clock on the wall ticking and the fluorescent lights as they hummed overhead.

It seemed an eternity before Emma could hear Jessie being led down the hallway in handcuffs.

Detective Kingman came back in, and Emma straightened up, sitting up off of Bailey's shoulder.

"Miss Landry, are you local? Do you still live in the area?"

"No, I live about an hour away."

"Can you stay local for the night? You mentioned that you are familiar with the location of the deer stand where the body is allegedly buried. Could you lead the team in the morning out to the woods?"

"I ... I have mediation in the morning. I have clients... I ...."

"I will call Greta for you. You can reschedule. I know you. I know you don't like to or want to, but this needs to be handled." *God bless Bailey.*

Emma looked at her watch. It was well past seven. She had been there only for four hours, but it felt like days.

Emma just nodded her head numb. *Of course, this bullshit will interfere with clients I've worked hard to maintain. I hope like hell they don't drop me over this.* Bailey got up and pulled her cell phone from her purse and left the small room to call Greta for Emma.

Emma was asked to run through the whole scenario again when Detective Kingman's partner arrived, who was a stodgy older man with silver whiskers and dull eyes, who went by Detective Bell.

It was another two hours before Emma and Bailey were able to leave the hospital and go check in to a local hotel. Bailey had suggested they stay at her mother's, but Emma didn't want to deal with it. She wanted her own space.

She called Detective Kingman when they reached the room so she would know where to meet her in the morning.

She stripped off her suit and threw it piece by piece over the back of the chair and climbed into the sheets.

Bailey slid in next to her and curled up against her, holding her tight. *At least I have Bailey. I can't believe she still wants to be here with me after today.* She held her tight throughout the night and had fitful dreams. She dreamt of her father choking her mother. In the dream, she was full grown, and she was trying to pry Bear off of Jayne, only for Bear to turn on her and strangle her instead of Jayne, while Jayne slipped out the door, not bothering to help Emma. She woke up and looked at the time on the digital clock next to the bed. It was only 2:30 in the morning. She rolled back over and tried to fall back to sleep.

She dreamt she was back in the deer stand. She was cold and could see her breath wisping around the barrel of the rifle. She saw the doe in her sight and she pulled the trigger. She watched the doe going down, but instead of going down on the ground, it fell upon Jayne's body and worms poured out of her. She saw Rhys's face laughing at her while she cried with wet pants.

She woke up feeling more exhausted than when she had laid down. Her alarm was set for seven, when she looked at her phone it was 6:30. She got out of the bed moving with quiet stealth so as not to wake Bailey.

She put her suit back on after a shower that didn't seem to get hot enough and weak hotel coffee. Her hair was flat, and she had no makeup since this trip was not planned and she had none of her products. She stared in the mirror at her reflection, with dark circles under puffy eyes, and heaved a sigh.

She kissed a sleeping Bailey on the head and made her way down to the lobby to wait for Bell and Kingman to pick her up. *All these years of wondering and missing and now I know. This will all come to a close. It doesn't really change anything though. Not really. I am still who I am, and my past still is what it is.*

When Detective Bell pulled up, she walked out and got into the car. He was dressed for the event, wearing jeans and a sweatshirt in lieu of a suit. She was jealous that she didn't have a change of clothes and would be traipsing through the woods of her childhood in a thousand-dollar bespoke suit, and four-hundred-dollar shoes. *I wish I had time to go home and change or go to the store and buy something more appropriate.*

"Good morning," he said gruffly as she got into the car next to him.

"Morning. Where is Detective Kingman? Oh, and can we stop by a Starbucks on the way? I need a real coffee before we do this."

"Yeah sure, I will take you through Starbucks. Kingman doesn't do woodsy things. She's at the hospital with your father."

Bell drove her through Starbucks, and she sipped her Americano as she led him to the best place to park, about a mile down the road from Jessie's shop and her old childhood trailer. She looked at them with cold and unfeeling eyes as they drove past. Both were looking far more dismal and run down than she had remembered. *I should just set both of them on fire. It would be the best thing for everyone really.*

After parking on the edge of the wood, they got out and Bell radioed for the rest of the team to meet up. Within a matter of ten minutes, a team of workers were there with shovels, and following them, reporters had started to arrive as well as the coroner's office.

Emma led them back through the trees and on a barely worn path Bear and Jessie used to this day. It was shaded and the grass around was tall. *These woods used to hold so much magic when I was little. There is the tree stump I had tea parties with Teddy and Brownie on. I used to pretend it was a grand*

table. Over in that clearing there is where I used to pretend a dragon lived.
We used to look for foxes and other creatures all through here. All this time.
All of that innocence. How different it all seems now. Now that I know this
whole time my mother was hidden in here. How sordid it all is.

The trees are all taller now, larger. It is still the same woods in a sense.
The magic is all gone though. This is the path they walked with my mother's
body. I hate this path now. I hate them for what they did. What they kept me
from.

It was just under a mile in when she found the deer stand. "He said he
buried her here. Under the stand." She pointed at the foot of the tree. The
rickety old deer stand that Bear and Jessie had built in the large tree above
looked as if it were ready to fall apart with a good windstorm.

The team with shovels dispersed around the tree under the stand and began
to dig. She envisioned Bear and Jessie digging for hours under the moonlight.
Her head continued to swim. The buzzing in her brain began again.

It seemed as if hours had passed, though she had no real concept of the
time, before the team came to a partially decomposed red sleeping bag with
the skeletal remains of her mother. Her hair was still there in the sleeping bag.
Like Emma's when she had worn it long. Thick, dark and wavy and silky.
Emma's legs went out beneath her, and she fell to her knees on the ground
below her. *All these years I've wondered why you had left and where you*
were. Bear lied to me. You never left. You didn't leave me. You were dead.
Dead and buried. Because Bear killed you.

The team carefully lifted the sleeping bag out of the ground after
photographing it and gently placed the remains into the body bag after taking
even more photographs of it. She could hear radio communications between
Kingman who was still at the hospital and Bell. She couldn't make sense of
what was being said. It was all jumbled and garbled in her head. Bell came
over and helped Emma to her feet.

"It's going to be a few days for the coroner to do his thing. We've charged
your father with manslaughter, but he's not going to live long enough to stand
trial. Your uncle, though, he confessed last night. He will probably plead

out..." Bell went on and on as they walked through the woods back to his car. The team with the body was behind her.

As they were loading the body on the stretcher, reporters flocked around and were flashing pictures and asking questions. News cameras were rolling, and microphones were shoved under noses. *You people are ridiculous. Absolutely no couth. I just saw the remains of my missing mother and you want me to answer questions. If only I could be invisible right now.* She stuck her hand up and shook her head as questions were flown at her.

She sat in Detective Bell's car and closed the door to avoid the circus so she could call Bailey who had met Mary Anne for breakfast.

"They found her. She still had hair," Emma said. Her voice was flat. She didn't have the energy for emotion.

"Oh my god," Bailey whispered.

"She's on her way to the coroner's. Bear was charged and so was Jessie. Jessie confessed. Where are you?"

"We are at the diner downtown."

Emma asked Bell to drop her off at the diner. When she got out of the car she made her way into the brightly lit, cheerful restaurant. Mary Anne stood up and hugged her hard. She had grown close to Emma over the years and could never deny that her daughter was head over heels in love with Emma.

Emma wiped a tear and sat down with them and recounted her morning.

"I guess I can claim the body and have a funeral in a few days. It's just so surreal," Emma finished. "I spent my life wondering where she was. Why she left. They knew. The whole time they knew. I would ask and ask, and they would just say they didn't know why she left. I questioned myself, my worth, all because I thought she didn't love me enough to stay."

Mary Anne shook her head in disbelief. "I never honestly liked your father or Jessie. I didn't. I can't lie. But I didn't think they would do something like that."

And bless you for keeping that to yourself all this time.

"Are you going to see Bear again before we head back?" Bailey asked.

I don't want to. I should. God I'm just really hungry. I can't even think about anything right now other than the fact I need to eat something. She flagged the waitress over to order a Greek omelet.

Televisions were mounted in the corners of the diner, and she could see the news footage of her morning displayed all around her. She saw the headline under the image of her walking out of the woods with the coroner's team behind her carrying the body bag "Missing Woman in Decades Old Cold Case Found Dead." She cringed in the booth as diners turned and looked at her.

"I guess I will go and say my piece. I will say what I need to say, and I will say my goodbye to him. He loved me. He killed her because he didn't want to lose me. He loved me in his own weird way."

After a mediocre omelet, Bailey drove them to the hospital and opted to wait in the car while Emma went up. There was now an officer in front of Bear's door. *Really? Where do you think he is going to escape to? He can't even sit up, much less escape.*

She asked the officer if she could speak to him. She was prepared to pull the attorney client privilege card if need be. The officer obliged and moved aside so she could go in.

"Wake up," she demanded.

Bear's eyes fluttered open. "Princess…"

"Save it. I'm not your 'Princess'." Emma sat down. "Jessie confessed. I led a team of cops to dig up my mother this morning. I'm only here because you are dying."

"Pri – Emma…" Bear started.

"No. You don't get to speak. My whole life I missed out on having her. I missed out on the love she had to give. I looked for her. I longed for her. You were selfish. But I still loved you. I do love you. I don't know that I forgive you. I don't know if I *can* forgive you. Maybe one day I will. But I need you to know that I loved you. I know you loved me. I saw her body today. What was left of it – and it almost broke me. You almost ruined my life in your selfishness. But I'm stronger than that. You did raise me to be strong. Self-sufficient. And for that I'm thankful. I will always love you, Bear. Always. And you are going to leave this life while I'm mad at you."

"I've made a mess of things, Emma. I did. But I knew you had a right to the truth before I died."

"I thank you for that. I thank you for what you did do for me. I love you, Bear." Emma stood and she bent over his ruined body and kissed the top of his bald head.

Before he could say anything else, she got up and left. She could hear him sniveling as she walked down the hall.

BEAR DIED TWO DAYS LATER. Emma had him cremated and unceremoniously dumped his ashes in the woods under the deer stand. She stood out in the woods in the light of day, looking at the holes that were dug to recover her mother as she poured Bear ashes. Some she poured under the stand in the hole where her mother was found, some where the doe went down all those years ago.

The coroner had released her mother's remains to her. Her wedding ring – a simple thin gold band was found still on her hand. Her purse and car keys were also shoved into the sleeping bag. Emma had her buried next to Teta in a beautiful pink coffin that matched Teta's. She did it discreetly to avoid the media circus.

~ 7 ~

Ever Mine, Ever Thine, Ever Ours

The Present...

CANDLELIGHT DANCED OFF BAILEY'S WEDDING rings. Emma was momentarily transfixed by the glittering of stones in the light the necklace and the rings dazzled her, hypnotizing her.

"You were there for me when I no longer had anyone. It has been you and me against the world, against all odds." Emma stood up and paced the length of the room. Back and forth. It was suddenly warm and oppressive. She unbuttoned the collar of her shirt and rubbed her hand through her hair.

"I never thought in a million years that you would stop loving me. That I wouldn't be your person. You used to look at me like I hung the moon... We built this life together. This beautiful, wonderful life. Around each other and together. I don't know when you decided I wasn't enough..."

Emma refilled her glass of wine. *I don't remember how many glasses I've had. Did I just finish my second or my first? Third? I don't even care. I can't even remember the last meal I actually ate.* Her head was swimming with wine and an empty stomach.

She picked up her glass and took another deep sip.

She looked at the stones in Bailey's ring again glittering in the light and set her glass down.

She paced up and down the room again, before leaning her back against the wall, sliding down to the floor. The floor felt unsteady beneath her, and everything was swimming around her. Her heart physically ached. It wasn't just an idiom. It was a real and stabbing pain.

The Past (2008-2010)

EMMA COMPARTMENTALIZED THE TRAUMA OF finding her mother's body, Bear's death, and Jessie's sentencing like a pro. She had a head filled with compartments that she tucked away all of her traumas. Rhys raping her went hidden inside one. Bear's confession in another. Seeing her mother's body in another. She threw herself into work and never brought any of it up again. Bailey would try to talk to her about it, especially after letters from Jessie started arriving from the prison. Emma would not even open them. She just ripped them up and tossed them in the trash. As far as she was concerned, he was as dead as Bear and her mom.

Though Emma had a penchant for bespoke clothing, she also loved investing and watching her bank accounts and investments and her "emergency stockpile of cash" that she stacked in her safe grow.

Emma was working nonstop. She barely took time off when Brandon married his paralegal at his firm, Savannah. She was a perfect match for him, witty and always seeming to be in an optimistic state of mind. It was an office scandal when they got together, her having a live-in boyfriend and he was engaged to Rebecca at the time. Emma didn't judge, love is love. She was just happy to see her best friend so happy.

Business, however, doesn't stop for love or happiness. Emma was almost late for the wedding because she was on the phone handling a client, and being Brandon's best (wo)man, she had the rings in her tux pocket. She came rushing into the church right in time to escort the matron of honor down the aisle and stand at the side of her best friend.

On a brisk fall weekend, she dragged Bailey to an open house in an upscale neighborhood. The houses were waterfront and spacious, reminiscent of the cottage Bailey had spent her summers in when they were young.

"I love our house though!" Bailey lamented as they drove into the neighborhood. "It's cozy and quaint. It was Teta's house!"

"I know. I love it too. But we can rent it out and it's profit straight in the bank, and we can get something new. Build new memories."

"Maybe. If we see the perfect one, then okay. We will do it."

They wandered into the open house. The back of the house faced west over the water. Emma pulled Bailey to the deck off of the master bedroom. "Imagine, sunsets here."

Bailey exhaled and looked up at Emma. "Maybe."

Emma dragged her into the room off of the master bedroom. "Maybe we have a kid? Nursery?"

Bailey froze. "I had never really thought about it until now."

Emma shrugged and dragged her to another room with floor to ceiling built-ins covering one wall and a window overlooking the lake. "*My* office," and through a Jack and Jill bathroom, "*your own* office..." and then down the hall, "guest room."

Bailey looked around at the upstairs space. "It needs different paint and new carpet. Maybe redo the floors for hardwood."

Emma smiled at her and took her down the stairs. *There you go. You see it, too! The vision is there.*

As they descended winding stairs down and around a large chandelier, "That would need to be replaced for something less gaudy..." Bailey noted. They stopped and assessed everything around them. The house was built over a decade ago and all of the decorations, colors, and fixtures were atrociously dated.

Sure, it looks like Liberace threw up on this place, but with Bailey's eye for decorating, and a hired team, this place could be beautiful. It wouldn't be Teta's house, it would be ours.

Emma took her through the dining room and living room space, downstairs guest suite and the large kitchen and out to the back yard that ended in the lake.

"Do you see it?" Emma asked.

"It being our future here?"

"Yes."

Bailey looked at her and feigned defeat. "Yeah. I do."

EMMA PUT AN OFFER IN on the house and it was readily accepted, and she found a property manager to handle renting out Teta's old home.

After moving, Emma gave a Bailey a budget for renovations and Bailey hired an interior decorator and a team and went to town on renovating the new home.

Emma was surprised how difficult of a transition it was for Bailey to leave the bungalow. "We have so many memories there. It was cozy. It was *ours.* Our *home,"* Bailey said after Emma pressed her to say what was bothering her one night as she tossed and turned.

"This can be our home, too…"

"It's not the same."

"You come from this lifestyle. I would think you would be happy to return to it." *I'm getting this huge sense that you are ungrateful.*

"I couldn't care less about lifestyle. I just want a life with you."

I'm trying to not take this personally. But can't you even recognize how hard I've worked to provide for you? Even with your PhD you don't make a lot of money. You work for peanuts at the museum and teach one maybe two classes a semester. I don't ask you to contribute to the household. I just want you to enjoy what you do and our life. Let me have this. Let me have a sense of pride in what I've accomplished and how far I've – we've – come.

Bailey propped herself up on her elbow and looked at Emma. "I know you are proud of what you accomplished. And I'm proud of you. And I'm grateful for what you provide and what you have built for us. I just got attached to our little home and our life there. This will be home for us, too. And I will love it when all of the renovations are done." She kissed Emma gently. "I promise."

RENOVATIONS TOOK ALMOST SIX MONTHS by the time Bailey had everything the way she wanted. *This house is almost not even recognizable from the day we bought it. It's beautiful. Just as I guessed it would be.* Bailey had bathrooms gutted and new fixtures and tiles put in. She redid counters and floors and painting. She had the atrocious gaudy chandelier in the front stairwell removed and replaced with an elegant and modern light fixture that suited her eye better. Aside from the bones of the structure, it was completely unrecognizable from when Emma signed the papers. Emma's favorite room, aside from her office and bedroom, was the large open living room. Bailey had exposed the beams of the cathedral ceiling and had them stained dark to match the hardwood floors and contrast with cream-colored walls. The large windows overlooked the spacious lawn, the deck and into the lake. Bailey had selected a black leather sectional and on the wall over it, a piece she purchased from an artist she featured at the museum. A modern piece that Emma had not originally liked, but now in its finished place, she appreciated. The artist had taken a white canvas and blurred different shades of blue with the darkest in the center fading to the lighter shades around the edges. It was modern and large, but looked beautiful in the space, accented by the blue throw pillows on the black leather sectional.

Emma and Bailey decided to throw a housewarming party to celebrate their new home being completed. The party was Bailey's idea. Emma worked so much that their social life was almost non-existent. "We need to socialize," Bailey rationalized. "All you do is work. Aside from attending Brandon's wedding like what seems forever ago, we've done nothing!"

Emma relented. *Anything for Bailey.*

Emma had invited Simone and Abby, though they were no longer together, they had managed to remain friends. Brandon and Savannah, and a few of her co-workers and friends from college and law school. Bailey invited her mom, co-workers, and lifelong friends and a few of their new neighbors.

The party spilled out the back side of the patio and to the lake. Their home was filled with laughter and conversation as the guests grouped together and talked and looked around, commenting on Bailey's good taste.

Emma watched Bailey in the golden light of the afternoon as she proudly showed off her hard work. *Today is the day and now is the time.* As the sun was setting, Emma pulled Bailey to the deck and called for everyone to pay attention. "Hi! Welcome everyone... I need your attention here for a moment, please. It's been a long road. Not just with all of the work my beautiful Bailey has put into renovating this place, but in general. Those of you who know, know. Bailey, I just want to acknowledge what you have been for me. You have been a dream come true. You have loved me through some unimaginable times and held me up and inspired me to make this life together. I can't imagine a better woman by my side. We've walked a crazy road that has converged together, time and again. You won me over time and again with your wit, charm, and remarkable beauty. But you are not just beautiful outside, you have this huge, beautiful heart that has a capacity for love and forgiveness I've never seen in another person. You, without question or hesitation, are my person. The only person I can imagine by my side for better or for worse." Emma dropped to her knee. "Will you marry me?" Emma presented her a deep blue sapphire ring with a halo of diamonds around it, set in a band encrusted with diamonds.

Bailey put her hands up to her face and looked at Emma as everyone cheered the proposal. "Like sapphire blue..." she whispered.

"Sapphire blue," Emma said.

"Yes, of course I will marry you." Bailey dropped to her knees and kissed Emma. Brandon and Savannah popped a bottle of champagne and began pouring glasses.

MARRIAGE EQUALITY, NOT YET LEGAL in all states, led Bailey and Emma to plan a destination wedding in Massachusetts for a year and a half out.

Bailey was excited by the prospects of planning a fall wedding, with a road trip up the East Coast from Boston to Portland, Maine to see the autumn colors for their honeymoon. Emma booked cozy bed and breakfasts along the route for them to stop at and enjoy the local flavor along the way.

Bailey and Emma traveled to Nantucket a few days before the small party of wedding guests were to arrive. Emma had to pull teeth to get the two and a half weeks off. It was a scheduling nightmare between bringing her associates up to speed and trusting her clients with junior associates handling their demands and needs. *Here we go again. She will not back down until I say yes. There is no need to be there that many days in advance. She has no clue how hard this is for me. Four extra days is a lot.*

Once they finally landed in Boston, got their rental car and drove to Nantucket, Emma finally breathed a sigh of relief.

They had taken short trips here and there over the years, but just long weekends or quick road trips. Emma had not actually been this far from home ever. She had never tried to take vacation days out of fear that she would lose respect from her colleagues, or a client would need her to handle something. And she would be dead before she took a sick day, working through colds, allergies, flues and whatever ailments plagued her.

Emma got out of the car and looked over the water and took a deep breath. *This is the first time in forever I don't have anything to do. Nothing. I've been nonstop since high school. Always working, planning, thinking. This moment to stand still actually feels good. And I get to have this moment of peace with Bailey. We are doing this.* The salty air smelled good, and the contrast of the fall colors around the waterfront dazzled her.

Bailey got out of the car and let out a squeal of delight. "I can't believe we are here. We are doing this!"

Emma pulled her in tight. "This is it! This is your last chance to run and hide."

"Not a chance." Bailey kissed Emma.

Once they had checked in and made their way up to the spacious suite, Emma threw the curtains back to allow the last of the daylight in. She opened the door to the balcony and stood outside. The afternoon sun was low and on the other side of the hotel, casting long shadows out to the water. The colors of the various buildings were muted as the sun was fading into the west.

Bailey came out and stood with her. Neither of them spoke for a long while. Bailey just held tight to Emma. *The first time I held you on a waterfront balcony, we ended badly. Now we are here to solidify all that we've been through and our future together.*

"This is nice…" Bailey murmured.

"I can't believe how peaceful and beautiful this place is."

"That's not what I meant," Bailey corrected. "The stillness of right now. This is nice. I don't think we've ever had this peace. This is why I wanted us to leave early. I wanted to just stand still for a moment with you. No agendas. No phones ringing. No juggling. Think about it. It's like what you said when you proposed. We've been on this crazy path since we met. I want this calm to last us through our day, and through our honeymoon. I just want us and the moment."

Emma laced her fingers through Bailey's. "You, as usual, are right. You had the right idea."

"We don't need to meet the wedding coordinator until the afternoon before, and none of the guests are getting here until that day. It's just us. Finally."

Emma found it hard those next two days to be still. She didn't know how to fully let go and relax. After the first 24 hours, she was antsy and looked for ways for them to fill the days. She read a book, she organized her clothes and belongings. When she went to check her email, she was met with a disapproving glare from Bailey, and she closed her laptop with a sigh.

Bailey had other intentions. She was wanting to linger in bed and just be together. Emma tried hard to accommodate Bailey's wishes, but after the first day, she couldn't.

"Let's go walk around the town or something… I can't be *this* still."

Bailey rolled her eyes.

"Room service for breakfast, and then we go for a walk. Just a walk. Maybe shop? Then come back and we can get back in the bed."

Bailey pouted for a moment. "Quick walk?"

"Quick."

Though the passion was far from waning for either of them, it was just not in Emma's nature to be idle. She was not used to sleeping in. She wasn't used to having nothing to do and no regimented schedule to maintain.

IT WAS EASIER FOR EMMA as the guests began to arrive and the meetings with the coordinator were time consuming. Emma had been extremely specific about the details for the flowers, the menu, the music. For every little detail, she expected perfection. *I'm doing this only one time. I want this to be just right. Not just for me, but for Bailey as well.*

She could tell Julianna, the coordinator, was irritated with her. *Julianna better not roll her eyes at me one more time. I don't care if she thinks I'm a bridezilla.*

Brandon and Abby would be her attendants. Bailey's cousin Monica and her best friend since undergrad, Nicole would be hers. Emma had Julianna drag them through two run throughs to make sure all timing and placement was correct.

The night before the wedding, Emma went to a local bar with Abby and Brandon. Abby sat at the table with Emma and Brandon bringing a round of drinks. "You knew from the beginning she was the one," Abby commented. "I was wrong. I told you to stay away from her."

"I can't say that I knew it would lead here. And you were not entirely wrong. A lot of pain and drama came from our early years. But I knew there was something more there. Well, more so Bailey knew. She wouldn't let it go."

"Honestly, I just wanted to see you take her from that little prick Rhys. I didn't think you would actually make it to this." Brandon lifted his glass in toast.

"Do you believe in fate?" Emma asked.

"In what sense of word?" Abby asked.

"Bailey's dad tried to separate us. He sent Bailey away. What are the odds that she would go to grad school where I went to law school, and she would find me in a coffee shop? She would pursue me like she did? I feel like it's deeper than we just met and settled with each other."

"Here's to love and destiny," Abby shrugged and raised her glass.

BAILEY HAD HELD TO THE tradition of not letting Emma see her dress beforehand. She opted to spend the night in a room with Monica. Before the ceremony, as they were getting ready in separate rooms, Emma sent Brandon to Bailey's suite with a floating sapphire teardrop necklace, delicate and beautiful, with a note card, a quote from Beethoven to his 'Immortal Beloved'. They had watched a film *Immortal Beloved* about his great love affair, they had both loved it so much it spurned much interest in the topic. The note card read simply, 'Ever Mine, Ever Thine, Ever Ours'.

Brandon returned with a box for Emma, containing a silver pocket watch, engraved on the back, 'Until the End of Time' with their wedding date etched in Roman numerals below.

Mary Anne had met a new love interest, George, a fellow surgeon at her hospital, and he was in attendance with her. She sat prim and proper dabbing her eyes in the front row, holding the hand of George. Bailey had not spoken to CJ since she had reunited with Emma. He had not approved of his sister's 'choices' and he had 'cut off' Bailey and Mary Anne, considering it disrespectful to his father's memory and wishes, he was obviously not in attendance.

The music had started, and Emma was standing with the Cape behind her, and the officiant to her side. Brandon and Abby stood beside her. The sun was slightly blotted out by puffy white clouds high above, and the waves lapped against the shore behind her.

Her tuxedo, like all of her suits, was bespoke and fitted to the highest precision of her details and specifications. The ascot was customized to the sapphire blue they had chosen as their color, and the boutonniere, a white rose with blue tips. The pocket watch from Bailey was proudly clipped into place, its chain glinting off the sun. Her hair was freshly cut yesterday and slicked back. Her trademark eyeliner perfectly accenting her eyes, she was as sharp as she had ever been. Brandon and Abby also donned tuxedos with deep blue boutonnieres and blue vests and ties. Abby lamented how she wished she looked half as sexy as Emma in the tuxedo.

Monica and Nicole came down the aisle in sapphire blue dresses and white flowers.

It has all led up to today. All of the pain, and all of the drama is behind us.

We are here to make it official. Forever. Emma's heart was beating loud in her chest as she waited to see Bailey come down the aisle. Her grandfather, Mary Anne's father, James, was giving her away.

It seemed an eternity until Emma saw them come around the corner. Grandpa James moving slowly with Bailey moving gracefully at his side. She was a vision of all that Emma had dreamed in white lace and gem stones hugging her bodice, gem stones and delicate feathers pluming out around her skirt giving her an ethereal look of nearly floating as the wind blew the dainty feather accents back as she marched with her grandfather slowly toward Emma. Her bouquet was all sapphire blue with peacock feathers added in, and around her neck was the sapphire teardrop Emma had gifted her.

Emma's knees were weak as she watched her walk. *She's so beautiful. She chose me. I am forever hers after today and she is mine. Stay still. I want nothing more than to run to her and take off. Just the two of us. We didn't need all of this. We could have said what we needed to say in front of a judge and just been off to celebrate alone. All that matters is that we are committed to be together forever. Til death do us part.* Emma struggled to keep it together, but her emotions were in high gear as she fought the tears of joy.

When Bailey's eyes met Emma's, she noticed Bailey's steps quickened as well, almost dragging Grandpa James down the aisle.

He told her to slow down with a good-natured chuckle. Their guests, having overheard, laughed lightly.

When at last she had made it to Emma and Grandpa James placed her hand in Emma's, Emma lost her battle with her emotions and a tear slipped out as she looked at Bailey smiling up at her. She bit her lip and focused on the feeling of Bailey's warm hand in hers.

The ceremony, by design was quick. They had written their own vows which were recited after a quick preamble of the officiant. Emma looked at Bailey after sliding a delicate eternity band of alternating sapphires and diamonds on her finger stacked above her engagement ring. "You have shown me, Bailey Anne Frankson, what it truly means to be loved. You proved to me that I am worthy of love and that I can love in return. I promise to spend the rest of my life loving you, honoring you, and being your partner, your wife, in life and all things."

Bailey placed a matching band, only thicker on Emma's finger, with tears in her eyes and a smile on her lips, "Emma Jayne Landry, from the first day we met I had to chase you down. When I found you again, I had to chase you again, and then again a third time. Not because you didn't love me, but because you were afraid of love. You showed me, though, what it means to be loved with a whole and pure heart, unconditionally. I never in a million years thought we would be standing here together, but as I stand here and look at you, I know you are the only person I could ever want to be mine. I promise to spend the rest of my life loving you, honoring you, and being your partner and wife in life and all things."

Emma wiped a tear from her eyes. The new weight from her ring on her hand not unpleasant or unbearable.

The officiant announced that they were now married by the state of Massachusetts, and Emma pulled Bailey in for a kiss. "I love you so much," Bailey whispered in her ear.

They walked together down the aisle as music played. Emma would never be able to tell you what song it was that was playing. She had made such demands and fretted over each and every single detail sending multiple emails and voicemails to Julianna. *I don't care about all of these stupid details. The minutia! I can't even tell you what song is playing. The only thing that matters right now is Bailey's hand in mine. We are together, legally and spiritually bound. Forever. She is my forever.*

They went into the restaurant that spilled out onto the covered patio for the reception. A deejay played music and announced their entrance. They walked in together to the sound of applause and champagne glasses being tapped. Emma spun Bailey around and kissed her again to an uproar of cheering.

There was champagne and food and music and laughter and love. Emma was satisfied as she danced Bailey around as Al Greene's 'Let's Stay Together' played and pulled her back in and held her close.

Brandon stood up to toast. "I am so proud of you both for making it to this point. You have been together for a while now. But marriage is different than just being together. When Savannah and I got married, Emma, you remember, you were there as my best woman. My father-in-law pulled me aside before the wedding and he said something to me. Do you remember it?" Brandon was looking at Emma and Bailey holding each other tightly. Emma and Brandon were alone in the dressing room. Emma was helping Brandon with his bow tie when he had come in and shook Brandon's hand and offered his words of fatherly advice.

Emma nodded and looked at Bailey and recited Savannah's father's words, "Hold on to this moment, always. Bad times are a guarantee, and so are the frustrations and anger and all the negativity that comes with life. Hold on to this feeling of today, and when those moments arise, lean back on this moment and remember the love that brought you here today."

Brandon beamed, shaking his head. "She forgets nothing. So, Bailey, Emma, remember this moment, always. Remember the love you share and the love you are surrounded by. When times get tough, remember the love that led you to this moment. Congratulations!"

The clinking of the glasses and the kisses and the dancing, and the shaking of hands and the hugs from guests seemed to go on all night.

How long are we obligated to be here? I just want to be up in the room and alone with my wife. Wife! We just got married. I'm done with entertaining now. Bailey was right to want those days before today to just be alone together. That's all I want now.

It seemed like an eternity before it was acceptable for them to leave the party and head up to their suite alone. Savannah, Monica, and Nicole had gone up to the suite during the reception and lit candles and spread rose petals throughout for Bailey and Emma. Champagne in a bucket and a tray of sweets sat on the table near the bed.

Emma languished in undoing the tiny buttons on the back of the dress, and admiring Bailey in the dim, dancing light of the moon and flickering candles. She was slow and deliberate in releasing each of the tiny buttons lined down Bailey's back.

When the white dress and its gemstones and feathers and lace fell away from Bailey's body, she guided Bailey one step at a time out of the pile on the floor and back to the bed. Bailey was resplendent in the moonlight and white lingerie, the sapphire teardrop in the hollow of her throat.

Emma stood on her knees at the foot of the bed and drank in the moment and the sensation. Adding it to the sentiments of the day. *I never want to take this moment, or how she looks right now for granted. What I feel for her, and for the magic of this day will always be cherished.*

The feeling of Bailey reaching up and pulling her down. The softness of her skin, the heat of her fingertips and taste of her mouth. The slowness of it all, like the clock had stopped and time was frozen. No one else existed and nothing mattered.

Bailey pushed Emma's jacket off and threw it to the floor. She slowly peeled away the layers of Emma's tux, relishing in the curves and skin beneath. Emma languished in Bailey's touch. *This is all I ever needed or wanted. Bailey is my everything.*

~ *8* ~

Unexpecting

The Present...

"DO YOU REMEMBER BRANDON'S TOAST to us from our wedding? To never forget the love that led to the moment?"

Silence met her question. Bailey had always been the queen of the silent treatment. It's how she dealt with her anger toward Emma. She could hold out for weeks if she was allowed to. And she had.

"The resentment that has been built up in you. You never came back to that moment. I did. Don't think that you have been the easiest person or a picnic to love all these years. You haven't been. But I always came back to that moment. I reminded myself of what you looked like. What you felt like. What you tasted like that day. That night."

Emma was leaning against the wall. Her wine glass in one hand, the near empty bottle in the other. She slowly slid down the wall so she sat against it.

"You let me go. You turned your back. This is not my fault. This is all on you. Your inability to have patience with me. I worked my ass off to provide this life for you. You never gave me the chance to fix whatever it was that was so broken that you felt the need to throw it all away. You never told me..." She pulled her knees up and put her head on her knees to slow the spinning around her. The world was slipping away from her, and she had lost control and lost her grip.

The Past (2010-2012)

AFTER THE WEDDING AND THE honeymoon life went back into its normal routine for Emma and Bailey. Bailey was busy with her classes and the museum. Emma was busy making money and building assets and growing her reputation as a fierce litigator.

Her reputation preceded her whenever she was assigned a case. She was the most requested attorney in her firm, and most of her cases settled as no one wanted to go up against her. She was savage and she was smart.

Being the only female to make partner at her firm, she worked twice as hard and long as her male counterparts to prove herself worthy of this coveted position.

Keeping a rigorous schedule Monday through Friday, she would wake up at 4 am and have her breakfast and coffee before going to the gym. She would come home, shower, change and make it to work by 8 am sharp, where she would stay often until 6 or 7 each night. She would come home, have dinner with Bailey and be asleep by 10 or 11.

Her weekends, if she didn't have a huge case pending, were devoted to Bailey and their social lives. They'd meet Brandon and Savannah for dinner, or Nicole and whoever she was seeing at the time, or they would take a road trip to visit Abby and her new fiancée. It was a busy life, which Emma loved.

Two years after the wedding, Emma had come home from a long day, exhausted, bickering with opposing counsel on her cell phone as she opened the door, kissed Bailey on the cheek and walked straight up the stairs continuing her debate into her home office. She dropped her Luis Vuitton attaché case on the floor next to her desk, threw her coat over the chair as she sat back in her chair, listening to the other attorney.

Bailey came in and sat at the chair across the desk from Emma.

Emma looked at her, rolled her eyes and made the talking gesture with her hand, then mouthed "Sorry," to Bailey. *Dude… shut up already. You are talking in circles and my wife is begging for my attention. To top it all off, I'm starving.*

Bailey stood back up and paced the room waiting patiently for Emma's attention. *I don't know what she could possibly be waiting for. Her pacing is going to wear a hole in the floor. It can't be good. He doesn't stop, does he?*

Emma spat coolly into the phone, "It sounds like we are not going to see eye to eye on this, Thomas. We will just have to sort this out in front of the judge. My client is not going to budge on this, and you seem to be misadvising your client to not come around on her end. Foolish on your behalf. You have no idea what you are up against. But that's fine. We are ready for court."

"Sexual harassment and quid pro quo in this current political environment are not something you want to play around with. My client—"

Cut him off before he gets back to his pontificating. "Thomas, seriously, there is not anything more that you can say that you haven't already covered. I have to go. Have a great evening." She hung up and smiled at Bailey. "Sorry, love. What's going on?"

Bailey sat back down. "I made dinner. It's ready…"

Nope. You want more than that. You never hang out in my office like this. "It seems like there's more on your mind than dinner."

Bailey was quiet for a moment with her hands in her lap and her hair falling in a shining wave of strawberry silk in front of her face. *Spit it out already.* She took a deep breath and looked up at Emma. "I love you. I love us. I want us to be a family. You mentioned a baby when we bought this house. I think it's time. I want to have a baby." She rushed the words out faster than Emma could comprehend them.

I don't think I heard that right. "Slow down." Emma smiled standing.

"Did you change your mind about that?" Bailey's brow furrowed with concern.

Emma shook her head 'no' and pulled Bailey back up so she could hold her close. *We will be a family. Something I didn't have as a child. We will be the best parents to this little one. We will provide for it in ways I only dreamed about as I was growing up. This is all I've ever dreamed for or wanted.*

"I talked to my doctor a while back about what we need to do, she did all of the tests. I didn't want to bother you with it if it wouldn't be a possibility. And it shouldn't be that hard. Just expensive. I didn't want to bother you, with how busy you have been. The doctor said our best bet is IVF given all of my tests and how things look."

"It's not expensive if it's worthwhile. It's an investment in our lives. Our future. Our family."

Emma was ecstatic about the thought of her and Bailey being mothers to a child. Brandon and his wife had just had a baby, Mason, and made Emma the baby's godmother. She loved watching Bailey fuss over tiny Mason when they would go visit.

What Emma was not prepared for was the fact that Bailey wanted her to be at every doctor's appointment, and it was her responsibility to give Bailey the shots every night which had to be delivered at the same time, and Bailey had become absolutely obsessed with planning for this new venture.

Books about babies were everywhere. The room that was planned as a potential nursery was undergoing renovations. It was all Bailey seemed to want to talk about. The shots were making her emotional and moody and being around her was a veritable land mine that could go off at any second if she said the wrong thing.

The doctor had harvested fifteen eggs from Bailey and was successful in fertilizing enough for three rounds of the IVF.

Bailey demanded that Emma be present for the implanting of the embryo, which was as it always was for Emma, a scheduling nightmare. She managed to be at the doctor's office in time, and had to return to work immediately after, which made Bailey an emotional mess. She wanted Emma home with her.

"I would love nothing more than to be there, but it's not possible. I have responsibilities."

"I have responsibilities, too. And I am one of your responsibilities. Starting this family together is one of your responsibilities."

Here we go again. "I paid for the procedure." *I should have said anything other than that.*

Bailey's eyes spilled over. "You are never home. You haven't been doing any of this with me. I'm doing this alone."

I pray this procedure worked and we can get back to some sort of normal. This is bordering on insanity. "I've been giving you the shots. I've been dealing with your new brand of nonstop crazy. Don't tell me you are alone. I have to work my ass off to maintain our life—"

"The life *you* think we should be living. I would have been fine to spend the rest of our lives in Teta's old house if it meant I got to spend some time with you every day. I never see you except at bedtime. When this baby comes, then what? It's going to be just me. I know it."

"We will cross that bridge when it comes. I have to go." She kissed the top of Bailey's head and left.

It was a tense few weeks waiting to see if the procedure took, which it didn't.

It was a Sunday morning and Emma was making pancakes for them. Bailey was sitting on a stool at the spacious kitchen island. She was flipping through a copy of *What to Expect When You're Expecting* when she got up and rushed into the bathroom.

Bailey came back out minutes later and put her head in her hands. "It didn't work."

Emma turned off the stove and made her way around to Bailey and sat down next to her, holding her close. "It's okay, baby. We will try again. We will try as many times as we have to or want to." *I don't know how to really make it known to you, that no matter what, I'm happy as long as I have you. Baby or not.*

"I was just so certain…" Bailey whispered as she cried into Emma's shoulder.

"I know… I know… But we are not going to be lucky every time we do something. We've been pretty blessed with everything else."

"I get that… I try to keep in mind how lucky we are."

The following six weeks were hell for Emma. She was in the midst of a high-profile sexual harassment case in which the media had painted her client

~ 184 ~

to be a certifiable monster given the political climate, and she was stuck defending him not only in the court but the court of public opinion. Emma was thrown into the national media spotlight on top of it all having to be on damage control for her client and defending him on national news networks as well as local. The firm was super pleased as she handled herself expertly and brought in even more business. She could have smeared the accuser and put her reputation on trial, but Emma managed to defend her client without disparaging the accuser, which was working to soften her client's image.

Most nights when she got home, Bailey was already asleep in bed. Emma spent the majority of her nights stuck in her office, sometimes until the early hours of the morning, getting only a few hours of sleep before she was up and out the door again.

Bailey would call the office and Greta would run interference. *I can't deal with her hormonal crazy bullshit right now. Thank God for Greta.*

The weekends were no longer free, as Emma was busy with her co-counsel and interns helping on the case preparing. They would be at the house taking over the kitchen with pizza or Chinese delivery, moving the kitchen table chairs up into Emma's office as they pored over the files. Bailey would pout and silently walk around them as they wandered from the office to the kitchen and back.

When Bailey was due to go in for her second attempt at IVF, Emma was due in court.

Bailey was furious with Emma. "Why can't this be as important to you as it is to me?" Bailey demanded.

These hormones really got her thinking that I can just cancel court to go with her. This has to work. We are going to end up divorced if this keeps up for much longer. "Baby, it is. But this is the type of case that makes or breaks a career. There is national media coverage of this trial. I can't just take a day off in the middle of it so we can get pregnant."

"*We?* Are you fucking kidding me?" Bailey turned to walk away out of Emma's office.

Emma stood up and cleared the space between her desk and the door to stop Bailey from leaving. *Nope. You don't get to keep acting like this. You need a dose of reality.* "Baby, I love you. I want this as much as you do. But you have to give me a little slack here. I can't just come and go and reschedule my life. You know what I deal with. You know I would be there if I could."

"No. No you wouldn't. You would be in your office. I haven't seen you in *weeks.* You are up at 4 and not home again until after 10. We haven't even had sex in over a month."

"Are we really keeping tabs of that? Because this is the biggest case of my career. In case you haven't noticed." Emma was annoyed now. She moved away to allow Bailey to pass. "It doesn't matter. You are just going to believe what you want and there is no swaying you when you are like this." Emma was past the point of trying to please Bailey. The hormones had made her completely unreasonable.

Bailey stormed out of Emma's office and down the hallway. Emma could hear the bedroom door slam shut.

While the court was in recess the following day and she found time to grab a sandwich at a deli down the street from the courthouse, she texted Bailey. 'Babe, you know I love you. I wish more than anything I were there holding your hand right now. You are my world.'

She was alerted that the message was read; however, Bailey didn't respond.

Emma dragged herself home close to ten that night. The house was dark and still. Not a single lamp or overhead light left on to welcome Emma home. Bailey normally left lamps on and a covered plate for Emma in the fridge, and tonight there was not one lamp lit or plate in the fridge. *I got it loud and clear. She's extra pissed off at me.* She found some leftovers and warmed them up and ate in the dark by herself.

She made her way upstairs and found Bailey sound asleep.

The next morning, on her way to court she called Greta. *I need to step up the damage control.* "Can you please have flowers sent to Bailey at her office? White roses dyed blue. The card should read, 'Ever thine, Ever mine,

Ever ours'." *When times get tough, and they will, lean back on this moment and remember the love you feel today.*

"Yes, Emma. Got it."

Emma texted Bailey later that day, 'I love you. That's all.' Read, but still no reply. *Wow. Okay. Not even a thank you.*

When she came home again, late and again to a dark house, she saw the flowers in a vase on the kitchen island. It had begun to rain, and Emma opened the refrigerator listening to the sound of the drops against the window pane.

There was still no plate left for her. *Damn. I don't even know what I can do at this point.* She rummaged around for leftovers and made a plate as she listened to the sound of the thunder rolling over the house. *Fitting.* The rain came down harder and lightning flashed lighting up the dimly lit kitchen in sporadic flashes as she sat alone.

Bailey was again sound asleep when she fell into the bed exhausted.

Emma nuzzled up to Bailey. "Babe, are you asleep?" No response but the heavy measured breathing of a sleeping Bailey and the rain beating off of the roof and windows and the moving thunder as the storm rolled west over the lake and away.

Emma rolled back onto her back and fell into a fitful exhausted sleep.

A week later, Bailey still had not spoken or responded to Emma in any way; Emma closed the case in court. She gave a riveting closing argument and took her seat at the table next to her client. He beamed at her and she smiled back confidently. *It's over. No matter what, it's over. I can work on Bailey and fix whatever it is that's bothering her. Get us back on course.*

Court was adjourned while the jurors deliberated. After giving a brief statement to the press, Emma went back to her office to handle loose ends on other client issues that had backed up while she was putting out this fire.

She couldn't focus on any of it though as she sorted through the stack of memos, notes and post its piled on her desk. Bailey had never gone this long without talking to her.

She picked up the phone and called Bailey's office.

"Dr. Bailey Frankson-Landry's office," her clerk announced.

"Hey, it's Emma. Is Bailey in there?"

"She's in a meeting."

Of course she is. "Have her call my office when she's free?"

"Yes, ma'am."

She's not going to. "Thanks." Emma hung up the phone and stretched back over her chair. She was annoyed now. She pushed her annoyances aside and began to work through the piled up miscellany on her desk.

She was notified that the jurors had not reached a verdict and called it a day and would resume in the morning.

Streaks of bright orange and pink clouds shot through the sky as the sun was setting as she drove home. It was her first day of getting home before dark in weeks. *I want nothing more than to hold my wife and make love to her. Just unwind and be together. It's been far too long. Order pizza and open a bottle of wine. Okay, so she can't drink it, but I need a glass.*

She came in and Bailey was in the kitchen. *We are right here nose to nose. You can't ignore me now.* "Hey, babe," Emma said as she approached Bailey.

Bailey turned and looked at Emma. "You're home." Her voice was flat.

Wow. That's a warm reception. I'm happy to see you, too. Trying her best to warm the cold reception, Emma reached for Bailey's hands to pull her in. "Yeah, I'm home."

Bailey pulled away from Emma. "I'm going to go upstairs and going to bed."

Oh hell no. "What the fuck?"

Bailey stopped and turned to look at Emma. "I need to stay away from stress. That's what the doctor said. Lately, it's been nothing but stress. I'm going to go lay down." With that, she left the room.

Emma grabbed a bottle of wine out of the wine fridge and uncorked it. She served a plate risotto from the pan Bailey left on the stove and sat at the dining table alone. *I have no clue how to fix this. I don't think I want to bring a baby into this, not if this is how life will be from now on.*

BY THURSDAY, TWO DAYS LATER, the jury ruled in Emma's favor late in the afternoon. They walked out of the courtroom to cameras and a large crowd of reporters from around the country, and Emma spoke on behalf of her clients as they made their way to a local Irish pub for a celebratory drink. She had not spoken to, nor attempted to speak to Bailey since she blew her off the other night. She had decided that she was not going to play games.

The music was loud, and the bar was dark, and time was seemingly indistinguishable from night and day to its windowless inside. The vodka soda and lime was refreshing and well earned. Emma was sitting at the bar waiting for a second drink when she felt a tap on her shoulder.

She turned around and was met with a stunning woman, looking up at her with wide dark eyes and a devilish grin in her personal space when she turned around. *Oh, hello!* She was stunningly beautiful in a tight tank top and jeans, and she was pressing in on Emma. *Back in the day, this would be a done deal and she would be coming home with me.*

"You are Emma Landry," the woman said, still smiling with a look that told Emma everything she needed to know – this woman would be hers for the taking if she so desired.

I don't think we've met before. Emma had nowhere to move, she was pressed against the bar as the woman encroached on her space. *Stop flirting. Stop thinking about it. You are married to Bailey, even if she's being a mega bitch right now. You spoke vows.* "Yes. Can I help you?"

"I just wanted to congratulate you. I've been following your case and your pressers." *Great. She's a fan. Awesome. I'm married and she's in my space. She can back up anytime now.*

"Thanks." Emma was uncomfortable with the bar to her back and the woman pressed to her front and the obvious struggle in her mind and body.

"Can I buy you a drink?" The woman was leaning into Emma. *I can literally feel every inch of her body against mine. My god. It's not a bad feeling. I haven't been touched in weeks now. Bailey hasn't even said a kind word to me in – I don't know how long. Bailey. Bailey is my wife. I'm married.*

The bartender handed Emma her second drink. "I got one. Thanks." Emma held the drink up so she could see.

"Well, maybe another time?" She had raised her eyebrow at Emma.

Oh... to go back in time. Emma held up her hand with her wedding band. "I'm married."

"Too bad," the woman said. She let her body rub against Emma's as Emma pushed around her.

Married. I'm married. Not going to fall for the bait. Damn. She is fine though. Emma walked away from her and back to the table where her co-counsel and her clients sat.

"What was that?" Jerry, her co-counsel asked. "She was hot!"

Yep. Yep, she was. "I'm married, Jerry," Emma reminded him.

"But are you? I mean it's only legal in Massachusetts."

You are a slimeball. Just because you cheat on your wife, doesn't mean I cheat on mine. "I am. I take it seriously."

"You need to loosen up..." Jerry teased.

You are disgusting. If I didn't work with you, I would not associate with you. Emma could see the woman at the bar side eyeing her. Emma smiled and winked at her, making her smile and look away in response. *Even if I'm not going to go there, what's it going to hurt to acknowledge her.* The woman turned back to see Emma still watching her and smiled at Emma – a smile that held promises of a good time if Emma would only give her the chance. *I wouldn't have done that if Bailey were here. But it's not like I'm going to really do anything with the girl.*

She paid her tab and left the bar after hastily finishing her drink.

She was not surprised to find Bailey was asleep when she got home. *Of course. The punishment continues.*

The next morning, Emma came home from the gym and did something she had never done before. She called in sick. *I need to focus on us. I need to do serious damage control before this ends in flames.* She made breakfast of home-made waffles and fruit, and had it ready for when Bailey woke up.

Bailey came down the stairs and Emma served her a plate with a cup of tea the way she liked it. Bailey looked dumbfounded at Emma. *You were not expecting this, were you?*

"I called in today," Emma informed her, leaning across the island. "Because we need to talk. You are going to call in today as well."

Bailey opened her mouth to object.

"No. This bullshit ends today. We are getting to the bottom of it. Eat your breakfast, go take a shower, call in, and meet me in my office."

Emma went up to her office and handled what she could from home and waited for Bailey to join her.

Bailey came in, hair damp and attitude resigned, she sat in the chair across from Emma's desk with her hands on her knees. Emma closed her laptop and steepled her hands under her chin. "I know you are frustrated. I am so sorry that that case consumed me. But you *cannot* constantly hold my career against me. Not when I'm doing this for us. I get it. You would be happy with us downsizing our lives, that the material is not important to you. But it is to me. It's not greed. It's that coming from where I came from, I feel like I have something to prove. I proved it. I'm more than Bear ever dreamed. I'm ambitious. You knew who I was when you got with me. Back in high school you pinpointed it when you compared me to Rhys. Back then, you loved it. I'm not going to stop. But I will do better to balance things going forward. When and where I can, I will step back. But you need to give a little, too. I sent you flowers. I called you. I did what I could, and you gave me nothing."

Bailey looked down. She didn't say a word. It was just an icy silence. *You would think that someone who has a PhD would be better equipped to deal with things in a healthy manner. Fucking say something.*

Emma waited a few moments to allow Bailey to respond and when there was nothing she took a deep breath and closed her eyes before saying, "I was approached at the bar last night. A girl came up to me and was flirting with me, and she was a solid ten. It felt good. It felt exciting to feel wanted, which is something I can't say I've been feeling much of here lately. I turned her down. I could have easily gone home with this girl. Jerry said I was stupid for not. But I love you. I've always loved you. But I'm not going to sit around and be ignored until you decide I've been punished enough."

Bailey still did not speak.

Still nothing to say. God damn she's bull headed. Emma stood up. "If you can get over your bullshit, we can go and have a nice weekend away, or you can stay in your funk, and I will go and have a nice weekend away without you. You decide." *But if you choose to not come with me, I can't guarantee that I will be coming home to you.*

Emma walked around her desk and made her way to the door. She went into the bedroom and grabbed her travel bag and began to throw clothes and toiletries in it.

Bailey came in and wrapped her arms around Emma. *Finally.*

Emma nuzzled Bailey's neck. "Is this done? Are we okay?" Emma asked.

Bailey nodded.

A WEEK LATER, BAILEY WOKE up while Emma was in the shower. She was sitting on the edge of the tub facing the walk-in shower with something in her hands waiting to catch Emma's attention. Emma looked over at Bailey, "Good morning. You are up early."

Bailey held up the small white stick with a digital screen in it.

"What is that?" Emma asked wiping the steam from the glass so she could see better.

Bailey got closer to the glass enclosure and held it up smiling. It read 'pregnant'.

Emma squealed in delight. *This is happening. It's happening.*

Bailey grinned. "I thought it worked. I could feel it. I know it's strange. But I felt like it... And I was scared to get my hopes up. But it's real. It's happening. We are going to be moms!"

Emma went to work on cloud nine. She had Greta send a large teddy bear to Bailey's office with a dozen blue and white roses.

Bailey texted her with the date and time of her first appointment. *I can't afford to miss it. I need to make this a priority.*

Emma had Greta add it to her schedule and made sure she was going to be there.

The first appointment the doctor did an ultrasound and on the screen, a tiny little heartbeat flickered, and Bailey cried as Emma held her close and tenderly kissed the top of her head. *This is more than I could have ever hoped for us.*

Emma went above and beyond to be everything that Bailey wanted her to be. She was doting, peaceful and loving. She came home early when she could, and she was there for the next doctor's appointment as well.

ONE WEEK BEFORE BAILEY WAS going to enter her second trimester, Emma was at work drafting a motion for a client.

Greta came in, "Bailey is on the phone, she said it's urgent."

Emma picked up the line, "Hey, little mama."

"I'm on my way to the ER." Bailey was sniffling.

"Babe, what's wrong?" *No. no. no.*

"Cramps… and bleeding." She was crying. "Not just a little spotting, but a lot of blood."

This can be anything. It doesn't always mean the worst. We read that in one of the millions of books. "I'm on my way. I will meet you there." Emma hung up and rushed to Greta's desk. "Cancel everything today. There's an emergency. I've got to go."

Emma drove like a bat out of hell and rushed into the emergency room doors. "I need Bailey Frankson-Landry."

"Are you family?" the clerk asked.

"She's my wife. She's pregnant. She came here with bleeding and cramping."

The clerk looked up at Emma. "She's your wife?" There was a tone of incredulity in her voice.

I will punch you in your smug, ugly face. Emma rolled her eyes. "Yes. My wife. We are gay. Whatever. Where is she?" *Tell me where I need to go before I lose my chill.*

"That's not legal here." The clerk smirked.

That's it. Emma slammed her hand down on the counter. "Save your sanctimonious bull shit. Where. Is. My. Wife?"

A manager had come around. "Ma'am, can we help you?"

Emma forced a fake smile. "My wife is here. I need to see her."

"Her name?" the manager asked scooting the old bitch out of the way.

"Bailey Frankson-Landry."

"Right this way." The manager came around the desk and escorted Emma back to a small treatment room where Bailey was dressed in a hospital gown, under the cheap cotton blanket. Her face was waxen and pale, eyeliner and mascara were smudged, and her eyes were red.

She is not okay. This is not okay. There is nothing I can do to fix this.

Emma crawled onto the bed next to Bailey on top of the blankets and held her close while they waited for a doctor to come in. Bailey cried silently in Emma's arms, neither of them spoke.

A young doctor came in after an hour of waiting. "I'm sorry to make you wait, Mrs. Frankson-Landry. What's going on?" He took a seat on a stool and scooted to the edge of the bed.

He's like twelve years old. What can he possibly do?

"I was at work and then I felt like really bad cramping. I went to the bathroom and there was blood. Not just a little spotting. But a lot."

"How far along are you?"

"Eleven weeks." Bailey's voice cracked. "I'm just a few days away from 12 weeks. Almost second trimester."

The doctor was taking notes. "Mrs. Frankson-Landry, it's very common for miscarriages to happen before 12 weeks. I'm going to send an ultrasound technician in, and we will go from there." Before Bailey or Emma could ask another question, he was out the door.

Emma held Bailey tight and stroked her hair. *This is the worst thing that can happen. We were so happy. This baby would have known so much love. Keep it together. Be strong. You need to be strong for Bailey. You can't both fall apart right now. Breathe and deal. You can cry later.*

The ultrasound technician came in with a portable machine. Emma got off of the bed and moved aside so the technician could do her job.

Emma stood where she could see the screen and watch. There was no heartbeat like last time. "How far along are you?" the technician asked.

"Eleven, almost 12 weeks," Bailey repeated, her voice a quiet whisper.

The technician nodded and kept moving the probe. Emma looked at Bailey's face. *She knows it's gone.*

The technician printed some images, and the doctor came in to observe.

"There's no heartbeat. The fetus looks about 10 weeks. When was your last appointment?"

"Last week. Everything was fine." Bailey had tears streaming down her face.

I have never felt pain in my heart like this before. It sucks about the baby, but to see my Bailey like this is beyond pain. Breathe and keep it together. This is about her right now. Every bit of pain I feel, she's feeling double.

"I'm sorry, this is not a viable pregnancy. We have a couple of options for removing the fetus since your body is not quite working it out—"

He has the bedside manner of a pet rock. What the fuck. "Can you leave us for a moment?"

"Of course." The doctor and the technician exited the room. Emma covered Bailey back up and sat down on the bed so she could hold her close again.

"I'm sorry, baby," Emma said softly. "We can try again in a few months if you want?"

"No. No. I can't do this again. It's too much."

Emma just nodded her head. *Maybe she will change her mind. Just listen. Don't argue. Don't persuade. This is about how she feels. Not what you want.*

"I just want it to be us. We don't need a baby. We don't need anything else. I just want us. Somehow the universe or God or whatever is telling us that we shouldn't be having a baby. It's not for us."

I really want this baby. I want us to be a family. "Got it. It's your call. I want what you want." She laid herself back in the bed with Bailey, feeling disappointed but unable and unwilling to express her feelings.

That night, after she tucked Bailey into bed, she closed the door to the room Bailey had lovingly redone to be the nursery, a door that would stay shut now, forever.

~ *9* ~

S e t t l i n g   I n

Present…

EMMA WAS LYING ON THE floor. Her body was stiff and cold. The bottle of wine was empty. *Am I awake? Am I dreaming?*

Bear was sitting at the table now. *I must be dreaming.* Jessie was there, too, and so was Teta. *Definitely dreaming. Jessie was shanked and died in prison years ago.* Bailey was laughing with them, and they were enjoying the dinner.

Emma sat herself up. *My body hurts everywhere. I'm too old to sleep on the floor now. I must be awake.*

"Well, there she is! Sleeping Beauty! Hey, Princess!" Bear called out to her. "It's been a minute, huh?"

No. They are there. Talking to me. I'm dreaming.

Jessie picked up his glass of wine and took a huge gulp. "I'm gonna need more of this if I'm finishing this meal. I don't know how you do that vegetarian shit. Couldn't you have made this with veal or chicken at least?" His blue eyes were glittering as he grinned.

Teta just looked at her sad. "You lost sight of who you are, who you were supposed to be," she said, her voice thick with disappointment.

"What do you mean?" Emma asked.

"She turned out just as she was supposed to," Bear announced. "Princess, you done me proud. Daddy's girl, all the way."

Jessie clinked his glass to Bear. "That's right. Our little girl."

"She thought she was gonna be better than us. Better than where she came from. Princess, you made a right old mess of your life after all, didn't cha? A true Landry after all."

Bailey just continued to laugh uncontrollably. "That's right. Exceeded all expectations just to meet them all in the end!"

When is the last time I heard you laugh like that? It's been so long. I never hear your laugh anymore.

The Past (2012-2017)

BAILEY DID NOT FULLY EVER recover from the miscarriage. When they came home, she spent a full week in bed. Not really moving except to go to the bathroom. She barely ate a thing, and just stared mindlessly at the television. Emma stayed home as many days as she could, working from her home office and going in and checking on Bailey and tending to her as best she could.

Emma finally called Mary Anne. "She's so broken right now, and I can't fix her. I need help."

"I'm so sorry for you both. I had a miscarriage between CJ and Bailey, and it was so difficult. All of those hopes and dreams you pin on this little life and when it doesn't make it, it's devastating." Mary Anne's voice was emotional on the other end.

"I have been home with her the last few days, and she won't even talk. She just sits in the bed and stares at the television. It's hard for us both, but I can't imagine how hard it is for her right now. I have to be in court tomorrow and I'm scared to leave her." Emma's voice held an edge of panic. *I'm terrified I'm going to come home and find her dead.*

"I will come and stay for a few days and make sure she's okay. I know you can't really take a lot of time off."

You were married to a workaholic. You know better than anyone what I need to be doing right now. But I need to start reevaluating my life and my priorities.

Mary Anne was there before dark that night. She laid in the bed with her

~ 198 ~

daughter and held her while she cried. She tended to Bailey in ways Emma just couldn't. *Sometimes you just need a mom.* Mary Anne was able to get Bailey up the next day while Emma was at work. Within the four days she spent with them, Bailey was almost back to herself, but her eyes still lacked joy and she didn't laugh as loud or as often. *I hope that one day you feel joy again. Truly feel joy. I want to see the laughter in your eyes again.*

After a week, Bailey told Emma she didn't want to return to work. "I can't handle being in the museum, walking around and seeing the strollers and families and moms."

"Bailey, are you sure you don't want to wait and give it time and try one more time? I understand not wanting to go back to work. I get that. You don't need to work anyway. But the doctor said we could try a full three times."

"How can you ask that of me? You have no idea of what it feels like. What I feel like. I feel like I'm a failure of a wife. I'm a failure as a woman. I couldn't do this one thing that I am supposed to be built to do. Everything in my body and in my heart and in my soul is cracked and open and in pain, and you are asking me if we can't try one more time. No. No, ma'am. No, we cannot try one more time. I won't survive another failure on this level."

You really are not going to revisit this. This is done. Emma sighed heavily. "I'm sorry. I didn't mean to sound insensitive in the question. I just thought maybe we don't take it completely off the table."

"It's completely off the table. I don't want to talk about it. It's not up for discussion."

Bailey submitted her letter of resignation and Emma sent two of her interns to go pack up Bailey's office and drop the boxes off at her house.

After a few months, Bailey seemed to come back into herself. She was laughing again, and she was more of the Bailey, Emma knew and loved. She had continued teaching classes at the university and picked up a few more classes at the small community college, and began to take classes herself, and her little office next to Emma's upstairs became a small home studio. It had canvases and paints stored in all the corners, a potter's wheel and brushes everywhere. She began to make art and not just teach its history.

Bailey's new obsession was dragging Emma to gallery openings and art shows put on by her new friends in the local artist community on Friday nights.

Before they knew it, five years had passed. Emma had quit the firm and started her own practice with Brandon, as they had planned as kids. She wanted to slow down and be with Bailey more. She had invested well over the last several years, and honestly could live off the interest of her investments, but she knew herself better than that. Having her own practice gave her more autonomy and less pressure. She and Brandon hired a few junior associates and paralegals, and Emma brought Greta with her. She and Brandon could pick and choose their cases and hand off the rest to the juniors.

Emma and Bailey were able to travel more. She would hand Bailey a budget and tell her to plan a trip. They had purchased an RV for road trips and would take cruises and travel to exotic places.

Bailey relished this new lifestyle of a more relaxed Emma.

One afternoon, a year and a half into their new chapter, Bailey called Emma's office. "Can you come home or are you like really busy?"

That's never a good call. Anytime I'm asked to leave work it's been bad. Emma looked over her schedule. "I can come home... Is everything okay?"

Bailey giggled into the other end. "It's good. Just come on home."

That laugh. You are up to something.

Emma rushed home to find Bailey sitting on the floor of the living room with a brown and white Cavalier King Charles puppy. "This is Charlemagne," she giggled tugging on a rope with the small puppy.

Emma laughed. "You brought me home because you got a puppy?"

"Yep. I saw an ad for them on Facebook and I couldn't say no when I saw the pictures."

Emma couldn't be mad. "Charlemagne, huh? That's a big name for such a little guy."

"It means Charles the Great. Get it? He's a Cavalier King Charles."

Emma had made her way onto the floor next to Bailey. "I get it." She picked the puppy up and held him to eye level. "What are we going to do with him when we go on vacation?"

"He's little. We can take him with us."

CHARLEMAGNE GOT HIS OWN TRAVEL bag, a collection of collars and leashes, and coats, and became their baby. The trips he couldn't go on, he went and stayed with Mary Anne. CJ had gone on to get married, have two kids, get divorced, get married again, have another kid and get divorced again. He had refused to reconcile his differences with Mary Anne and refused to allow her time with his children in fear that they would be exposed to what he claimed to be the immorality of his sister, so Charlemagne was the closest she had to a grandchild, and she doted on him as any grandmother would.

After considerable debate and planning, and given a budget and told to just plan a trip somewhere, anywhere, Bailey had set up a trip for them to go to New Orleans. Neither of them had ever been there, and they were excited.

Bailey had booked them at a boutique hotel in the French Quarter (that allowed dogs) and researched all of the restaurants and bars and tours that they had to make it to. She knew to plan an itinerary that would balance downtime with activity to keep Emma engaged.

Emma stood in the French doors that opened to the balcony of their room holding Charlemagne and looking up at the sky. "Is it just me, or is the sky bluer here in New Orleans?" *There is an entire energy here, a vibe that I can't place my finger on. It's almost like this city is a living being.* The air was humid, and the smell of spices and rich foods hung about, and the blue sky was speckled with puffy white clouds.

Bailey came out and looked up. "It seems so."

Jazz music filtered up around them from somewhere below mixing with the voices of other visitors laughing and reveling in the atmosphere of The Quarter. The city had a certain energy and that hummed around them. She could hear the crowds from the restaurants and bars and groups wandering the streets. The energy of the city welled up from beneath and wound its way within her. *This is my kind of city. It is brimming with a constant energy and restlessness. This is the embodiment of how I feel constantly. A restlessness that is never seemingly sated.*

Bailey snapped Charlemagne's leash on his collar and dragged him and Emma down to the streets. People were coming and going out of the various businesses. The smells of sweet liquor and spicy foods emanated from everywhere around her. *This is perfect for a person like me who never likes to be still.*

"This reminds me of half of the cities we saw in Europe. It's like it's not even really the United States," Emma remarked taking in the brightly colored buildings and the ornate wrought iron balconies. Trees lining the streets were draped in bright green, purple, and gold colored beads. *Not only does the city itself seem to be alive, but it's like it has its own character and personality.* Emma eavesdropped on a pair of locals standing on a corner. She loved their unique accents, a mixture of New York, and deep south. Their banter made her smile, and she was inclined to want to join them in conversation, but was detracted by Bailey handing her Charlemagne's leash.

Emma watched as two young boys tap danced with bottle tops fixed to the bottoms of their shoes in lieu of taps. Bailey wandered up to a daiquiri stand on the corner and ordered two drinks for them. Emma handed the boys each $10 from her pocket as Bailey came back out with two go-cups filled with sweet frozen rum drinks. She handed Emma one and they continued to walk. Street vendors and performers were up and down the streets. Mule drawn tours carted tourists around spilling the details of the city's colorful history.

They found their way into Central Grocery and Emma waited outside with Charlemagne while Bailey went in and purchased a muffaletta. They found a spot to sit across from St. Louis Cathedral to enjoy their lunch.

Emma was obsessed with watching all of the people as they ate the sandwich. *Of all the cities and trips we've been on, this is my new favorite. There's so much to watch and see.*

"I could lose myself in this town. Maybe we should buy an investment property here? We could Air BnB it. I could see us coming back," she commented. She was eyeing an old Creole lady at a card table with a crystal ball and tarot cards. "Hey, I think we should get a card reading."

Bailey shook her head 'no. "Those things are scary. What if they tell us something we don't want to know? Besides, what more is there?"

Emma shrugged. "I don't know. Just for fun. See what they say."

"People get readings to find out about money. You've got plenty of that. Love. We've got that. Success... what more can there be? Let's go look at the cemetery, if she's still there when we get back from that, fine."

They walked hand in hand through The Quarter and to the St. Louis Cemetery No. 1. Bailey snapped pictures of the ornate and crumbling tombs. They tagged along behind a tour and listened in on some of the facts and stories before dipping back out of the cemetery and back into The Quarter.

Emma navigated her way through the streets back to Jackson Square to the old Creole woman. *I bet she's still there. She's got her hustle and she's not going to be gone. Not when the streets are this crowded. And look, I'm right. There she is.* The chair across from the old woman was empty and waiting. Emma bee lined it and sat herself in the chair across from the woman. She had a strange accent that was not Southern and not quite French either, her voice had a resonance of gravel from years of hard liquor and smoking. "Hello, *mon petit.*" Her wispy white hair blew in the breeze and her cataract covered eyes had a milky quality, she was small and shriveled looking, with gaping holes where teeth had long gone missing.

Emma's heart started to beat hard and fast. *Maybe Bailey was right. I think this is a bad idea. Something about this woman is starting to freak me out.* Emma moved to get back up.

The old lady's hand reached across the table faster than Emma expected she could move. She snatched Emma's wrist. "*Non. Non.* Stay, *mon petit.* I've got a message for you."

Emma sat back down. *A message? Alright. I will bite.*

"Babe, I think we should go," Bailey said. Her voice was quiet and anxious.

"*Mon cher,* I mean no harm. Not ever," said the old woman. Her hot little bony hand flipped Emma's hand over. "Sylvia is my name. I tell no lies. I don't seek to hurt." She flattened Emma's hand on the table examining Emma's palm, her sharp fingernail tracing the lines of Emma's palm.

I want to leave now. This is wrong. But I can't move. This little old lady is not going to hurt me. She can't hurt me. She has me compelled to see what she has to say.

Charlemagne was on the ground trying to pull Bailey in the opposite direction on his leash.

"You have demons. Death surrounds you. You were born into death," Sylvia said. "You fight those demons every day. But for you, it's a losing battle." She let go of Emma's hand and began to shuffle the deck of tarot cards. She shoved the deck to Emma. "Cut the deck."

Emma obeyed and handed them back to her.

Sylvia flipped over three cards in succession. "You think you have it all. You worry about losing it. And you will. Love. Money. Life. It will escape you. You will not see the end coming, it will come when you least expect it."

"That's it. This is over." Bailey grabbed Emma and attempted to pull her away.

Emma was frozen in place. *No. She knows. She absolutely knows.*

"Sylvia can help you, *mon petit*. I have spells. I learned under the best voodoo queens in New Orleans. I have a direct line to the Queen, Marie LaVeau."

"Emma, this is a scam. Let's go."

I don't think it is. She knows something we don't. She can see it.

Emma stood up and threw a hundred-dollar bill on the table. The old witch snatched it and put it in her fanny pack. She grinned her toothless grin at Emma. "You will not wait for my spell?"

Just in case. I hope that's enough. She walked off with Bailey and a sizeable pit in her stomach.

Her head was buzzing as she followed Bailey into an antique shop. She held Charlemagne under her arm as they walked, and Bailey appraised the sparkling estate jewelry in the cases. She was on autopilot as Bailey tried on a sparkling fleur de lis necklace. She didn't question prices, she just pulled out her black AmEx card and handed it to the clerk.

Her stomach ached and she felt nauseous that night as they sat at dinner.

Bailey adorned with her new necklace. She blamed the feeling in her gut on eating the muffaletta when she has spent the better part of her life as a vegetarian.

"She was right," Emma said. "Think about it." She was pushing her red beans and rice around her plate with a piece of cornbread.

"She probably says the same shit to everyone," Bailey countered.

Such a skeptic. "Maybe."

"No maybe about it."

For as much as Emma loved New Orleans, the rest of the trip held a shadow of that reading over it. Emma had nightmares every night, waking up in a cold sweat. When she would awake, the visions from her dreams that woke her would be gone, dissolving as quick as her eyes flashed open. Try as she might to recall them, only for nothing but a sense of dread in her heart. She could feel Sylvia's hot bony hand in hers, her sharp nail tracing patterns in her palm. She would look over at Bailey sleeping soundly next to her and listen to the soft snoring of Charlemagne at her feet and lay there with her chest tight and her heart beating loud and fast in her ears, covered in a cold sweat.

~ 10 ~

The Fruit Never Falls Far From The Tree

Present...

EMMA'S EYES FLEW OPEN, AND she was looking up at the crown molding on the ceiling. Her head hurt and the room was spinning. She turned her neck and looked at the table. Bear, Jessie and Teta were no longer there. *It was just a dream. An alcohol induced dream.*

The music was still playing on an endless loop. Ellis Marasalis soulful piano playing. She normally loved the sound of his piano, it would resonate through her chest and fill her soul, but now she just wanted it to stop, every stroke of the keys was a jab of pain in her head.

She propped herself up, knocking the wine bottle over. The empty bottle rolled loudly across the floor and her teeth were set on edge. Her stomach lurched. She had barely had two bites of dinner last night, what could she possibly have to throw up now? Wine. She drank two bottles of wine. She tried to remember if she was the only one who drank... *Did Bailey even have a sip? It was her favorite wine...*

Emma felt the heat and acid creep up her chest, and into her throat, her mouth began to water. She scrambled to her feet and over Charlemagne who had been lying next to her on the floor and barely made it into the kitchen before she threw up into the sink, gripping the counter and trying to stay up on her feet as the room continued to spin.

Emma grabbed a glass of water with her trembling hands and rinsed her mouth out before taking a few gingerly sips and rinsing the sink back out.

How long have I been passed out? It couldn't have been long at all because it is still dark outside.

She splashed cold water on her face and leaned against the counter. She had to get a grip.

The Past (2017-2021)

EMMA HAD NEVER BEEN HUGE on social media. It wasn't her thing. She would wonder at Bailey who would spend hours a day scrolling and posting.

Bailey posted everything. Pictures of Charlemagne. Pictures of Emma. Pictures of Emma and Charlemagne. Pictures of the food she made. Pictures of her art. She would look up friends. She would like their posts. She would comment and get into long discussions. She would do reunions.

Emma would roll her eyes and go back to reading a book, or flip the channels on the television when Bailey would show her posts she made, or comments people said or posts their friends had made.

Bailey wasn't the only one trying to persuade her to join social media. Brandon would encourage it, and so would Simone. Emma would just say, "Bailey's on there enough for the both of us. You are friends with Bailey, you know everything we are up to." *Not to mention, I don't really think everyone needs to know everything we are up to all the time. It's really rather lame.*

When they came back from New Orleans, there was a perceptible shift in their dynamic. Emma noticed that Bailey was spending longer on social media. She was spending more and more time chatting with anyone that was not Emma. *What on earth is so all consuming on that screen? I get it that you are a social creature, but what about what is right here in front of you?*

She was also getting moodier and colder. Emma would reach for her and be shirked off. "No, honey... I just can't right now," Bailey would say as Emma tried to nuzzle her or even hold her hand. It was a slow but noticeable cooling in their relationship in the months that followed the trip.

Someone is hormonal. It's normal for relationships to ebb and flow.

When the pandemic hit, it was even worse. The first two weeks, that's all Bailey did was scroll on her phone. She vacillated between Twitter, Facebook and Instagram in an endless loop. Suddenly, Emma was home every single day. *Since day one, all you wanted was for me to be home with you every day. Now here I am, and you could not give a shit.*

Emma took on projects around the house and met with clients virtually, attended court virtually. She was home all of the time. Bailey would lock herself in her studio and avoid Emma most days.

The room that was set to be a nursery, had been sealed off and not touched years ago. Emma finally went in and gutted it herself. She took all of the furniture out and hauled what she couldn't sell to the dump. She repainted the room, built shelves and purchased expensive couches and turned the room into a library, where she color coded their collection of books on the shelves. It was her haven while Bailey ignored her in lieu of her rich social media life.

Emma suggested that they take the RV and go on a road trip to while away the time. Bailey said no.

Emma tried to suggest days of binging Netflix and snuggling. Bailey said no.

Once the world started to re-open from the shut downs, Bailey started going out without Emma. It was like she couldn't get away from Emma fast enough. She would stay out after her Art classes. She would go out to lunches with friends Emma didn't know. *Whatever it takes for her to be happy. She needs a life and hobbies outside of us. I get that. I have the firm and I have my workouts and my friends and colleagues, and Bailey doesn't give me shit about it.*

Increasingly these lunches turned to dinner, which turned to drinks, which turned to Bailey returning long after Emma was in bed.

Bailey would slip in and come upstairs and get ready for bed in the dark, and slip under the covers. Emma would reach over to touch Bailey, and she would whisper, "Shhhh... no... go back to sleep..."

Emma would roll over and feel the coldness of loneliness slip over her. *I never realized marriage could be so lonely. We've been together 21 years. But these last few have grown increasingly cold.*

After six months of this treatment, Emma had had enough. She tried to talk to Bailey about it.

"I just don't feel... I don't know what I feel. I just am not really feeling it right now. I'm sure it will pass..." Bailey blew her off.

"Maybe we can go get counseling or something?" Emma suggested.

"No... I mean... I just don't think we are there. We've been together a long time. It's just a low point for me. I think it will pass."

It needs to pass, because I can't handle much more rejection. "Maybe I can come with you sometime to meet some of these new friends of yours? I mean you are spending all of your time with these people, and I have never even met them."

"You wouldn't like them. They are artsy people, and you would be annoyed because you will think they are flakey and stuff. Just like I don't like your work friends because all you do is talk about law stuff and politics and it's always so serious and boring."

So that's bullshit. You get into long drawn-out discussions about politics and social inequities and through osmosis you could almost pass the Bar. "Bailey, we need some time together. To reconnect. I can't even remember the last time you kissed me, much less the last time we had sex." *Actually, if I try really hard, I can remember. It's been months. Multiple months. I'm craving my wife. I'm craving some intimacy. I need her. I need to feel that connection.* "It's like you are not even my wife any longer. You are a roommate who shares a bed."

"We will... Just give me some time. I need time."

How much time? Hasn't it been long enough? Do you not hear me or see me?

The day after she was rebuffed by Bailey, she went over to watch the football playoffs with Brandon. Bailey had gone out to hang out with some friend or another. Emma again offered to cancel with Brandon and go with Bailey.

Bailey gave it no thought before telling Emma no.

As she flopped onto the deep cozy couch in Brandon's rec room, he opened the mini fridge in the corner and pulled out two craft beers. He handed one to Emma and sat next to her. "You look stressed," Brandon said as they waited for their team to kick off.

Emma sipped her beer and put it on the coffee table in front of her and spread both her arms over the back of the couch. "I think I'm losing Bailey."

Brandon grinned at her. "That's not even a remote possibility. She worships you."

Ha. Maybe at one time she did. Emma shook her head. "She used to. Past tense. Maybe this is TMI, so I'm sorry. But I need to talk to someone. We haven't even had sex in like six months, maybe longer. And that was lackluster, which is not like us. I can't even remember the last time she kissed me. Like really kissed me. She is gone all the time with these new friends from her Art classes. She doesn't talk to me. She just scrolls on that goddamn phone when she is home. It's like I don't exist in her world anymore."

"It's a phase. You will get through it. Savannah and I have gone through those patches. It comes and goes."

"It's never come and gone with us. Normally I have to beat her off of me with a stick."

Brandon looked down and paused for what seemed like a long time before he shook his head. "I can't even believe I'm going to ask this, because honestly, it seems so implausible. I mean this is *Bailey* we are talking about. Do you think she's having an affair or something?" His tone was serious.

Emma had not ever considered that. *Duh. It's textbook. Emma, how did you not even consider that? Because it's Bailey. Bailey would never. Would she? It makes so much sense.* She felt her blood run cold.

Brandon was able to read the expression on her face. "I mean, I'm not saying she is. But I mean, Emma, based on what you are telling me and what we know."

Emma looked over at Brandon slowly. "It never occurred to me that it would be a possibility until now, but now that you mention it. It could be. It's textbook, isn't it?"

"We have investigators at our disposal. Just call one in. It can't hurt."

Emma shook her head 'no'. "I wouldn't involve them. I can do a lot on my own."

"What are you going to do?"

"I don't know yet." Emma grabbed her beer and took another sip.

FOR THE NEXT WEEK AND a half, Emma watched Bailey and her habits. *It is all so clear. The secrecy, the coldness. It really is plain as day. I have just never thought in a million years Bailey would do that to me.* Emma just had to wait for Bailey to leave for an afternoon with her anonymous friends.

On a Saturday where the sky was dark and the clouds hung low, heavy winds swept around and forced the trees to bow in submission, Emma sat and watched Bailey as she got ready to leave. "I'm going to go shopping and get lunch with Jeannette and Sheree," Bailey announced.

"Who are they again?" Emma asked, leaning against the counter. The wind was howling outside against the windows and thunder was rolling in from the distance.

Bailey secured her scarf around her neck. "Friends from my Art classes."

"Okay. I can come with you. I have nothing going on."

"No. It's a no spouses thing. I can't bring you if they aren't bringing theirs."

Emma moved across the kitchen and sat down at the island, sipped her coffee and put her book down. She slipped her wire frame glasses off and looked at Bailey. "You don't want to stay home? We can light a fire and maybe get naked and have some one-on-one time?" *I need you. I need you to say you will stay with me. I need to feel you. I need to feel loved by you.*

"No, I already promised them I would meet them. I don't want to be rude." Bailey put her coat on and grabbed her bag. "I will be home later today. In time for dinner for sure."

She was out the door. No kiss. Not another word.

I can't believe I'm doing this. I need to know what is really going on. This is not right. Emma waited for her car to pull down the street before she went up to Bailey's studio. She opened the door and grabbed Bailey's laptop as she sat herself at the drafting table Bailey used to sketch. Looking out the window, over the lake that appeared black, reflecting the darkness of the sky and impending storm, Emma exhaled as she opened the laptop.

The password was easy enough. Sapphire00. It was her password for everything.

She clicked the icon for Facebook. Bailey had over 300 friends. Emma scrolled through the names and links to profiles. A lot of the names she recognized from their three years of high school together before she fled to Teta's house.

One name stood out as she scrolled through the list. Rhys Mills. *She is really friends with that douche bag?*

She went and clicked on the option that showed all of their interactions together on the site. He 'loved' all of her pictures, except the pictures of her and Emma together. She loved all of his pictures too, except the ones of him and his wife together. Comments read almost like coded messages. She wrote on one selfie of his, 'Coconuts'. He wrote under one of hers, 'Cherries'. *They are random, seemingly harmless words. But I need to be real. I know better. I've argued enough divorce cases over the last few years. This is classic cheating behavior.* Her chest began to ache slightly. She felt cold despite the heat blowing through the vents and her cozy law school hoodie she had donned this morning.

She pulled up Rhys's profile. He was married with two kids. He was working for his father's business – the heir apparent to inherit the company.

He was fit, and his hair was thinning. Looking at his face made her stomach sick. She just thought back to the day he pulled her into the alley with his cronies. He was still friends with all of them, too. She had not seen him since that night, nor even given him another thought since then.

His wife was pretty. She had an 'exotic' look similar to Emma, but not as striking. She had the same olive complexion and dark hair, but her eyes were dark, and her nose more prominent. But she was stylish and had an excellent figure, and a dazzling smile.

Their kids were both boys, they were in middle school. His wife was a stay-at-home soccer mom.

Emma clicked off his profile and opened the messenger feature. When she opened the messenger app, she saw a message thread between Rhys and Bailey. After opening it, she scrolled to the top. The first message was over seven months old. Thinking back through the timeline, this was the biggest shift in Bailey's behavior. With her heart sinking, Emma began to read the messages.

Rhys Mills: Hey stranger! You look great!

Bailey Frankson-Landry: You don't look so bad yourself! *Really, Bailey?*

Rhys Mills: It's been a while, huh?

Bailey: Yeah. You really screwed me over.

Rhys: I was young, and you broke my heart. What do you expect? I'm sorry. Friends?

Bailey: Friends. :) *Why?*

Rhys: What have you been up to?

Bailey: I got my PhD, got married. Now I'm kind of a housewife who makes art and cooks a lot.

Rhys: I see you "married" Bloody Mary. (Emma bristled when she saw that old epithet, and the quotes around the word married, as if it were not legitimate.)

Bailey: You still call her that? LOL Let it go already. (*LOL? What the absolute fuck, Bailey?*)

Rhys: You are still super hot. I remember when I took your cherry. *I think I'm going to throw up.*

Bailey: Thanks. You look good, too. I saw you just did an Iron Man, congrats.

(Days' worth of endless banter back and forth) *So this is who you are spending so much time talking to on your phone.*

After a few weeks of daily harmless chitchat, Emma found what she was dreading.

Rhys: I had a dream about you last night. It was hot. I want to tell you about it.

Bailey: Stop! You are making me blush!

Rhys: I woke up and I could almost taste you. I never forgot what you taste like. Can you believe that?

Bailey: I can't believe that.

Rhys: Can I call you?

Bailey listed her number and the messages ended there. *You have to be fucking kidding me.*

Bailey had synced her laptop and cell phone and tablet, so she could get her messages on all platforms. Emma pulled up the text app and found where their thread continued via text. Bailey had never in a million years thought Emma would go through her devices and violate her privacy this way, so she never thought to delete these messages or change her passwords.

Emma continued to read. They met for lunch four months ago, after a month of messaging about meeting up and what it would be like to fuck. *My heart actually physically aches. It's not cliche. It's a real pain. This is what it feels like to be betrayed.*

Shortly after they met for lunch and ended up in bed together after, Emma scrolled and saw Rhys sent her a picture of his dick, hard and in his hands. She flashed back to him stroking himself in the alley before he forced himself into her. Her stomach lurched and she ran to the jack and jill bathroom that separated Bailey's studio with her office and threw up. She gripped the cool tiles of the counter top and tried to ground herself as the acids settled.

Before going back to the laptop to read more, she went downstairs and made a vodka soda and lime. *I can't look at any more of it. I need to – I don't know what I need. I need a drink.* She let Charlemagne out to relieve himself and let the cool air refresh her senses. It was misting outside, as a precursor to the rain that was coming in. The rumbling of the thunder was coming closer, and she could feel it through her whole body as it got closer and louder. The wind whipped around her as she tried to breathe and calm herself. She could see the messages that hurt the most, burned into her brain every time she closed her eyes. 'Rhys: you know I'm in love with you. Bailey: I think I might love you, too.'

She felt numb and disconnected. She watched Charlemagne hop around to avoid the puddles, he never liked to get his paws wet, and make his way back to the door. She would normally pick him up and dry his paws before letting him come in. She didn't bother. He tracked wet paws against the otherwise immaculate tiles on the kitchen floor.

She tossed back half of her drink, refilled it (more vodka than soda) and went back upstairs to pick up where she left off. After Rhys's dick pic, was a response of Bailey's naked body. Emma's eyes blurred with tears. *The body I have been denied these many months is being given wantonly to Rhys Mills.*

Messages and pictures and meetings. More than half the times Emma took for granted that Bailey was with her art friends she was with Rhys at a hotel.

Including right now. Today.

Emma opened Bailey's email. Mostly junk mail, except for a message from a name she recognized: David Arthur. He was a prominent divorce attorney that Emma had gone toe to toe with a handful of times. He was known to be tough. She braced herself and opened the email it was dated three weeks ago.

'Bailey: Hi David,

I'm hoping you can be discreet in this communication. I'm just looking for information on possibly divorcing my wife. You know her and you know her reputation. Emma Landry. She has mentioned your name a handful of times, so I know that must mean you are good and can handle going against someone like Emma. If I go through with this, I'm not looking to wipe her out. I just want what's fair. She has accrued considerable assets over the course of our marriage and at great personal cost to myself.' *Great personal cost? You haven't worked full-time in over a decade. You take classes, teach classes once in a while, and make art and spend my money.*

David: Good Afternoon, Bailey,

I do know your wife well. She is, for a lack of better terms, a bull dog of an attorney. I would definitely be interested in meeting with you to discuss this. Call my office to set up an appointment.'

Emma opened the calendar app and saw the various meetings with Rhys entered, her Art classes, dates for gallery openings and shows, but she never went through with meeting David.

She went back into the text messages and saw a thread between her and Rhys from a week ago.

Rhys: Hey babe. Did you contact that divorce attorney? You know I can't follow through with that right now. You know why. I got too much to lose. You, babe, you got everything to gain though.

Bailey: I emailed him. But I'm not sure I'm ready to make that decision. It's not so easy and it's not so cut and dry for me either.

EMMA CLOSED THE LAPTOP. SHE stayed still for a long moment. She was trying to assess her feelings, but she couldn't feel anything.

There was a vibration or humming in her head. Her breathing was shallow. Her drink was empty.

The room grew progressively darker, occasionally flashing bright with lightning. Emma finally forced herself to move. She looked out the window and the rain was falling harder, torrential as the wind whipped loud and furious.

She made her way downstairs and let Charlemagne out one more time. The little dog had difficulty in moving far with the wind and rain. He came bounding back in fast.

She made another drink and sat in the living room. She turned the television on for some noise, but couldn't follow what was going on. *Considerable assets at great personal cost. Everything to gain. It's worth nothing without you, anyway.*

She sipped her drink and every time she blinked or closed her eyes, she saw the picture of Rhys's junk, followed by Bailey's beautiful body.

Her phone buzzed with a text from Bailey. 'The roads are terrible, and we've all had too much to drink. We are all staying at Sheree's. I will come home as soon as the weather clears in the morning.' *Not even a phone call. Just a text. I don't even get the benefit of your voice.*

Emma's eyes spilled over with tears. She pictured Bailey wrapped up in the blankets of the hotel room with Rhys snuggled in his arms. *What did you tell your wife, Rhys? Who does she think you are with? What does she think you are doing? Does she care?*

The house felt suddenly hollow and empty. She refilled her glass with vodka, soda and lime over and over again, increasingly more vodka and less soda with each refill, until it was straight vodka. She lost count of how much she had drunk. The humming in her head wouldn't stop. The words from the messages replayed on an endless loop in her brain. Emma sat in the large living room overlooking the lake. The room that was her favorite at one point now seemed hollow. She looked up at the cathedral ceiling and it seemed to spin above her. *Worthless. It's all worthless without Bailey. She never gave me the chance to make whatever was wrong right.*

The sky went darker, and the rain eventually stopped falling and the thunder quieted.

Emma hadn't eaten, and she hadn't slept. The sun started to come up. She was numb. She was drunk. The humming in her head was intense. Her eyes were red and dry. Her eyeliner smudged and her hair disheveled. Her brain was numb, and her head was just filled with a loud humming noise that she couldn't silence.

In the early hours of the sunrise, the door from the garage opened and Bailey came in. Charlemagne jumped off of the couch and ran to her tail wagging, and she bent to pet him and scoop him up into her arms. When she looked up, she saw Emma. Her breath caught audibly at the sight of Emma's disheveled appearance.

"Hey, babe!" Bailey said with forced cheerfulness.

"Sit down." Emma's voice was hoarse.

"Are you okay?"

Don't you dare act like you are fucking concerned about me. "Sit. DOWN," Emma commanded.

Bailey's hair was damp, and she smelled like hotel shampoo. *At least she had the courtesy to shower and not come home smelling like Rhys.* Bailey sat and looked at Emma concerned, releasing Charlemagne to sit next to her on the couch, he circled twice before making himself a ball next to her thigh.

Emma pulled out Bailey's laptop and opened it. She began to read the messages between Rhys and Bailey. "'It felt so good being inside you yesterday. I can't wait to see you again.' 'Baby, you make me hot when you talk to me like that!' 'I can still smell you and hear your moaning in my ear…' 'I love the way you make me feel when—"

"Stop! Stop reading!" Bailey was crying, her hands over her ears to block the sound of Emma's reading.

"You don't get to cry! You really want to leave me. Leave what we've built together to be his whore?" She turned the laptop in her hands to show Bailey the pictures of Rhys's dick. "This, do you even know what it was like to see this for me? Do you remember what he did to me?"

Bailey covered her eyes and looked down.

"*Look. At. It.* He *raped* me with that thing in the alley by the train station after your dad sent me away from the cottage. He had his friends hold me so he could do it. All because of you. Because CJ told him what he saw. He did it because of CJ and because he was so threatened by you wanting me then. And you just went running to it." Emma's voice was hard.

"No. He wouldn't have done that. I know you think that's what happened. But he wouldn't," Bailey whispered, shaking her head disbelievingly.

Emma threw the laptop against the wall so hard it shattered. "You have been fucking him behind my back for months. And now you are defending him? When… When did you stop loving me? When were you going to tell me you chose him? You used to *love* me! You pursued me! You made me love you. And now you defend *him?* Love *him?*" Emma was pacing with her hands in her hair.

Bailey flinched and cried, "I'm so sorry!"

Emma cleared the space between them, and her anger was at a fever pitch. *This humming needs to stop. I need peace. I need quiet. I can't think.* "You don't get to be sorry! You did this!"

Bailey looked up and met Emma's eyes. Emma was standing over her. "Forgive me! You have to forgive me. Forgive me!" Bailey cried, shaking. "I still love you. I'm just so confused. I'm sorry. I'm scared. You are scaring me. I'm sorry!" She was shaking and crying.

"Shut. Up. Don't." Emma was nose to nose with Bailey. The humming in her head was loud. *I need peace. Just be quiet. Shut up. I need quiet.*

"Emma... Babe... I'm so sorry..." Bailey was shaking hard and so pale.

"You told him you *loved* him." Emma was standing looking down at Bailey.

"I'm sorry. I'm so sorry..." Bailey was sobbing.

"Stop fucking crying!" Emma roared.

Bailey sniveled loudly trying to stop herself. "I'm so sorry! Forgive me. Forgive me. You have to forgive me!" she whined.

Emma lunged at Bailey and put her hands on Bailey's throat and began to squeeze. "Shut. Up. Shut! Up!" *I just need quiet. I need peace. I need this to be over. Just be over. Just stop fucking talking.* Charlemagne was barking, and the humming in her head was all consuming.

Bailey was struggling under Emma, clawing at her wrists, writhing and gagging. Emma just squeezed harder, straddling Bailey with all of her weight. *I can't stand the crying and the apologizing. It has to stop. I need to stop. Bailey has to stop. I need to stop but I can't. That incessant buzzing in my head needs to stop. Charlemagne needs to stop. Everything just needs to stop. Why won't it stop?*

She could eventually feel the hyoid bone under her hands crack as she watched the light in Bailey's eyes slowly dim and the writhing stopped. Bailey was limp under her. *How much time has passed? Time stopped. It did.*

It's so quiet now. Blessedly quiet. It had to stop. The apologies and whining and sniveling. The barking. It had to stop. The humming had to stop. It's all quiet now. Everything is blissfully quiet. Bailey is quiet. Bailey. Bailey.

Emma stumbled off and backwards and Bailey's head lolled to an unnatural angle as Emma fell backwards onto the floor. Emma sat for several minutes with her knees up against her chest staring at Bailey. All was silent except for a loud ticking from the corner of the room. Countless ticks as Emma stared in silence trying to make sense of what she was seeing. The blue painting behind the couch. On the couch Bailey, with her head back in that sickening angle. Unseeing blue eyes fixed and staring at the blue painting behind her. Slowly as the ticking continued, clarity returned to her, and she had the understanding of what had just happened. *Oh. No. No. I killed her. She's dead. I've seen that look. The doe. She has the look like the doe. That's what Jayne probably looked like. Jayne my mother. Bailey.*

She let out a yell from the depths of her soul. It roared through the room and caused Charlemagne to run from the room. "No... No... No..." Emma was whispering. She scrambled to her feet and ran into the kitchen to vomit again in the sink. She could still feel Bailey's throat crush under her hands. Tiny red scratch marks on her wrist from Bailey's nails – but she couldn't feel them. The humming in her head had stopped and the stillness and silence was suddenly oppressive. She could hear the ticking of the grandfather clock in the living room, and the soft breathing of Charlemagne at her feet. She had sat in this kitchen morning after morning in silence having her coffee and never once noticed how loud that damn grandfather clock in the other room was. Now the ticking was like a hammer inside her head. She stared at her wrists another moment and her hands. *I just killed Bailey. I just took her life. With these hands. I couldn't have. This is not real. It's not real. I love Bailey. I've always loved Bailey. This is not real.*

She slowly walked back into the living room and saw Bailey's body on the couch, her head back and to the left. Her blue eyes faded and staring up at that blue painting, unblinking and unseeing. Black and blue, Emma's handprints had come up on her beautiful white throat, accusing her.

She swore she saw Bear in the corner of the room laughing, giving her a slow clap. She walked through the room and to the stairs, not looking at Bear and not looking at Bailey. *It's so quiet. Except for that damn clock. It's quiet. I am losing my mind.*

Emma went upstairs and took a shower. She was numb. She put the water on as hot as it would allow and stood in the heat trying to feel something. Her skin was red and raw when she got out, but she felt nothing. She dressed herself and did her hair and her eyeliner.

She went back down the stairs and avoided looking at Bailey's lifeless form on the couch. She fed Charlemagne and let him out.

After letting Charlemagne back in, Emma went and lifted Bailey's slight body and placed it on a blanket on the floor. Using the blanket, she dragged Bailey to the guest suite off of the living room, her neck made a sickening cracking noise as it rolled back and forth over Emma's forearm as Emma set her in the bathtub. She left Bailey there in the tub and went upstairs to the master suite and gathered Bailey's favorite dress and her shampoo and conditioner and body wash and brought it back down to the guest suite.

Emma took Bailey's clothes off and washed her body gently. She washed the smell of the cheap hotel shampoo and body wash and washed the evidence of Rhys off of Bailey. She lotioned Bailey with her signature smell of sweet strawberries.

She blow dried Bailey's hair and curled it, and dressed her in her favorite dress. When she was done, she sat Bailey at the dining room table and made them dinner.

Part II

Reckoning

~ *11* ~

U n d o n e

EMMA WENT FROM THE KITCHEN back to the dining room. Bailey's lifeless body was slumped now on the table. A fly was making his way up the side of Bailey's ashen face and landed on her lifeless, unblinking blue eye.

Emma slowly and systematically cleared the plates from the table ignoring the fly. She carried them one by one back into the kitchen and scraped them into the garbage. She rinsed the plates and put them in the dishwasher. Her mind was blank, and she worked slow and ordered on autopilot. Clearing the mess from the dinner seemed normal. Mundane. After what she had done, it seemed like that was what she should be doing.

She went back into the dining room and picked the wine bottle and her glass off of the floor. Emma threw the bottle in the trash and put the glass in the dishwasher and started the cycle. It was all so conventional and routine, aside from the fact that Bailey was dead.

Emma wiped down the table and turned the music off.

Emma took the trash bags and loaded the bags onto a trailer she had purchased when she was renovating the nursery to the library. She had used it to haul the baby furniture that did not sell to the dump, and when she was purchasing lumber and other big items for building the shelves.

She walked back into the house and made her way to the dining room and picked Bailey's body back up, placing it again on the blanket. She dragged it to the garage and dragged her limp body into the trailer. She pulled Bailey's wedding and engagement rings off and held them to her heart, before placing them safely in her pocket, leaving the glittering fleur de lis around her neck.

Emma bent down and kissed Bailey's cold and unresponsive lips. "I'm so sorry…" Emma whispered as she covered Bailey's face with the blanket. *You deserved better.*

Emma grabbed Bailey's laptop, tablet and cell phone and made sure they were all sufficiently smashed and destroyed and threw them in the bag inside the trailer with the food trash, followed by a shovel.

She hitched her truck to the trailer and threw on a ball cap and sunglasses and made her way to the dump. The rain had stopped, it was still unseasonably cold. The ground was wet, and the sun was too bright for Emma. The reflection from the sun off of the lake was blinding in shades of blue, reflecting the too bright sun. Driving in utter silence, her head hurt, and her eyes burned. Her tongue was thick and dry in her mouth. Her mind was still blissfully blank and empty.

After pulling to the gate of the dump, she was directed where to go to drop her load.

She navigated around the hills and narrow winding roads until she got to the spot where she had been directed. There were only a handful of other trucks dumping loads and she was grateful for that, and even more grateful that none were near where the spot she was tossing the bags filled with last night's uneaten dinner and Bailey's electronics, and the trailer containing the dead body of Bailey. Overhead, flocks of crows and seagulls were circling and calling out. The incessant noise from the birds made her headache worse. Emma released the button on the trailer, and it tilted up so the contents could roll out. The sound of the gears grinding to lift the trailer grated her nerves.

Even though it was cold outside, and her breath steamed around her, she was sweating, and her stomach was sour with the smell. Her face mask did little to reduce the cold and the thick smell that initially didn't seem like it would be so bad, seemed to get worse the longer she was out in it, and the deep breathing that came with her physical exertion as she tossed the bags with the smashed electronics hidden under food waste. She looked into the trailer and could see Bailey's body was still tucked into the blanket in the front end of the trailer. She could see tendrils of strawberry blonde spilling out of the blanket.

Back in the truck, she sat after dumping the load, driving, still numb, staring at the road for an hour and half, back to the woods she had known as a child. She passed the now dilapidated and crumbling, empty shop and the trailer that was now sagging in the middle. She pulled to the spot she had parked with Detective Bell all those years ago and pulled her truck back as far as she could go.

She opened the back of the trailer and dragged Bailey's body off and into the woods, using the blanket as a makeshift sled. She dragged without stopping until she was under the crumbling deer stand. She dug for what seemed like hours. She was sweating and weak when she finally felt the hole was deep enough. She gently laid Bailey's body inside and covered her back up.

I just killed my wife and hid the body. I'm no better than Bear. Bailey, like Jayne, deserved better. Her father was right. CJ was right. Rhys was right.

She was feeling the weight of her exhaustion, but she couldn't sleep just yet.

The sky was already darkening again. It had been days since she slept or ate now. She unhitched the trailer and parked her truck and went up to the bedroom. She grabbed Bailey's overnight bag and threw in clothes and lingerie and went back down the guest bathroom and threw all of Bailey's toiletries on the top. She grabbed Bailey's keys and threw the bag in Bailey's car. *I should just take myself to the police station. I'm not doing myself any favors right now.*

Navigating on autopilot, she drove to the hotel that Bailey and Rhys had met at, and parked toward the back, where she could see there were no cameras. Emma adjusted the seat to where Bailey set it, and wiped the steering wheel and handles down. She threw the overnight bag in the dumpster and then walked to the bar across the street from the hotel.

With her facemask adjusted over her face she found a booth toward the back and ordered a vodka soda and lime and an order of French fries.

After three cocktails and picking at the fries, she called a taxi thinking it would be less traceable than an Uber and went home. She had the taxi drop her off a block away from her subdivision and walked in the bitter cold home.

She went upstairs after feeding and letting Charlemagne out. She texted Brandon and told him she was sick and not coming in in the morning. *I just need some time to think. I am not ready to face the consequences of my actions right now. I need time.*

Emma turned the shower on and stripped off her clothes. The water steamed around and out of the enclosed shower, and she stood under the scorching hot water. No matter the heat of the water or scorching of her skin, she was unbearably numb.

The humming in her head long gone, she still felt anesthetized. *I will not get away with this. I know that. Nor should I, really. But I'm not ready. I need to reconcile who I really am with what I thought I was going to be. I need time to understand. Not that I even deserve that time. I'm so sorry, Bailey. My beautiful Bailey.*

Her body was red and raw from the hot water. She got out and dried off and laid with Charlemagne in the bed. She pulled Bailey's pillows over to her so she could smell her.

Emma slept deep and dreamless that night.

THE NEXT MORNING, SHE WOKE up late. She flew out of the bed in a panic – it was past ten in the morning. She had wanted to be on the road by eight. *I'm already off to a bad start. I should have been up hours ago.*

She threw as many clothes as she could in a suitcase and then went to her safe in her office. She grabbed the stacks of cash she had piled up in there over the years. It was close to $110,000. Bailey used to laugh at her for depositing money into the safe. "You never know when you are going to need cash. The banks could fail, anything can happen."

"If the banks fail would the cash be any good?" Bailey had laughed.

"You never know."

You never know. You could kill your wife and need to go on the run after dumping her body.

Emma piled the stacks into a separate bag. She took the suitcase and the bag to the RV they stored in the back and threw them on the king size bed in the fifth wheel and came back out. She loaded food and Charlemagne's supplies inside as well. She had felt this particular RV was excessive when they had purchased it, but it was the only one Bailey would agree to. It was almost 41 feet in length, with multiple slideouts. Emma had often referred to it as The Ritz Carlton on Wheels. It was decked out with every imaginable luxury that could be included. The selling point for Bailey was the reading nook in the master bedroom, which was perched in the forward window.

She went out to the garage and opened the deep freezer and started pulling out the containers of food Bailey had pre-made for her for meal prepping. She lined them up and then pulled out the three pints of ice cream. Butter Pecan. Bailey's favorite, and loaded them into the refrigerator of the RV.

When she was done loading up and hitching the fifth wheel to the truck, it was well past one in the afternoon.

She loaded Charlemagne into the truck and pulled out. She would start heading west. She didn't have a destination in mind, so much as just west.

She emailed Brandon and requested that he handle the business and that she was going to take some time off. After she sent the email, she destroyed her own phone and disposed of it along the route west.

She stopped at a convenience store four hours away and bought a burner phone, and filled up and kept going until she was well clear of the state lines.

Emma pulled into a big box store parking lot where other RV's were also set up for a nightly pit stop. *Anonymous and alone. This will do.*

She walked Charlemagne and fed him and made herself a bowl of soup. It was the first real thing she had eaten in days, and it sat in her stomach like lead.

She patiently waited for the other campers to fall asleep. In the dark of the night, she slipped out of the RV and took off her plates and deposited them in a cabinet in the rig. She snuck over to another trailer and took their plates and affixed them to her rig and her truck. She made sure she was on the road in the morning before they were awake. *It's almost like I was born to do this. To be a common low life criminal.*

She drove from dawn to dusk that night, stopping only for gas and to let Charlemagne relieve himself. Towns came and went, and she just kept driving. Sunlight glittered off windshields and buildings in a bright blur, until that began to fade, and the sky darkened around her. Stars littered the sky and Emma began to feel the weight of her exhaustion. She found yet another parking lot and pulled in with other campers. Another bowl of soup that again sat like lead in her belly.

That night, she dreamed of Bailey. Bailey was sitting in the bed next to Emma. She was not broken. She was not crying. She was sitting quietly. She was looking at Emma intently and with this look that Emma couldn't explain. It was not love. It was not hate. It was somewhere between curiosity and pity, as if she didn't even truly recognize Emma.

Emma reached out to touch Bailey and pull her in. She just wanted to feel Bailey by her side and in her arms again, but by the time her hand met with where her body appeared to be, she was gone. Emma woke with a start, causing Charlemagne to jump from the bed and scramble around.

AFTER DAYS OF DRIVING, AND waking up in random spots, she looked out the window and dawn was breaking over the horizon. She was in a rest stop parking lot somewhere in Oklahoma. *Or am I in Texas now? I don't know anymore. What day is it or how long has it even been since I killed Bailey? I think it might be Tuesday today. I've been driving for days or was it now weeks?* It was all so unclear. She had been zigzagging a westward route, driving all day and stopping at night. She threw on a sweatshirt and took Charlemagne for a walk.

Her stomach felt hollow, and she pondered that she had barely eaten since Bailey stopped living.

She had gotten another new burner phone and had no idea if the police had found Bailey or suspected anything. She had not checked her email or contacted Brandon since she had taken off.

She was back to being invisible and it wasn't so bad. No one paid her any mind when she stopped to get fuel, walked Charlemagne, stopped for the night, or stopped to dump and fill her tanks. She slipped under all radars and stuck to herself. She paid all cash for whatever she needed and didn't speak unless she needed to. The mask mandates around the country helped her blend into anonymity. *There is a positive to all of this Coronavirus stuff after all.* She kept her ball cap on, dark sunglasses and a mask. She was just a lone white woman in a truck with a fifth wheel and a dog.

She hadn't touched a drink since being in the bar after dumping Bailey's car. She was scared that if she drank too much she would sink into a hole of keeping herself drunk and numb. But she was numb anyway.

Several more days slipped by. Several more towns. Several more sunsets. Several more early mornings. Days and weeks blurred together as she kept on zig-zagging around the country aimlessly and stopping only to sleep, dump tanks, add water, buy food, relieve Charlemagne. Emma had not spoken to a single soul aside from her ever faithful companion, Charlemagne. Emma drove into New Mexico and stopped at a nondescript little town and wandered into the library. She inquired about the computers and the librarian pointed to a bank of them along the back wall.

Emma sat down and pulled up the local news sites for her hometown. Bailey Frankson-Landry, and her wife, Emma Landry were missing, officially. Mary Anne was tearfully pleading for information or for Bailey and Emma to return, or some form of contact or any information about them or their whereabouts. One story included tidbits about Emma's family history of a mother that had been missing for decades before being found dead after her father's deathbed confession, and Emma's rise to prominence with a successful law career.

Bailey's car had been found at the hotel, and the videos of her walking through the hotel lobby, and her overnight bag found in the dumpster behind the hotel, led them to believe there was foul play. They did not say if they had any official suspects at this time. It did not bode well for Emma that she was missing. But the police were concerned that the both of them were now unreachable.

She had downloaded the messages between Bailey and Rhys from Bailey's laptop to a jumpdrive in her haze. She hadn't anticipated killing Bailey so much as probably filing for divorce, and using the messages to protect her assets, especially after Bailey had reached out to a divorce attorney.

She took the files and printed them, and anonymously mailed them to the police and a local reporter. It would keep them busy and keep them from thinking too much about her. Best of all, it would throw a wrench in Rhys's life. *I should send a copy to his wife, too. But that's going a bit too far. She will find out soon enough with all of this going on.*

She sent a vague email to Brandon, ignoring all of the emails he had sent her (over 200 to be specific), and let him know she would be gone for a little while longer.

Back on the road. Her body was beginning to ache from the hours of sitting and driving endlessly with little rest in between. Charlemagne just sat in the passenger seat and slept in a brown and white ball, or stood on his hind legs to look out the window.

She missed Bailey. She missed the steady stream of conversation, and the effortless laughter. Bailey was not just her wife, but her best friend.

She pulled onto the side of the road somewhere – maybe it was New Mexico or maybe it was Arizona – she had long lost track of days, time, or location – and got out of the truck. The landscape was barren, and the dirt and dust had a reddish color to it. Strange looking plants and shrubs sporadically dotted the landscape that included bizarre looking rock formations. The sky was cloudless and pale blue and the sun hung bright and hot above her. Looking out into the alien-like landscape she let out a cry of anguish that seemed to echo into the distance.

Emma took off her ball cap and ran her hands through her hair and fell to her knees in the dusty red dirt. The full weight of what she had done was pressing in on her from all angles.

Bear was standing next to her. "Princess, you done fucked up your life good. All that you worked so hard for. Now you are no better than me."

Emma looked up at him. *I have to be going stark raving mad. He's dead. I know he's dead. I scattered his ashes in the woods, where he had buried my mom. Years ago. Another lifetime ago. Where I just buried my Bailey. But he's standing there. I can see him. I can smell him. Cigarettes and that musky smell that was unique to him. That's Bear.* He was not the wasted and sickly Bear from the hospital, but the Bear of her youth. Large and loud.

"Princess, did you really think you were going to escape your past so easily?" He laughed crouching down next to her.

She stood up and looked him in the eyes. "Fuck off."

And he did. He was gone. The cigarette and musky smell of him lingered for a moment but vanished.

She stretched and cracked her back, walked Charlemagne and got back on the road.

She suddenly felt foolish. *I've never done anything without a plan. Here I am wandering like a goddamn gypsy. No itinerary. No plan. Just in the wind. Not even knowing what day it is. This is stupid. I need a plan. I need an agenda. I need to have something down.*

"Tomorrow..." she said to Charlemagne. "Tomorrow we are going to make a plan and an itinerary. We need to know what we are doing and where we are going."

He just panted and looked at her with his large black button eyes.

WHEN EMMA AND CHARLEMAGNE WOKE up in the morning, they were outside of Phoenix at a rest stop. The dry heat felt good. Emma opened the windows of the fifth wheel and took extra time to clean up the RV. She swept and wiped the surfaces down, organized her clothes, and made toast and jam and coffee for breakfast. *It's been some time, but I feel normal. I know I shouldn't. I know I should feel bad about what I did. It was an accident. I didn't plan it. I was in shock. I was hurting. I can't change it now. I need time to heal. I do. Then I will go take accountability for what I've done. But I need to enjoy the peace for a little while.* She had managed to tuck what she had done into a nice neat little compartment somewhere in her brain and move past it, just like she did every other traumatic experience in her life.

She sat down at the table with the warm breeze pouring in. She pulled out a map and looked at where she was and where she could go. She tried to make sense of the timeline of how long she had been gone, but she had no clue. The days had run together and the best she could tell was that it had been probably two weeks now, maybe three. No matter how hard she tried, she could not even remember what the date was when she had killed Bailey.

Charlemagne gnawed at toy at her feet, and she spoke to him as if he had a say in the matter. "We are going to go to California. We will cut up the 101 to San Francisco. Stay there for a few days, and then maybe go down to Santa Barbara, San Diego and then into Mexico. End at Ensenada. Or maybe north into Canada if they reopen the border to Canada. Go up through the Pacific North West. Let's see what happens in California, first though, eh?"

Charlemagne didn't respond. His tail wagged happily as she spoke to him though, so she took it as his consent to her plan.

She put the slideouts in and got back behind the wheel with Charlemagne copiloting. For the first time on this journey, she put music on and put the sky light open and the windows down for fresh air.

~ *12* ~

California Dreaming

EMMA STOPPED AT A GAS station/truck stop somewhere in the middle of California. She walked Charlemagne and put him back in the truck and wandered in. She was waiting in line to pre-pay for her fuel and a box of dog treats for Charlemagne.

The fluorescent lights seemed to buzz louder than she could tolerate, reminding her of the incessant buzzing in her head when she killed Bailey. The sun was bright outside and pouring into the already brightly lit station, and she was antsy today. Emma rubbed her temples as she stood in line.

Two young women came in together. They were loud in their chattering and giggling and Emma was annoyed with them instantly. *Why won't this line move?* The cashier was carrying on a conversation with the person at the front of the line. The way they carried on implied they knew each other personally. There was only the one cashier on duty. She pulled her ball cap lower and suddenly her facemask seemed to be suffocating her. *I can't breathe. Those gaggling nitwits are so damn loud.* She adjusted the mask and shifted her weight in her feet and looked at her watch. The two girls chattering and giggling incessantly went to the slushie machine and filled cups with bright red iced slush and got in line behind Emma.

They are standing too close, she thought. Through her mask she could smell sweet strawberry scent. It was overwhelming her, and her head began to swim, and her vision blurred. The scent was choking her. She thought of Bailey and the feeling of nuzzling into her neck and being consumed by the sticky sweet scent. Cold sweat beaded onto her forehead. Her mouth was watering fast and hot, and the acid rose from her stomach and the floor spun underneath her. She pulled her mask off and vomited on the floor, splashing up and spattering the girls behind her.

"What the fuck?" one of the girls whined.

Oh, shut up.

Emma didn't bother to apologize, wiped her mouth with the back of her hand instead and put her mask back in place. *Get out of here before you make a scene and people recognize you.* Before she could give anything a second thought, she pulled $20 out of her pocket and slammed it on the counter and walked out with the dog treats and got back in the truck and pulled away without fuel. *It's not urgent. I can get it somewhere else.*

She drove another 40 miles and stopped somewhere else. She ran into the RV and brushed her teeth before going in to pay to fill her gas tank. Her heart was still racing, and she still felt unsteady, and her hands shook as she paid. She pulled her facemask off as she stood outside and waited for her tank to fill. The dryness of the breeze and dusk slowly cooling off the world around her, the world began to slow back down around her, and she regained a sense of calm. She breathed in deep and tried to calm her nerves.

That night when she finally stopped for the evening, she snuggled Charlemagne and tried to control her breath. Her pulse would not slow, and she couldn't control her tears. She missed Bailey. She missed the sound of her voice and her laughter. She missed the smell of her and the feel of her body next to hers.

As she finally drifted off to sleep she smelled the sweet strawberry scent. She felt a touch on her face and a coolness around her. "I really was sorry… I never meant to hurt you…" Bailey's voice was soft, she could feel Bailey's breath on her ear. Emma clung to the moment and kept her eyes shut. "I loved you," Bailey's voice continued to whisper in her ear. "Forgive me. I forgive you… You couldn't help it. I promised to never hurt you, and I hurt you."

Tears slipped out of Emma's closed eyes, and she curled into the fetal position wrapping around the small warm furry body of Charlemagne. *I fucked up. I killed her. I had no right to take her life. I can't fix this.*

The next morning Emma got onto the road early and made her way to a place she could park just outside of San Francisco.

It was overcast and cool. She was north of the city along the coast at a place she could pay cash for in a box by the day. She unhitched for the first time from the truck and set up. She wanted to stay still for a few days or even weeks. She had a nice view of the bay and the bridge. She could just see the orange red color of the bridge peeking out from the heavy gray fog.

She and Bailey had come for a long weekend to San Francisco to celebrate Pride month years ago, right around the time The Supreme Court ruled that gay marriage was to be federally recognized. The two of them had walked hand in hand down through The Castro and wandered into the exotic shops in Haight Ashbury. She pushed the memories aside as she felt the pain in her chest and the heaviness of what she had done weigh on her.

Emma put on a hoodie to fight the chill in the air and sat on the picnic table in her campsite facing the water. The fog and gray swirling around her was suiting her mood.

Days began to blur together at her small site. She didn't wander far, and she lost track of how long she had been parked in the spot. Campers had come and gone, and she didn't socialize with any of them. The fog in her brain was just as heavy and all-consuming as the one that wrapped around The Bay Area. She spent most of her days sitting in silence, staring at the bridge desperately trying to make sense of something that would never make sense.

She had a few books in cabinets in the RV and she would flip through them, trying to focus on the words on the pages.

She found a notebook with Bailey's handwriting – flamboyant and swirling. A to-do list for when they returned from a road trip on one page, and a grocery list on the opposing page. Emma stared at it, letting her fingers trace the markings. She closed the notebook and put it back in the cupboard feeling a new level of pain and sorrow for what she had done.

After an indiscernible number of days, she walked Charlemagne down and out of the camp area into a small quaint town area and picked up a coffee and croissant from a bakery. Finding a seat at an outdoor table, she picked off small pieces and fed them to Charlemagne between her own bites.

She was lonely. Not just for Bailey, but in general. Since college she had lived a social life. She had been surrounded by people who admired her and lauded her. She had grown accustomed to having her ego stroked constantly, so falling back in line with a solitary lifestyle being invisible was beginning to take a toll on her. She also missed Brandon and considered calling him but thought twice about it.

She sat at the outdoor table with her mask off, sipping coffee. A woman walking by slowed her pace and smiled at Emma flirtatiously. Emma winked at her and smiled back. The woman kept walking and glanced once over her shoulder. It was all thoughtless and reflexive.

It had been months since she felt appreciated and attractive. Bailey had been distracted by Rhys and she had been set to the back burner. She hadn't been touched, or kissed in as long as she could remember.

Bear was suddenly sitting at her table with her. "Princess, you got to just move past what you did. Move past what that traitorous bitch did to you. Go meet some people. Get some lovin'."

Emma shook her head trying to make him go away. She finished her coffee and tossed the cup in a trash bin and walked back to her RV. As she walked, she heard Bear behind her in a steady stream of dialogue though she was not responding.

"I mean, the woman was going to leave you. She *cheated* on you. You can't beat yourself up forever over this. You were *justified*. Besides, it's not like what I did to your ma. Your ma didn't do anything to deserve what happened to her. Bailey deliberately hurt you. You couldn't help it. You are your father's daughter. You should go out. Shake the dust off. Go out. Meet a nice girl and get you some…"

"Gross. Shut up," Emma said under her breath. She went back to her rig and turned the electric fireplace on and put the antenna up and tuned in some local television channels to see if anything about her or Bailey had reached this far west.

She watched the local news broadcasts and nothing new was discussed. Politics and Corona virus were all anyone was talking about.

She was antsy. She wasn't driving and she wasn't working. She had nothing to do and nowhere to go. She cleaned the RV again. She brushed Charlemagne.

Finally, she got into the truck and went to the local grocery store and bought fresh food to make herself some dinner. She had long since eaten through the meal prep food Bailey had made, the butter pecan ice cream – she couldn't bring herself to touch stayed in its containers in the freezer. She had burnt herself out on canned soups.

For the next several days her life followed the same routine: walk Charlemagne to the bakery – sit and have coffee and a croissant, walk back, clean the RV, watch the news, read a book, make dinner, sleep.

Finally, after dinner one night, she looked at herself in the mirror. Based on how long her hair was she tried to estimate how long she had been living on the road. *It had to be at least a month, maybe six weeks now? Eight?* She cut her hair the best she could in the mirror, using clippers to shear the sides, keeping the top long, almost the same style she wore in high school, only shaved higher up. She slicked back the long hair on top.

She took herself into town and wandered into one of the many gay bars in The Castro. It was small and dimly lit. She had opted to not wear her ball cap and dressed herself in a nicely fitted button-down shirt and jeans. She put her makeup on and looked like herself. *This is a huge risk if they posted my picture on the news. I don't care though. Honestly, if I get caught, I will face the consequences.*

She walked in and took a seat at the bar and ordered a vodka soda and lime.

The bartender served her drink and she looked around the bar. It was not crowded because of pandemic restrictions, but there was a decent sized crowd. Just being out in a crowd made her feel less isolated and the vibe in the bar was positive. Poppy dance music played loudly, and a few people were up and mingling, and a group was making use of the pool table near the bar. The occasional sounds of the billiard balls hitting and the thrumming of the bass in the music and background chatter gave Emma a sense of normalcy.

She turned back around to face the bar and fiddled with the paper straw in her drink. Several minutes seemed to pass before someone sat down next to her. She was petite, with thick curly brown hair, and in the dim light her eyes appeared chocolate brown, her toned arms were sleeved in old school sailor style tattoos. She removed her mask and ordered a Jack and Coke with a slight southern accent.

"I'm Tawney," she said to Emma.

Emma panicked. She didn't want to give her name suddenly. "Jayne," Emma said, extending her hand. *That's the worst possible name you could come up with. Dumb.*

"Do you live here?" Tawney asked.

She's interested. Look at the way she's looking at me. I'm not here for a hook up. I just needed to socialize. But it feels so good to be wanted. "No, I'm just passing through. You?"

"I'm here for work. I'm a travel nurse. I'm here for a few months to help with pandemic support and such."

"That sounds like it's tough."

Tawney shrugged. "I've been here two weeks, and this is the first time I've gotten out for a night." She moved herself on her stool, so she was facing Emma directly, leaning in slightly to indicate her interest.

It's been over twenty years since I've been with anyone other than Bailey. I don't even know if I can be with anyone else. I don't know that I want to be with anyone else.

Emma was sitting with her knees apart, feet perched on the stool, so it was almost as if Tawney were leaning into her. Emma could smell that she was wearing a vanilla scent and it reminded her of warm fresh baked cake or cookies.

"Where are you from?" Tawney asked, trying to make conversation.

Emma had to think fast. "New Orleans," she lied.

"You don't sound like you are from New Orleans."

Fuck. "I didn't grow up there. I just live there now. Where are you from?" Emma was trying to volley the conversation back. *Answering questions was something I was not prepared for, nor wanted to do in general.*

"Atlanta. What do you do?"

"I just quit my job. So I don't do anything. I was a litigator though." *Look at me being all honest.*

"Why did you quit?"

"You ask a lot of questions."

"I want to know you... You intrigue me."

You intrigue me as well. Emma laughed. "I intrigue you?"

"You are definitely hot. You know that it shows in how you carry yourself. And you look so alone. Sad. I want to know why."

Of course. She's perceptive. "I'm not alone. You are talking to me."

"But when I approached, you looked sad and alone."

"I'm dealing with a break up..." Emma felt a pit in her stomach. *I mean, it is a kind of break up.*

"Who did the breaking up?"

"Are you sure you are not an attorney?" Emma asked. "I feel like I'm on the witness stand." She was grinning at Tawney. *I guess since I killed her, I did the breaking up.*

"I told you... I just think it's strange that someone who looks like you would be here alone and sad."

"My wife cheated on me. With a man. So, I found it unforgivable..." Emma had to stop herself from finishing with "who happened to have raped me, so I killed her." Instead, she took a breath and said, "I left. I up and left everything. I figured I would take some time to be on my own and come to terms with what happened. Try to figure out who I am without her. We had been off and on since high school. It's a long time to be with someone and then not be together." *Twenty-seven years of back and forth if you want to be honest.*

Tawney licked her lips and leaned further into Emma. "I'm sorry. I don't think I heard you correct. She cheated on you?"

"We were together for a very long time. I think she got bored. Got complacent. Whatever. It was unforgivable. I don't deal well with that kind of thing. What's your story? Aside from being a traveling nurse from Atlanta?"

"It's been a long time since I've been involved with anyone. I broke up with my last girlfriend a year ago. We were together for five years, but we ultimately wanted different things. She wanted kids and a white picket fence... I wanted the relationship, but not the conventional life. I like to travel... I like adventure. I'm kind of an adrenaline junky." She grinned at Emma. *She could be fun for a fling or something short term. This is not a bad thing.*

"What do you mean adrenaline junky?"

"I like to skydive and hang glide and mountain bike, stuff like that. When it's not a pandemic, I actually work in the E.R. I guess you can say I thrive on chaos," Tawney was grinning as she spoke.

"That's so not me..." Emma said. "I'm a workaholic. Or I was. But I am a creature of habit and routine. I like to know what I'm doing or about to do at all times. I usually have every second of my day planned out."

"Your drink is empty. Do you want another?" Tawney asked.

Emma looked down at it. *It can't hurt. Better than going back to the RV alone. She's hot, and she's interested. Maybe even go home with her for the night. This is the best I've felt in months. And having this attention is nice. She is definitely into me. Bailey was so absent in regards to us, all the way up to when she died – which yes, I am responsible for.* "Are you trying to get me drunk?" Emma asked raising her eyebrow. *I still have game.*

Tawney laughed, "Maybe." She bit her lip in a seductive manner as she met Emma's eyes.

They had two more rounds and steady conversation, at which points bordered on direct innuendo, before Tawney looked at her phone. "Wanna grab a bite to eat? There's a diner down the block."

Emma nodded and they left the bar after settling their tabs. The street was cold and dark and quiet compared to the bar. The fog was settling in, and the air was cool and damp. After the heat of the bar, it was surprisingly refreshing. Emma tilted her head back and breathed deep, filling her lungs with the coolness.

They had walked almost half the block without saying much when out of the blue, Tawney grabbed Emma and pushed her against the building, before Emma could think twice Tawney's lips were on hers. In the first few moments, she enjoyed the sensations of Tawney's body against hers, the taste of her lips and the warm sugary vanilla scent. Her heat and intensity and aggressiveness were reminiscent of the urgency in which the girls threw themselves at her in college. *It's not sweet strawberries. It's not the soft yielding body of Bailey. That's because that body is rotting in the ground below the deer stand in the woods I spent my childhood in. This body is hard, and this kiss is aggressive, and demanding. Nothing about this feels right. I can't do this. Not now. I'm not ready.*

Emma put her hands on Tawney's shoulders and pushed her away gently.

"I can't do this. I'm so sorry. I just can't."

"Jayne…" Tawney pleaded. "I'm not trying to get married. I just want to have a good time for a night or two."

Being called her mother's name further set Emma on edge. "Tawney, you are amazing. You are beautiful, smart and funny. I think in another life, another time I would be willing to go there with you. But I'm not in that space now. I can't. I thought I could. I really did, but I can't."

Tawney was reluctant to move away from Emma and it was making her feel suddenly claustrophobic. Her hands were on Emma's hips.

Emma put her hands on Tawney's and moved them off of her. "I'm sorry…" She moved aside and started to make her way to her truck so she could go.

She could hear Tawney's footsteps chasing her up the street. "Jayne! Wait!"

Emma didn't stop. *Please just let me go. You don't want to get tangled up with me anyway. I killed my wife. God only knows what I would do to you.*

"You can't even talk to me?" She caught up to Emma.

"Please, just respect where I'm at with this. I can't. I thought I could. But I can't. I'm truly sorry."

"You can't even give me your number?"

"No. I can't. I'm leaving in the morning anyway." *I hadn't actually planned on that. But it sounds good. I think I am leaving in the morning. Maybe I won't even wait until the morning. It's time to get out of this area.*

Emma got into her truck and started the engine. Tawney backed away slowly and stuck her hands in her pockets and made her way back down the street shaking her head.

THAT NIGHT EMMA DREAMED OF Bailey again. They were sitting on the bed facing each other, cross-legged.

"You didn't wait very long," Bailey reprimanded.

"At least I waited until we weren't together any longer."

"You choked."

"She wasn't you. I never imagined being with anyone other than you. Not since that night when you cooked me dinner…" Emma's voice cracked.

"Well, you certainly made sure it would never be me again."

"I didn't mean to… I don't know what came over me."

"You were hurt. You were sad. I shouldn't have defended Rhys… I had no excuses."

"I shouldn't have done what I did. I love you. I will always love you." Emma wiped the tears away from her eyes.

Bailey smiled at her. "You can't help who you are, or who you were meant to be. My dad warned me all about you and loving you when we were young, and he sent me away."

Emma reached out to touch Bailey, and she was gone. She awoke with a start. It was dark and a heavy fog hung over the bay as she looked out the window.

She took a shower, got dressed, and got on the road. She needed to get away from here. She had stood still long enough.

EMMA DROVE STRAIGHT THROUGH THE morning and found a place to dump her tanks and refill her water, and a place to park near Santa Barbara. She was facing the ocean and the warm salt air was welcoming after the chill and gray of San Francisco. It was warmer in this area and the sun was bright. She hadn't eaten since before going to the bar the night before. She made breakfast and fed Charlemagne.

She snapped his leash on and grabbed a blanket and took him down onto the sand and watched the waves. Charlemagne sprawled on the blanket next to her and dozed off. Emma absentmindedly stroked him and talked to him as if he would respond to her.

"The color of the waves... Bailey would say they match my eyes. Like sapphire blue. What did I do, Charlemagne?"

Charlemagne just continued his nap.

Emma was trapped in a tug of war with her conscience. *I destroyed her. I wasn't a good wife. I didn't prioritize her when she needed me. When she felt low and neglected she sought attention elsewhere. But she did not talk to me. She didn't verbalize what she needed when she needed it. I can't change what I did. We both made mistakes. I don't even know how I am to go on now. Do I go on? Do I turn myself in? Do I keep moving? I don't know what's right anymore.*

Emma went to the grocery store and restocked the RV and grilled vegetables outside in the afternoon sun. She had stopped hiding under her ball cap. She was daring someone to recognize her.

She basked in the sun on the beach, watching sea lions frolic in the waves and roll around on the beach. She walked Charlemagne around the local area and lost herself in memories of Bailey.

Several days into her stop, she took herself to the library and sat in front of the computer and pulled up the local news from home.

There was a video with an interview with Rhys. She put her earbuds in and clicked the link for the video. Rhys was standing in front of his daddy's business in a suit looking smug. "Mr. Mills, what do you have to say about the disappearance of Bailey Frankson-Landry?"

"Bailey was a very confused woman. She didn't know what she wanted. It could be that she just ran off. It could be that her bitch wife killed her." *Rhys is not doing himself any favors with his arrogant attitude. If he were my client I would have raked him over the coals for even answering the questions on camera. Everything he is saying could be used against him.*

"Mr. Mills, is it true you were having an affair with Bailey? There have been message threads released to us and they are quite, well, steamy."

Rhys visibly bristled at this. "Bailey and I have been friends since high school. We dated when we were kids. We reconnected as friends on social media."

"From our sources, Bailey left you more than once to pursue a relationship with Emma Landry. Is that true?"

"And recently she was pondering leaving Blood – uh – Landry to pursue a relationship with me."

Your attorney hates you right now.

"So, there was a relationship between you and Bailey Frankson?"

You are so stupid, Rhys.

"I didn't say that. I said we reconnected on social media. Bailey was pursuing me."

"The excerpt of this message, where you reference a meeting with her at a hotel indicates that there was much more. I would read it aloud, but it would be censored."

His face reddened. "I will not answer any more of your inane questions. Any further inquiries can be directed to my attorney. Thank you," and he ducked into the building.

Emma was satisfied. The reporter went on to talk about how the hotel Bailey was seen on camera coming and going from had a room rented in the name of Rhys Mills, and how her overnight bag was found in the dumpster of that very hotel, as was her car.

"Bailey Frankson-Landry's wife Emma has been missing since the same date. She is not currently a person of interest; however, the authorities are interested in speaking to her if and when she is found."

Emma grinned and sat back in her chair. She exhaled. *Rhys is the person of interest right now. But that's only going to last so long. Most of the people in these comments below the article know I'm the one to blame. Trial by media and the perception is less than great right now.*

She made a point after the first three comments to not read any further. Her anxiety couldn't take it.

She logged into Bailey's email account and drafted an email to Rhys and CC'd the reporter who had cornered him outside the office.

'Rhys,

You know what you did to me. You know what you did to Emma in the alley, too.

Shame on you.

Bailey.'

EMMA CLICKED SEND. *JUVENILE FOR sure. But whatever. He deserves whatever he gets.*

Emma went back to the RV feeling smug and self-satisfied. She grabbed Charlemagne and made her way to the boardwalk.

She walked the dog up and down and passed a small building with a bright red neon sign that read 'Psychic'.

Emma stopped and stared in. The room was dimly lit and done in shades of purple and reds with gold accents. An incense burner emitted a graceful trail of smoke, and candle light danced from the corners. New age spa music filtered through the speakers faintly.

Emma tucked Charlemagne under her arm, put on her facemask and walked in the door and a chime tinkled softly.

An older woman, Emma guessed to be in her fifties or maybe sixties, walked out. She was dressed in long flowing skirts and a tight tank top. Her hair was dyed a deep brilliant red with black lowlights. Her golden-brown eyes were lined thickly with black, peering up above her face mask that was bedazzled with rhinestones. Several crystals on silver chains varying in length were layered over her decolletage.

"Do you have availability for a reading?" Emma asked as Charlemagne sniffed the scented air around them in her arms.

"Hello, good afternoon… Let me check…" She went to an appointment book and looked. The heady incense and soft lighting soothed Emma's nerves.

"Can you come back in 2 hours?" the woman asked.

Emma nodded, "I can do that."

"What's your name, dear?"

"Jayne," Emma said reflexively. "J-A-Y-N-E. Mansour. Do you need my last name?"

The woman shook her head as she wrote in the book. She looked up, "My name is Callie. I'm the only one here today. Just come back, and if no one is out here, sit and wait." She smiled warmly.

Emma took Charlemagne back to the fifth wheel and made something to eat to burn the time. She started getting nervous. Her only other experience with a reader was the one time in New Orleans and that did not exactly go over well. *I feel like Callie's operation is a lot more legitimate than the old Creole witch in New Orleans. Although, in hindsight, has not all that the old Creole lady said come to light? What am I even hoping to accomplish with this? For her to negate what the old witch said? Tell me everything will be okay? I know everything is not okay.*

She made her way back to the boardwalk and back into the shop. She sat and fidgeted in the seat waiting for Callie. She tried to breathe deep and take in the scent of the incense and watch the dancing candle flames. *Maybe I should just leave. This is not the smartest thing to be doing right now.*

Callie came out with an older man. He was dabbing tears from his eyes, and he hugged Callie, as Emma watched from her seat. "Thank you. I needed that."

"You are welcome. Be safe and be well." Callie, on her tiptoes, returned the hug.

The man walked out and stood outside the door. He exhaled, letting his shoulders drop, and made his way down the boardwalk.

"Jayne? Are you ready?" Callie asked softly.

Emma stood. "I think so." *No. I'm not ready. I'm lost and I need to go home. Whatever that means.*

"Relax. Come with me." Her throaty and warm voice washed over Emma, giving her a sensation of calm and comfort.

Emma followed her into a small room with a table. A tarot deck and several crystals sat in the center.

"What brings you here today to see me?" Callie asked as they both sat down.

Emma took a deep breath. "I don't really know." *I killed my wife, and I don't how to feel. I feel guilty. But I don't feel guilty because she cheated on me and now I'm seeing things and hallucinating my dead wife and father.*

"Have you ever had a reading before?" Callie asked shuffling the cards and looking into Emma's eyes.

Emma nodded. "In New Orleans, several years ago. It wasn't good." *But now that I think about it, she was spot on. Just because it is not what I wanted to hear, it doesn't mean it was not good.*

Callie nodded. Her eyes closed as she continued to shuffle the deck. "Your name is not Jayne. A woman is here. She said she is Jayne, not you. She will not tell me your name though."

Emma's heart raced. "That's true. My name is not Jayne." Emma looked around.

Callie set the cards down and pushed them across the table to Emma.

"I will not pressure you for your real name. No worries. I respect your need for privacy. Jayne says the woman in New Orleans was not altogether wrong, was she?"

Emma shook her head slowly. "No. She wasn't."

"She said she's been watching you your whole life. She is proud of what you accomplished, but sad about how it all turned out. Shuffle the deck." She pushed the deck across the table to Emma.

Emma shuffled slowly and handed the deck back to Callie.

"You are lost..." Callie said flipping over a card. "You don't know where to go, or what to do. You are scared." She flipped the cards slowly as she spoke. "You are hiding a big secret. It's dark. You are dangerous and you are in danger. You are like a ticking time bomb. What you did, is unforgivable." She looked up at Emma and her eyes locked. "You have to either come to terms with what you did or return and make amends. You are not going to be able to outrun what you did. Those are your only choices."

"What do you mean I'm dangerous?" Emma asked.

Callie closed her eyes like she was listening to something far away. "You know what I mean. You know what they mean. She says 'you know what you did. You know what you are capable of. You are your father's daughter.'"

"Does she hate me?" Emma whispered.

Callie inhaled deeply and there was a long pause. "No. She doesn't hate you. She is sad though. Disappointed. She said you threw it all away needlessly."

Tears welled in Emma's eyes. "Are you able to talk to anyone else? Or is it just Jayne?"

Callie with her eyes closed, reached for a crystal from the center of the table and brought it to her forehead. She rocked back and forth slow and rhythmic. "You are surrounded by the dead. They circle you." She continued to rock. She was quiet, continuing to move back and forth in perfect tempo. Her rocking started slow, but then became more frantic and faster. She stopped suddenly. Her hands were grasping at her throat as if invisible hands were strangling her. Her eyes flew open. "Leave. I need you to leave." There was urgency in her voice. Fear.

Emma scrambled out of her chair and backed against the closed door.

"I will not say anything. It's not my place. But I know what you did. She showed me. She told me. You are a killer. You killed her. Get out. Leave." Callie was crying. "She showed me. You strangled her. You took her life because she hurt your pride."

Emma backed out of the door and tossed a couple hundred-dollar bills on the counter as she walked backward out. *Why I even bothered is beyond me. There was nothing that I could have expected to gain from this. It's not like Bailey's spirit was going to pop in and tell me that it was okay that I killed her. My mom was not going to pop in and tell me she's proud I killed my wife in the same manner my father killed her. My only hope and prayer is that Callie keeps her word and doesn't say anything.*

Emma made her way back to the RV and closed all of the shades and blinds. She sprawled on the bed and drifted off to sleep.

She was back in the living room with Bailey. But she was watching from afar. She was not inside herself.

She was showing Bailey the screen with Rhys's dick pic. She was watching herself tell Bailey what Rhys did to her. She had only ever discussed it the one time with Bailey. She could hear Bailey defending Rhys, saying he would never do that. That Emma was mistaken.

She watched her own face go blank. She watched as her eyes took on a cold, hard soulless appearance – the light had gone out within her, and she was on autopilot.

She saw Bailey's expression for the first time – really saw it. She saw fear, sadness, and regret.

She saw herself throw the laptop. She heard her own voice and heard Bailey's sobs and Charlemagne barking as if he knew what was going to happen. She saw herself lunge on Bailey. She heard Bailey's gasping and gurgling, she heard the hyoid bone snap and crush in her grip.

Watching it all from a distance was terrifying for her.

Bear was sitting in the reading nook. She was unsure if she was awake or asleep. "Princess—"

"Don't call me that."

"You need to let it go. You can't keep beating yourself up over it. It's over and done. Move on."

"Like you moved on? Visiting hookers and strip clubs? Leaving me home alone to raise myself?"

"You turned out just fine, until you freaked out. I didn't want another woman holding me down. You a Landry, girl. Like it or not. You are not meant to be held down either. Move on. Keep moving on. Besides, that spoiled little bitch asked for it. She didn't care that she hurt you."

"That's not true," came Bailey's voice, almost a whisper as she was suddenly standing in the corner by the nook, next to Bear.

Emma sat up in the darkness of the RV and moved through the pitch black into the living room. Anything to get away from Bear and Bailey in the bedroom. Moonlight made its way into the living room of the fifth wheel through the blinds, weak and silver.

She opened a bottle of wine and poured a glass. *Callie was right. I am lost, dangerous and in danger. I'm in danger of losing my damn mind. I'm a danger to myself. I need to figure out how to come to terms with what I've done. Am I just going to roll on past it like Bear did or am I going to go back and turn myself in? I need a sign. I need something to tell me what to do.*

She went outside under the moonlight. *I miss Bailey so much. I ache for her. I ache for the Bailey who was my doting wife, before she iced me out. I ache for what we used to have. Not that we were guaranteed to ever get it back. Realistically, I most likely would have filed for divorce. There would be no going back. No matter what. Not once I knew.*

Seated alone in the dark, staring up at the moon she finished the bottle of wine. She took her drunk and sorry self back inside and passed out in a deep and blissfully dreamless sleep.

The next day she took Charlemagne on a road trip into Paso Robles and wandered the wineries. She sat alone in the tasting rooms tasting, buying bottles of expensive wine with no one to share with. The back of her truck was beginning to resemble a wine cellar as she added bottle after bottle, more with each stop.

She flew under the radar. The wine servers would try to make conversation with her, and she blew them off.

She sat outside with Charlemagne at one populated winery. It was decorated with statues and art of local artisans everywhere. Kids were playing on the lawn and Charlemagne was laying at her feet.

The sun was warming her face and she felt the familiar buzzing within her brain and all through her body. The heady smell of jasmine was everywhere, and bright pink bougainvillea bloomed up a lattice near where she was sitting. It felt good to be around the liveliness, though she was alone.

Emma curled her long legs underneath her on the large high-backed chair and she adjusted her sunglasses, removing her beige straw fedora hat pushing her hair back underneath before setting it back in place.

She exhaled a deep breath and took another sip of wine as a butterfly flitted over her head and landed on the bougainvillea. At first glance, the butterfly's wings were brown and black. As it rested on the bright pink flowers and opened its wings they were bright blue. "Like sapphire blue..." Emma whispered. *Those butterflies don't live here. This has to be a sign from Bailey. Sapphire blue. It has to be. She's telling me something. Even after what I did, she is there for me.*

Tears fell from Emma's eyes. She removed her sunglasses and wiped her eyes.

A man came and sat near her. "Are you okay?" he asked. He was attractive, about her age. His brown eyes were soft and compassionate, his face wore a salt and peppered five o'clock shadow, and his dark waving hair had graying flecks along his temples.

She nodded slowly.

He looked over at the butterfly. "That's a blue morpho. They are not native to here. They are from South or Central America. That little guy is far from home," he said, setting his wine glass on a table between their chairs.

Emma didn't respond. She just stared at the blue shining wings as the butterfly filled itself on the nectar of the bougainvillea and opened and closed its wings in a rhythm that seemed to match her heartbeat.

"Seriously, are you okay?" he asked.

"Yeah. I'm just dealing with ... I don't know. A lot, I guess."

"Do you want me to leave? I can let you be. You just look like you need a friend right now."

"I am pretty alone." Emma smiled through her tears. "Just me and my boy Charlemagne here."

"Do you want to talk about it?"

Emma almost looked at him and spilled that she killed her wife. She took a deep breath and wiped her eyes. "My wife left me. I'm trying to come to terms with it."

He gave a quiet chuckle. "Mine, too."

They clinked their glasses together. "Here's to starting over," Emma said.

"Mid-forties, two kids, and here I am. Did you guys have any kids?" He sat himself in the chair next to hers.

"Just Charlemagne here. I didn't give her a choice. He's mine." *It isn't really a lie. Bailey didn't have a choice.*

"Charlemagne? That's a big name for a little dog."

"He's a Cavalier King Charles. The name means Charles the Great. Get it?"

The man laughed and said, "Yes." He stuck his hand out, "I'm Salvador. They call me Sully though."

I could give him my real name. I can just start being honest about all of this. I'm just not ready for that, though. "Jayne. Just Jayne." She shook his hand.

"Are you from here?"

"No... I'm from a long way away. I came out here to escape and regroup. Try to figure out what to do next... I guess you can say I'm having a midlife crisis." *That's one way to call it. Midlife crisis. I could have bought a sports car and fucked a younger woman. Instead, I killed my wife and went on the run.*

Sully smiled at her. "I'm from San Francisco. I'm kind of doing the same thing."

Sully and Emma finished a bottle of wine while talking about politics, football, and everything other than their ex-wives. Emma was at ease and the conversation was easy and flowed effortlessly. Sully was good company and being with him was reminiscent of hanging out with Brandon.

The sun was sinking lower in the sky and the wine server came out to tell them they were closing for the evening.

Sully reached out and touched Emma's hand gently. "I have an Air B'N'B not far from here. Would you like to come over? Order pizza and keep talking?" Sully was hopeful. "This is the best time I've had in … a really long time."

"You know it won't go anywhere. I'm not into men."

Sully half smiled and blushed. "I was kind of thinking you would say that. I was hoping it wasn't so black and white. You are a perfect woman. Your wife was a fool."

"It is that black and white for me. I'm sorry. My wife wasn't a fool so much as I was over sensitive. I made her leave." Emma stood and picked Charlemagne up, cradling him in her arm.

"Can I at least get your number? We can be friends?"

Emma shook her head. "I don't think that would be good for either of us. I had a great time, Sully. It was a fun afternoon. You made me feel human for the first time in a long time, but I have to go." She threw two twenties on the table and turned and left.

She didn't look back. She just walked to her truck and left.

Sitting back in the RV after storing all of the bottles of wine she had purchased throughout the day she looked at the map again.

She looked at Charlemagne. "I know we said south and into Mexico… But hear me out. I'm thinking Tahoe? What do you think?" she asked the little dog. He just looked back at her with his large black button eyes. "I think that's a yes," she said folding the map back up.

~ 13 ~

Pretty Wounded

EMMA DROVE FOR HOURS STOPPING only for fuel and to let Charlemagne out. She finally made it to South Lake Tahoe in the early evening, found a campground and walked into the office.

The woman at the desk appeared to be slightly younger than Emma, with dark blonde hair streaked with shades of pink. She was propped behind the desk reading an Anne Rice novel. Emma stood there for a few minutes waiting, attempting to have patience before clearing her throat.

The woman placed a bookmark in the pages, closed the book and looked up with hazel green eyes over her mask. "Can I help you?"

"I would like to park for a few days... Or weeks."

"Which is it? A few days or a few weeks?" She was dry, reopening her book.

"I don't know. Can I pay cash? Go day by day?"

"We are renovating the grounds, so we only have spots on the lower level." The woman pulled out a site map and indicated where on the map. "There's only about five other rigs here. So, you can take your pick. Fill this form out, please, and I need to see your license."

"If I pay cash, can we skip all of that?"

The woman raised an eyebrow at her.

"I just am trying to lay low for a while. Understand?"

"Are you on the run?"

"I don't think so. I just don't want a paper trail. I need to be away for a bit."

"We aren't supposed to do that, but I guess."

"Thank you."

"Honestly, you picked a good place to go off grid. This place is full of characters and stories of its own. No one will bother you here."

This is exactly what I am looking for. "Good. It's what I need."

"Once you find your spot, come back over and let me know where you are, and you are set. Just come bring cash daily."

"I appreciate your accommodating me."

Emma walked back and parked her RV and set up camp. The campground was almost completely vacant as the woman had described. There were only five other campers, and they were all distant from her site.

Emma chose a spot toward the back of the lower level where she could back in. Large pine trees and boulders surrounded her site, and it was a quick walk across the street to the office and the lake. If she walked to the upper level of the grounds she could actually have a view.

Emma walked Charlemagne across the street to the office and camp store noticing that it was attached to a bar and grill as well. She walked back in and up to the desk.

"Did you find your spot?" the pink-and-blonde-haired woman asked.

"Site 1170."

"Normally, that site would go for $70 per day. With cash, let's just call it $55 a day."

Emma counted out $275 and handed it to the woman. "I know I'm not going anywhere for the next five days."

The woman counted it and put it in her pocket.

Emma raised an eyebrow at her. *You are a bit shady, aren't you?*

"It's not like that. This is my dad's place, which means it will be mine when he retires."

Emma didn't say anything. She just walked out and dropped Charlemagne off at the trailer and went back to the bar and grill.

She ordered a tomato soup and grilled cheese and a white Russian. She was sitting next to the fireplace and looking out the window at the lake. *The color of the lake is so beautiful. I've never seen a turquoise quite like that in life. Bailey had always wanted to come here. She would have loved it.* A paddle wheeler was coming into dock and a smattering of tourists were clamoring to shore.

The bartender was the only other person in the restaurant, and he was busy scrolling on his phone. *Indeed, this is the right place for me. It's quiet, calm, and everyone seems to keep to themselves. I can heal here and decide what it is I need to do.*

She walked back through the camp store on her way out to buy some dog treats and toys for Charlemagne.

"So, your dad's place?" Emma asked as she placed her purchases on the counter.

"Yeah. He bought this place after he retired from his corporate world job in 2008. He would drag us up here every summer for vacation when I was a kid. I got burned out on teaching a few years ago and came out here to run the place for him."

Emma handed her more cash and she put it in the register and gave Emma change.

"What did you teach?" Emma asked her.

"English. But the politics of the job and parents killed it for me. I'm Morgan, by the way." She pointed to a name tag that was partially covered by her pink and blonde hair.

Emma thought about giving her an alias but chose to just be honest. "I'm Emma." She smiled under her mask. She felt like even if Morgan watched the news she wouldn't be likely to notify anyone.

"What do you do, Emma? For a living? Other than walk around with a lot of cash and hide out." She was leaning over the counter on the edge of her chair.

I feel like I'm picking up a slight vibe here. "I'm an attorney. I need a break."

"Sounds awful." Emma could see Morgan was smiling under her mask.

"It wasn't that bad." Emma took her bag and put her change in her pocket. "See you." She nodded and went out the door. *She's definitely cute. But the last thing I need is to get involved right now.*

Two days later, Emma built a fire in the fire pit and poured a glass of wine and sat at the picnic table with Charlemagne in her lap. She hadn't had dreams or visions of Bailey or Bear or anyone since she made her way up here. *I haven't slept this good since long before the pandemic. I have no idea how long I've been gone now, though. It has to have been months now. Bailey died (I killed Bailey) – when? When was it? No matter how hard I try, I can't make sense of the timeline or when I did it – I only know I did it. I know I've been on the road for a long time now. It's fall here, looking at the colors on the leaves. They are starting to change. And it's slightly cold now. I've spent months in and out of a haze.*

If I search the depths of my soul, it feels like my life that I had with Bailey was lived so long ago. It wasn't even me, or my life. I am so far removed from all of it. I should check the news to see what is being said or known. My life as I know it, no matter what, is over. Done. My accomplishments and who I was – it's all moot. I'm not even that person any longer.

She was sitting in her quiet contemplation when Morgan showed up at her campsite. "Hey…" She sat down across from Emma.

"Hi?"

"I'm bored and I have nothing else to do. Dad is in the office, and I am not wanting to be micromanaged. So, I'm doing a 'site inspection'." She used air quotes around the words site inspection.

So, you are drawn to come over to my campsite and sit with me. You are interested. "Do you want a glass of wine?"

"I would love one." Morgan pulled her long pink and blonde hair up in a ponytail.

Emma went up into the RV and came out with a second glass and poured for Morgan.

Morgan inspected the bottle and took a sip. "This is good."

"Thanks. I picked it up a few days ago in Paso before coming here. So... Outside of walking away from a teaching career to work for your dad, what's your story?" *Emma, you are opening a can of worms. You know this is a slippery slope. When you ask someone questions about their life, they will want you to reciprocate. But I can't help it. She's interesting. And she's quite pretty.* Emma analyzed the features of Morgan's face sans mask for the first time. She had lips that were full and perfect teeth. When she smiled, her features softened in a way that was disarming.

Morgan smiled, but this time, the smile didn't reach her eyes. "I've been up here for just over a year now. I came up here to escape, too. My fiancé killed himself two weeks before our wedding, which was four years ago. I've just been trying to rediscover what I want and who I am supposed to be."

"That's harsh."

"What about you? What are you running away from?"

Emma smirked. *See. Now you have to share.* "It's so complicated. I don't even know where to start. I'm kind of having a midlife crisis, I guess. My wife cheated on me – with a man... With a man who actually raped me when we were younger – if you can believe that... I just had enough. I had to go. I needed some time and distance." *That's a way to dance around the full truth.*

"Are you going to forgive her? Reconcile?"

Emma took a sip of wine. "I forgive her for the cheating. I think I came to terms with that. She needed something and I couldn't give it to her, apparently. I was too self-consumed, I guess. But there's no going back." *Because what I'm not telling you is that I killed her.*

Morgan cocked her head to the side. *You know I'm leaving information out. I can tell. I know that look. I want to tell it. I need to tell it and let it out. But I'm not ready for what that means.*

"What's this little guy's story?" Morgan asked to change the subject, ruffling Charlemagne's fur.

"That's Charlemagne. He's my copilot. He was my wife's dog. But I took him with me." Emma smiled warmly. "Did your fiancé leave a note? Did he say why?" *Redirect. Keep the focus on Morgan.*

"He did leave a note. But it wasn't much. It just said, 'I'm sorry'. He battled with mental illness for pretty much his whole life. He was tired of being strong, I guess. I forgive him. I found him. He hung himself with a belt. It was scary and sad. I freaked out for a while. But this past year... Well, I think I am finally better."

She has a beautiful smile. "It's a process, right?" Emma smiled.

"It is. So, you said five days. It's three now. What are you thinking?" Morgan swirled the wine in her glass, appraising it.

Emma bit her lip. "I think I'm staying beyond that. I have nowhere else to go and I think I like it here. Charlemagne likes it, too." *That came out way more flirtatious than it should have. But honestly now, it's been over a year since I've been touched. Bailey had deprived me of any and all affection for months before I realized she was cheating. Had I not lost my mind and killed her and just done things the way they should have been handled, it would not be too inconceivable that now would be a good time to start maybe dating. I'm definitely picking up something from Morgan. And I'm so damn lonely. Though that's completely my own fault.*

Morgan stayed around for another hour making small talk with Emma. *The longer she's around the more I like her. She's easy to spend time with. I think she's definitely into me, but she's not all high pressure about it. She's not forcing it. She's feeling me out, too.*

When she left, Emma felt good for the first time in a long time. *I'm staying here until I'm caught, or the money runs out. Whatever happens first. I'm not running any longer.*

She went to the office on her fifth day with a stack of bills and handed them to Morgan. "This should keep me for six months."

Morgan looked at Emma with big eyes. "That's a lot of cash. Did you rob a bank?"

No, I killed my wife and went on the run with my cash holdings from our safe. She smiled instead. "Maybe," and winked at Morgan and walked next door to the bar for lunch.

I can feel her eyes on me. If I look around right now, I know for a fact she will be looking at me. I will not look though. I really want to. But I'm not going to.

As she sat at the bar, Morgan made her way in and sat next to her. *I knew it. Not only were you looking, you were compelled to follow.* They chatted and laughed, and Morgan followed Emma back to her RV and walked the dog with her before leaving for the day.

It became a daily event that Morgan would either come by Emma's rig or Emma would stroll up to the store and hang out while Morgan worked, for the next two weeks. *Being around Morgan is a breath of fresh air. If she only knew how much I really look forward to being near her. She gives me something to look forward to every day. She's smart and funny, but her spirit is light.*

On a rainy and unseasonably cold day, Emma felt cooped up and restless, and Charlemagne was not liking his brief walks outside to relieve himself, dragging Emma back inside as soon as he finished. *Do I really want to walk in the rain to the store to see Morgan?*

Before Emma could answer herself, Morgan was knocking on Emma's door. Emma opened the door and let her in. She had been making a vegetarian chili in the slow cooker and cornbread was cooling on the counter, while she played a silly rom com on the DVD player to fill the silence in the background.

Morgan came in and sat herself at the table, "It's so shitty out there. Sometimes I wonder why I stay here! I miss San Diego... Sunny and 70's every day."

Emma smiled. "It's like this a lot where I come from. Colder in the winter though."

"Where is that, exactly?" Morgan asked. *That's what I get for giving information. It leads to more questions. More questions I need to eventually answer.*

Emma shrugged. "Back east. The Midwest."

Morgan did not pressure her further.

"Are you hungry?" Emma asked. "I made more than enough."

"You cook. You are handy. You were an attorney. You are smart. You are hella good looking. What was that wife of yours thinking?" Morgan asked.

Emma shrugged. *If I had a dollar every time someone asked that. If I only knew the answer to that.*

"Yes... I would love to have dinner," Morgan answered.

Emma turned on the electric fireplace in the living room under the television and opened a bottle of wine before serving the both of them bowls of chili and sitting with her guest at the small table.

After they had finished with dinner, Morgan offered to wash the dishes for Emma. "I mean you cooked... I don't cook. So I am in awe of people who can and do. The least I can do is clean the dishes. I'm really good at doing dishes, by the way."

Emma laughed. "Yeah, sure. I will let you do the dishes if it makes you feel better." *Her presence really is a gift. Having her around makes me feel happy. At ease.*

When Morgan was finished, she sat on the couch next to Emma facing her. "I came here for a reason." She was serious and her brow furrowed over her pretty hazel eyes.

"Okay..." Emma leaned against the couch, facing Morgan. *I think I can tell what this reason is. But I want to hear her say it.*

"I think... No... I know. I have feelings for you. And it's really confusing for me. I've dated women before, but nobody like you. And I find myself really... in to you. I haven't really been with anyone, in any real sense of it, since Jonathan – that was his name – killed himself. I've just been on my own and up here and not really thinking about anyone or anything. But over the last few weeks, I feel like I'm falling for you. And it's confusing for me. It's weird to feel this way again after all this time. But I think about you. All. The. Time. Like I find myself finding excuses to see you and talk to you. When we part ways, I don't want to. I look forward to the moments I am with you. When something happens, I want to run and tell you first. And I seriously just want to know what it feels like to kiss you..." Her words came out fast and frantic.

Emma reached over and took Morgan's hands, lacing her fingers through Morgan's. *Here it goes. I need to be honest. I want her, but I don't know it's the right thing for either of us.* Electricity seemed to pour from Morgan's body into hers through the lacing of her fingers. She felt charged through the center of her body – a feeling she had unknowingly been missing. "I would be lying if I said I didn't think there was something between us at this point. But my issue is this, I'm not wanting to be your experiment back into the dating world after what you've been through. I don't want to be a fling or a one-time deal to salve your wounds. I didn't mind that dynamic when I was young and in college, but I'm not that person anymore. I'm not the kind that does well with games. I'm in a fragile place right now and I don't think I could handle it."

"That's not what I'm saying. I don't want you to think that is what I think you are or what I want for you. This is not coming out right at all." *She is beautiful when she's vulnerable.*

Emma pulled Morgan close and brought her lips to Morgan's. *Not what I had planned to do.* Morgan's whole being yielded into Emma soft and fluid. *Everything about her is different than Bailey. The way she feels, smells, her kiss. It is not a bad thing, either.* The electricity that had shot through her in just the intertwining of their fingers, turned into a small flame, lighting from her center. Emma broke the kiss and looked at Morgan for a reaction.

Morgan was trembling.

"Are you okay?" Emma asked her.

Morgan just looked at her. "That was the best first kiss ever." Her voice was a soft whisper.

It was pretty amazing. But I can't play with her. She's fragile. I'm fragile. We can't go barreling into this. "If we are going to do this, we are taking it slow, okay? I can't jump into anything. And I like you. I like you more than I thought I could at this point. But there are a lot of complications with me."

Morgan leaned in and kissed Emma again. "I can take it slow," she said.

The bedroom is just a few steps away. I could take her. Have her. I want nothing more than to see her stripped down and laid out across the bed. I can only imagine what she could be like. And if we keep this up, I will have no choice. I feel so whole and alive for the first time in forever. She stood up and moved across the room in her long easy stride and leaned against the counter facing the couch. Her body was astir and vibrating with heat and energy. *I forgot how good this feels. Feeling wanted, and that mutual, all consuming, desire for someone.*

"I could find it very easy to push this too far too fast."

"I understand." Morgan was quiet.

I don't think you do. "This is not against you. This is not personal. I want to see where this goes. I do. And I'm so honored you think the way you do about me. But I don't want to hurt you. It's the last thing I want. And I think if we sit here on this couch and drink wine and keep kissing like that, I'm going to go faster than I want, and things are going to get messy, and you are going to end up hurt."

Morgan nodded. "I understand and I respect that."

"Can we see each other tomorrow? Lunch? I will come find you."

Morgan nodded.

Emma grabbed Charlemagne's leash. "I will walk you out to your car and this is to be continued." *If I'm smart I will pack up and get on the road the moment she leaves, but I need her just as much as she needs me. I need to feel this.*

Emma kissed Morgan good night at her car, neither of them minding the falling rain. Emma watched Morgan get into her car and waited for her to drive out of the park and onto the main road.

She went to bed that night with the expectation of having a dream of Bailey or Bear, but to her surprise and delight, she slept like a baby in a deep dreamless state.

The next day was bright, sunny and much warmer than the previous days. The sky was a vibrant blue with bright white clouds. *Nothing screams romance and taking it slow like a beach picnic on a fall day. Emma, you are a fool. But seriously, this woman is everything I need right now.* Emma put together a picnic basket and grabbed a blanket and took it over the office.

"Come on, beautiful," she coaxed. "It's lunch time."

"You made me a whole picnic?"

"You are rollin' with Landry. That's what I do," Emma grinned.

"Landry?"

"My last name."

"I don't think you ever told me that." Morgan locked the store and put a sign up that she would be back in an hour.

Emma shrugged. *I highly doubt she's going to do a Google search on me. She doesn't even have social media accounts. She thinks it's a waste of time just like I do. However, a curious woman may feel the need to know more before getting hurt. Fuck it. If she looks me up, she looks me up. It's no longer in my hands, I can't unring the bell.*

They walked around the building and to the shore where Emma spread out the blanket and put out the lunch.

"How are you? Since last night?" *She doesn't seem to be freaking out. But you never know.*

Morgan smiled at her and the wind blew her pink strands away from her face. "I feel good. I was happy all night. Like a kid at Christmas. I've been waiting all day for lunch. Why? Do you regret it?" Morgan looked at Emma concerned.

Emma smiled at Morgan. "I was just wondering. You said it yourself. You haven't been with anyone since Jonathan. I don't regret it. I just wanted to make sure you were not all freaking out questioning things."

"Believe it or not, it's the most healthy, happy, and right thing I've done in four years. What I haven't told you is the bullshit I did to cope in the first few years, which led me to being here and quitting teaching."

"So tell me," Emma prompted. *I might not be the only messed up person present. This is good.*

"When I found Jonathan dead, hanging by his belt in the closet, I had nightmares. I didn't sleep for days. I couldn't sleep. Because every time I closed my eyes, I saw him, swollen and purple and…" Her voice trailed off and she paused for a long breath and took a sip of the wine Emma had poured.

"So, to keep myself from sleeping or even feeling anything, I started doing Adderall and other uppers, which led to meth and coke, anything that I could get my hands on to stay awake. I was on a stress leave from work, but I just stopped even caring. I eventually stopped getting the paperwork filled out and I didn't care. So, I wasn't very truthful when I told you it was the politics of the job. But it's not something I'm proud of, or something I like to even really talk about. So, yeah. Hi, I'm Morgan and I'm a recovering addict.

"But that was about two months after I started using, so three months after Jonathan took his life. So, I traveled around for a year or so, high and out of control, and continued to do a lot of drugs, sell a lot of drugs, and act a fool. I joined a cult for a short time, believe it or not, which did at least get me clean. I wound up here because I had nowhere else to go or be. I relapsed back into using after getting up here. Finally, my dad gave me an ultimatum. Rehab, therapy, or leave. He was tired of seeing me ruin myself. So, I did six weeks of in-patient treatment, and then a year of outpatient and meetings and grief groups and now, here I am. So, when you say you need to go slow, I respect that. I will respect that. But I will not, nor can I regret falling for you or kissing you."

Emma put her hand over her heart and dropped her head. "Wow. I never would have guessed that you went through all of that. I've been so wrapped up in my own bullshit I never thought to consider what you went through after Jonathan." *That Reader's Digest version of your last four years leads me to believe that there's more you are not telling me. Which is fine. I don't need to know. Just like you don't need to know my atrocities.*

"I'm not proud of it. I don't talk about it. I don't like that part of who I am. Who I was."

Emma gathered Morgan into her arms and kissed her softly. "I appreciate who you had to be to become who you are now."

After lunch, Emma packed everything up and walked Morgan back to the office. "I wish I could close for the day and just lay on the shore with you." Morgan pouted.

"We will see each other tomorrow."

"It's so damn difficult knowing you are literally 200 yards away from me."

"I will see you tomorrow." Emma kissed her and walked back across the street. *Restraint. We both need restraint.*

And the courtship continued for another ten days. Emma and Morgan met daily for a date or a rendezvous. Emma was finding it harder and harder to walk away from Morgan and keep herself composed. Emma literally had nothing else to fill her time with, so Morgan was her new drug.

Morgan had invited Emma (and Charlemagne) over for dinner at her small apartment near downtown. Emma parked her truck and made her way up the three flights of stairs holding Charlemagne. *I am shaking like a nervous bride. It's not like I haven't been spending every day with this woman. But it is the first time I'm going to her home.*

Morgan opened the door and kissed Emma lightly on the lips, and stepped aside to let her in.

Emma looked around, and after several months in the RV, this space felt big to her. Though it felt spacious, the space was small but cozy and inviting. A cream-colored chenille couch with sherpa throw blankets and cherry wood end tables in the living room, and a matching cherry wood round table and chairs in the small dining area. The walls were decorated with framed posters of classic films Morgan loved. She had bookshelves in the living room filled to capacity. Emma immediately loved the space for its coziness. The space smelled of the scent found in new age shops, and the scent that always hung faintly to Morgan's skin, Nag Champa.

"So, I already warned you, I don't cook. I picked up carry out. A veggie burger for you! A real burger for me! And you said you haven't seen *Breakfast at Tiffany's*, so I'm changing that tonight." She closed the door.

Emma couldn't wait any longer. She pushed Morgan against the wall and kissed her deep.

"I'm not hungry." Emma's voice was a low whisper in Morgan's ear.

Morgan's eyes were big. "I'm not either." She led Emma to the bedroom. Emma could see that Morgan was shaking as she had after their first kiss. She lacked the confidence and overwhelming sensuality of Bailey, and Emma was glad for it. The difference between Bailey and Morgan helped keep Emma in the moment.

Morgan's gentle hands and lips swept over Emma, and she lost herself in the sweetness of her.

Time became irrelevant and she melted in Morgan's touch, taste, the sound of her breath and moan. Morgan seemed to give herself over in complete abandon and surrender to Emma, and Emma took it all in. Seconds blended with minutes and into hours. Both of them were seemingly insatiable and lost in each other.

Emma, body wracked and exhausted, pulled Morgan into her and caressed her hair and kissed the top of her head. *If only I could erase all that I had for the last two decades. No Bailey, and replace them all with Morgan and this moment. It's crazy to think such things. It really is. But her sweetness and her gentleness come from her soul. She is all anyone would ever want or need.*

Propping herself up on her elbow, Morgan was still in the glow of the moonlight through the window making her skin glow an ethereal shade of blue against the darkness. Emma traced the cursive words tattooed along Morgan's ribcage, just to the side beneath her breast, 'Dum Spiro Spero'. "While I breathe, I hope," Emma translated with her voice soft in the darkness.

"You know Latin?"

"It was another lifetime ago, or so it seems."

"I think I might be in love with you." It came from nowhere, with her voice barely above a whisper.

"You are in love with orgasms," Emma teased her. "Not me." *Stop trying to be so cool. You know what you are feeling.*

"That's not true. I mean. It is, but it's not." Her long pink tendrils were brushing against Emma's chest. Her hands caressed Emma's chest and down her belly.

Emma caught her hand and held it still. "Morgan, I could easily fall in love with you. I'm trying hard not to. I just caught myself wishing I could wash away the last twenty years of my life and replace it with you. You are everything my wife was not. You are everything I've needed. You are what I need to heal. I just worry that we have two very broken people fitting our broken parts together to be whole and ignoring the holes and cracks."

"I don't understand."

She is so genuine and feels so completely, this is over her head. I'm over thinking and if I keep this up, she is going to take it personally.

Emma shook her head. "Maybe I'm being over cautious and I need to just shut up and enjoy this moment. Maybe I just need to eat that veggie burger. Just forget I said anything."

Emma looked at the clock on the nightstand. It was well past midnight.

~ *14* ~

Downfall

EMMA AND MORGAN SPENT NEARLY every night together, either at Morgan's or Emma's for the next three months. The winter was cold around them, and the holidays came and went. They were peaceful and happy, and the past was a seeming non-issue that neither of them spoke of. It was as if the only thing that mattered to either of them was the present and the future. *It is so easy to just be with Morgan. There's never any guessing or drama or demands.*

Emma found herself not even concerned with the past or what she had left behind. It had now been since before she went to Lake Tahoe since she checked her email or the news.

Her hair had gotten long and shaggy, and she had had enough of trying to trim it herself. She went into town and had her hair cut. The stylist kept looking at her as if she knew her. *She's making me nervous the way she keeps looking at me. She has to recognize me. It could be on the news out here now. I should go check on the status of things 'back home'.*

After her haircut she went to the library and sat at the computer and pulled up social media pages for Rhys and his wife. They had separated and it was nasty. Emma smirked. She went to the news and a pit formed in her stomach. The letter she sent to the reporter was traced back to Santa Barbara. Bailey was not seen in Santa Barbara, but a woman matching Emma's description was. She was wanted for questioning. It was reported that she had gone completely dark, including not even checking in with her law firm. Brandon, bless him, was doing all he could to do damage control. *I know I said that if I got caught, so be it, but that was before Morgan. I should have been up front from the beginning. Not like that would have been good either.*

She went back to the campground and hid in her RV. Morgan popped in after work and was excited by Emma's haircut, but annoyed by Emma's obvious distraction.

This is why I never should have gotten involved with Morgan. I now have something to lose, and it doesn't feel good. There is no way out of this without a lot of hurt. I was so stupid to think that I could just forget what I did and have a future with this woman. There will be a reckoning for what I did. There needs to be. But I don't know how to navigate my way through this. I'm not ready. I'm not ready to leave Morgan. I love her. But if I truly love her, I need to let her go, no matter how much this hurts.

"What's wrong?" Morgan pushed her. "You are like a thousand miles away right now."

Emma shook her head. "It's just something I need to come to terms with and deal with. I'm not sure how, is all."

"I can help you."

No. No you can't. And I don't want you to. I don't want you to even know what I did. You will think differently of me. "No... Not with this. I'm sorry. Let me deal with this." She kissed Morgan on the top of the head.

That night Morgan slept, warm and sweet, wrapped around Emma.

A light in the corner of the bedroom switched on. One of the reading lamps over the nook. Emma looked over and saw Bailey for the first time in a long time.

Charlemagne was in her lap, and she was petting him. "Bailey?" Emma asked sleepily.

"So, you've replaced me."

"No... But I couldn't mourn forever."

"You love her?"

"I think so."

"So, when she hurts you, will you kill her, too?"

"I think it was more about who you cheated on me with. If it was anyone else, I don't think I would have done what I did."

"Keep telling yourself that. You are a Landry. You are a killer by nature. You are your father's daughter. Somehow or some way, you are going to hurt that poor woman, too."

"I won't. I can't…"

"You can run all you want. You can't escape who you were born to be."

Emma put her hands over her ears. "That's not true."

Bailey laughed hysterically. "Keep telling yourself that."

Morgan was now up shaking Emma. "You are having a nightmare. You were saying the name, 'Bailey'."

Emma rubbed her eyes and fell back onto her pillow. She didn't sleep the rest of the night. After two hours of lying next to Morgan, looking over at the nook every now and then to see if Bailey was there, she got up and went into the living area of the RV and made a cup of coffee. *This is not good. I need to let Morgan go. I need to cut it off and go back and handle my business. Enough is enough. I just don't want to. I'm being selfish. I know that. The longer I hold on, the harder this is going to be.*

When the sky began to lighten she made breakfast for Morgan and woke her up.

Morgan came out and sat at the small table and let Emma serve her coffee and a fresh yogurt and fruit parfait. Emma had been determined to get Morgan into a vegetarian diet.

"What are you doing today?" Emma asked Morgan.

"I'm getting my hair done today. The color is faded so I need a refresh. And my dad will be here so he will take over the office for the day."

Emma smiled at her. "That sounds like a good day. I will meet you after your appointment at your place, okay?" *Here I am acting like nothing is happening. Everything is great and normal. I need to tell her I'm leaving. I need to leave. She can keep the money I prepaid, but I have to go. God. I don't want to go. I want this. I want her.*

"Sounds like a plan." Morgan finished her breakfast and made her way back home.

Emma tried to take a nap and rest. Every time she closed her eyes, she saw Bailey sitting in the corner of the room shaking her head in disappointment.

She walked Charlemagne over to the shore and sat by the lake. Her chest hurt and her eyes were burning. *This is all coming to a head, I feel it. I have to stop running. I have to stop pretending everything is okay. I need to go be accountable for what I've done. To think I have a future with this beautiful, sensitive, kind woman is comedy. I have to go. I have no rights to a life with her. Not now.*

She checked her watch and saw that Morgan should be back from her hair appointment. She made her way back across the street and took Charlemagne over to Morgan's.

Her legs felt heavy like lead as she walked up the stairs to the apartment and knocked on the door.

Morgan answered and her appearance took Emma by surprise. Instead of the soft shades of pink, her hair was streaked with a deep blue. The buzzing in her brain was loud and she couldn't think.

"Wow... That's a change!" Emma managed.

Morgan laughed. "I loved the color... It was listed as Sapphire Blue. It reminded me of your eyes," she said.

This all ends here. Now. Emma felt dizzy, the floor under her feet was unsteady and her vision blurred. "Like sapphire blue..." she whispered. She saw Bailey sitting in the corner of the living room with a large, disfigured grin. It was horrid and toothy, too wide for her face, not the pretty and mischievous grin of days past.

"What?" Morgan asked her face showing the obvious confusion.

"Nothing. It was a thing from back in the day. I need to sit down. I don't feel great." The room was spinning, and Bailey wouldn't stop leering at her from the corner.

"What's wrong?" Morgan asked concerned.

"I don't know. I just feel dizzy. Probably because I didn't sleep great last night. I think I'm just over tired." Emma collapsed onto the couch, where everything around her seemed to go dark.

She didn't even realize that she had passed out. When she woke up still on the couch she was wrapped in one of the sherpa throw blankets Morgan kept draped over the back, with Charlemagne snuggled under.

Morgan was sitting in the chair across from her with a laptop on her lap. The room was darkened, and Morgan was lit by the glow from her screen.

Emma sat up and looked at her watch. It was almost midnight. *I've been out for hours.*

"We need to talk." Morgan's voice was ominous.

Emma sat up and stretched her neck. "Okay. Talk." *This is it. This is the reckoning. I can tell by the look on her face and the tone in her voice.*

Morgan turned the screen around and it was headline reading 'Local Couple Missing for Months, No Answers', with a picture of Bailey and Emma from an event they attended before Covid for charity. Emma was dressed in one of her fine suits and Bailey was dressed in a cocktail dress, glowing. Bailey was looking adoringly at Emma as she looked directly into the camera, smiling. *That was such a great night.* A fundraiser for a local charity, a silent auction. The byline read, 'Emma Landry and Wife Bailey Frankson-Landry Still Missing Without a Trace'.

Emma sat up straight and sucked in her breath. *This was an unfair way for you to find out that I'm not a good person. I should have never done this to you.*

"You don't ever talk about your past. You never told me her name. You never once talked about Bailey, really. You never talk about memories or life before coming here. I was fine with that because I was so wrapped up in us in the moment and thinking about a future with you. I was busy building fantasies in my head about us and what our life would be together.

"And then... then last night when you said her name, I thought I would look her up. I knew, the way you said her name, that was your ex-wife. I became curious about your past and what kind of woman she could be that would hurt you like she did. I wanted to see what she was like. I typed in her name, and she's been missing for months. You both are. I saw the man she had the affair with. I saw he was questioned and then ultimately not a person of interest. But you – you've been missing since the start. You are here, and she is not."

Emma's eyes misted with tears. *The fucked-up part is that I'm more upset about what I did to you than Bailey at this point. I should have left you alone.* "I don't know what to tell you. I never wanted to drag you into any of this."

"What did you do?" Morgan whispered.

It's time to come clean. Speak the truth. "I killed her." Emma's voice was barely a whisper. It was the first time she had said it out loud.

"How?" Morgan asked, fat tears falling from her pretty greenish hazel eyes. She leaned forward closing her laptop. The room was dark now, the only light coming in from the security light on Morgan's balcony.

Emma was silent for a long moment. *I don't even know what to say or how to say it. Either way, I come out as a monster.* "I strangled her. I found out she was cheating. I found all of the messages and pictures. I confronted her. I asked her how she could do that to me with Rhys... Especially after she knew what he had done to me. She defended him. I don't know what happened. I don't know why. But I did." Emma's voice was still quiet, she looked through the darkness and into Morgan's eyes as she spoke. *I swear I'm not a monster. I'm not. Please don't hate me. Please don't turn your back on me.*

"Where is she?" Morgan's voice was a fragile whisper.

Emma broke her gaze and tilted her head back and put her hands over her face, and up through her hair. She exhaled. *There is no way to tell this part without you truly thinking I'm a horrible, evil, disgusting person. I am a monster.* "I panicked. I buried her in the woods where my father, consequently buried my mother. She deserves better than that. She does."

There was a heavy silence for what seemed like an eternity in the dark.

"I need you to leave. I can't believe this. You need to go. Get out of my house. Get out of my campground. I loved you. I was in love with you. And it was all for nothing. I can't believe this." Morgan's voice was surprisingly calm.

Emma moved to comfort Morgan, and she shrank from Emma. This small gesture of not allowing Emma to touch her, stung worse than any words ever slung at her. Hurt more than a fist to her gut.

"No! Don't you dare touch me! Not ever again. I can't believe you just came here and did this. You acted like you were the victim. You were the one that was hurt. You made me love you. You acted like nothing was wrong. Have you no conscience?" Her pitch had begun to rise.

"I have no excuse. I wasn't expecting to meet you or to fall for you. That was not part of the plan."

"The plan?" Her laughter was dripping in sarcasm. "What, pray tell, was your plan? Oh, please do tell me!"

"I was just going to hop around until I figured out what I wanted to do. Maybe go to Mexico. Canada. I needed to make sense of what I did. I don't know. But, Morgan, listen to me. Everything that happened between us was legit. It was real. How we felt and what we had was honest, and raw. It brought me back to life and gave me something I didn't even know I needed."

"What you need? You *killed your wife.* What you need? You need prison. You need to not be here. Please. Just go." Morgan's laughter had morphed into tears.

Emma got up and picked up Charlemagne and let herself out the door. Her head was spinning and buzzing again. She made her way back to the campsite and loaded up as quietly as she could so as not to disrupt the other campers. It took her just over an hour to pack up and hitch back to her truck.

Bailey was sitting in the passenger seat. "I told you that you were going to hurt that woman. You broke her."

"I didn't mean to."

"What are you going to do now? Are you going to keep living like this?" Bailey asked.

Emma didn't answer. She just kept driving. She didn't stop until she was four hours away. She was southeast in a small town called Lone Pine at the base of the Sierra Nevadas. She was in a parking lot, and she went to lay down for a few hours.

Her heart was beating so loud and hard in her chest. She dozed fitfully and when she woke, she knew what she had to do.

She picked up her burner phone and called Brandon.

"This is Brandon Fitzgerald," his familiar voice came through the phone.

It's so good to hear your voice. I've missed my best friend. "Hey, it's Emma," she said quietly into the phone.

"Emma? What the fuck!" Brandon whispered. "Hold on." She could hear him talking to a group of people excusing himself. When the background noise had faded, he was back on the line. "Where the fuck are you? The cops are looking for you. They are all over everyone who knows you. They've searched your house. They are sitting in front of our offices."

"I'm somewhere out West. I'm coming back. I'm turning myself in. I need you to represent me."

"Turning yourself in? Oh my god. Emma. You did it…"

"I can't tell you that. Not if you are representing me, not until I decide how this needs to go down. I am coming home. I will be there in three days' time, maybe four. Buy me time. I will call you when I get in."

"Okay. Okay. I got it. Fuck. *Fuck.* Emma. What did you *do?*" His voice was anguished.

"Brandon, keep your chill. I need you to stay calm. Don't say anything to anyone. I will be in touch."

Emma hung up with him and went to a local library. She sat for hours drafting her paperwork. She had considerable assets she couldn't just leave hanging. She drafted that all of her assets be left in trust with Brandon as the executor, and instructions to sell the lake house, and keep Teta's house managed. She emailed him the documents.

He emailed her back, "Thank you? Will notarize when I see you?"

The question mark was all she needed to know. She wasn't sure she still even had an ally with her oldest and closest friend.

She got back on the road and kept going. She drove until she couldn't see straight any longer. Her stops were short, and she was barely sleeping. Bailey seemed to be there all the time. She ignored all of it, keeping her focus only in the moment and nothing else.

She finally pulled into the driveway of her home, and she called Brandon to meet her before she even set foot back into the house.

While she waited for Brandon to arrive, she wandered from room to room. Bailey had always been left to decorate the homes. She had impeccable taste. The house screamed with her presence in every room and every corner. The house that was normally kept obsessively clean and orderly was ransacked from the searches. Drawers left open, footprints from shoes coming and going. Fingerprint dust on surfaces. A year's worth of dust clung to the surfaces. *It is all real. This is it. I killed Bailey. Our life here is over. This mess says it all. I did this. This is all because of me.*

Emma collapsed on the sofa in the living room, sitting next to where Bailey had sat when she killed her. The blue painting looked dull in the dusk light coming in over the lake and through the large windows. She looked to her side and saw Bailey sitting quiet, looking around at the damage. "Everyone dies, Emma. Some make it decades, and some make it a matter of minutes. You know the cliche. People come and go for a reason, a season, or a lifetime."

I can't do this right now. I can't handle seeing you. Not in that spot. "What I did… What I did – there is no turning back. There is no making it right. I killed you. I hurt Morgan. I need to pay for what I did. What is my reason? My purpose?"

Bailey sat unmoving in her spot. Emma just stared at her as the room got progressively darker.

"Emma, you look like hell." Brandon's voice coming through the door broke her from her reverie.

"I know. I haven't hardly slept in days." She was collapsed on the couch in the murky darkness, the only light coming from the porch light on the patio that had been set on an infinite timer years ago.

Brandon turned on the lamps and was next to her. "You are like a sister to me. I am here for you. But you need to come clean. What happened?"

"I need to start with Junior year," Emma began. She told Brandon all of it, reminding him what she endured in the alley and how she felt all the way up to the moment she killed Bailey and on through Lake Tahoe. Brandon sat listening as Emma went through calmly and patiently telling it all over the span of several hours.

To finally get it all out feels so good.

"We can plead temporary insanity," Brandon said when Emma had concluded.

"No. I'm not doing that. I'm just going to go in and turn myself in. I need you to negotiate my sentencing. I want manslaughter. Not first degree. I didn't plan this. I want parole eligibility. The whole nine."

"Emma, sleep on it. You look rough. You were in a frenzied state. You were completely dissociative. You said so yourself. You said you've been hallucinating Bailey and your father since it happened. You can go away to an institution for a few months, maybe a year tops and be back out living your life. You can resume your practice. It was an accident, Emma. You loved her so much. Anyone who's ever known you knows that. You were hurt, drunk, exhausted. The pictures brought you back to a traumatic event that you never properly dealt with." He was building her insanity defense as he went. "It would be nothing to get an expert witness to evaluate you and testify to that." His voice reflected his pain and disappointment.

"Brandon, it's done. It's over. I did what I did. Take Charlemagne for me. Take care of him. You have control of my assets. I'm done. Go call the prosecutor and arrange it for the day after tomorrow. I'm going to sign these papers, you notarize them." She motioned to the file he had set on the coffee table while she had confessed to him.

After Emma signed the papers giving him control of her assets in trust, Brandon sat back and dialed the prosecutor. Emma listened as he negotiated her surrender.

She stood when he was done. "I'm going to enjoy my last hours in this house." She walked up the stairs without saying another word.

She heard Brandon and Charlemagne leave. The door snapping shut.

~ 278 ~

She turned on the shower and sat on the bench in the enclosure and let the hot water wash over her. She cried with relief. It was done. She spent the remainder of the evening cleaning up the mess left behind by the various searches. She sat for a long time in the library room she had made. She loved this house. She loved this room.

She watched the sunrise over the frozen lake. The shades of pink reflecting from the scattered clouds reflecting off of the ice. Bailey was by her side, quiet. Emma could smell her and feel her presence. She didn't say anything but sat quietly.

She went back to her bedroom and changed the sheets. She slept deep and peaceful in her bed. She could smell Bailey still on the pillows next to her. She didn't long for Bailey, or Morgan. She just wanted rest.

The following day she spent time covering the furniture of the house. After everything was said and done, the house and all of its contents would be sold, and the money would be added to the trust. Teta's house would remain in her name. Brandon would manage it all.

In the morning she donned her favorite bespoke suit, her grandfather's Rolex, and did her hair. She walked downstairs and waited patiently for Brandon.

When he arrived, he hugged her tight. "Emma, this is your last chance."

She shook her head 'no'.

"You are throwing it all away. Everything you've worked for all these years."

"Brandon, I'm a Landry. I didn't deserve any of this." She motioned around her. "It was all pretense. I tried to live the life, but I am my father's daughter. He was a killer and so am I."

He sighed and led her out to his waiting car.

She watched as the city went by out the window. She didn't have anything more to say, and Brandon didn't say much either. That was the thing about Brandon. He always understood her, and right now, he respected her need for silence.

He got to the complex that housed the police and the prosecutor's office and walked in with Emma. Reporters were surrounding the building and snapping pictures. Emma, used to dealing with high profile cases, didn't look at them, just kept her eyes ahead. She didn't block her face or make any remarks. Questions were fired at her, microphones shoved at her. She just walked with her eyes forward.

They were seated in a conference room with the detective, the prosecutor, Emma, and Brandon.

"Emma Landry. Where have you been?" the prosecutor asked. He was a short man, with salt and pepper hair, and an upturned broad nose that reminded Emma of a pig. She had gone toe to toe with him since opening her practice. She had always won, and he never cared for her. She presumed he was on a high having her at his mercy.

Emma sighed. "Let's skip the pleasantries. Let's negotiate this."

Brandon put his hand on her back to stop her. She nodded to him. She wasn't used to someone else handling her business.

"Manslaughter, with a recommended sentence of 10 years, eligible for parole in 5, and my client will tell you where Bailey Frankson-Landry is, as well as a full allocution, or we take this to trial, where you will not be guaranteed a win, and we all know your record against our firm is not great, as my client has an easy case for insanity."

The prosecutor looked at Emma and Brandon. He stood across from them. "Deal. I will go write it up." He left abruptly.

It was nearly an hour before he came back. In that time, Brandon and Emma sat and talked about the firm and what she missed out on, and Mason's newest skills and accomplishments.

When the prosecutor finally came back in, Emma looked over the deal with Brandon. She nodded to him and signed her name.

She sat back and looked at the detective and said, "Bailey Frankson-Landry, my wife, who died by my hands, who I strangled, is buried in the woods behind my childhood trailer. Under the deer stand my father buried my mother under." She drew a map, with remarkable detail from her memory.

"You buried her in the woods?" the detective asked with a tone of incredulity.

Emma told the whole story beginning with Rhys's rape, to uncovering the affair.

The detective just looked at her at the end of it and shook his head.

They stood Emma up and she took her suit jacket off handing it to Brandon. She was handcuffed with hands in front of her, Brandon draped her jacket over the cuffs, and they led her from the building.

The reporters clamored sticking microphones and cameras in her face and Brandon's. Neither of them spoke a word or answered a single question. *He has no idea that his friendship is the biggest blessing I could have ever asked for in life.*

She was placed in the back of a cop car and taken to the county jail. She put her head back against the seat back and closed her eyes. She tried to feel something but was utterly empty. *It's all done. It's over. I've come full circle.*

Stripped of her expensive suit – her armor – and placed in an orange jumpsuit, she was processed at the county jail. They cataloged her belongings and put them in a box and escorted her to a cell.

She made her rack and looked around her. There was another rack, but no one was in it. It was not assigned to any other inmate. In the common room, there was a television with several other inmates around it watching the local news. After making her rack, she slowly made her way out. Some of the inmates were playing cards and some were just hanging out. Their conversations buzzed around her, and she tuned it all out. She sat at a table near the television, and no one paid any attention to her.

She stared at the television, as she saw herself escorted out of the prosecutor's office with Brandon at her side on the broadcast. Her jacket 'hiding' the handcuffs as she made the "perp walk" to the squad car. A few of the women turned their heads and looked at her and made some comments quietly. *Here we go again.* She ignored them.

There was a cut in the footage to an interview with Rhys. "I always knew she was crazy and dangerous. Just like her family. Trash," and he turned and walked away from the camera. As he walked away, a savvy reporter asked him about the alleged rape of Emma. He froze as he was walking away and flipped his middle finger at the reporter as he continued to walk. *That reporter must have one hell of an informer to have had that information so quickly.* Then it was a cut to Mary Anne. "I'm just happy we can finally put my daughter to rest properly. I never thought this would happen. Bailey and Emma always loved each other so much." A reporter shouted a question to her. "Yes, I plan to meet with Emma at some point and find out what happened. Emma has been my family for over two decades. I loved her. I am hurt by what she did. Confused. Sad. But she was a broken girl and the best way to deal with broken people is to love them."

They cut to CJ, "I warned my sister about Landry when they were kids. My dad and I went to great lengths to keep those two apart. We knew. God rest my sister's soul. She deserved better."

Emma's heart felt heavy. She got up and went back to her cell and laid down. *I'm so sorry, Bailey. We did have something special. And yes, you fucked up. But CJ is right, you deserved better.*

It seemed she was on the news all the time. The story just kept getting bigger. Given their social status, the story was now national. It was a salacious story about wealthy white women that had sex, scandal, and murder. Everyone was talking about it, and everyone was talking. She saw clips of Tawney and Sully talking about meeting her while she was on the run. Morgan spoke in her own quiet manner. "I loved her. God, I was so in love with her. I had no idea she had that other side. I didn't know what she did. We never talked about the details of our histories. We both knew we had baggage from our past. We both just wanted a fresh start. I still find it hard to believe she could have done it. But she confessed it to me. She did." Her hair was still streaked with a deep sapphire blue, her eyes and her voice wounded. The footage cut from there back to the reporter who showed the body being carried out of the woods, just as it had years ago when they dug her mother out of the woods.

Emma received word that there was a funeral for Bailey. She saw clips of it on the news the night of the funeral. Rhys and CJ were there in the crowd. Mary Anne and George were walking in front of the casket and several of her friends poured out of the church, including Abby and Brandon and Savannah.

The day after Bailey was buried, Mary Anne was seated in front of Emma in the visiting room of the county jail. The small metal table was between them, and Emma sat in her bright orange jumpsuit. She couldn't look at Mary Anne through the tears she was fighting.

"Emma, will you please just look at me."

Reluctantly she looked up.

"I feel responsible for this."

"Mary Anne, please, no. This is not you. This is me. I own this. I can never make this up to you or Bailey. You did nothing but love me and treat me like your own. How can you even say that?"

"Remember ... remember back at the cottage when CJ discovered you and Bailey were together? Charles was so angry. He threw a fit and he sent you away."

"A day I can never forget."

"And then CJ went inside and called Rhys and told them what train you were on. I overheard him later that night talking to Charles about how he sent Rhys out to meet you at the train station to deliver a message to leave his sister alone for good. My god. I could have said something at the table that morning. I could have stood up for you. I could have stood up for you both. Don't think that I didn't suspect what had been going on between the two of you. I knew she was in love with you at prom. I knew that look. I was weak, Emma. I was afraid of my husband and his temper. I was afraid of losing the life we built if I stood up to him. I was a coward. If I stood up to him, none of this would have happened. Bailey would not have been sent away. You would not have been on that train. Rhys wouldn't have done what he did to you. So many things would have never happened. I am every bit as guilty as you are. That is why I don't hate you. I forgive you. I have grief in my heart for losing my daughter, but I am always going to be here for you, because I own this with you."

~ 283 ~

"I appreciate your love and support, Mary Anne. I do. But you cannot own this. I wish I had the answers for you. I wish I could explain to you how it's not on your shoulders. I don't deserve your support or forgiveness. You don't deserve the guilt of my actions."

"You will never convince me otherwise. I will be at your sentencing. I will give a statement that explains how much you mean to me and how I support you. I know how much you loved Bailey. I know you didn't plan it. You didn't have anything to gain. I can see the pain you feel when you talk about her."

SEVERAL WEEKS LATER, BRANDON HAD brought her one of her suits and she was in front of the judge. Mary Anne, Abby, Simone, and a slew of their mutual friends sat in benches behind Emma. No one stood to say that Emma was a bad person. Everyone painted a picture of a loving and kind woman who just for some reason they didn't know or understand, snapped, most likely due to the unresolved trauma.

Before she was set to speak, Mary Anne reached over the back of the bench and gripped Emma's shoulder. Emma touched her hand lightly. She stood and looked around the room. She didn't have a script and didn't want to plan her words. She wanted to speak from the heart.

"So many of you already know my story. And my story with Bailey. Bailey had been my world when we were in high school together and she became my whole world again in undergrad and then again when she found me in law school. I have no excuse for what I did. I've heard the word 'snapped' thrown around a lot. Maybe I did. I don't know. I wasn't crazy and what I did wasn't calculated. I realize this may sound like a cop out, but I have no words to describe my state of mind during, or even after what I did. But I regret it. I regret it every single day." Emma paused as her voice cracked and she wiped the tears that began to fall. She waited a minute to compose herself before continuing. "I extinguished this beautiful, vivacious light from the world. I miss her. I miss our life. A life I worked so hard for that I took for granted ultimately.

"I killed my wife. It was unintentional, but it is an act I must own. The day before I killed her, I found out she had been cheating on me with Rhys Mills, a man who Bailey had known, had raped me in an alley, as a means to threaten me and keep me away from her years earlier. I saw a thread of messages and photographs that illicitly detailed their long-standing affair. I drank heavily to cope with it. When Bailey came home the next morning, I was drunk and I was exhausted, I confronted her." Emma paused as her voice broke again with emotion. She took a deep breath before continuing. "I reminded her that Rhys had raped me. It was not the first she had heard of it. Yet, she defended him. I then acted on impulse, and I strangled her. Several hours later, I put her body in the trailer, and then buried her in the same woods my father had buried my own mother. I then took off for several months in a panic.

"Am I sorry for what I did? Every day. I miss her so much. The love I felt for her was rare. It doesn't exist in most people's lives. It's the kind of love that electrifies and energizes you. It is so powerful you depend on it like a drug – and when it is withheld, you are but a junky, lost and craving what you can't have. Losing her at that moment, my life was over. That is not an excuse for what I did. What Rhys Mills did to me, is not an excuse. I have no excuse, other than I was outside of myself in so much blinding pain at the time." Tears were streaming down her face, and she sat down. Mary Anne put both hands on Emma's shoulders and gripped.

The judge spoke after a few minutes of silence. "Emma Landry, the prosecution recommends a sentence of 10 years, with eligibility of parole in five. I have known you for several years. I followed your brilliant career, and I was, for a lack of better terms, a fan. I figured at some point we would be peers and you would be here on the bench someday yourself, or at least I had high hopes for you to be seated here one day. I believe you when you say it wasn't calculated and I believe your remorse to be genuine. I am going to uphold the recommendation." He hit his gavel.

Emma was taken back to the county jail until she could be transferred to the state correctional facility for women in a week.

The women from the county jail were watching her on television as she came back in. They whispered and made comments. Emma ignored them and went to her bunk, where she collapsed and slept. *It's over. It's done. I'm done.*

It took almost a month before she was sent to the women's correctional facility. After a week of processing, she was given her final uniform for the next several years pending parole. A deep blue jumpsuit. "Like sapphire blue..." Emma whispered as she was escorted to the changing area.

~ *Epilogue* ~

MOST OF THE MAIL EMMA received was thrown away being 'fan mail'. The letters came mostly from women around the world pledging their undying love to Emma. She even received some from a few men. She never read it, but she liked to look at the envelopes and see where the letters were coming from. Occasionally she would get letters from Mary Anne, or Brandon, or Abby, so she had to be careful to not throw them away in the piles of fan mail.

Mary Anne and Brandon and Abby also came to visit regularly. Emma also began a pro-bono law clinic for the women she was serving time with. She noted the inequities based on the races and socioeconomic statuses of the women she was serving time alongside with as she listened to their stories. She knew had she not risen up with the help of people like Coach Adame, she could very well be one of them. She helped them write briefs and motions and reviewed their cases giving them pointers and information and questions to ask their public defenders to help them with their appeals. Given what help she was providing them, allowed her to be left alone and not messed with.

For her actual job, she was assigned to work in the education department and helped teach GED classes to her fellow inmates. It kept her busy day after day and she found herself in a routine that gave her a sense of purpose.

The networks loved to feature her case even though she declined interview requests. She had given Brandon permission to respond on her behalf. She would watch with curiosity as they were aired on the televisions in the common room. Her fellow inmates would side eye her as they sat and watched. Everyone had an opinion about her and what she had done. It was puzzling for her to watch her entire life analyzed by people who never knew her, starting from her childhood. Other than Rhys and CJ they could never find anyone to speak negatively about her.

She was amazed that they analyzed every detail of her life, including the fact that she was vegetarian ever since she was 8 years old – they knew the story about the doe. Pictures of her life, mostly cultivated from Bailey's social media profiles, were on display for the world to see.

Everyone interviewed always sang Emma's praises. Rhys's reputation was destroyed by Emma's allegations of his raping her. His ex-wife spoke up about allegations of marital rape while they were together and what a cruel person he could be. He was forced to step down from his father's company by the board of directors. Their affiliation with him was hurting their business. One by one people in her life were trotted in front of the camera: coaches, teammates, teachers, coworkers, friends. Her life was up for everyone's speculation. Pictures of Bailey. Pictures of Bailey and her together. She would sit and watch and try to make sense of it herself.

She was forced to see a prison psychiatrist and attend an anger management group. She didn't mind. It helped pass the time between her teaching classes and helping her fellow inmates sort out their legal affairs. She saw it as mildly helpful as she discussed and analyzed her life.

Almost a year into her sentence, with talk and speculation it was reported that given her assistance helping her fellow inmates, her work with the GED program and her outstanding behavior, they may release her after another year to a halfway house. Emma ignored the speculation and kept on her routine.

After mail call one afternoon, she was filing through her stack of mail when she saw one from Lake Tahoe in the return address. She looked at it again, it was from Morgan. She had willed herself to not think of Morgan since she saw the interview on television. Morgan was off limits in her mind. She had done enough damage to that kind and beautiful soul. She opened the letter, and she could smell the faint Nag Champa fragrance from the paper as she read it.

"*Dear Emma,*

I have started this letter and thrown it away so many times over the last few months. I didn't even know how to address it. Dear? Dearest? Anyway, here it all is. The words I feel that need to be said. What you left behind in your wake.

I don't know what to say. You turned my life upside down. You woke me up and you made me love you. I fear that I will never love another like I loved you. I believe there was a reason us two broken people came together. I understand now, what you said about two broken people trying to mash our broken pieces together, ignoring the cracks. I have so much that I never told you. So much I left out when I told you about my own past. But that is for another time. Another letter, maybe? I want to focus on you right now.

You said in your sentencing (I could not help but to watch every single bit of coverage), that the love you had with Bailey was electrifying and like a drug. I laughed out loud because that was how I described what loving you was like when they interviewed me. They didn't play that clip on the news. It must have been left on the cutting room floor.

I believe you. I believe, also, that you loved me. Maybe not in the way you loved Bailey. But no two loves are the same. But knowing you as I knew you, watching you go through what you went through, I know you have remorse, and you are a good and beautiful person. I know that you speak from the heart, and you feel things so very deeply. When you told me you loved me, you meant it.

I watched the documentaries about your case, and I read the articles. Everyone tries to figure you out. But I knew you. Even though you never talked about your past, so much of you makes so much sense now.

I have missed you so much in the days since you have been gone. I feel like I'm mourning a death again. I was harsh and judgmental when I sent you away. That was wrong. I should have listened to you and listened to my heart. Hurt people hurt people. You didn't mean to, plan to, or want to kill Bailey.

It's evident. You were hurt. After a lifetime of hurt, the betrayal of the person who pledged to love you and protect you sent you outside of yourself.

I'm sorry for not listening to you. I'm sorry for not asking questions to clarify or seek to understand. I'm sorry for pushing you to turn yourself in. I understand why you did. I understand your need for penance.

You deserve love. When you get out, I will be here waiting for you, because I never could stop loving you.

Love Always,

Morgan.

PS. I know you are thinking you don't deserve my love. I've been there and felt I didn't deserve forgiveness or grace either. This quote has gotten me through the worst of times, "Each of us is more than the worst thing we've ever done," Bryan Stevenson

Emma folded the letter and put it back in its envelope. She held it close to her heart before putting it away within a book on her shelf in her cell.

~ *Afterword* ~

AS WITH MY FIRST NOVEL, *This Too Shall Pass,* I found myself wrapped up in a soundtrack that helped influence the story and the characters. I must give credit to the following artists and their work:

Joy Division – Love Will Tear Us Apart

Marilyn Manson – Kill4Me

Abney Park – She

Madonna – Sorry (Remix)

Young The Giant – Something to Believe In

Mad Season – River of Deceit

Duran Duran – Come Undone

Moby – Like a Motherless Child

Delerium – Once in a Lifetime (feat. JES)

Raving George – You're Mine (feat. Oscar and The Wolf)

Ellis Marsalis – Heart of Gold

BONES UK – Pretty Waste

Talking Heads – Once In a Lifetime

The Score – Born for This

Pink – Beautiful Trauma

Dead Can Dance – The Ubiquitous Mr. Lovegrove

Alice In Chains – Hate to Feel

Leonard Cohen – Nevermind

(This playlist and the one for *This Too Shall Pass...* are both available on Spotify.)

Connect with me on social media:

Twitter: @MarisaBillions

Facebook: @AuthorMarisaBillions

Instagram: @AuthorMarisaBillions

Helpful Links:

Scan to purchase a copy of *This Too Shall Pass*

Scan to access playlist for *This Too Shall Pass*

Scan to access playlist for *Like Sapphire Blue*

Join the conversation by joining the group on Facebook

~ *Other books by Marisa Billions* ~

This Too Shall Pass... A Mother Will Do Anything To Protect Her Son

Into The Blue Again (Coming Soon)

Made in the USA
Las Vegas, NV
06 September 2023

77136902R00177